AWAKENING

Jacob M. Callcut

Dedication

To all those in search of their true self.

CHAPTER ONE

THIS WAS NOT THE PLAN. I'd be wearing my boots, *that's* for certain, and some proper clothes. Such luxuries, though, are for those not in the middle of getting ready for bed and far from their room. Then again, had I been anywhere else, I'd not have overheard that the watchmen were hunting for the two. Then we'd have no plan.

Thank the stars I'd hidden them not an hour before, intending to leave at first light. Instead, we'd a restless night of cat and mouse that now has us reeking of—well—what you reek of after a wrong turn ends with you wading through sewage. How the guards even found them out baffles me, but at least we made it to the docks unseen.

I think.

My lungs suck in the fresh morning air. "You certain that the guard outside the incinerator room didn't see us?"

Paul slides his hand through his light brown curls and flings the wetness drenching his forehead to the side. "No," he huffs as his eyes peek back at the blackened steel door from which we entered the dockyard, "but I imagine she'd be after us by now, had she." He shuffles further behind the stacked crates the other side of the meter gap between us and faces me. His eyebrows shoot upward as his chin drops along my profile. "You're cut—bad."

"Huh?" Follow his eye-line to a jagged ten centimeter slit in my blackened nightgown. "Crud." A ruby red streak crawls from my right thigh. "When'd I do that?"

"Here." Paul removes his undershirt and latches onto its hem. The lines of his chest sharpen. *Oh, my!* His biceps swell. *Close your mouth.* With a slow *rrriiiippp*, the garment's threads surrender into halves. "Use these." *For serious, close your mouth and stop gawking!* He tosses the improvised dressings at me with a quick underhand flick.

Snatch the rags from the air—"Ah… thanks."—and angle away from him, both to hide my burning face and my modesty. I kneel on my good leg and shuffle the hem of my gown up and over the toppled L that my other leg forms. I spread one cloth over the cut, then—

"Pack it first. You should know that."

Stop and twist to face him. "I should know what?"

Paul rushes over and drops to his knees in front of me. "To staunch the blood, you need to pack it first." The satiny tips of his fingers tingle across my skin as he lifts the dressing from my thigh. He folds it over, then dabs at the liquid already escaped the cut.

My eyes shut as shaded memories, long ago lost, wash over me. A likewise bright, soft-faced man with delicate hands. A child fresh-fallen from her bike with an asphalt-burn to her knee. Not just any man… and not just any little girl. An adoring dad attending to his daughter. My Papa… my Papa nursing my swelling wound with his tender touch… *How could I've ever forgotten you?*

A wet path runs over my cheek.

"Crush me!" Yank my thigh sideways and fling my lids open. "What are you doing?!"

Paul grimaces. "I know it hurts."

Sure, now that you're goading my thigh… thank—you—very—much. The fire ants chewing at my flesh concur, but to say as much would be rude. I wipe a tear of pain from my cheek with one hand while tugging the gown's skirt back over my crotch with the other as I angle the injury back to him.

Pajama pants… you couldn't have grabbed some pajama pants. Rather, in this heat, some shorts.

Paul pushes (*OW!*) the dabbing cloth in deep and wraps the other tight over the first, knotting it twice at the back of my thigh. "That should hold for now," he says as we rise, our eyes engaging. He flashes me a small but short-lived smile, then glances over my shoulder.

I turn. "She okay?"

Paul's fiancé is butt to the ground, back crushed against the pile of crates on the other side of the gap. She glares at us, but her eyes are stony and unresponsive. The woman hasn't more than mumbled for hours, since we first squeezed like toothpaste out of its tube through some air vents… along rat-tiled drainage gutters… and those fetid sewer pipes… Blah! Took the depths of my willpower to not puke. She was less fortunate, thrice. Her face still colors the inside of a ripe cucumber.

Paul goes to her and kneels. "We're close, sweetheart." The encouragement passes like neutrinos through her, soliciting not a grumble of acknowledgment. His head droops, a sigh slips from his mouth.

I move across the opening and lay a gentle hand on his bare shoulder.

A long second passes, then he sighs again and stands, my fingers tracing down the ridges of his firm, gleaming shoulder blades, along his spine, and to his—

What are you doing?!

I rush my hand to my side. He circles at me and, in a low tone, as if burdened by a secret he can't share, says, "She's not gonna make it."

Harden my jaw, if for no other reason than to excuse my radiating cheeks. "I'm getting you *both* outta here." I eye a mound of wooden crates further across the yard, shake out my legs, and set to drop into a sprinter's stance.

Paul latches onto my arm. "Not so fast, Miss Speedy; that gash's doing you no favors. Besides, I'm the older of us." *How's that matter?* "I'll go."

"Look, I"—don't know how old I am—"appreciate the concern." No student does. The Facility doesn't celebrate birthdays, and no one foolish enough dare ask. They measure our growth, and thus class progression, solely by our abilities. I graduated into Class Three just this week; my birth year is immaterial. "I've worked down here before, so *I'll* scout the docks."

Paul's searching leer seems to suspect my over-boast. Fact is, I only once helped unload the monthly containership, four years ago. That week I worked the pier is one of my earliest memories. Few students recall experiences before the Facility. Nothing of family or friends. Of riding bikes and skinning knees. Only the "business" of life: skill sets, physical abilities, book knowledge.

As our instructors often profess, "One is what one is because one is that."

The few glimpses I have into my past before the Facility's molding re-enforce as much. In Gym, I outlasted everyone in fore-handed chin-ups. In math, I answered convoluted story problems in a flash, dumbfounding my peers. The depth of my literary essays left mouths gaping. Skills that the Facility's rigorous training has enriched and refined. Not that I'm some beacon of super strength—the jacked proportions of a bodybuilder don't interest me—but my physique gives the toughest of opponents pause. And my noggin, it could give the brightest of PhD-bound graduates an academic smackdown.

Typical young woman, by whatever meaning, I am not.

"We both go," Paul says. His crunched forehead betrays an inner conflict.

"You can't leave her."

"She can't help search, and time's too short for you to find us a suitable hideaway alone."

He's right. For the last half hour, only his prompting kept the woman moving. I can't let her believe we're abandoning her, though. I scoot around Paul and rest my hands like cotton balls atop her own. "Katherine," attempt my words, "we *will* be back for you." The woman's tear-filled face turns and, with a slight tilt of her head, she acknowledges my presence. I brush the strawberry locks glued to her wet cheeks behind her ears and offer a smile. "We will."

A hazy gray fog wrapped my early visions of the two. Not much of a *who*, no distinct *where*, no *why*… save the vague imprint of a crucial, yet-to-occur event. Worthless little detail to guide me. I've clairvoyance, yes; an ability to see, no.

We students have few unsupervised moments, though, so I first searched those locations I'm allowed. Thereafter, I had to craft unique ways to avoid the watchmen—and more challenging, the Facility's instructors—to search those areas I've no access rights. The barrack's duct work proved the perfect roadway, yet success eluded me as eight months of tedious, fruitless exploration passed.

Clogged by failure, I let the intense training regimen required for my Class Three advancement all but erase the mission from my consciousness. Then, as I eased into sleep on the eve of graduation—my abilities at a peak—a young, soft-faced woman with reddish hair and her gruff, warm maple syrup of a man, projected upon my mental movie screen. The pair huddled inside a small, poorly lit room in need of urgent relief. The surge solidified my obligation to this unknown couple to free them from this constrictive place. A vision that drove me to further scour the vents in search of the pair…

The hushed giggles of a youthful woman bounce against my eardrums, guiding me to the grate from which they originate. Peek into one of the many ambiguous storage rooms within the building. No one. Huh, I swear—*Another giggle. A man's* uummm *joins a warm, feminine* ooo-ah. *A most intimate exchange.* It's them, *my heart insists. Ease the grate free and slip into the room. Edge against a stack of boxes hiding the couple from me.*

"Now stop that," the female says, though her giggles proclaim no such reservations. "We're supposed to be planning—"

"Your escape!"

I race out from behind the cardboard wall. A shirtless Paul nibbles on the neck of a likewise bare Katherine. Face on to me, she screams, then pushes her beau away in an urgent search for her blouse. Paul, meanwhile, pivots at me with a "What the frick?!", his fists balled.

"Wait!" Throw my hands up. "I'm here to help!"

Mutual embarrassment aside, my timing was critical. The day prior, I heard the dock supervisor say today's ferry is the last for a year. *No matter what, you need to get these two safely on board.*

I rotate to see Paul moved twenty-five meters to the left and behind a stack, four-crates tall. Sucking in two deep, oxygen-rich breaths, I launch after him… and smack dirt as my right leg gives out. A restrained "Yip!" bursts from my mouth. Pain races through my thigh and into my hip, along the arm that braces my fall. *Well,* that's *gonna boost his confidence in you.*

Paul scans the yard in a rush, then the security camera mounted atop his shoulders stops on me with a *told-you-so* grouse. I ignore the wordless remark and push up and into a left leg-favored jog. As I hobble toward the cover, Paul re-adopts the role of lookout. Not that it matters; anyone he spots will spot me, there being nowhere in-between to duck and hide. Five seconds later, I reach him and sit. To my relief, the strain on my leg subsides straightaway.

Paul leans back-first into the mound. "You sure you don't want to wait here? You've no obligation to help us."

His sincere baritone, so similar to Papa's, wraps like a cozy blanket around my heart. I glance downward and take two deep breaths, forcing the puffiness from my cheeks. My forehead eases upright. Thank the stars, Paul is again busy scanning the shipyard. "The pain's minor."

Paul's head turns at me, but his eyes drop to the reddened rags on my leg, doubt flooding his face.

"For real," I say, masking whatever agony my face wears as best I can.

Paul rolls his eyes. "Fine." He huffs. "Where next, then?"

Flit my tongue at him, then crouch to my feet and survey the path onward.

While the crates spread around the yard provide abundant coverage, the gangplank onto the freighter is exposed. Not an option as we're dressed, but, if I remember right… Scan the western wall. "There." My finger points at a gap fifty meters away. "The workers' locker room is through that archway. Should be spare overalls inside."

A laugh trumpets loudly thirty meters to our right, the first of the day shift arriving. *How'd you not hear them sooner?* Paul presses my back. "Go then!"

We shoot at the archway, he at my side for five meters, when my pained thigh commandeers my pace. Within seconds, the space between us grows from five to ten meters. As he passes through the opening, Paul is a good twenty meters ahead. I dig deep, lengthening my stride despite the talons scraping at my thigh. *Pain's a weakness you'll not give into.*

"You—stop now!" booms across the shipyard from behind.

Slide to a stop ten meters short of the passageway. Can't risk Paul and Katherine being discovered on my account. Destiny may demand we part ways, but I can still act as your diversion. Paul'll get them through the last step. He presents resourceful, as capable as any of us students. He can do it.

"I said freeze, now!"

Perplexed, I turn around. Not the guard, but Katherine's anguished face greets me. She followed too late.

"On your knees, now!" The guard is to my left, hidden as I'm to him, behind another pile of crates.

Katherine obeys and drops to her knees. Her arms struggle to raise.

Need a distraction! Twist, finding nothing of use. *No, sneak around and subdue him quick, before he can call for backup.* Should he radio anyone, the ferry won't depart without a thorough search.

My intentions rush around the crates, but my actions ice in Katherine's *I'm-gonna-hurl-again* gaze. Instead, she mouths, *Run!*

Shake my head no. I can't fail you like this.

Her eyes bulge as the guard steps out from behind the crates. *For Paul!* her silent demand hits me.

Tears stream the hills of my face and *thump* onto the ground. Her sacrifice should be mine. Fight the urge to strike the man and instead rush for the archway as best my leg allows. Paul *has* to have that door open. How do I comfort the man, though? I've no experience offering condolences. I only know that now more than ever we need a sanctuary, even if for a mere instant.

My body shoots into the archway, only to barrel into the open arms of Paul four strides in. He hugs me to a stop. Bury my face into his chest, my tears mixing with his sweat. He radiates—despite the grimy path we traversed—a warm, cinnamon-muffin-short-out-of-the-oven scent. I wrap my arms tight around his midriff.

"Locked," he says.

"I—I should've never led you down this path," chokes my lips.

Paul's grip loosens. His hands raise to my shoulders and ease me from his chest. I soak into the raw umber of his eyes. "It's okay," he says. "We'll find another way."

"No, it's… it's…," my mouth resists. I point back through the short hall.

Paul's hands drop, his shoulders sag. No more words need to be said. He walks to the archway and peers out. His shoulders could scrape the stone at our feet.

You dope, comfort him! I weave my arms under his pits and across his firm chest. Lay my head against his upper back and hold him tight against me. "I'm so sorry, Paul. I—I—" Did nothing.

He stiffens and twists, forcing me to loosen my grip and step back. "Where are they taking her?" bursts from him. My body jerks back. "Come on, for certain, you know! Where will they take her?"

"Mmm…" Stretch my brain. "The holding cells, for processing," pops from my mouth.

"Can we intercept them?" Paul's eyes glisten as if he won a giant stuffed elephant in some carnival game. His exhilaration refuels me. *Certainly with the proper shortcut…*

I thrust deep into my recollection of the greater complex and its lesser-known passages. "They'll use the main path to the upper courtyard," I hypothesize, "then to the security center. So…" My brain runs through the route again. *Yes, it will work.* "North of here is the kitchen supply elevator. We can head the guard off, free Katherine, and be back before the boat's departure."

Without a word more, Paul locks my upper arm and hurtles us from the corridor and left. My leg screams as the cut pulls apart. A fresh, thin stream of liquid red races out of my thigh. Bite my lip and push hard—for Paul's sake, for Katherine's—to stay in step with him for the twelve painful meters to the lift. He careens us aboard the elevator before relinquishing his grip, slams its grated door shut, and punches the button arrowed *"UP".*

The elevator clanks skyward.

Two, four, six levels of stacked crates drop below us. Sol's morning rays break over of their shadows and warm my cheeks.

Oh, crud! *How could you forget?*

I yank at Paul's arm—"Get down!"—then crouch to the cart's backside as we level with the stack tops. The cranky elevator demands at least a glance from the dock workers; we cannot let them see us.

Paul puzzles at me, then out of the basket. "Right!" He bends at the knees. The dock workers, now a good forty meters away, have little chance to notice us through the basket's weave, yet I keep a close eye for quizzical fingers pointed in our direction. The smaller their figures become, the greater the success of our ascension.

I recall the lift running two minutes from dirt to sky the few times I used it in the past. Paul picks at the grime under his fingernails, shifts his weight, fidgets, picks again. Part of his pointer nail lifts, and he rips the free edge off. He lets the piece fall and shifts to the nail of his middle finger. Realize I've ripped the tip of one of my own.

"Paul…"

"Yeah."

"Paul… look at me, please." Grab his hands so he stops tormenting his nails, before I destroy my own. "We need a plan. There'll be two, maybe three, guards escorting Katherine."

"A plan—yeah, sorry—right, we need a plan." Paul shakes his head as if to clear whatever thought is lingering there. "The kitchen has to have knives, a cleaver or two—"

"No knives," I say.

"No knives?"

"No knives. Restrain and gag them, even knock 'em out if need be. But no killing."

"As you request," Paul says, though the *huff* and flippant hand gyration he includes leaves no doubt of his desire to do more than give the watchmen concussions.

The elevator shudders to a halt. As we stand, Paul reaches for the rear door, to have it open not by his hand. A Redwood of a man gawks at us, the hat of a sous chef atop his head, an empty cart at his rear. "You're not my asparagus."

Paul's fist springs at the poor guy's face. The chef stumbles back, catching his right Achilles on the cart, and topples to the ground as if a soggy piece of Italian loaf. Paul glances back and says with a drone, "No killing, right?"

I giggle. "Yes, that will do."

Paul scoops the chef under his arms and dumps his generous stature into the supply cart. "He'll be out for now," Paul says as he works, "but see if you can find a rope to bind him. We'll need to head back this way once we've secured Katherine."

He read my mind. All the crates littering the yard, the ferry has to be empty. We've perhaps another half hour, forty-five minutes tops, before the dock crew has the ship prepped for departure. We need to be quick… and this is the quickest way back.

"Gotcha." I hasten along the hall that joins the elevator to kitchens. Short of the kitchens proper, a series of supply closets and food pantries line the hall. In none of them, though, is any twine or rope that can restrain the chef. Rope of the wrist-binding variety is not a common staple of cooking.

The worn wheels of the cart rattle and clank against the pockmarked floor in my direction, one with the squawks of a dying goose. Dang, could that wheel ever use some of that vegetable—Wait!

Race two rooms back and into one of the storage closets. Shove two boxes aside. There rests my quarry: a thick roll of cheesecloth. No effort to shred when spread thin, the material's easy to overlook; but when rolled tight, it's tough to sever. Used right, the ferry will be well on its way, Paul and Katherine stowed safely aboard, long before the chef can get out of his bonds.

"You designing to wrap him up as a mummy?" teases Paul as I emerge with my prize.

"Huh… oh, funny… yeah, that would work, too. No, I was thinking more of this…" Kneel and rip a meter of the material from the bolt. Lay the piece flat to the floor, triple fold the edges, then roll the cloth as if working a length of dough.

"Genius." Paul joins me on the floor. "We'll need nine."

"Right." Rip off another piece and hand the bolt to him. Set the piece flat and cross over the ends, pinching the seams into a thin tube. Flatten my hands against the material and rock them back and forth. The roll tightens, massages at my palms. Papa and his ever-curious daughter, covered in flour, laughing away, drifts into my mind's eye. The two in the middle of yet another experiment gone not quite to the recipe. *"Think of a recipe more a guide than instructions,"* he nurtures. *"The results are so much more interesting."* My heart warms, his comment more than a mere lesson in baking.

"Thanks, Papa," I half whisper.

"You finished with that one?"

"Oh, jeez!" I jerk, half raveling the cloth. Paul is standing again, his left hand held out, the right holding the first two of our pseudo ropes. He nudges his chin at the cart stopped at the first of the closets.

"I'd like to get him outta sight."

"Ah, yeah." Shake my head and quickly fix my gaffe. These fresh visions—*Memories?*—demand more attention than I've capacity for at the moment. "Here." I hand Paul the rope, then latch the bolt and pull another length of the cheesecloth loose. From my left, the squeak of the overloaded cart no sooner disappears into the storage room there, when the service elevator comes to life.

I wrench at the unexpected noise to see Paul jump from the room. He slams the door shut and turns to me. "Run!"

Launching upright as Paul joins me, we rush for the first kitchen proper. The hall rises with a gradual slope before emptying into the ground-level kitchen. Though a short distance, the angle is such that a person in a rush, as we are, gets winded. I stop us at a split in the hall.

For the first time, I'm glad I've worked as each a busser and dishwasher often. The hall to the right connects the kitchens. Halfway between, doors open to the cafeteria's food kiosks, which, given the murmur of voices that carry up the hall, are busy serving students. Clearer are the clanks, whirs, and buzzers of food preparation emanating from the other kitchen. As few attend breakfast, fortune is on our side that the one open kitchen is not this one.

"Come on." I secure Paul's hand and move us straight on to a door bearing the title "Dish Room". There is no lock, not even a handle. Just a two-way swing door with a small window centered three-fourths of its length from the floor. Don't expect to find anyone in there, but still check. The room is vacant, so I slide my way through the doorway. Not ready to relinquish his firm, comfortable hand, Paul's no option but to remain glued to me.

"Where are you taking me?" He asks.

Small windows line the outer wall of the dish room. The morning light beams throughout the space. A thin dust dances in the rays. Unlike the kitchen, the room has but a solitary, one-way door. To our gain, that singular way is outward.

"That," I say, "opens into the upper courtyard. They'll cross through there to access the security hold. From the right spot, we can get the jump on them."

Paul huffs. "That's a big 'if'; most of that field is wide open space."

"Most days, yes, but today there's training. The added barricades will provide plenty of cover." I edge the door open and find my assertion confirmed. Scan the yard for the scantest of movement. "Not how I expected to use the equipment today," I continue, "but hey, who am I to argue?"

Paul squeezes my hand. "You are… indispensable."

Oh, such music to a young woman's ears. Swallow. *Why are your cheeks tingling?* Push the door further open, the rising sunlight floods in. Paul masks his eyes with his free hand. My lungs bath in the crisp morning air, averting the awkwardness.

The nearest barricade—twenty meters off—is not a military apparatus, but a generous pile of rubble. We hurry there in mere seconds. The pile's angle gives us a perfect view of the gate from the docks, while keeping us hidden from anyone passing through. Paul insists he take lookout, an implication that I—the "indispensable" one—am to plan the next phase of our ambush.

Huh... "'Indispensable'. That's the best you've got to offer?"

"Sorry? You say something?"

Crud, did I say that out loud? A pit opens in my stomach. "Ah... you see them yet?"

"No, nothing."

Three minutes. Nothing.

Six minutes. Nothing.

Almost ten minutes and nothing.

Paul picks at his fingernails again, the ground owning more of his attention than the gate. "Where is she?" he asks in a gloomy tone. I ease him further behind the mound, then peek around the rubble's side. No one is there, and the gate is still shut.

"I don't get it. I thought for sures..."

"Hey, you!" booms from the distant side of the courtyard. Turn on my heels; a boyish man points at me. He wears a dark blue t-shirt, the mark of a Class Four student. His first three steps toward us stretch into a lazy run. His mop-like, dark brown hair bobs as his pace quickens. "I know you!" The boy-man's voice jingles with familiarity, but I've no time to deplete brain waves over him: his troops' instructors rush at us, quick to assess our malicious intentions. One commands, "You... stop NOW!"

The chance to intercept Katherine lapses; not, though, the prospect of making good with Paul. Grab his hand and tug him upright. "We need to go!"

Paul's eyes lock onto the closing staff and his body limps. "Forget it. We're burnt."

"Sol's fury we are!"

Locked from the kitchens as we are, going east is no option, though that's no loss; people'd be occupying the space at this point anyhow, if for no other reason, in search of the sous chef. South through the gate is also no alternative; save the guards hauling Katherine, the path is often buzzing with passersby, even in the early hours of the day. The archway northwest catches my eye.

The girls' restroom!

Leagues from a proper exit, the restroom's windows are large enough to work a body through. With the instructors closing in from the northeast, I yank Paul toward our sole refuge. "Come on!"

Tow him ten meters trying to break his sandbag pace, when he snaps out of the funk and scurries ahead. Painful as a knife blade, sweat stings at my leg. The makeshift dressing on my thigh struggles to hold back a free flow of blood. The passageway grows nearer. Over my shoulder, the instructors draw close; with a generous leap, one could latch onto my ankle.

Ten seconds more pass, me still on my feet, as the partial darkness of the passage besets me. Blink through the salty wetness cascading my vision. Paul races a good twenty meters ahead. Battle to close the gap, to extended my lead from our pursuers. My leg sears as if being torched.

"Paul, no! Stop!"

He's passed the turnoff to the restrooms by five meters. He skids to a stop and flips around, his face contorted in confusion. "Come back this way," I call as I reach the intersection and cut left. With a snap change in plans, I bullet past the women's room into the guys' farther along the hall. The lifeline is straight ahead, waist high in the middle of the wall. Step at the window as Paul busts through the door.

"They're close!" Paul sucks at the room's stale air as he nudges past me. *Hey!* He pries the window open. "I'm first."

For serious! So much for chivalry. Besides, am I not supposed to be leading us?

Before I can protest, he boosts his legs through and sits on the ledge. "I'll ease you down," he says as he contorts his body around such that his hands brace against the frame, then slips his butt off the ledge until his body hangs loose. "Hurry!" he says as he lets go, his head disappearing out of sight.

"Sure," I say to no one, "'cause I just lazying about."

From outside the window, a slight grunt and the *clunk* of loose rock mark Paul's landing. At the same moment, the entrance to the girls' restroom slams open. Hurry, indeed! I launch through the window in a mimic of Paul and dangle in the air. My thin shoes scurry around in search of a solid resting place.

"I have you!" A hand secures around my good leg, another against my buttocks.

My buttocks—under my gown! Crush me! *You're flashing the man!* My thighs clench. "Let me down, now!"

"Not yet," Paul grunts as he boosts me higher. "Shut the window."

My modesty a lost cause, stretch for the bottom of the windowpane. Thank the stars, it seals with a minor effort. "Done!" Now get me down!

Paul's hands slide to my waist. The stones below rock and slightly give. Paul shifts his feet to compensate; my body falls flat against his. My back brushes along his bare chest; his heartbeat drums through my torso. My skin tingles, desires to stay within his secure grasp, but his hold vanishes as soon as my feet touch solid ground.

"Where now?" bursts from his lips.

I survey our surroundings, instantly glad Paul went first. They'd built the complex atop an elevated layer of massive boulders, upon two of which we stand. The ground, another two-and-a-half meters lower, looks parched and solid. My leg would have given out and sent me tumbling hard to the ground had I gone first. At least the rocky platform angles out from the walls, creating enough of a pathway over which to make our way ground-ward.

At last, something easy!

From there, though, our prospects remain limited. South along the wall will lead us to the entrance of the courtyard we just left. North along the wall will lead to the lower courtyard entrance on the other side. The open field to the southwest, the only remaining direction to go, lacks any cover. Worse, the stall doors of the boy's room slam open.

I fasten onto Paul's hand and work us from the rocks to the ground and into the openness. Hasten into a run as we reach ground-level. Sweat explodes from every pore of my skin. The cut on my leg rips wider. Tears attempt to wash away the sting of the salty water dripping into my eyes from my forehead with scant victory. I wipe the mixture away with my free hand and scan ahead.

Salvation!

A blackness two hundred meters on calls to me… as a coarse voice demands from behind, "STOP NOW!" To believe the guards wouldn't follow us out the window is a fool's wish.

I don't live on wishes.

I squeeze Paul's hand, a gesture he returns, and quicken our pace despite the screams from my right leg. A fresh, wide stream of red liquid trails from thigh to foot. *Not the moment to dwell on your injuries!* Now pulling me more than me pulling him, Paul shoots at the hole as if a freight train with no breaks. I hoick back on his arm just short of the pit.

He turns at me, his face contorted as if he's stepped in dog poo. "What?!"

I nod at the hole. He peers at the shadowy abyss, then over his shoulder. Our pursuers have covered a third of the distance we just completed. He turns back. "That? For real?"

I release his hand and grab a nearby stone, near to fifteen centimeters in girth, and toss it into the jagged oval. Two seconds pass before the stone kerplunks into water. "Ten, maybe fifteen, meters deep…," I say, "survivable if you pierce the water feet first."

Sure, the realist in me replies, *presuming the water is deep enough.*

I peer back. The guards are closing quick, seeming unaffected by their heavy gear. Next to me, Paul stands Roman-column stiff and glares into the depths of the pit. He sighs as he looks again at me. Crunch my face in one of those half-smiles that radiates a lack of options.

"So be it," he says in a sober tone. "Before we die, though, it'd be nice to know your name."

"Crush me!" My hands fling over my gaping mouth. I forage through the mental videos of our meeting. Despite my ill-timed intrusion, he and Katherine were gracious in their introductions. Me—I spat out a *"Hey"* and lunged into my (*not so*) sure-fire escape plan. Mom would have scolded me to no end; she is so judicious with proper etiquette. Papa's view would be more practical: admit the mistake, apologize, and move past the *faux pas.*

Mom… Dad… my parents! Bounce on my toes. I remember *both* my parents! Did I just squeal? Don't care!

Though now is not the time for such memories. I address Paul's bewildered face. "The trainers call me…" I sense my birth name straining to burst forth, but sups from my lips the only designation I know. "They call me Jay-N-oh-four-four-nine."

He smirks. "Ah, yeah—I don't think so!"

Don't think what?

Paul leaps into the hole, its mouth salivating, eager to consume me too. JUMP!

Yet nothing.

Dammit, girl! You can do this! Just jump!

A whizzing *crack* echoes past my ears. Several pebbles near my feet spray into a mini dust ball, stinging my ankles. "Ouch!" Crouch to rub away the discomfort.

Blood slams to the front of my cortex. A dazed clumsiness overtakes my legs. The lip of the hole passes. Darkness sucks away my sight. Exhilaration tickles at my skin. *I'm flying!* my brain dupes me; my flailing arms better reflect the truth as my body plummets toward the bottom of the pit.

Yet I've no fear, no panic. Only calm. Only belonging. That despite an ungraceful entrance, I'm where I need to be: unencumbered, eyes closed, absorbing the odd hospitality of free-fall.

Impact, though, is inevitable.

Did Paul's weight splash into the water yet? He should have hit bottom by now… unless the pit is deeper, much deeper!

His splash ripples over me as if passing through pudding… making it seem we'd jumped minutes apart as opposed to seconds. The syrupy air sticks to my skin. Fingers, arms stiffen. This cannot be real? The deeper into the earth, the slower I fall. Gravity doesn't work this way!

The pool of water below grows close, maybe ten meters away…

No, nine… Eight…

And the pool is deep enough!

Six… Five…

At least a good four meters deep!

Three meters… Two…

As I hit the icy water, joy sprays over me… how everything is now different… so very different.

CHAPTER TWO

THE WATER IS ICY, NO surprise. Any guarantee of warmth only comes to those that aim to be first into the locker room showers, but Coach held me after P.E. to discuss the weekend's gymnastics meet. Twenty minutes later, I rushed into an empty locker room, threw my gym uniform into my locker, and jumped into a stream of water that's struggling with the concept of heat.

The water temperature doesn't bother me as much as having to rush. I enjoy my gym showers. They're the one time each day that I can find some peace. The Universe knows I can't get that at home, there being but one bathroom for six of us, three being my obnoxious brothers. I'm already late for Calc, though, so need to be quick. I skip my hair and instead lather my legs, only for a smug voice to barrel down the steps to the locker room entrance.

Come on… her… now?

Like a runaway freight train rushing through a tunnel, Katie Matters roisters into the room. "… and she didn't have a clue what hit her!" she guffaws as she and her cackling cohort slide through the door.

I kill the water.

She and I are parsecs apart from being on the best of terms.

Four years ago, courtesy of an abrupt company-wide reorganization at Papa's employer, my family moved to New Grigny near summer's end. Despite our kid-rich neighborhood, between getting our house unpacked, last-minute school shopping, and a reckless younger brother… I know I have to love him and all, but the kid's more exasperating than a nickel-sized cyst on your butt that just won't pop. *Ugh! No matter how hard you squeeze it.* The turd had us sitting in the emergency room for half the day before school started, leaving me no opportunity to meet any of my future classmates. The next day, I walked into middle-school as a friendless, unknown face among my new peers.

Strike one.

As if that alone wasn't bad enough, Mother Nature would force me to have my eleventh birthday earlier that summer. Sure, I'd a slight bit of height over the other girls and was more toned than most, thanks to eight years of gymnastics, but for eleven peaceful years I blended with ease into a packed playground.

Then I woke on that first day of my twelfth year feeling sore and stiff and—hands to the stars—somehow two full centimeters taller than the day before. By summer's end, I shot skyward another fourteen (and added several kilograms of muscle), frustrating mom to no end, as my wardrobe became a river of donations. First day of school, I towered fifteen centimeters over my female classmates and could hold firm in an arm-wrestling match against the strongest of my male counterparts. No longer was I just another nondescript kid fluttering about the schoolyard.

Strike two.

The tipping point, though: my brain. Make no mistake, I'm no straight-A student. Like my peers, I've challenges with homework, study long hours for tests, and am a regular at office hours. For me, though, puzzles that baffle everyone else just fit together in indescribable ways. A trait that earned me the label "academically gifted" as a sixth-grader and enrollment in eighth-grade classes. More exacting, a sixth-grader enrolled in Katie's eighth-grade classes.

Strike three.

Thus, Katie interjected her most unwelcomed self into my life; the two of us becoming intertwined in a detrimental interconnection ever since.

That first day of school alone, the witch targeted me with snide comments on everything from the flowery shirt I wore to the applesauce in my lunch. I mean, come on, what's so wrong with applesauce? As friendships with my peers blossomed (despite her badmouthing), she recruited her cronics to join in the harassment. For an entire week, they laced the pages of my textbooks with Super Glue. They once even tried sticking me to my seat.

A fortnight after, I started the day engaged in another heated argument with my older brother over the bathroom. He bit extra sharp that morning, claiming me as the unwanted child that should have never been born. Mom—no surprise—sided with *her* son; any delay had to be of my doing. As if! He was the louse barring me from the bathroom, from getting ready!

I bloodied the mole at the nape of my neck while obsessing over the incident during the bus ride to school, only to have Katie take the baton of intimidation without a misstep. Not five minutes of taunts into first hour, she glimpsed my red-strained collar and out came: *"Chick can't even manage a proper period."* I wanted to hide in a closet. My only relief was Papa, who took off the second half of work to pick me up for a mid-day gymnastics showcase. I struggled to reach the car before the tears stormed forth; yet over each of the full three hours there and back, I couldn't bring myself to confess my anguish, even to him.

I couldn't have performed worse in a showcase.

Katie won that day.

Papa didn't press the matter. Even when he found me in bed later that night, my pillow saturated in the failures of the day. He gave me one of his patented bear hugs, a gentle kiss on the forehead, and said, "I am the luckiest man alive to have such a special, talented daughter like you." Buried my misery under his words and let the day's struggles fade away as I drifted to sleep.

A week later, while weeding the flower garden and sowing some terrible jokes (*Papa: "What flower does everyone have on their face?" Me: "What?" Papa: "Tulips!"*), find Papa locked on me, a big smile on his face, a chasm of warmth radiating from his eyes. Everything pours out. No, please don't tell mom, I would hate for this to affect her employment. No, don't call the school; that would make things worse. No, she hasn't beat on me. Yes, she is an insecure bully, and yes, it is best to ignore bullies. Yes, one day, in some karmatic way, someone will put her in her place. And, yes, I'll handle this myself. Thank you for your support, no matter which path I choose.

I ignored Katie, which sufficed to the end of our first marking period.

No matter how insecure a bully, Katie is no scholastic slouch. She'd long set the curve in each of her subjects and took exception when I, a lowly sixth-grader, jumped to the top of the class. Her displeasure rocketed from trivial put-downs to fierce attacks on my yet-to-develop feminine form. Her infamous cronies soon joined in on the "fun" by targeting my parents' jobs and financial means. Katie avoided direct physical attacks, but coaxed (with cash when necessary) as much from several boys and the huskiest of girls: an "accidental" bump into the wall during passing time; a "chance" trip while in the lunch line; an "unavoidable" hit during gym. There's nothing she wouldn't do to underscore how unwelcome I was in *her* school.

Embracing Papa's continued guidance and heartwarming hugs, I steeled myself against the onslaught of relentless cruelty. When I couldn't avoid or ignore, I held my ground—sometimes dishing back what she was serving, but more often by spreading kindness, which infuriated Katie all the more. Her deep-rooted need to make my life miserable never faulted though, cementing our relationship as one of tormentor and tormentee.

She never has, however, won the day again… perhaps until now.

My nervous hand latches the musty curtain shielding me and shifts it the slightest bit to the side. Reflects in the restroom's mirrors the unmistakable reddish-blonde waves of Katie Matters' ponytail dancing between her shoulders.

"Did you see that preacher's wife dress Samantha had on last night at McNaily's?" Katie quizzes of her companions. "Who was that slut trying to fool with that outfit—us or herself?" Her cackle drowns out the giggles of the girls with her.

Another recognizable voice grinds, "Had to be trying to mock me, don't you think? Ann told me, according to her brother, Sam hooked up with Dewey just last weekend, and she was down for more than mere petting. I swear, if that is even half true…"

Denise Brightford, field-hockey co-captain and Katie's best friend, has reason to worry, being the two-year on-again, off-again girlfriend of one Dewey Rogers, a.k.a. my eldest brother. The two are off again, owing to her being—per rumor, and counter to her promiscuous facade—quite the conservative prude. From what I gather, she won't even let Dewey french her. Samantha Collins has no such reservations in living up to her licentious reputation. And Dewey… well, despite the high esteem to which my mother holds him, our shared bedroom wall speaks the secrets he hides from her, not to mention Denise. My lack of clothing aside, I've no desire to tell Denise that the joke is, without a doubt, on her.

"Oh, for goodness' sake D, give it up to the poor boy already!" Katie holds back with no one. "By the stars, at least let him give some attention to more than the lips on your face." Picture her punctuating the statement with the same eye roll she so often throws my way. One of life's ironies, Papa once mentioned, is ending up knowing your deepest rivals with as much intimacy, if not more, than your nearest friends.

"That's easy for you to say," Denise retorts. "You've known your soulmate for years now! Might as well get married already."

Katie Matters in a long term—monogamous!—relationship... *that* I didn't know.

"We *are* made for each other, aren't we?" comes Katie's smug reply.

Denise huffs at the comment before a third, unfamiliar voice teases, "Stop picking on Denise. If she wants to envelop herself in a chastity belt until she's married, that's her choice. It's... honorable."

Katie seems to ignore the comment's sarcasm and replies, "Yeah, whatever." Her voice drops in tone. "Don't make me have to remind you of the pact we made; there are relationships to maintain."

A discomfited hush thickens around me. I dare not breathe.

Denise saves me from suffocating. "Anyhow, what was with that dress..." her voice enthuses, "she rummage through her grandma's attic, searching for a Halloween costume?" The trio giggle as the cattiness carries on.

Katie turns to a sink, snaps open her purse, and pulls out a lipstick. With the simultaneous snaps of two other purses, the girls take up their second favorite pastime and begin primping themselves in the mirrors. With my gym class being the last scheduled before lunch, they've the privacy of the locker room to glory in their shallowness.

Goose pimples spring to life as an uncontrollable shiver overtakes my body. I dare not turn the water back on to rinse my legs before Katie and her crew leave. *Come on bell, ring already!* Draping against the wall opposite the stall, my towel is too far away to grab. With no alternative, I hug myself and rub my hands up and down each arm.

The shriek of the bell comes and goes; the girls do not. *Idiot, of course they're skipping class.* They continue to tweak their looks while snickering at the perceived flaws of their fellow female classmates. Papa echoes in my head, "*They torment in order to feel better about their own inadequacies.*"

An extra chilly (and mind-numbing) fifteen minutes of banter passes as my arms turn pink, as if lugged back and forth across a stubbled carpet. My legs itch, the soap they bear having set. I so want to dig my fingernails, had I any, over them. Drag each over the other, my body wobbling as I shift from one foot to the other. My arm knocks my bar of soap from its holder. Though well used, its thin girth still hits the wet floor of the stall with a *splash*.

"What was that?" the unfamiliar voice says.

"What?" Katie fusses, her story cut short.

"I think there's—"

"Hey!" Katie's voice elevates. "Whoever's here, make yourself known now!"

A shadow shifts across the shower curtain. I stiffen.

"Janson, if you and your loser buddies are in here trying to spy on half-naked girls again, I'm gonna have your hide!"

Chance to peek around the curtain. Katie—who's ten centimeters shorter than I—is strutting toward the locker bay, the bulked muscles of her legs flexing as she moves. Aiming to be the center of attention as always, she wears her school uniform at least two sizes too small. The outfit looks a mini-dress, fighting to keep even her meager bosom contained. Its flared skirt sways side-to-side as she walks. Denise is following her characteristic step behind, dressed in the school standard white blouse and brown-green plaid pinafore. Their third companion remains hidden.

The pair proceed past each locker row, Katie searching to the right and Denise to the left. For a minute, the *clump-clump, clump-clump* of their designer ankle boots echo throughout the locker room. Four rows deep, Katie stops. She glares at the row, then disappears into the section. A moment later, her mischievous voice calls out, "Well, looky-looky what we have here!"

Denise gives up her own search and meets Katie as the latter comes back into view, a reddish cloth clenched within her hand. *Oh crud!* Loosening her grip, the full length of my hair ribbon comes into view. Consumed by my more immediate predicament, I'd shelved the memory of my locker being down that row. In my rush to get out of my P.E. outfit and into the shower, the ribbon must have fallen out.

"You don't think..." Denise looks from Katie's hands to her eyes, a devilish grin creeping its way across her face. Katie glances from side-to-side as if the two are standing among an enthralled crowd and leans down to whisper into Denise's ear. Denise giggles in reply and the pair disappears into the row. Locker doors slam open. In moments, my belongings will confirm their suspicions. In moments, a mere curtain will prove false protection. The true irony: the lockers have no actual locks.

There's no way from the showers past Katie's mystery companion, only the hope of some mercy in an otherwise terminal situation. I slip first my left hand, then leg, past the once white shower curtain. A slickness caresses my nakedness. Grimace. Slide my torso and cheek around the edge of the cloth, grime latching to my skin. A damp, dirty socks aroma stings my nostrils. A shudder ripples through my body.

Disgusting.

Almost free of the curtain, yet my towel is still *(Come on—really!)* out of reach, I freeze solid, desperate for rescue. Angelica would, was she not visiting her sister at University. As protective of me as she is, for certain my best friend would be on the search by now. The plaid yellow-green skirt and canary blouse lighting into view, however, offers no such reprieve. My eyes squeeze shut. So cruel this day has been, I can't absorb the look of ultimate victory upon an adversary's face.

"What are you two doing?" are not the words a girl exposed to the eyes of the world expects to hear. Brave a peek out of my right eye, then open both wide. I'm alone, so to speak. The dull *clunk* of what has to be the girl's low-heeled shoes prod toward the locker bay.

Go now!

Snatch my towel from its hook and rush around the wall that segregates the showers from the adjoining toilet bay. Sneak a glance at the lockers. Hmm… thought I knew all of Katie's committee of vultures.

A cut-to-the-shoulders arctic blonde glides toward her companions. Similar in height to Katie, the girl wears the same school-standard flare-skirted dress, but in a size more compatible with her physique. The dress complements her subtle hourglass shape, she with more natural proportions than the artificial, ballooned shape many a female celebrity creates for herself. As with the other two, the girl's arms and legs are all muscle, but with less bulky, more statuesque curves. She complements the outfit with a cute neck scarf matching the plaid of the dress along with white knee-highs and forest green oxfords.

File the clothing combination under *charming-outfits-for-the-future*. Adjust my focus to a more relevant topic: neither Katie nor Denise have yet exited the locker row, so with this unknown girl's back to me, I complete the first steps of my withdrawal with success.

Continue my blitz into the toilet bay to find that all three girls left their purses on the perches above the sinks. Katie's handbag I've seen flaunted many times before: a two strapped *Finesse La Model* made of genuine taupe-beige alligator skin. She boasts the purse was custom designed by her mother, a gift from their last trip to Manhattan mere days before the irrevocable failure of the island's dikes.

The spinach green purse furthest to the left must be the blonde's. The largest of the three by a good five centimeters all around, the bag's exterior is one-hundred percent leather; save the gold-toned hardware that attaches its handles at four points along the sides of a slight parabolic top. A *Prada* logo embellishes the front.

Thus, the remaining handbag is Denise's, though I've not seen her with it prior. A rigid lung-shaped structure runs its outside length, with a hinge at its base and metallic clasp at its top. The silver lame cloth clutch bears a single silver-toned metal handle. At both ends of the handle, where it attaches to the purse, garnish lion's heads with sparkling crystal eyes.

All three purses are wide open.

Lean forward. What secrets might you girls be—

"Well, what have we found here?"

Spring back as Katie's jubilation bounds throughout the locker room. I listen as the pages of books—my books—whip about with a rush, then fling onto the floor with a thud. Paper crinkles and rips, the contents of my brown-bagged lunch following my books. Someone kicks my orange across the floor, and it rolls into view. Denise cackles. My pencil case unzips, its contents clink and clank upon the bench.

"Oh my," howls Denise, "look at those panties! Are those ice-cream cones?" Another unruly laugh before she says, "How old is this chick?"

A tear traces the curve of my cheek. "Bitch."

I say it quiet-like as I reach for Katie's purse. After all these years as the butt-end of her cruelty, dammit if I'm not overdue some kind of revenge! An eye for an eye.

My free hand about lock upon her purse straps, a glimpse of me latches onto my eye. "*A mirror always reflects truth,*" Papa once told me. The naked girl reflecting in this mirror is no exception. She is a vivid reminder of how vulnerable I am at this moment.

Draw my hand back. Now is not the time for revenge, but to embrace what meager dignity I've left to salvage. Grab two corners of my towel lengthwise and wrap it around my torso as best as possible. Lock the corners together in what limited cleavage my body sports. I'm no example of modesty—the towel's width hangs mere centimeters past my hips—but the alternative leaves nothing to the imagination.

"Wait a minute…," Katie's voice sparks, "dirty gym clothes… red hair ribbon… prudish bra, children's underwear… No way!"

Her words erase any advantage my silence granted me. Turn. My legs fatigued, the toilets provide but a single, risky hideaway: squatting atop a bowl, feet slipping off the lid. Even tougher: leave the stall doors cocked open and hazard partial coverage or close one in the hope none of the trio notice the change. The stars forbid should one of the three need to use the facilities.

The stalls are a poor option.

Surrender being a non-option, the only choice is the hunter green door at the far end of the room: the exit leading to the gymnasium. An inferno aside, I'd never dare venture from the locker room dressed in only a towel. Alas, desperate times… desperate measures. Spring for the door as *clump-clump-clump* hurries from the locker bay.

"Come out, come out wherever you are," Katie's devilish voice teases. "I know you're in here."

More clumping—louder, faster.

"But then," Denise cackles, "perhaps it's better you stay put. Would hate to burn my eyes out!"

Her voice rings in my ear as if we are standing shoulder-to-shoulder. The exit is too distant, the time too short. With no seconds to spare, I slip into a stall and press myself as far into the back corner as possible. No sooner, two pairs of clumping boots come rushing by. A second after, the first shower curtain—the one I only moments ago stood within—whips open.

"Come now, my little sewer rat, I know you're in here!"

The jibe is one of the many "nicknames" Katie's saddled me with over the years, that one in particular a play on my initials. A little *puff* of disbelief escapes my lips. Resorting to such a juvenile gibe, Katie must think she's hit the *I'm-going-to-stick-it-to-her-this-time* jackpot.

Another curtain whips open.

The shuffling at my locker continues, but in a more deliberate and thoughtful manner. Blondie hasn't returned with her cohorts. Nor has she spoken since walking back to the lockers. She is still poking through my stuff, but if I'm not mistaken, she's returning each to their place in my locker?

Who is this girl?

No time to dwell on that: a third curtain whips open. Few to go!

I move out of the stall with nimble feet, my eyes again catching the open handbags before me. So want to snatch them, but that'll only fuel Katie's search.

Although… inflicting a touch of payback seems justified.

The ideal play, something subtle, yet infuriating to the likes of Katie, peeks out from her purse. The gold tipped, purple and light blue alternating lined cap of her favorite lipstick. It once fell from her purse during passing time, yet she, thinking it stolen, had the hand of the naïve freshman returning it, broken. To think if her lipstick was forever gone…

Grab the tube, ready to carry it right out the door, then eye the lung-shaped purse again. Perhaps more delicious… if her best friend was to take it, that'd confound Katie. The depth of her reaction, who knows, but the entertainment factor when that confrontation comes to head, one not to be missed. I chance a second to stuff the tube deep within Denise's own handbag.

Mischief complete, I hurry to the hunter green door, edge it open enough to slip past, and feather it back into place. As the locker room's light cuts out, the last of the curtains whips open and Katie—dumbfounded—complains, "Where the shits is she!"

If only you knew!

No time for complacency—Katie could bust from the locker room any second—I hurry through the short, dim hallway and up the steps to the gym floor proper. Pause a second to peep over the topmost step.

Thank the stars, the basketball courts are empty, but I'm far from home-free. They did not design the gymnasium for a naked girl wrapped only in a less-than-concealing towel. Scan for a solution.

Along the far-right wall, the gym has three sets of double doors, all of which lead to the rear of the school and its athletic fields. The far-left wall has two sets of double doors that open into the classroom hallways. Passing through those will make an already grave situation much worse.

The boys' locker room is ten meters away, along the same wall I kneel. On the one hand, it is a solid choice: Katie will never figure me for going in there. On the other, a nude girl caught in the boys' locker room… not only a call home and definite suspension, but bright oils with which Katie can further paint her distorted portrait of me.

The only plausible solution is the hunter green door to the immediate left of the coaches' offices.

A growing commotion echoing from behind me, I grab tight the knot at my chest and dart across the gymnasium floor. No more do I launch when my towel rides up my hips. Halfway across the courts, I'm nothing less than bare-butted. I slow and let loose the knot to pull the towel back down.

Pull too much.

The knot gives way before I can restore my grip. As the towel falls, my legs wrap around the loose fabric. Stagger twice and go down hard, sliding forward across the floor a mere meter shy of my sanctuary. The wooden floor rips at my forearms. The towel, for what little it's worth, shields my legs from equal punishment. I lay there, my rear irradiant for any full moon enthusiasts to enjoy. Bite my cheek to stifle a scream. Tears stream down my face.

At once, the locker room door crashes open as a furious thunder roars overhead. I jump to my feet, ignoring the sting racing through my arms. Grab the towel and bolt for the green door. Behind me, Katie's heels pound up the steps. "… have sworn she'd be down there!"

"Maybe those were spare clothes," what I now know to be the blonde's voice points out. If only that were true, then I'd be in Calc right now. *Crap!* We've a big test today; twenty-five percent of the semester's grade! *No— your GPA!* The Nursing Corps accepts only the two top-most from each high-school.

The pounding heels go silent.

"Are you delusional? A spare set of clothes or not, there is no way *she'd* leave all those books behind." The elevated accusations continue. "I'm damn certain that bitch was down there. Believe me, I will figure out what the shit is going on!"

The stairs again thunder as another lightning bolt explodes outside.

Pull the door open, a dull yellow light painting over me. Chance Coach forgot it was on and launch into the equipment room as Katie's voice breaks the stairway. Ease the door shut and back into the room. Find the giant parachute we use in class tucked behind some boxes. Free it, heap my towel down in its place as a pad, sit, and cover myself.

Rain pounds down on the roof of the school.

Sit as still as possible, stretching my ears into the gym. Please, let me have avoided Katie.

The downpour dominates anything else that there may be to hear. I let what I guess to be five, then another five minutes pass, motionless. My body cramps, my buttocks ache from sitting huddled as small as possible on the floor; a small price to pay to remain undiscovered.

Flex as much as the cramped area will allow. My legs itch again. Pull the towel out from beneath me and do what I can to wipe away the soapy residue. Dab away at the spots of water still clinging to the rest of my body, the towel having earlier soaked up most of it.

For sures they're gone, right?

I'm more than tardy and desperate to get back to the locker room and dress. Not to mention, I don't know when the next P.E. class starts. I no more stand halfway up when the sound of shoed footsteps approaches the equipment room door. I halt in the semi-hunched position as the closet door opens.

"Just grab one cart," a close masculine voice calls out.

"Sure thing," a much closer—dangerously close—male voice returns.

I pull on the lobe of my right ear.

The cart sitting not a stride away from my toes moves, its tiny wheels screaming for grease. Within seconds, the sound dampens as the cart exits the room, the lights extinguish, and the door again clanks shut. The gym fills with the *badadump* of dribbling basketballs. Bathed in darkness, I can only sit back, shaking my head.

Of all days to thunderstorm.

No way am I making it to the locker room. Sense I'll not be making it anywhere for a while. I pull off the parachute, stand, and re-wrap my torso with the towel. *At least with Katie hyper-focused on you, she won't be injuring naive freshman girls.* Shift some boxes to make room enough to lie in a partial fetal position. *Or shaming some poor boy into harming himself, or worse.* Suppose in an ironic way, the longer I hide, the longer I'm protecting everyone.

Being protector, though, is exhausting. I restore the chute and close my eyes. Rub my temples between my thumb and middle finger of my right hand. It finds a plump lump at my hairline.

Another pimple, of course.

Dig what of my nail-tip there is into the spot, which, after a painful second, pops with a *plip.*

Keep doing that and you're gonna scar.

"Oh, shut up."

Another crack of thunder roars outside, shaking the building and my body alike. The rain slams even harder against the roof of the school, its tin-like response drilling against my eardrums. A drip of water plops on a box near me, then another and another. If the box was keeping time, it'd have the most irritating second hand ever. Push my palms into my fore-head.

So, this is what a migraine feels like.

CHAPTER THREE

A DRIP OF WATER BEATS at my dazed senses. *PLOP* the drip bangs. A silent second passes. Another *PLOP*, then silence. *PLOP… PLOP… PLOP!* Each drop a sledgehammer slamming in my head. My backside is sore, body stiff. The floor underneath is cool and hard. What thin cloth drapes my body provides no padding, no insulation. Shiver; the chill of my damp gown magnified by a slight breeze. I lean on my side, pull my knees up to my chest, and embrace myself to stave off goose pimples.

"Ow! Shit, that hurt."

I sit bolt upright; the voice sounds like it's on top of me. Open my eyes to nothing but darkness. "Paul? That you?"

"This place is a damn maze," the voice says. "How the frick does the commander expect us to find anyone?"

"Can it, Walters," a second, gruff voice demands, "I just heard something." There's a shuffling of boots from behind me. I glance in the direction, but there's nothing but black.

"Walters has a point, Captain," a female voice joins in.

"Dammit, Brayberry," the Captain says, "didn't I just tell Walters to shut up?"

The voices, and the shuffling, are getting closer. I try to stand, but my head clouds, forcing me back to the ground.

"For serious, Captain?" Brayberry says, seeming too comfortable in disobeying orders. "You know as well as us they cannot survive down here. This is a shit assignment, even coming from the commander."

The voices are getting closer. I raise on my hands and knees and crawl to the right, away from the exchange. My left hand sinks into a shallow puddle. *Crud!* My gown a worthless towel, fling what water I can into the mossy air.

"Shit assignment or not," the Captain says, "it's the assignment. Now shut it."

I crawl on, guided by the contour of the right wall. Ridges and dimples litter the floor. Loose dust scoops into the webbing between my fingers. A pebble digs into my left hand. Bite my lip to keep from calling out. My knees ski across a damp, spongy patch. A bitter stench lingers in the air, teasing my nose. I fight back a sneeze, silence being crucial.

Thirty seconds along, the wall curves to a sharp left. The voices fade as I follow the angle and, twenty seconds more, navigate another wall that veers a decisive left.

A beam of yellowish light blinds me.

"Hey!" Raise a hand to shield my eyes.

The light beam angles to the floor half a meter in front of me, then again half that much back toward me.

"Paul?" I lean butt to ankles and gawk up. Where he found a flashlight, I don't care. The search party can catch up at any moment. Unless these are soldiers, too! Three meters off, though, the shadow behind the light is too diminutive for a soldier, and certainly is no man the likes of Paul. *Is that—a boy?*

Rather, a teenager; but all the same, how can that possibly be?

"Hello," I say.

The flashlight beam jerks upright and tangos across my eyes. Sweat breaks through my temple. A warm, bitter taste burns in my throat. Turn away and double over, a dagger piercing my stomach. Heave. Liquid splatters against the wall and floor, its misty residue sprinkles across my thigh.

"I'm so sorry," I blubber to the light bearer, then suck in a deep vat of stale oxygen as I struggle to fight away a dry heave. Spit what residual phlegm is in my mouth to the floor. Wipe away the last of the spittle that dangles from my lips.

From behind, boots slam into puddles in a rush. Spots of light dance upon the far walls in the direction. How not could they have heard me puke? I fight through the nausea to my feet and face the teen. "Please, help me."

The boy takes a step forward, then stops, perhaps now noticing the lights and boots of the search party. He whips around, a stuffed sack strapped over his back, and takes off in the opposite direction.

"No, wait!" I sprint after him. "I won't hurt you." Where in the Universe is Paul?!

As the teen runs, his light flings from floor to ceiling, making his red, spiked hair look like sputtering flames. He pulls farther from me with each second, perhaps being faster, but more likely having the advantage of a familiarity with the caves. Not that the cut on my leg is of any cruddy help. That there is just enough residual glow from his flashlight keeps me on his trail, and from slicing my skin against the stubby outcroppings plaguing the cavern.

What seems fifteen meters ahead, he stops, looks back, then launches left. A static-laced exchange between the search party and headquarters hits my ears from behind. *Human puke, fresh, no question,* the Captain reports. I double my efforts to get to the boy. I round the corner he took, but there's nothing to see, not even the halo of his flashlight.

This has to be the turn, I'm certain.

I think. My head's still groggy. Maybe I misjudged the distance? Am I a turn too early? The *clump, clump, clump* of hustling boots and rattling gear nears. *Come on—stay or go? Make a choice!*

My stomach tightens. I move my hand to—*Wait! What the crud!*

Though only the faintest of grays, there are my fingers. I look down, see my worn, torn gown, my bandaged thigh. The wrap is black stained, a bad sign. Lower, there are the edges of the cavern's floor and, looking up, the walls draw into focus. Only two meters in any direction, but I can distinguish the passable areas from those not so passable.

Almost everything radiates even the slightest of a heat signature, but the human eye cannot perceive in the infrared. *How can this possibly be?*

A question for later. The boots are bearing down on me, maybe twenty seconds behind. I move forward with caution, testing my unaccustomed eyes. At once, I see the heat from what seems a residual hand print, next to a tight crevice on the right, two meters away. It's a smart choice of escape. Even should the headlamps and flashlights of the search party find the hole, only the most slender of them could make it through, and only without gear. I've no gear, but with my curves?

You've no choice!

Twinkles of light ping from the dust hanging in the air just outside the turnoff. Maybe ten seconds, twelve tops, before I'm done for. I squeeze sideways into the crevice. Narrow even had I no breasts, I force the air from my lungs and wiggle in. The lips of the passage pull at my gown, scrape at the skin beneath. Boobs only compress so much.

Well, this one time, they'll have to compress a little more. My brain fights against my lungs to not take a breath.

"There's a side-tunnel," the voice I know as Walters says. The boots close fast. Spots of light dance through the entry.

I contort left, twist right. Slip a little deeper.

You can't breathe!

The circles of light grow bigger, brighter.

You're gonna pass out!

My gown snags on the spiky outline of the crevice entrance. Half of the back doesn't want to go through. *Oh, come on!* I make a final push. Threads *pip* and *pit* apart. *Push!*

Rrrriiiippp!

Crap!

The remains of my frock spill to the sides like a hospital gown as I pop into the other side of the crevice. No sooner, the tunnel floods with light. I back-foot into the wall opposite the opening and suck at the stale air as quietly as I can. A chill runs up my backside.

I don't care.

At least I'm safe for the moment. Where, though, is Paul? Did they catch him?

The lights outside the crevice swing back and forth between the walls, but none directly into the hole. "Damn," the Captain says. "I could swear we were trailing them."

"This way or the other, Captain?" asks Brayberry.

There is a pause of quiet as a light sweeps the immediate area again, then the captain says, "The other, though, Walters, be sure to mark this one. We'll be back."

"Yes, Sir."

You're one lucky chick.

The lights dim and disappear in seconds, but I hold still, despite my chattering teeth, until the boots fade. Stones suck away heat fast. I butt off the wall and slither free of my now cape. The rip is from the hem almost to the neckline, but I have to make it work. I tie one knot, then two, three, four between the halves, a simple task as the gown fluoresces in waves of my body heat. I slip it back on, barely. Both my hips and boobs complain about the tight fit.

I move deeper into the new tunnel, scanning for any signs of the teen. Not five steps along, the gown is riding up. Yank it back down. *Good thing Paul's not here now, eh?* At any moment, I'm sure my chest is going to pop loose the knots.

Bet you look like that one girl from high school—what was her name?

Crud. What was her name? Ugh—and that friend of hers… what was *her* name? She was dating my brother. "Wait! I have a brother." No, a trio of brothers! *Come on, girl, you know their names.* The youngest was a "J"-name… John… no… Jake… um… Jim… Jim, James. James, that's his name!

Wish you had all those curls, don't ya?

The passage splits into a rough Y. I pause and scan as best as my magic eyes allow each direction, but there is nothing to see. Strain my ears to hear nothingness other than the occasional faint drip of water from the left arm. *Let's go that way.*

No idea why.

My older brother, the one dating the friend of that girl, he's always so engrossed with that tease—Debbie? Denny? No, he's a play on her name… Denbie. That's it. That ridiculous nickname he baby-talks. Denbie, this; Denbie, that. Ugh! What girl allows such a thing?

The hall weaves right, then left, and right again. Still no sign, though, of the teen or Paul.

Ooo, and my younger brother has the jolliest smile, ear to ear. Makes you want to give him sloppy smooches every time he walks into the room. How can I not remember his name? He's my favorite brother, for goodness' sake!

Who am I?

From *where* am I?

I take a deep breath. This isn't healthy… neither the lamenting nor the stale air.

Rather, is that lilac?

I rush forward, letting my nose lead me down a break-off ten strides from the first whiffs of the scent. I turn right twice, left, and right once more, then close to trip over the body.

Leaned half against the side of the tunnel, her head dangles in an unnatural arc to the side. I saw a dead body only once before. A training accident: a novice Class Two mistimed a grenade throw. Blew his arm and half his torso off. I helped triage two of his squad mates who were worse off: they survived the blast. Threw up four times that day. Couldn't eat for a week after.

Death by a broken neck is nothing.

Still, the sight tightens my stomach. I swallow hard and caution forward.

"Son of a—!"

Not with caution enough. My flimsy slipper-shoes offer no competition to the pebbles that litter the passages, let alone stones of any substance. Pop the shoe from my right heel and rub the ball of my foot. Cruddy—crud—crud! Is that shattered glass?

I glance at the floor, but there is no rock. Squat down and grab the metallic, rectangular casing laying there. To the back of the casing attaches a cloth band; the front bears a hard plastic. I aim the plastic face down the tunnel, close my eyes, and flip its switch on. Seconds pass as my sight adjusts to the yellowish glow filtering through my eyelids. As the yellow fades to a brownish hue, ease my lids apart. Bit by bit, my pupils adjust to the light.

The woman is hips-down exposed except for plain underwear. A crumpled pair of cargo pants lays next to the body. Her footwear is gone (Crap!), along with any weapons from her nearby kit belt. I grab the pants and slip them on. The woman is petite, but we otherwise share a similar figure. They are snug in the hips and short—more like capris than trousers—but shouldn't ride up. Her shirt fits even less so, the guard's chest much flatter than my own. I work the hair band from the short ponytail atop her head and slip it over my wrist, then search for anything else of use. A basic first-aid kit remains in one pocket of the pants, three protein bars in another. There's nothing else of value.

Latch my arms through her pits and shift the body flat to the ground. Guide her head into a more natural angle, as if she is looking off to the side. The flowery scent of her shampoo is stronger so close up. I close her eyelids and drape my discarded gown over her body. She deserves some minimum of modesty, not that she'll know the difference. All the same—woman to woman—it seems right.

I stretch my ears, not expecting to hear the boy—he's long gone—but also hoping to not hear my pursuers. There is nothing to hear save my own exhalations. I work the headlamp past my ponytail and move further along the tunnel. It curves a gentle left several meters before splitting into a lopsided T. The left side angles obtusely for about four meters before turning a sharp right. The right side stretches nine meters into a dead end.

"Okay, left it is."

I turn. The pale freckled body of who seems to be the woman's teammate, lies face down not two meters in. Like his companion, he's stripped of his gear. The black sports boxers protecting his modesty aside, all his clothes are gone. A sizable pool of blood teases out from underneath his body. Flip him to his back. His left lung leaks of a wide knife wound. For certain, he's the worse of the two deaths: suffocated in his own blood. I step over the body and down the hall before my stomach twists further.

There's an unfamiliar scent hanging in the air. I take a deeper draw of the mixture.

A thick hand, a man's hand, smacks over my mouth. The muscles of the other wraps my arms around my thorax and thrusts me off my feet. An unnerving chill races down my spine as his breath tickles at my left ear. Kick back at his crotch with my right foot. He shifts; my sole catches his tougher inner thigh. "Arg!" we both grunt as his grip loosens. Arc left and outward, breaking his grasp. Bullet the open palm of my left hand toward the man's chin. He jerks to the side to avoid the blow, but stumbles and snaps his head against the wall, then plops to his behind.

"Oh, shit!"

Paul cradles the back of his head.

"I'm so, so sorry." I lift his red stained hands from his head and kneel to assess the damage. A seven-centimeter cleft runs diagonally through his curly hair. It already swelling and with no way to wash the blood away, I can't tell how deep it goes. Thank the stars, most of the cut appears to be shallow.

"Man, am I glad that left hadn't connected. Though…" He reaches for his head and cringes. "I'm gonna have a pounder of a headache."

"Jeez, Paul, why didn't you call out? What in the Universe was that about?"

"Now wait a minute there, missy, look at how you're dressed. Can't see for crap in this darkness, and I've got nothing but this penlight. So, whaddya think I was doing?"

"Well—that's not—ugh!" Did someone turn up the heat in here?

"Hows about we call it a miscommunication and get a move on. I may have found somewhere we can hide for a bit." Paul reaches his right hand out. "Help me up, will you—with a gentle hand, if you please."

We lock palms around the other's elbow, and I bring him to his feet with a cautious yank. He wavers and, in a twist of roles, leans into me for balance. His head rests against my shoulder, his breath again plays at my ear. A chill, more pleasant than the last, meanders down my spine.

Crud, did I step into the sun?

Armed with the headlamp and Paul's penlight (Where'd he find that?!), we move through the passageway with ease. He pulls ahead several steps, as if he's well-traveled the route. A thin river of red weaves from his head through his back muscles. My leg, irritated by our scuff, fares no better. A small stain of blood leaks through the capris. Medical attention—any medical attention—is an urgent priority.

Paul halts and leans against the tunnel wall. "I need a minute," he says. I come about his front. He looks up and forces a smile. His face is pale. "Don't worry, I'm fine. Just need a breath. We're close. Twenty meters— I think."

"Those two back there… you do that?"

Paul chuckles. "Funny, I've the same question for you… well, about the guy. There was another one?"

"Yeah, a woman, back around the corner. Best I can figure they got jumped from behind."

"Hummm… who else would be down here?"

"I saw this boy, a teen," I say. "I don't think he could have done it, though. The woman has a twisted neck, and you saw what they did to her partner."

"That makes no sense. How can anyone survive down here, let alone some boy?"

"Well, someone no good is down here. No one passed by you?"

"Nope, but these caves split all over. Any of these crevices could be the secret entrance to some whole other branch and no one would know the better." Paul pushes off of the wall. "We should get going."

Twenty meters is more like thirty-five, but who's counting? He ignores three cut-offs along the way and turns down a fourth split, which thereafter divides again into a Y. "Down this way." He takes the route to the left, but not far through the passage, we face a dead end.

"Wrong turn?" I tease.

"Quite the opposite," he says. "You feel it?" Paul stands proud, a glisten in his eyes.

Or is that just from the headlamp?

"Well…" I beam the headlamp around.

Nothing obvious or unique comes into focus. The ceiling arches upward a meter and a half higher than the rest of the corridor, but similar spots exist throughout the cave. All three walls are as nondescript as any other part of the caverns we've passed through. There are some pockets that are a touch sweatier than the rest, and the air seems a touch heavy with moisture, but a little fresher and easier to breathe. My headlamp catches a green moss growing on a slight ledge in the upper right corner, where the dead end intersects with the side wall. I reach up. A warm breeze flows through my open fingers.

"Exactly," Paul says. "Hop up and look." Paul crouches down as far as he can, his back toward the wall, hands cupped and waiting.

"You sure about this?"

"Trust me," he says, "I *am* a lot stronger than I appear."

Ugh! Did he just flex his biceps? His strength is not my concern. Already spent half the morning with the man shirtless; I'm well aware of his physical capabilities. His paling face, though, is a red flag. "It's not that— well—oh, fine. Whatever. Let's just do this."

Rest the ball of my left foot into his hands and half-kneel, palms resting against the wall. How's this keep happening? A little more light and Paul'll have a front-row show of my cleavage.

"Count of three then," Paul says. "Step up to my shoulders. Shouldn't be an issue for you, gymnast and all." He takes a breath. "One…"

My body shudders as Paul's warm breath finds its way down between my breasts. Suck at the air, attempting to clear the distraction.

"Two…"

Hold a minute! What did you just—

"Three!"

He grunts and heaves upward. My right foot darts to the top of Paul's shoulder. Push up, my left leg flexing into a clean tuck before my foot finds his other shoulder. He grunts again and rises. The mossy edge draws closer and closer. "Almost there," I say.

"Ga—oood," strains Paul's voice.

The closer comes the hole, the warmer the air. Its moistness tastes alive. A touch of salt floats into my nostrils, a refreshing change from the dankness of the caves. I grab a hold of the edge and ease off Paul's shoulders. The beam of the headlamp crests the edge.

"I think it's…" I eye the width of the opening. *You know these dimensions.* "It's a ventilation shaft."

"Did you say…" The headlamp bounces side-to-side. Grab at the mouth of the shaft to keep steady. "Sorry 'bout that," Paul calls up. "Cramp. Anyhow, did you say a ventilation shaft? Down here?"

"The edges are rough, irregular—but with what time I've spent in air vents of late, I'm certain this is one. In fact…" Just inside the opening, a raised lip calls out to my fingers. I glance down toward my left foot; spot a groove in the cave's wall about a third of a meter up. Shift my weight to the right and edge my left foot into the groove.

"What are you doing?" Paul says.

With a hefty push from my left thigh, my body shoots up. My hand locks onto the lip while my right foot finds enough of a divot for another boost. I heave my chest clear of the ledge and reach forward with my right arm. Latch a rocky handhold, then shift divots with my left foot. I yank my torso into the vent, then my hips. The bulk of my weight forward, I wiggle the rest of me in, then flip over to my back and take a deep breath.

"Easing your burden," I tease.

"Funny," Paul says without even a chuckle. "And had you slipped…"

"You'd have caught me. You like me too much."

"Oh, for certain." Paul's soft chuckle clears the ledge. "So, what now?"

"Let me scope this out and, if it's promising, we get you up here."

"Ten minutes," he says, all business-like. "Fifteen at the most, if we've even that long."

"Right."

The vent's height keeps me on hands and knees. Like the main tunnel, it weaves and turns with no obvious pattern, widens and narrows in irregular lengths. The sharper stones that line the path make progress slow. One wrong placement is a slice across the palm or a pin digging into a knee.

Three major turns in, a large-slated register, two centimeters narrower all around than the passage itself, separates rock from metal. Though no obvious screws or clips lock it in place, the piano hinge at the grate's top appears fused shut, the salty air having long worked its chemistry on the metal. This will take some effort.

Tug my shirt off and wrap my hands. Grab hold of a slate near the bottom. Yank hard. The grate shoots up with a squeal, close to smashing my hands against the roof of the rocky vent.

Like the register, patches of rust splotch the visible length of the metal enclosure. The grate balanced with one hand, contort myself so as to not drag my back across its rough surface. Reverse into the vent, ease the grate back into place, then snake face-forward and replace my shirt. Though the surface smooths not far past the entry, I snail onward; don't want a missed protrusion to cut into my skin or, worse, to rip my fresh shirt.

A minute after entering, the vent splits into a V. I choose right. Two meters along, the vent cuts back left, parallel to the original vent. Another three meters further, find the end capped with a large vent fan. Enough light squeezes past its blades that the headlamp is no longer necessary.

The fan bears a healthy reddish-brown hue, its blades solidified in place. The unit's seal, however, has two centimeters of play. Flip to my behind and rest the flat of my feet against the arms of two fan blades. Scoot my butt forward such that my knees tuck up toward my chest. An "Urrggg!" escapes me as I push.

The fan resists, tattooing its mark upon my shoulder blades as they grip against the rusty surface of the venting. Rev my legs against the unit. The metal pops and my limbs jolt out as metal slams against glass and metal. Light fills the opening. *Thank the Universe.* Arch my head up then lie back, close my eyes, and suck in three deep breaths. Not too far off, a rhythmic, soothing swashing eases my mind.

The metal vibrates as Paul's voice slices through the brief peace. "Out" and "time" reach my ears, but the distance between us mutes anything else.

Maneuver to the opening. The mid-morning sun fills the room through an enormous window running most of the length of the eastern wall. With a sluggish rhythm, whitecaps roll up the beach outside. Below the opening, the metal table that wraps the parameter of most of the room has crumbled. Just beyond, the fan lay on the floor, gnarled, surrounded by broken glass. Scattered about the untouched portion of the table are an array of beakers, flasks, and test tubes. Metal stools stand under the wall-side tables, others butt around a metal table filling the center of the room. A deep sink with a long-necked spout bulges from the bottom of the tables every couple of meters. Across from me, a double set of tall lockers borders each side of the room's single door, itself ajar.

Ease out of the vent, careful to avoid what cracked glass remains on the table. Pivot two meters left and jump down to a glass-free patch of floor. A puff of dust shoots into the air. *Perfect!* The thick layer of soot that covers everything proves the room is the sanctuary we need.

Now, how to get Paul here?

Nothing on the tables is useful for scaling a rock wall. One locker is empty. In another hangs a trio of tattered lab coats and a pair of long rubber safety boots. The boots are big, but with slippers on, my feet don't slide in them. Rummage through the room's drawers and cabinets. The diversity of lab supplies is vast, but for the immediate need, are worthless, except for the Bunsen burners in the next-to-last cabinet. Or, more exactly, the tubing attached to the burners. Grab a fist full and head for the vent opening.

Glass crunches under my unconcerned feet as I near. Throw the tubing up into the vent and grab the closest stool. Sit it atop a level part of the table before joining it. The stool slides with a *sqweerk* into the opening. Metal on metal is far from stealthy.

"I know!"

Go to the lockers and pull out all three lab coats. Return to the opening and stuff the lab coats in, then heave myself up. With what workspace I can create, open the coats lengthwise parallel to the vent floor, fold them side-to-side. Sit the stool over the makeshift sound-proofing, then secure the robes to the stool with some tubing. I make a crude harness of the remaining rubber, snug it at my waist, then wiggle past the stool and into the dark.

The cloth sled snags on the trail's rustier spots, lurching my stomach each time, but otherwise works despite its battered state. One of the more brittle tubes snaps as I transition from metal to rock, but otherwise travel well on the loose gravel and dirt. Shy of the vent's end, I pause, listen. All is quiet.

"Paul?" I whisper. Nothing. Perhaps it's too quiet. "Paul," I say louder, but not too loud. If something happened to him…

"Could you've taken any longer?" he calls.

I crawl to the edge. "Hey, I'm doing the best I can!"

"I'm certain you are. Did you—" Paul flips his penlight off. "Kill that headlamp! And don't move!"

For a half minute, there is nothing… no light, no sound… only anxious breaths. Then, from below, a shuffle and two rocks smacking together. "Shit, that hurt!" Paul's light comes on, pointing at a large rock on the floor. The beam travels forward, his toes poking into view with each step. Ten slow steps later, he slides from view.

Where's he going? Whatever draws his attention does not bode well for either of us. I loosen the tubing around both myself and the stool. Tie the pieces into a rope, secure one end to the stool, and dangle it over the ledge.

Wait.

Not long.

With much less caution than when it left, the light beam comes busting back into the passageway. I flip my headlamp on to find Paul panting below. "They're"—a deep breath—"They're at the bodies; we've maybe two—three—minutes."

"Here." I lower the stool.

Paul's light follows its descent; he grabs the seat once within reach, frowning. "What am I supposed to do with this? 'Stool' these guys to death?"

"No, you ass!" *Can't believe you just said that!* "Use it to boost yourself to the divots; climb from there."

"Ah, sure." Paul places the stool on the ground, rests a foot on one of the stool's cross beams, and pauses.

"Get a move on, Mr. Tubby."

Paul chuckles. "Well, aren't you Little Miss Spunky." He flips off his light, stuffs it in his waistband, and climbs atop the stool. "You know," he says, more to himself than me, "I like that—'Little Miss Spunky'." A distant, unfocused smile flashes across his face. He reaches up, finds a divot, and yanks. He finds another and—"I…"—a grunt interrupts as he ascends—"knew there'd be…"—another hold, another grunt—"a feistiness in you somewhere."

"Oh, shut up and climb."

He latches another divot and, as if he's each handhold committed to memory, scales the rest of the wall in a flash. A meter from the lip, he whitens. "Paul!" His left hand slips. Shoot my hand out and lock his forearm. He reciprocates and together we finish his climb. He drops to his stomach, breathing hard. Red—much more than when I left him—drenches his back. A tiny stream of blood flows without restraint from his laceration.

"Give me a sec," Paul says.

He needs patching quick, but I've the stool to retrieve. Though the stool is light, the tubing shreds against the edge of the outcropping and flakes off in my hands. I stop pulling and peer down the edge. The seat dangles two-and-a-half meters from the lip, well out of my reach. "You ready?"

"Already going." He sounds as if speaking through a sponge, not a good sign. I turn at him, but he's already hands and knees down the rocky vent.

Must hurry. I return to the stool. "What to do about you?" It curls left, right, and left again, mocking me. That the improvisation has survived at all is a gift. The tubing, though, can't handle any more abuse. I leave the chair hanging, hoping it is high enough to be inconspicuous, and run the tubing to a small outcropping on the right wall. The primary line locked in one hand, use the other to wrap the remaining frayed portion around the stalk. It crumbles after four passes.

The moment of truth… Hold my breath and let the line free.

And nothing.

Nothing! I'll take it! No concern for the pebbles digging into my hands and knees, I rush after Paul. Well, rush as much as the vent allows. I find him slouched at the metal lip to the vent. His breaths are hard, chest and arms drenched in perspiration.

"Sorry," he labors. "Just needed a minute."

I edge past him to pull open the grating, my arm brushing over his. It's clammy. "We're close," I tell him.

"I'm fine."

"You're not." Damn men always think they have to look so stoic. "But I can't help you here." It's idiotic. I brace the grate open with one arm while balancing on my hip with the other. Paul squeezes past. His bicep brushes my chest. His back muscles glisten as they flex in the headlamp's beam. The lines of his glutes press out against his pants. A shiver races along my spin. *Darn these rocks are cold.* Or so I tell myself. "Stop that," I say under my breath. "Not appropriate."

Paul stops short. "Huh?"

"Ummm—sorry—nothing." I follow Paul through the opening and, once he's out, twist around onto my behind and scoot through. I restore the grate, then start after him, only to pause. "Paul, I need a second here."

He pauses and arcs his head around. His eyes look weary. "Sure," he says.

"You keep going. Not far up, the vent splits. Go right."

"Right." Without another word, he continues on his way. The vent gives a little with each of his moves, then pops back into place as he shifts to the next spot.

As much as Paul needs attention, an interruption will make all for nil. I inspect the inside perimeter of the cover. There is no latch, no lock. I sigh. "Was a good thought." My capris snag on the vent's bottom as I twist. With a small hip jerk, snap the caught threads free, then reach along my leg and finger a fresh hole. "Damn."

I glance down. A couple strands of broken thread cling to one of the rusty spots decorating the vent. I wonder…

Slip off the headlamp and wrap the band around the unit's casing. Palm the result, arch my right arm back and slam the light hard into the center of the rust. The spot gives way with an odd *crunch*, like almost-stale potato chips being stepped on. The light flickers twice, but otherwise stays lit. I unwrap the band and inspect the hole. A slight depression in the rock contains a tiny pool of water, now littered with fragments of rust. Crude, but will make a decent brace all the same.

I unhitch the band from itself, then thread one side through the lowest slat of the grate, then re-latch the two halves. Stuff the light under and up the inside of the hole as a bulwark. Snag the band against its edge; extinguish the light. I yank the fabric's adjustor tight, then lie back and push my feet against the grate. The slight give is not enough that someone might otherwise believe the grate stuck shut.

Now for Paul!

I scuttle toward the lab and go right at the split. *Please have remembered…* There are no clanks of compression or pops of relief signaling which path he took. My gut hopes he followed the light. The opening, and a large speed bump, pop forth as I cut the last turn.

"Paul!"

He is flat on his stomach, his head about half a meter short of the exit. I hurry forward and shake his leg.

"Paul!?"

No response, save the slightest of back movement as his chest balloons against the bottom of the venting. Thank the stars! How many more breaths he has, injured as he is, I've no want to discover, but the roadblock he's made prevents any treatment.

There's no pushing him. Even if the fall—which will end on the vent fan—doesn't break his neck, the glass fragments will rip into him. He need not lose more blood. There is only one most unladylike option. *You've gotta crawl over the man.*

I compress against the roof of the vent and slither my way over his backside. Latch his shoulders, then slide across his back. The swirls of sweat and blood resting there soak into what otherwise dry spots remain of my top. Clinging all the more to my body, the already tight shirt fights against my breasts as they rub their way forward. *Could this be any more inappropriate?* Every curve, every bulge, every firmness of Paul's muscles dance across my abdomen, toward my malnourished loins. *Any more unbecoming a young lady?* My focus fogs over in the cloud of his musk. *No!* The bottoms of my feet tingled. *Not like this!* My thighs constrict…

"Ugh! Do *not* go there. The man's not only passed out, but engaged, for goodness' sake!"

Gulp at the air—three times—then I crawl past his head (So awkward!), contorting as best I can to avoid more damage to his scalp. Not to mention, maintain some degree of feminine decorum. He'll not know the difference, but I will. Nonetheless, he catches a prime view of my cleavage, a generous survey of my rump—and an unfortunate knee to the ear—before I escape the tube.

The first-aid kit contains the essentials—antibiotic gel, gauze pad and wrap—but the cut needs an urgent cleanse to make effective any other treatment. I check three different faucets. No water. The safety shower in the lab is likewise dry. I sort through the various jars and jugs of liquids stored in the cabinets.

"Distilled Water" reads one gallon's label. The liquid within is clear. I twist free the lid. There's no actual smell. I risk a swig. Flat, tasteless, stale; all the same: water. I grab a fistful of cloths and a trio of pipettes from a nearby drawer, then climb back upon the table in front of the vent opening. Paul's motionless. A tiny pool of blood now rests on the vent floor below the back of his head.

I wash away what blood has not yet congealed. A pink stream trickles out of the vent, first plinking onto the crevice of the table where the fan has hit then splattering onto the floor. Use the cloth to loosen the clumps gummed into Paul's hair. The blood cleared, the cut appears overall superficial. Tiny rock fragments impact the worst of it. I suck into the largest of the pipettes a full draw of water, then lean close to his ear. "Sorry," my lips soothe as I force the water into the depth of the cut.

"Urg!" Paul calls out, attempting to swat away the irritant.

That's positive.

Even more positive, the table clinks three times. Some sediment, though, remains. I refill the pipette and lean into Paul a second time. "Just this one more."

I brace his head with one hand, rest the tip of the pipette at the edge of the cut, and squeeze its bulb. The water shoots into the cut. Paul grabs at my arm and tries turning his head away. A fresh stream of blood leaks from the cut, carrying two more clinks against the table. Paul moans at first, but settles as the rush of water fades and the pipette drains. I rinse the wound one last time with a gentle stream from the jug, then dab the incision dry and shine his penlight over the deeper portion. No other debris remains. Before any fresh blood escapes, I coat the cut in the gel, apply the gauze pad, and secure it in place with several passes of the wrap. Wipe up what of the water and blood I can from the vent floor, then rest Paul's head on what dry clothes remain.

"That should do," I sigh, "for now." I take a breath of relief, only to have my condition smack me. Everything is sore, if not from cuts and bruises, from stress and overwork. My inner thighs burn from the wide straddle they have of the dent. My behind begs of a stool. Paul isn't going anywhere, so I oblige.

The bright beach looks inviting. Just lay there and let the waves soothe me off to a pleasant dream world. Let the sun's warmth bury into my skin. For a moment, forget reality. The reality of sitting among what is now a lagoon of glass, blood, and water. Of my aching body, craving an intake of calories. Of having separated a loving couple—one of the pair lost to who knows where, and the other almost lost of life. All for what? Some baffling vision far from the reality in which I sit.

How did such a beautiful morning turn so sour?

Self-pity solves nothing, including my chattering teeth. Even with the growing warmth of the day, the sweat and blood that bathes me chills my skin. Even more so for the water-coated, bluing Paul. We need dry clothes... a dry place to rest. I jump off the stool, grab the penlight, and head straight for the lab's proper exit. Flash one last check of Paul, then push through the half-open door and launch once again into darkness.

CHAPTER FOUR

BETWEEN AN OVERCAST SKY AND pulled shades, our family room is dark.

Darker than usual.

Quieter than usual.

My younger brothers should be rampaging about, laughing over some oddball shoot-'em-up game they invented. Else, at each other's throats in an escalating insult shootout. Either case proves frothy entertainment, at least until the kicks and punches start.

Yet nothing. "Hello? Is anyone here?"

I planned to make a break for the locker room once the class that trapped me in the equipment closet ended. No such luck. No sooner did that class vacate when another took its place. And so repeated, through lunch. They had frozen lemonade today. *You know you love frozen lemonade.* None for me today, the tennis team having commandeered the facility for an impromptu practice during the break. Hungry and bored, the rhythmic *pong* of tennis balls lured me to sleep. Awoke well over four hours later to not only an empty gym, but an empty school. Retrieved what of my belongings hadn't gone missing, excluding for some inconceivable reason, my underclothes, and walked home, the school buses long departed.

While the heaviest of the storms had ended, enough light rain still falls that—given the long trek to our front door—it soak my clothes through. My once loose blouse stresses *all* my curves; my skirt plasters my thighs.

Goose pimples paint my skin. My teeth won't stop chattering. Good thing there is no audience to welcome me home. The only agenda item right now: a warm, soothing bubble bath. *Well, that and figuring out how you're ever going to convince Ms. Luis to let you make up the Calc test.*

I close the door and turn one-hundred eighty degrees to the stairs. Take the first step, then pause. Was that someone laughing?

"Hello? Stevie… James? Mom?"

There's no response. *Shoo!* I take the stairs two at a time. Cut left at the L halfway up then, once at the top, angle northwest toward my room at the back of the house.

"Stop right there, young lady!"

I try to ignore the squeak behind me as the sounds of a well-aged house, but the sudden flood of light is harder to dismiss. Half a meter more and I'd been secure in my room. Anyone else, I might make a dash for it. Instead, my feet freeze.

"Where have you been? And what is going on—Hey! Pay attention when I am talking to you."

I glance down my front side. Turning will not end well, though, much worse awaits me should I not. "Sorry, Mom."

As I pivot on my left heel, shift my book bag up and across my chest with my right hand. The heat filling in my cheeks does nothing to diminish the fact that a cold rain does a bra-less girl in a thin white blouse no favors.

"You ought to be. I'll not be late because of you."

Oh, no! Tonight's the party!

An elegant a-line, floor-length gown drapes Mom's figure. The bodice is a princess scoop-neck cut with beaded sequin embellishments across the chest and down the chiffon arms. The skirt of the dress is a simple, solid gray crepe fabric. Not that she ever presents as wearing lesser quality outfits, but I've never seen Mom in a first-rate dress of such excess. No wonder the kitchen cabinets have been so barren for the last six months. Even if the party wasn't at her employer's home, she'd not care if I starved.

A shift in shadows from her room catches my eye. "Is that Dad?" He'll save me.

"No." Mom shifts her weight left to block my view into her room. "He's meeting us."

"Oh." I glimpse down the dark hall toward my brothers' rooms. "Where's everyone?"

"Does it matter?"

"I guess not. It's just that—"

"Not that it's any of your business," she cuts in, "but Dewey's having dinner with his girlfriend's family. Steven's at a friend's house for the night. James is with us."

"Oh. I'll—ah," I half turn toward my room, hugging my bag tight, "go get ready then."

"Wait a minute." Mom surveys my profile. "Why are you standing like that? What are you hiding?"

"Mom, you don't—"

"I what? Don't understand? Oh, I understand young lady. More than you'll ever realize. Drop the bag, now."

"But, Mom…"

She hasn't always been like this. I was a little over two when she and Papa married. For many years, she cared for my every need: an instant daughter whom she had not born, yet knew no other mother. When she became pregnant with my youngest brother, James, she changed. She would snap at the smallest of mishaps, but only with me, never with the boys. Denied me when I ask for—well—near anything that Papa didn't already okay. Offered no preparation, no guidance to a petrified preteen who one day awoke in a blood-soaked bed. She begrudged me a day's worth of her pads because she "didn't want me ruining another set of *her* sheets" along with a scolding over how I should have already had my own.

How was I to know?!

Her once deep love she replaced with a chasm of disinterest. Nowadays, there is no arguing with her, no explanation that will suffice. The furrowed brow, pin-pointed lips, drilling stare will not allow for one. I doubt any love ever existed.

The bag slides down to my hip as a tear slides along my cheek.

"Oh, my." She shakes her head. "Is this what you girls are doing these days? Get out of the house and off comes the bra. Showcasing your womanhood for any passerby to gawk at?"

"Please, Mom, I'd never…"

Chit! "When I'm talking," her voice gruffs, "you're listening." Her finger of blame shoots up. "What if your brothers saw all that? Huh?" She waves her hand at me like she is painting a narrow wall with an over-worn paint brush. "No one wants to see *that.*"

My entire body shakes, but she pays no heed. If only this one time, you'd listen, sympathize with me—try, once again, to bond with the only other female in the house. Papa would give me one of his firm embraces, tell me all would be okay, that there's no reason to be ashamed. At this moment, though, some feminine support is what I need. Dig my nails into my palms to distract me from full on tears.

Can't recall the last she offered any such support.

"Twenty minutes," she says, "and the taxi will be here. You get fifteen and not a minute more, or so help me! And for goodness' sake, put on some proper undergarments. Never do I want to see this display of indecency again."

The signature red of Mom's Christian Louboutin's flash as she spins to her room. Other than her *precious* sons, the shoes are the only other thing she cares about. One of the few things she walked away from her first marriage still possessing, my older brother Dewey aside. She never talks about the marriage, or divorce, with me, though she'll seldom let an opportunity pass to remind Papa how opulent her life had been. Any time we've no money for the extravagant item of the moment, her oration begins. He always takes the rants in stride, a meager "Yes, Dear" and he moves on. Whatever endearing quality she has that Papa willingly married, the woman escapes my understanding.

"Damn, you *are* a straight up bitch."

She pauses at her door. Can swear that was under my breath. I don't wait to find out and turn on my heel and rush into my room. I bang the door shut behind me and aim as best my tear-filled eyes and the darkness allow for my bed, to crash stomach first against the corner of a stiff box. Roll off my bed and onto my knees, trying to regain my breath. I reach over to the bedside table and flip on the lamp there, then pull up the front of my blouse. There's a reddening scrape running from the center of my abdomen to the right side of my torso.

Nothing like layering injury on top of insult.

Turn back to the bed. A large, decorative—now dented—royal blue box sits there. While only seven or eight centimeters tall, it is over half a meter wide and almost a meter long. A wide sky-blue ribbon binds all four edges, coming together in an enormous bow at the box's top. The box itself has a soft velvet texture, embossed with vines budding rose profiles.

The signature style of a single, legendary designer. Right there, in the lower left corner: *Jeffrey DeVoe.*

"Whoa!"

But who?

Only one person in the entire world would ever give me such a gift. But how? DeVoe's are well outside anything our family can afford.

Sit on the bed, next to the box. The bow gives way with a small tug. Inside, a silvery tissue paper protects the contents. A card rests in the center, Papa's handwriting on the outside.

For my daughter.

Flip the card open.

Something special for a girl who has grown into the most lovely of young women—both on the inside and out. As am I, your mother would be so proud. You will forever shine, our Galactic Princess.

All my love,

Papa

Oh, Papa. I grab a tissue and dab at my watery eyes, then free the dress of the wrapping and stand to let it unfurl in front of the full-length mirror attached to my closet door. "So stunning!"

Not me. I'm more of a ragged mess than usual. The dress is perfect. It has a shoulder-less inner black velvet layer with a dark purple sheen, over-laid by a midnight purple-blue mesh covered in tiny, multicolored faux gem flakes. The gems are thickest in the o-neck bodice and thin out into random groupings the further down the bell-shaped silhouette of the gown they go. Each shimmers with a rainbow of colors as they catch the light of my table lamp. A long ribbon, similar in color to the inner layer, wraps around the waistline.

"Papa, how did you ever…"

Peel off my soaked uniform and throw it to the side. Slide the dress on in its place. It's classic DeVoe. The cut flatters in all the right places, yet stays young-lady modest. Provocative, yet classy, at the same time. The fitted corset hugs my midsection and breasts with a firm, yet comfortable, embrace. The hemline rests a centimeter above my knees. Sits on me as if he made the gown for no other.

He did, you goofball.

DeVoe guarantees each dress unique to its owner. Most want something boisterous, but for those who shell out the cash, only a vigilant appraisal will reveal the dress's individuality. I've seen nothing like what now covers my body, but then again, it isn't as if I've ever been to events where I would.

Such a shame I can't wear it. Not without sleeves. *But you've done so well lately.* I check my arms. I *have* done well: there are just a couple of small sores, not even that irritated. Plus, I want to do this for Papa. How long must he have saved? But what is that spot? My pointer finger runs over the tiny, dull lump on my forearm, to be joined by my thumb. They trap it and squeeze. Harder. It hurts.

Outside my door, the floor squeaks twice, and someone swears. What is going on? I leave the tissue and move to the door. Twist its knob and crack it open the slightest bit. My door, being diagonal to the staircase, can observe the comings and goings of the family. Mom is standing outside her door, looking toward the staircase.

"Thanks again," she says. "I most desperately needed that tonight."

Halfway down is not one of my family, but one of Mom's work assistants. Recognize his curly brown hair. He comes by the house from time to time with this or that paper for Mom to sign. His name slips from my mind, but not those captivating eyes… warm, welcoming smile. And so cute!

"Sooo much my pleasure," he replies, before disappearing down the stairs.

He's no more gone when my brother James shoots out of mother's room. He is only half dressed for the party.

"Get some pants on!" Mom yells at him—a rare event. "We don't have time for your clowning around!"

She pushes James into her room and slams the door, jilting me back to the task at hand. Seven minutes already gone, the walk home appears to be my first and last shower of the day. My hair, however, can't sit pasted to my head. Grab a brush and work out what tangles that will give way. Find a pair of hair ties along with a handful of bobby pins and manipulate my black mane into two twists. Stop each next to an ear, then bring the two halves together at the back of my head in a single, low ponytail. Work my right hand halfway down the center of the ponytail, bunch the remaining loose hair in my left, and tuck it into the pouch created within the ponytail. The pimple I ripped apart earlier is nearly invisible, but I still tug my left bang free and let it drop along my cheek. After a spritz of hair spray, consider my hair as done as it will get.

Five minutes are gone, with still much yet to do.

Though the style doesn't call for one, after the evening's run-in, there is no way Mom is letting me leave the house brassiere-less. Dig deep into my underclothes drawer, shuffling the boring bras to the side, to retrieve the one non-flesh colored brassiere I possess. It's a black, lacy bandeau Angelica insisted on buying me during one of our parent-less shopping trips. My protests ignored, she'd once riffled through my dresser drawers, ultimately declaring she would not let me go through life without some "creativeness" to my undergarments.

Whatever that meant.

Loosen the dress' side zipper and let it fall to my waist. I wore the bandeau only once before, one of the rare times the house was empty. Just to see. It was tantalizing, making it a prime candidate for confiscation by Mom. So I buried it until now. If this isn't a moment that called for a little "creativeness", then no such moments exist.

Breasts covered (*Hmm… this bra's a little tighter than I remember*) and dress back in place, grab underwear and a pair of nude stay-ups from their respective drawers. Head to my closet for one last item: shoes. I've a couple pair of black flats, some clunky two centimeter heels, but (*Darn*) nothing to compliment the grandeur of the dress. Be a shame to taint this charming gown with sub par footwear.

Wait! Bounce on my toes back to the box.

Every DeVoe includes—right there at the bottom of the box—two heels in a color coordinating with the inner layer of the dress. They are taller, a good five centimeters, than anything I've ever worn. With their wide top lift, though, nothing this gymnast won't be able to learn straight away.

As the shoes come free, a small jewelry box pops loose. Sit everything on the bed and reach for the box. Hinge it open. Inside, a shiny golden neck chain adorned with a two centimeter diameter marble-shaped charm. Its odd reflection seems as if to glow from within. Even in fuller light, the mystery doesn't lessen. Centered within the sphere rests a replica of the Milky Way. Not, though, a mere flat picture, but a spinning 3-D illusion of dust and stars. An amazing trick of optics. I waste no time latching the chain around my neck, the charm dangling atop my cleavage.

"Oh, Papa, what a wonderful surprise. I love you too!"

Puh! Puh! rattles my door.

"What the…!" Close to yank the charm off at the sudden disruption.

"Let's go!" Mom calls through the wood.

"I only need…"

"Nothing." She no longer sounds right outside my door. "They charge premium prices for this service."

Well, maybe you shouldn't have spent so much on that dress! Snatch up those accessories still to put on and make my way into the hall. Mom and James are already near the end of the stairs. Whose she aiming to impress anyhow? We are *not* important.

Make it to the mid-stairs landing as Mom opens the front door to a suited, gray-haired gentleman standing on our porch. "Good evening, Madam," he says with a slight bow. "I am Jasper, and will be your driver for the evening."

"I don't suppose you have something for *that*?" Mom flicks her hand at the rain falling around our porch. It's grown thick again.

"I am most prepared, Madam," Jasper says as he opens a large black umbrella.

"Given your prices, I'd expect so."

Jasper's demeanor remains unaffected. His arm sweeps forward in a motion that says *after you.* "Very good, Madam." He glances at me, a fresh arrival at the doorway, smiles. "I shall return for your lovely daughter in a second."

"Eh," Mom replies.

At the sacrifice of his own dryness, Jasper ensures Mom and James remain centered in his umbrella. He ushers them to no "taxi" I've ever seen.

The vehicle is a stretched sedan, two-thirds the length of a limousine. As Jasper opens the rear door to allow his clients to enter, a soft, golden-blue glow fills the passenger compartment. Mom stuffs James in first. He skids across a bench seat running along the back of the compartment, then juts forward and disappears. Mom leans down into the compartment, yells something the rain hides from my ears, then sits on the far side of the bench. James is again next to her, door-side, as it shuts.

Jasper starts back toward the porch. He shakes his head in a slow arc as a chuckle shakes through his shoulders.

Yeah, I know that feeling.

I step onto the porch intending to meet Jasper partway, only to have the cool cement remind me that my shoes, stuffed with my stockings, still hang from my hands. I back into the entranceway to slip them on—*Crap!* My underwear still occupies the other. *Can you not do anything right?*

There is no option to excuse myself to the bathroom. Mom will have my hide if she waits any longer. Jasper's too close for me to step out of view and pull them on; and I've not grabbed a purse that I can stuff them in.

The couch!

Fling the wad toward the far wall of the family room. They hit the top corner of a framed photo of my parents with a *plut,* unravel, slip… then latch the frame's braided motif.

Crap! Crap! Crap!

"Miss."

My burning face turns. Jasper waits at the threshold of the door, his hand held out for me to take.

"Um…"

"Do you need a moment, Miss?" Jasper winks.

"Well, um…" Did he see that? Oh, please, *don't* let him have seen that.

I dare not shift my pupils at the underwear's landing spot. There's no need to draw his attention all the more to the embarrassment. Perhaps there is some way I can make it into the house in time after…

"Your shoes, Miss. Do you need a moment?"

"Oh—ah, yeah—my shoes."

Liberate the stockings from the toe pockets, slip the shoes on, and step onto the porch. Turn to pull the front door shut, taking a quick glance at the wall. *Shoo…* the underwear is no longer hanging from the portrait. Can only hope they've fallen behind the sofa. One more thing I don't want to explain today.

No sooner does the door close, when its lock clicks into place via Mom's remote. I hustle to the waiting car, having no interest in shouldering any more of her fury. Jasper does well to keep up.

I discretely point toward the car as we draw near. "Sorry about that."

"No worries," he says with another wink. "In my profession, I see all kinds. This one gets a night to play dress-up, so thinks she also has to play a role. The key is to not let her draw you into what is a one-person show."

Jasper releases my hand and opens the sedan's door.

"Thank you, Jasper."

"Miss." He tips his head again.

Opposite Mom and James is a second leather bench about two-thirds of the other, being bordered on the far side by a narrow drink bar. One glass, marked with James' fingerprints, is out of line with the others. Blonde-stained wood trim accents the compartment's tan interior with a translucent encasing along the joint between the walls and ceiling. The casing gives off a soft blue hue. As the door shuts, the overhead lights dim to a gentle, warm glow. Not much more brightness than you get from a night light.

I settle myself in the middle of the bench as the car rolls forward. Mom stares out the side window, not even glancing my way. Across the compartment, a goofy grin on his face, James won't stop staring at me. Like he knows some secret he's eager to share, but only if you ask.

"What?" I mouth at him.

He flashes his pointer finger in my direction and giggles. His eyes glance down my body, betraying him.

Oh, no!

It isn't abnormal to me to be sans underwear. Plenty of times I've gone such for gymnastics meets. Most gymnastics leotards have high cut hips, making it prohibitive to wear typical underwear. In fact, it is common for judges to deduct points if your underwear flash out of your uniform. Tried some specialized underwear twice, but found going without is the most comfortable. Don't even think about it anymore; is as natural as wearing a swimsuit. This, however, differs from anything else I've done before— *How's that for "creativity", Angelica?*—and nothing I intend to broadcast, in particular, to my brother!

The skirt of my dress, though, lies conservatively across my thighs and under my behind. Cross my ankles just to be sure; there is no way he can know the truth beneath. Check that the rest of the dress is as it should be. The bandeau provides more definition to my cleavage than is natural, but the bodice more than covers the bulk of my chest. Just to be sure, I give the top a tug upward.

James giggles.

"Crush me!" shoots from my mouth before I can check myself. "Are you staring at my breasts?"

James giggles again. Mom whips around. "For the love of... Young lady, you best have a bra—"

"I *do*, Mother."

These days, I'm not in the habit of cutting Mom off. My focus, however, is not on her. James stops giggling and turns a bright red under my glare. He might be Mom's baby, but that cannot help him this time.

"Then what is that in your hand?" Mom asks.

"Oh, ah..." I unfurl the stockings as my attention shifts to her. "I hadn't time to put them on."

"I see." She rolls her eyes with a huff. "Well, get them on then."

I clear my throat and jut my head toward James, who is still staring. As spacious as the compartment is, it won't be trivial to both preserve my modesty and get the stockings on under his gaze.

Mom turns at James and the drool about to plop from his gaping mouth. She bats him alongside the forehead with the back of her hand, breaking him from the trance.

"Stop looking at your sister like that!"

"Sorry, Mom." He droops his head.

"Look out the window," she says before turning back to me. "Now get it done—then back at me. I see your stockings are not the only thing you 'didn't have time' to put on this evening."

She couldn't... "What?!" How horrible of person she must think I am.

"Don't play dumb with me." Yikes, she knows! "Do you think I'm blind to the ridiculous gobs of makeup you girls wear these days? I'm sure you're dying to fit right in."

"Ah, yeah." No makeup. That works, for no way am I revealing what's really missing. While I often wear a modest application of makeup to school or on special occasions, I'm just as comfortable without. Tonight is very special, deserves much more than nothing. Under mom's tight timeline, though, I didn't think to grab even a lip gloss.

Mom pulls her purse out from her side, pushes two glasses atop the wet bar to the side, and retrieves several tubes and cases from the bag. She glances at me with a glow in her eyes I haven't seen since I was a little girl. For once, her misunderstanding could be a good thing.

"Let's do this in the proper manner," she says in an almost jovial tone. Her chin nods at me. "That would be easier if you turned sideways."

Heed the advice and turn away from the two, parallel with the bench. My womanhood now shielded, finish pulling the stockings on with little effort. Mom waits with lip balm ready in hand as I pivoted back.

"All right—lesson one," she says. "When applying lipstick, you want to start with lip balm."

"Lip balm?"

"Yep. Bet you didn't know that. Not only moisturize your lips, but will soften and smooth them, so lipstick goes on level."

"Oh." I have to be dreaming right now. No way this is for real.

"Let that sit for a minute, then dab any excess residue with this." A small cotton pad presents before me. "If we were at home, I'd recommend using a makeup sponge to apply a thin layer of foundation to your lips. It's inessential, but helps bring out the natural color of the lipstick. Oh, and be sure to smile when you apply the foundation."

"Smile?"

"Right, smile. Helps fill in any little cracks in your lips." Mom picks up a red pen and pulls its cap off. The tip looks like a thin marker head. "Lip liner," she says, "is an imperative part of applying lipstick. Extends the life of the application by giving it something to grip to—and prevents the lipstick from bleeding." Mom nods at me. "Now dab."

Do so as Mom shifts to the edge of the seat. This is me, though. The nightmare has to be lurking nearby.

"This," Mom pinches the pen between her fingers, "is all I have with me, but when possible, you'll want to use a liner that complements the lipstick and image you intend to convey. For a bold lipstick color, use a liner that is a touch darker. If you've primed with foundation or want a more natural look, use one that matches the natural color of your lips." She holds her free hand out. "That should be good."

Place the pad in her hand, which she then hides in her purse.

"Now," she says, "hold your mouth open, like this." Mom relaxes her face, her mouth opens just wide enough that you can see but a hint of her teeth.

Mimic her.

"Excellent." She places her left hand under my chin to hold my face steady and works the lip liner. "The magic of lip liner is you can make your lips look bigger, smaller, rounder, wider… whatever you want depending upon where you apply the liner. For tonight, let's go narrow. Apply it along the inner part of your natural lip line. For bigger looking lips, apply around the outside instead."

Do what I can to keep my jaw locked in place. "Ah, huh."

"And then the lipstick itself." She pulls out a tube of the same red she is wearing and twists out the contents. "Hold your mouth open further. Now, don't make the mistake of trying to go side-to-side. You should always start at the center of each lip and move outward toward the side, like this."

Mom presses the slick against the center of my lower lip and glides it to the right. She next returns to the center and glides it left. Repeats for the upper lip.

"Okay, rub your lips together and apply a second coat." She hands me the tube and a small makeup mirror. Replicate her actions, the result much better than I've ever done alone.

"Thanks, Mom!"

She smiles at me as I return the items.

"Absolutely! There are some other tricks you can experiment with. For example, pucker your lips around your finger and then pull. That helps prevent the lipstick from getting on your teeth. Or you can make the lipstick last longer by pulling a tissue in half to get a nice thin sheet. Press half against your lips and then dust on a translucent setting powder before applying the second coat. Lots of variations I can show you at home."

"I'd enjoy that."

"Me too. Now, let's talk cheeks and eyes…"

Of all things, who'd ever guess makeup would bring my mother back to me?

But has it?

Mom dusts my left cheek.

For certain, the iciness that coated the early evening has melted away—but why? Am I some show piece, some decoration?

The dusting pauses as gentle fingers swivel my chin left, then the brush tickles over my right cheek.

Stop that—stop tainting the moment. Let her pamper you. When can you say that last happened?

The dusting stops. "That is quite a mesmerizing charm," Mom says. "I don't recall ever seeing that before?" She leans in toward my chest.

I scoop the charm up and hold it up as far as it will go. "It's part of my gift from Dad—with this dress."

"I see." She bends further forward. "Is that… spinning?"

"An illusion. A good one, granted, but it's nothing more than a trick of light."

"Hmm. Something unique about that one. Anyhow, back to your eyes. Close, please."

Let the charm fall back to my chest as Mom disappears from my view. A couple moments of silent dabbing pass as she works. Hold on! This isn't about me. Is this mom, nervous?

"Mom?"

"Daughter?"

Wow! Hadn't realized just how much I missed that being said with such tenderness. "Is this odd for you?"

"Putting makeup on my daughter?" she asks. "Well, no—my mother did the same with me when I was learning."

I chuckle. "No, not *this*. The party, you being the house manager for the Matters."

"Oh." Her application of eyeshadow to my left lid hesitates. She takes a deep breath. "Well, I oversaw the party preparations, but that's business; this is pleasure."

"I suppose. Seems strange, though. Not sure I'd ever want to eat at the same restaurant where I waitress, you know?"

"Hum." Another hesitation. "Perhaps back in the day, when I was the one washing the linens and cooking the meals, I'd see tonight in a different light."

One-third a minute of nothing passes.

Ease my lids apart.

Hovers before my right eye, Mom's fingers pinching a thin brush. Her other hand holds a small silvery cosmetic case, its lid propped open. She pulls her hand away. A puzzled look decorates her face. "Are *you* concerned about tonight?"

Is this really my mother asking how I feel? Oh, how therapeutic it would be to free myself of the years of Katie's tormenting. Even just the disaster of the day. But is that fair? How will she react, knowing the person her employer's daughter is? To have such a sour taste in her mouth soon to arrive at an event that means so much to her?

James coughs, an abrupt reminder that now is not the right time. At least I've one precious half-hour with the struggles of the day wiped away.

"I was just curious," I say. "I know so little about your actual work day."

"Well—close your eyes, please—I oversee all the domestic needs of the Matters' household. I do everything from scheduling work hours for the staff, to coordinating with Mister and Misses Matters for major events, like the party tonight. I'm in charge of ensuring the cleanliness of their mansion, verify the grounds crew maintain the landscaping… I even act as concierge for guests of the family. Anything and everything to do with keeping their home up and running."

"That sounds overwhelming."

"It was when I first started a couple of years back. Now, though, I've got it all working like clockwork."

"Must be nice to have the help of an assistant."

"Assistant?" she mumbles to herself. "I don't have…"

"You know, Mommy," James busts into the conversation, "Mr. P.J. He was just…"

"Ow!" The applicator mom is using pushes into my eyelid, then out to the side.

"Oh, crap!" Mom says. "James, you shouldn't interrupt like that. Just watch out the window."

Humph, he replies.

"Sorry about that," Mom says to me. "Close back up and I'll fix it." Sense she's searching her purse given the sudden rustling of papers, plastics, and keys.

"Mr. P.J.?" I say after a moment.

"There they are." There is a small *rip* and then a damp, cool pad rests just to the side of my eyelid. "Yeah—ah—P.J., my assistant…" Mom swipes away the excess eyeshadow. "He's more an intern than an assistant."

"Intern? At a private residence?"

"Private, yes, but no typical residence." Mom's eyes light up. "The Matters' household is like running a mid-sized hotel. People come and go daily, all with diverse needs that require multiple staff to accommodate. Though it's a non-traditional environment, for a Hotel Management student, the experience is the same. And, yes, he's been an *immense* help to me."

"Will he be at the party?" The question shoots from my mouth with more eagerness than I intend.

The pad pauses. Mom chuckles. "Ah… no, he'll not be at the party." As if we share a mind, she says, "If I recall, he's on a date with a young *woman* tonight."

My cheeks burn. "I just thought," I sputter, "with him being your intern and all…" Not sure the words could be any less convincing.

Mom pulls the pad away. "I see." Her humoring tone does little to diminish that she can see right through me. *Click. Ping* of the metal case against the drink bar. "Okay, enough questions. Open your eyes and let's see what we have."

Open my eyes in time to see her mouth, *wow*, a big smile across her face.

"Now," she says, "you look stunning. You will woo tonight. Make all the other girls jealous." The *jealous* she draws out, as if stretching taffy.

Unable to contain myself, I wrap my arms around her in my best replica of Papa's bear hugs.

"Thank you so much, Mom. You've made my day." For serious, is this a dream, some joke?

A brief static sputters overhead, shocking my grip loose.

"Madam, we shall arrive in ten minutes," Jasper calls out. "The weather has cleared. The temperature is warm."

"Thank you, Jasper," Mom replies. She takes my chin between thumb and forefinger, leans in, and kisses my forehead. "And you are ultra-welcome."

CHAPTER FIVE

AT LAST, TEN MINUTES. TEN minutes to soak in the sun before it disappears behind the cliff face for the afternoon. Our clothes are almost dry, thank goodness! The ocean's salts have done a marvelous job of agitating out most of the blood, albeit a chilly and painful job to undertake. Tried to not wander too deep, but found it impossible to avoid the spray of the waves from stinging into the scrapes and cuts scattered about my body. The worst of my abrasions, my thigh, stabbed anew courtesy of each watery crest.

Flip onto my stomach. The sand underneath the tablecloth has cooled, though enough of the morning sun's warmth still radiates from it to soothe my sore muscles. Plus, need what direct sunlight remains to finish drying out the backside of my underwear. Even with Paul well passed out, and those sections of the building I can access otherwise empty, can't bring myself to "put it all out there"—so to speak. Who knows how long our hidden oasis will remain so?

Or maybe you're just chicken, you prude!

"Oh, shut up."

Undo the clasp of my bra and slide the shoulder straps off my arms. Tan lines and all. Cocoon my hair forward over my shoulder in a pillow against my right arm. Close my eyes. The mellow sway of the waves against the beach rock draws the mental strain of the morning away. Pulls it adrift. Washes it out to sea. Disappears at the line separating sky from sea…

"Well?"

"I—I just don't know. It's so—revealing."

"What'd you expect, silly—it is a bikini."

Big white dots on three navy triangles stare back at me from the half hexagon of mirrors. Pull at the bowed ties sitting on my hips. They hold, being stitched together at their knot. Adjust the similar rose violet-colored strings looping my neck for more lift.

"Mother would kill me just for trying this on, let alone wearing it anywhere!"

"Good thing I'm not your mom. Now, are you coming out, or am I coming in?"

Without waiting for a reply, the curtain slides open.

"What the—" My hands raced over my breasts.

"Damn, Girl!" Angelica says. "You look outstanding! Put your friggin' hands down already."

Drop my arms. Twist to the side, seeing the whole of my hips and curve of my buttocks in the mirror. "I can't Geli. This just isn't—"

"Don't you dare go there," Angelica says. "That is your fuddy-duddy mom in your head. This is you. You just don't want to admit it."

Angelica steps into the changing room and turns me about face, straight on the main mirror. The suit is cute and compliments my curves in all the right places. All the same—a string bikini—that's not me. "Maybe if there's one with more coverage. What am I saying! I don't have the cash for this."

"Hogwash. And I already told you…" She looks into the mirror with me, shoulder to shoulder. "It's my treat. You know who's gonna be at the party, don't you?"

"Ah, everyone. That's why there is no way I can wear this."

"Whatever. At least half of those snobs deserve to be jealous of what you are. No, I'm talking about Abraham."

"Abraham?" I shrug. "We're just friends."

"Not from what I hear." She pinches my side. "He's got quite the crush on little old you."

My face burns red. "It's not like that!"

"Yeah, keep telling yourself that," Angelica says. "Unless, perhaps…" She pulls the curtain shut and steps between me and the mirror. "It's someone else you are interested in?"

She wraps one arm around my waist, pulls us tight together. My breasts slide across the top of those of her shorter frame. With the other hand, she brushes a loose bang of her black-brown hair from her cheek, then angles up and lays her lips upon my own.

I can't resist the sugary sweet taste of her breath—like the cross between a mango and strawberry—and kiss her back. The electricity cycling through my body forces my *eyes shut. One of her hands weaves up the center of my back. She tugs on the neck strap of the bikini top. The pressure holding my chest in place loosens. A coolness shivers across my skin. I wrap my arms around her warm, inviting body, but stop midway. Geli's my best friend and all—but she's not like this. I'm not like this. We're not "friends" like this, are we? Yet so pleasing and natural it feels to be in her embrace.*

No!

I grab her hips and thrust her back toward the mirror. Open my eyes to see I've thrown her off balance. "I'm sorry, Angelica, I—wait, who are you?"

The girl—no, woman—regains her step, brushing her reddish-blonde hair from her eyes as she again faces me.

"Oh, you know who I am." She steps forward, I back. "And for another kiss like that, I might forget the way you keep looking at my fiancé."

She steps forward again. I back another. The pits of my knees brush the wooden bench in the room. "I would never."

"Oh, but you would and have." The woman's sweet tone gives way to a bitter grating. "I know girls like you. Just flash your goods around"—she waves a hand toward my exposed breasts, the undone top now fallen toward my waist—"and take what you want without regard for anyone else."

Her hands ball up. "Now, you will pay!" She rushes forward. I leap to the side, tangling myself in the privacy curtain. The curtain rips from its rod and together we fall toward the floor. The carpet provides little cushioning as my head hits the floor. My vision goes brown and fuzzy. Someone in heels is hurrying toward me.

"Miss," the heeled hurrier says, "Miss—are you all right? Miss?"

The hurrier shakes my upper arm. "Miss?" she says again. I want to respond, but I can't. "Miss?" Another shake. "Miss, please?!"

Peek with my right eye. The feet before me wear boots, military boots. One lifts and jiggles my shoulder.

"Miss?"

Have to protect Paul!

Swing my arm in an arch to the side and lock on the heel of the planted boot and yank in toward my side. The body falls back as its owner yelps. I scurry over and straddle the fallen body, locking my hips over the soldier's and keeping her pinned in place. Clasp my right hand over her throat like a vise. She struggles for air.

"You don't want to die today, do you?"

As best she can, the woman shakes her head no. A tear runs down each of her cheeks. From fear or lack of oxygen, it doesn't matter.

"I'll loosen my grip if you don't scream—understand?"

The end of a round pipe presses against the back of my head. "I think instead," a man's voice says, "that you will acquit yourself of my wife. Unless *your* goal is to die today..." *Click—whir—*a pulse rifle primes with a round.

The fight in me wants to tighten my grip, but flight wins the day. Raise my hands. The woman coughs as her lungs struggle for fresh air. The man grabs my arms and pulls them behind my back, then locks them together with a plastic pull tie. She twists onto her side and snakes her way out from between my thighs. The nails on my left hand start picking at the nails of the other.

"What the scraig," she manages between breaths. "We're trying to help you."

The rifle shifts off of my head but otherwise stays trained on me as the man circles around and helps his wife to her feet. She rises, half turned away from me, rubbing her neck, taking deep breaths.

"You okay?" he asks.

Her head bobs with a rough nod as she sucks in another vat of oxygen.

They are both dressed in a mismatch of guard camos and gear. Neither, however, looks like any guard I've seen before. The man bears a thick, unkempt beard and similar scraggy hair (unlike the religiously clean-cut guards). He's a tall, husky physique, at least two meters high. His wife stands about a meter and a half tall with a solid, pear-shaped frame. She's a rounded face that hints of softness, yet etches with stress and struggle. Both look to be in their late thirties.

"Vasquez." The man points to his side. "My wife, Mariana."

Having regained her composure, Mariana is busy brushing the beach from her olive skin. "Hi," she says, her tone more forgiving than a person who was the twist of a wrist away from death moments before. She swivels to face me; her eyes bug open. "For scraigs, Kaden! Let the poor girl cover herself!"

Not waiting for her husband to take the lead, Mariana unsheathes a gut hook from its pouch at her waist and steps behind me. The cool blade slides between my cuffed wrists, stopping just shy of slicing through the bindings. She puts her lips near my left ear, her long black hair mixing with my own. In a hushed, determined tone she says, "I—we," her head jerks toward her husband, "are choosing to trust you." Her potatoes and garlic breath streams past my nose. My stomach growls, longing to appease its hollowness. "Don't make me have to draw this knife on you again."

With a sharp flick, the bindings fall loose. My hands rush forward to hug my breasts in an X of crossed arms.

"Here." Mariana drapes the tablecloth along my shoulders and over my chest, then steps next to her husband.

"You're the one from the facility," Vasquez says. "Yes?" He waits, the smugness in his words begging for validation of what he already knows. My only answer is to pull the tablecloth tighter to my chest. I mean, come on, where else would I be from?

"You're fresh. Probably don't remember your name yet, eh?" he asks.

Turn away, my cheeks puff with a mix of frustration and loss. Not knowing one's own identity eats away one's core. At whatever it is within you that makes you, you. Much more embarrassing than—well—being close to all skin in front of two strangers.

"No worries," Vasquez says. "We'll call you Jane Doe, at least until the drugs wear off."

My face flings back at the two. "Drugs?!"

"Ah, so you haven't gone mute."

Mariana slaps her husband's shoulder. "Kaden, stop trying to harass this girl. Lord knows what she's been through getting here." She smiles at me. "Please allow me to apologize for my ass of a husband…"

"Hey!"

As if he isn't even there, Mariana continues, "We'll cover the drugs later; right now, though, you're in danger here." She reaches out a hand. We lock forearms and she pulls me up to my feet.

A genuine curiosity breezes over me. "How so?" Before the batteries in the headlamp died, I completed a thorough search of the building. There is no obvious way in or out, save the entrance that opens onto the beach, itself only accessible via water or air.

So how then…

I glance down the beach to find nothing anchored to the shore. Anything from the air would have wakened me long before this curious encounter. A question about to emerge from my lips, the male Vasquez says, "You're a desirable commodity." His wife nudges him, earning her a side glance before he continues, "The eyes and ears we've within the Facility say there's a search on for you like no other they've seen of any previous escapee."

Me? "I'm no different from anyone else."

"That's an opinion you need to adjust," Mariana says.

My head flinches back, nose crinkles. "I don't understand?"

"There will be time for understanding later," Vasquez jumps in. "Though I'm most curious to hear about your escape, our priority needs to be getting out of here, out of the open. For now, they've presumed you lost in the caves—and there are *a lot* of them—but they'll search the rest of the island soon. At least one flyover in before it gets too late in the day. I'm surprised they haven't yet."

"My husband, abrasive as he can be, has a point, dear. You're fortunate we found you first, given your rather *exposed* situation."

The female Vasquez appears to have already put our near-death meeting behind her, but the pun is too soon. With a renewed grip, encase within the tablecloth all the more. My elbows compress my ribs. Breaths struggle past my lips. If this isn't like wearing a straightjacket, I don't want to know what is. I twist around, seeking my brassiere.

"Let me help you with that." Mariana moves past me and grabs the undergarment—buried from our altercation—off the beach. A grapefruit's worth of sand pours from one cup. "You'll not want to wear this, dear. When we get back to camp, we can find you something from our stocks."

It's generous, but presumptuous, of the woman to include me in this *we*. Who are these people? How can I trust them any more than the guards? And if I'm such a "hot commodity", why risk helping me? Of what use am I to them? Besides, there's Paul... "I appreciate all that, but..."

The hurt flaring in Mariana's eyes cuts me short. She places her free hand on my arm and peers up into my eyes with a mother's compassion. A small part of my resistance melts.

"I—we..." she glances toward her husband, "appreciate that giving someone your blind trust is difficult, and risky. It's a lot for us to ask. Believe, though, we've the sad experience of knowing that if you don't come with us now, you'll not see the end of this day."

Her words are heavy but seem to come from a place of sincerity. A relief, as I've not much of a choice. Given Paul's condition, she vocalized what I already know, deep down: without these people's help, this day will not end well. "Alright then."

"Good!" Mariana lights back up. "Let's go then!" Wrapping an arm around my waist, she directs me toward the laboratory entrance. The male Vasquez is already several steps ahead.

"I have some clothes drying out down on the dock."

"Perfect!" Mariana says, then squeezes my waist. "I wasn't sure how to make this tablecloth last until camp. One of my boys can grab those for you. Better to get you under cover, *rápida*."

"Boys?"

"Paterson and Mahoney. Joined our team over three years ago, two months apart. Peterson's not much older than you. You may know him."

Why would that mean I know him? "Doesn't ring a bell."

"Perhaps you'll recognize the face." Mariana gives me a little squeeze. "We found him lost in the caves, dehydrated, near death. He'd been only a year at the facility, so overcame the indoctrination in short time, after which he joined us.

"Mahoney's the older of the two. Worked on one of the supply ships. As he tells it, one night he and some crew-mates were having a few drinks when someone suggested they break into the training grounds. As you know, they restrict the sailors to the docks."

"Ah—sure." I don't, but whatever.

"Anyhow, too much booze and the need to flex their masculinity overtook logic. What originated as a prank on the newbie ended with Mahoney caught and banned from service. More than that, they instructed his captain to leave him for the sharks once they were at mid-sea. Before they got the jump on him, Mahoney abandons the ship in a lifeboat and makes his way back here, to this exact beach. And the rest is history."

Right. No gaps in all that.

"Let's go, ladies!" Vasquez's quicker pace already has him at the facility's main entrance, pulling its glass door open. The *GGC* printed on its surface teases at my memory, only to fall away as a pudgy young man—dressed the likes of the Vasquez pair—rushes out.

Like the male Vasquez, his hair is a fluffy mess, but blooming with the color of a cornflower. He salutes Vasquez who, himself, returns the acknowledgment before stepping into the building. The young man starts down the steps when he notices us and stops. He scans up and down as if I'm some circus oddity. He giggles. "One-of-a-kind dress you got there."

"Stow it, Paterson," Mariana barks the order before I can retort. "Go get her clothes off the dock and beat it back here double time."

"Yes, Ma'am!"

With a second salute, Paterson rushes past us and toward the docks. We proceed up the stairs and into the building. Inside, Vasquez is standing next to a counter studying some papers with a just as tall but more defined man. While the second man wears fatigues similar to the others on his lower half, a biscuit-colored tank top covers his upper body. The choice showcases the crimson tailed mermaid painted onto his dark-skinned biceps. Great—a narcissist.

As we approach, the man snaps straight and salutes. "Ma'am," he says with a gruff.

Mariana returns the salute. "At ease. Jane, this is Mahoney. Best spelunker in this part of the Pacific. Saved our asses more than once." She nods at the man, her face awash with gratitude. "Mahoney, Jane Doe. Our latest escapee."

The man shoots out his large hand. Padlock the tablecloth as best I can with one hand and clasp onto his offering with my other. He wraps his other hand over mine and gives it a gentle but firm shake. "Pleasure to meet you, ma'am."

Huh, perhaps not so self-absorbed. "Likewise." I smile.

"Jane Doe, huh?" he asks.

Why's it always about my name?! "So it seems." I snap my hand away.

"No worries." Mahoney flashes me a bright smile and a wink. "We'll help you find the real you."

The *real* me. What is the real me? What does that even mean? My visions hint that there's more to me than the person standing here. But are they genuine reflections of some past reality, or just the daydreams of a girl trying to delude herself into believing she's someone, something, else? Too many questions, too few answers. How this man, this group, can bring clarity is hard to envision.

"Mahoney says the guards have spawned out this way," the male Vasquez's voice pierces my thoughts. He's addressing his wife, who steps closer to the counter. With her arm still wrapped around my waist, I've no choice but to join the pair.

With her free hand, the woman circles the southwestern corner of the hand-drawn picture laying atop the counter. "We should go around this way, then." The picture is full of twisting and turning corridors laying atop a grid. Abbreviations and numbers of unknown meaning mark the various intersections and rooms scattered across the page. Near the bottom of the page, just left of its center, there is a recognizable cove containing a boxed off area labeled *Abandoned Labs*.

"Are those the caves?" I ask.

"You bet," Mahoney boasts as his big thumbs shoot at his chest. "Courtesy of yours truly."

"The detail's amazing."

"It is," Mariana chimes in. "Sixteen months of much appreciated, careful work by our Mr. Mahoney." Mariana gives the man's bare shoulder a squeeze, then turns back to her male counterpart in reviewing the map.

"Thank you, ma'am." Mahoney gives me a small bow. "Miss Doe." He pulls a large apple from his pocket and rubs it against his shirt. The apple has a beautiful light-red sheen with a bright yellow undertone. After a quick inspection of his polishing work, Mahoney digs his teeth deep into it with a crisp *crunch*. Juice drips down his chin, which he wipes away with the back of his hand.

"Surray." His lips struggle between keeping food in and letting words out. "Can be bitta slob, sometimes." He flashes a small smile, then grinds away at the treat. Crunch after crunch, his mouth works the chunk down. His cheeks bulge in alternation as he shifts their contents from side to side to work the bigger pieces.

My cheeks flush with saliva.

Crunch! In goes another bit before he's even finished the first. As he crunches away, he scopes the apple for the next area to indulge in. About to take a third bite, his eyes catch mine. "Good apple." He raises it toward me as if we are toasting in celebration.

My tongue darts across my lips of its own accord. I swallow hard, the liquid about to overflow my mouth.

"Oh, jeez!" Mahoney says. "Did you want one?"

"Yes, please!" *Darn straight!* my stomach echoes. Not sure how fast my head bobs up and down.

Mahoney pulls another of the oval apples from his pocket and—as with his own—gives it a brief polish. He extends the fruit to me, but stops just shy of my waiting hand. An odd grin plays across his mouth. "Be sure to take your time and savor each sweet taste."

As if you're one to talk about savoring each bite, you horse! "Thanks."

I grab the apple from his hand and dig my mouth deep into its skin. Juices shoot in every direction, into and out of my lips. My stomach doesn't care. The apple is mildly tart but sweet. Cannot help but close my eyes, letting the crisp texture of its flesh play across my tongue. I may have moaned.

Mahoney laughs, but Mariana's troubled "My gosh, dear, when did you eat last?" steals me from paradise.

Open my eyes to find all other eyes on me. Swallowing the chunks left in my mouth, my stomach torn between nausea and glee. "Lunch yesterday."

"Goodness, you should'a said so!"

As genuine as the concern in her voice, seems one of those deflective statements people say to absolve themselves of your dilemma. Regardless of her motivation—*You're keeping me from the food!*—free her of any responsibility. "I'm all good," I sputter, then take another big bite from the fruit.

Mid-chew, Paterson blows into the lobby, his mouth struggling to find oxygen. His hands hold my clothes. "Boats!" He takes a depth breath. "Two, and they're close; give'em ten minutes."

"Shit!" the Vasquezes echo the other.

"And that's our signal to leave," utters a pragmatic Mahoney.

"Her clothes," Mariana shoots at Paterson. He tosses them at us. Mariana releases my waist and snatches them out of midair, then butts her husband toward Paterson. In the same moment, she commands, "Mahoney, shield her."

The tablecloth rips from my hand and plucks from my shoulders. Before I can protest, a weak breeze flutters across my back as Mahoney spreads it wide behind me. Still at my side, Mariana stuffs the clothes against my again unclothed chest. "Make it quick."

Against my stomach's demands, sit the rest of my apple on the counter and curl my right arm over the clothes. Mariana turns away. A kind gesture, but what little of my modesty that exists between us is long lost on the beach.

Heeding Mariana's words, sit the pants on the counter, then slip my arms and head through the shirt's holes. Tug at its waistband; was never an ideal fit, but don't recall it being so hard to get over my chest. What originally fit as a crop-top yanks no lower than a tube top. The pants are worse, unable to conquer my hips, let alone button even if they did. "Crap!"

"What are you doing?"

Look up from my struggle to see Mariana peeking at me. She seems torn between frustration and laughter. Straighten and, with a *huff*, fling my hands down to my sides in a whip motion.

Mariana twists to face me and snaps, "Peterson!" She snatches the pants he throws and flings them at me in a single motion. "Wear these."

"Those are Paul's. They're too big."

Mariana crosses her arms and shifts her weight to her right leg. Her lips go thin and tense. "So?" Her foot taps… taps… taps…

The uncomfortable moment feels too familiar, yet distant. Memories from a younger me chafe at my heart. Fight the visions back into subconsciousness. There is no mistaking that Mariana is not in the mood for any defiance or further delay.

Step out of the tight pants, slide into Paul's… to have them fall to the floor once left to their own devices. *Told you so!*

"Mr. Vasquez, your belt, if you please," Mariana says without pause. She sticks her right arm out to the side, all the while not taking an eye off of me. Within ten seconds, Paul's pants are back at my waist, secured in place with a deep brown, wide rawhide belt. Paul, being taller than I, adds several unnatural cuffs to each pant leg to avoid tripping. Pair the outfit with the slippers and rubber boots I left next to the door before heading to the beach. Thank goodness there are no mirrors here; this is not an outfit I care to reflect upon, with neither my eyes nor my mind.

A growing rumble carries across the beach. Paterson glances out the glass of the door. "They're around the cove, aimed for the dock!"

Crud me! Is *this* my life now?

"Paterson, brace the doors behind us, as always," Mariana says. "The rest of you, let's move!"

The woman grabs my biceps and hauls me through a vestibule next to the counter area that was once a security checkpoint to get into the building proper. The others hurry to gather what little they have out and follow, save Paterson, who first rushes to the main door and pops the bolt lock at its foot into place. Most of the door is a traditional glass panel—unlikely to provide much resistance to our unwelcome guests, or protection for Paul and I.

The security checkpoint doors Paterson retreats to, however, appear made of a mix of metal and polycarbonate. A bear grunt leaves Paterson as he tries sliding the first of the two doors shut. The foot of the door squeals as its rusted metal wheels budge.

Grunting, his arms and legs straining, he huffs, "How'd you get these open?"

"I didn't." I'd help, but Mariana's grip is firm. "They were this way when I came through."

Mahoney slips past us and joins in the effort. Between the two, the door squeaks shut. While Paterson regains his breath, Mahoney bends down and twists a knob built into the bottom corner of the door. A moment later, a firm *cha-cumpth* signals the manual lock securing into place. The second of the checkpoint doors again takes the pair to maneuver it, but shuts with less resistance than the first. Despite his best efforts, though, Mahoney cannot get its manual lock to engage.

"Just leave it," the male Vasquez instructs. "We'll be gone long before they can get through that first door." He has Mahoney take the lead toward the laboratory.

"Behind Kaden," Mariana says as she at last releases my arm and takes the second spot within our quintet. Paterson falls in last as we head for the laboratory. Each of them carry a flashlight. Shy of the office within which Paul rests, Mahoney's light turns left and starts down a flight of stairs.

"Wait! Where are you going?"

Everyone stops, but Paterson speaks first. "To the caves, through the basement."

"But Paul's in an office down the hall. We can't leave without him."

Mariana steps around her husband. Her flashlight beam pokes at my face, close to blinding me. "Sorry, dear, but your boyfriend—"

"He's *not* my boyfriend."

"Fine!" She's snooty. "Boyfriend or not, he's a liability and will only slow us down. I'm sure you can appreciate the urgency of our situation."

She isn't wrong: the moment is urgent. The boat motors have subsided, for certain the soldiers disembarking. Conversely, Paul's not moving of his own volition; it took my full might to get him onto that couch. To move him is an enormous burden—an obvious risk—but not doing so seals his death sentence. To remain behind with him, suicide.

"I'm all he's got," I say between tears. "I—I can't leave him here to die." I can't fail Paul again.

Mariana steps closer and takes one of my hands in her own. The ambient light streaks in her own wet eyes. "Sweetie, he's running a fever with a head injury. Even if we had proper supplies, we don't have the know-how to help him. The Facility does; the guards will take him back there."

How can she not help? "They'll kill him," I fling back.

Mariana drops my hands, her face stiffens. "Fine! Then stay and share his fate. We're leaving!"

"Mariana!" The female Vasquez snaps toward her husband. *"Por favor, ven aquí, mi amor."*

The woman flashes a glare my way, then steps over to her husband. They share a whispered exchange in Spanish and, with a kiss on the forehead from her husband, Mariana's shoulders drop. She wraps her arms around his torso and buries her head in his chest. He returns the embrace, but looks over her head to his team. "Mahoney, you know the rec room?"

"Yes, Sir."

"Good. I'm sure I've seen a surfboard or paddle board or something like that in there before. Go grab it."

"Sir!" Mahoney salutes and rushes back in the direction we'd come.

"Paterson, you're with me. We need to figure out how to turn a surfboard into a stretcher. You," Vasquez's stern eyes lock upon me, "take this." He holds out his flashlight, which I accept. "Follow Mariana downstairs. When you reach the bottom, circle the staircase and head down the center passageway. Fifth door on your left is a small storage room. Third cabinet along the rear wall has a false back. Remove it and wait for us there. Understand?"

"I do." I wipe away the tears from my cheeks. "And thank you."

The glass of what can only be the front door shatters. Everyone jerks to attention and stares down the hall. Only blackness stares back.

"Don't thank me yet," Vasquez says, bringing us back to the task at hand. "Let's go!"

CHAPTER SIX

OUR SEDAN JERKS TO A rest, clanging the glasses on the bar against one another. James, who sits twisted atop his legs so he can better stare out the window, slides forward and off the leather seat. His knees smack into the floor—"Ouch!"—as his upper body tilts forward in a slow motion arc. His head bounces with a muted thud onto the seat next to me.

A small giggle leaks from my lips.

"Apologies, Madam," Jasper calls over his speaker.

"No harm." Irritation laces mom's reply, but she smiles at me with a giggle of her own. James twists his body, struggling to release his legs from underneath himself. "Can you help him, please?"

"Sure."

Grab him under the pits and boost his behind onto the bench beside me. Begin brushing dust and lint off the knees and lower half of his pants' legs.

"Stop touching me!"

"Oh, stop it. I'm just trying to help you."

"I don't need your help. *Maaumm!*"

"Quiet, James." Mom's focus is out the window. "We're pulling up."

I twist and look through the window. Our sedan queues fourth behind those guests whom are more timely in their arrival. Vehicles unload two at a time, meaning my once dreaded but turned pleasant ride is near conclusion. As exciting as the party will be, part of me wants Jasper to loop around, to have just that little more girl time with mom.

"I'm bored," James says. "Can we get out?!"

"No!" mom and I say in unison.

"Jinx!" I call out.

Mom laughs. "Guess that means I owe you a Coke."

"I guess it does." I smile. As tasty as a Coke sounds, some food sounds better. The emptiness in my stomach gurgles and yelps at my brain. Breakfast was so long ago and dinner's not in the immediate future. Of course, a party like this will float with appetizers. James may have it right! Can we get out yet?

"That is… different," Mom says.

From the first vehicle emerges an elderly couple, he in a handsome swallowtail jacketed tuxedo and she in full-length, ruby red Rococo. The couple leaving the second car, though, is for certain what grabbed Mom's attention. They are much less in years than the first pair, an adolescent daughter—perhaps ten—standing between the two. Mom and daughter wear complementary pink polka-dotted dresses, draped shawls, and hair ribbons. The father wears a black suit, a pink polka-dotted vest peeks out from underneath his jacket. All three wear black heels of varying heights.

A tuxedo-dressed porter leads each of the parties away from their vehicles and toward a dual gated entrance into the estate. The first two cars pull away. Jasper pulls into the furthest forward of the vacated spaces. As we stop, two more porters move into position. Both are clean-shaved, have a crisp, close haircut, and are wearing the same midnight black tuxedos as their peers. The porter at our vehicle first consults a wrist pad and then pulls the door open.

Artificial light pours into the passenger compartment, the sun having set in the time it took us to get to the party. My eyes squint as they adjust to the brightness. After two quick blinks, find the porter offering his hand to assist Mom from her seated position. "Mrs. Rogers."

With the porter's help, Mom lifts free of the car; she pushes her chin forward and puffs out her chest as he leads her to the side. Her heels click across the bricked walkway fronting the gateway, stopping about four meters from the car. She stands there prim and proper, glaring past her nose, though at whom is unclear. She downplayed the circumstance, but how

could it not be odd attending a party at her employer's home? To be min-
gling with the very crowd she serves? For her sake, I hope her pageantry is
not for nil.

The porter gives her a small bow, then moves back toward the car.

Primp at the skirt of my dress. The bright light from outside twinkles
off the flakes like stars on a dark, clear night. Reds… greens… blues…
yellows flit over the ceiling and edges of the compartment. My eyes dart
from side to side, trying to keep track of them all.

"Pretty," James says.

"For certain she is."

Oh, jeez!

Jerk to attention. The porter is bent at the waist, his milky green eyes
locked on me. His face reflects that of a college student, but reads an older
man's maturity. Pale brown freckles dot his neck to forehead, and the outstretched hand awaiting my own. "Miss."

I take a deep breath and smooth the skirt of my dress, then turn my
legs toward the door and scoot nearer to the exit. Layer my right hand with
a polite arch over the porter's. With a similar gentle, yet firm, manner, his
grip replies.

"Get outta the way!" James yanks my right shoulder back—breaking
my grip with the porter—and bulls past, stepping on my foot, cracking my
knees together.

"Ow! Dammit James!"

The porter grabs James by the arm as he shoots out of the car and whips
him around to face the two of us. "Master Rogers," he says in a quiet but
commanding voice, "that is disgraceful behavior for a gentleman. Please
apologize to the young lady."

"You're not my dad," James retorts. He tries, with no success, to pull
away from the porter.

"James," I say, "your manners."

"Let me go!" James squirms back and forth, trying to break the porter's
grip.

"Apologize," the porter insists, "and you are free to go."

James looks me dead in the eyes. "Never." His face contorts in what
could only be anger. "I'm gonna tell Mom!"

In the right or not, Mom getting involved will not end in the positive for any of us. Well, for anyone other than James. He'll twist the story, make this all my fault. Mommy's baby can do no wrong. "You can let him go."

James' face cringes, the porter giving his arm an extra squeeze before he relinquishes his grip. Free, James rushes over to Mom and buries his head into the ruffle of her dress. Mom wraps an arm around his shoulder but doesn't otherwise seem to notice his distress. He says nothing despite his threat.

"Allow me to apologize for the young master," the porter says. "He has much yet to learn about being a proper gentleman."

Ugh, those lights are bright, so hot. Reach down to rub the top of my sore foot, an excuse to hide my face. It isn't much of a hiding place. The porter's outstretched hand grabs at my peripheral vision and draws my full gaze on to him.

"I think I am the one that needs to apologize," I say. "And thank you for that."

"It was only the proper thing to do, Miss." The porter follows his comments with a small bow. "If your foot should permit, it'd be my honor to escort you to your party."

My hand returns to his, with which he helps lift me from the car. Clear of the door, he pushes it shut and steps to my side. His right fingertips rest with a gentle touch on the small of my back as he guides me toward Mom and James. The help unnecessary—my brain more than capable of directing my legs four meters without straying—the personal attention is a welcomed diversion to what, until an hour ago, was an otherwise unwelcoming day.

The porter aligns me next to Mom, James fidgeting between her and me, then straightens in front of our small group. "On behalf of the Matters' family," he addresses us, "allow me to welcome you to Avalon Estates."

"Thank you," Mom says.

"Mrs. Rogers, your husband is already at the pavilion. Would you care for me to notify him of your arrival?"

Please, yes!

"No, the children and I would care to surprise him."

Darn, I could so use one of Papa's hugs ASAP.

"As you wish, madam," the porter replies. "Now then, shall we go to your waiting carriage?"

The porter offers his arm to Mother, who weaves her hand through the opening. They step toward the gate, James and I trailing close behind. The scowl on his face aside, James allows me to take his hand; more than once, he's taken off in random directions when not guided otherwise.

Pass through the gate, after which the wide, well-lit ingress collapses to a single walkway bordered by authentic gas-feed lamp posts. All give off a soft, yellowish glow. A thick flotilla of bushes and trees delimits the sides of the walkway. Catch a deer out of the corner of my left eye, but cannot otherwise make out any of the many animals that scurry away as our small group passes.

We walk in silence, save for the odd mix of rustling foliage and two sets of clicking heels for seven meters, before the porter speaks again. "As you can see, Avalon Estates is more than a mere home, but a sanctuary for wildlife of many kinds. While most of the plants and animals are harmless, there are some exotic and predatory among the woods. For both your own and the wildlife's safety, the family insists that you remain in designated areas only during your visit."

"Naturally," Mom says.

"Very good. Not far ahead, we shall find your waiting carriage."

"Not far ahead" is another seven meters before the walkway again widens and ends at a platformed boardwalk. Along the raised structure, two long, horse-drawn, open-top landaus wait.

The first is a rich green color, ornately trimmed with silver-colored embellishments. Gas-lamps, similar in style to those that stand along the walkway, perch on each corner of the passenger compartment. A large, detailed crest—that of the Matters family—embosses on the side of the cart. Its passengers: the elderly couple paired with a young woman bearing a headful of long whitish-blonde hair, highlighted in a rainbow blend of blue, green, and purple. The driver takes his place at the front and mushes the carriage's two horses ahead.

Our coach twins the first but is instead a deep royal red color with gold-colored accents. Our driver, an average height man in his late fifties, has the side door open. He wears a classic, double-breasted livery, accurate to that of a Victorian coachman. His coat is in the same royal red color as the carriage, with an elaborate golden trim. Our porter stops us just short of the waiting driver. "This is where I must bid you *adieu*," he says with a slight bow. "Mr. Tosetti shall take you from here."

"Thank you Adrian," Mr. Tosetti says before turning his focus to me. "Miss, if you would please."

His hand offered for balance, Mr. Tosetti assists me up the pair of steps ascending to the carriage. The pink polka-dotted family has already boarded and situated themselves on the bench seat facing toward the rear of the carriage. As the first of our party into the compartment, I move to the far side of the forward-facing bench, across from the couple's daughter. The girl is fanning out the dress of a doll—pink polka-dotted, like her own. She looks away from the grooming and gives me a polite smile.

I smile back. "Your doll's precious."

The girl sits up a little straighter, her smile widens. "Her name is Martha."

I take hold of the doll's hand and give it a small shake. "Pleasure to meet you, Martha."

The girl's eyes grow into plump grapes, crinkling her forehead. "Your dress is *so* beautiful."

"Ugh!" James snickers. "Disgusting."

He sits just inside the door, as far to the left side of the bench as possible. His favorite pastime is to fire off subtle backbites anytime I do anything nearing girly, presume James' comment intended for me. Discretion, however, is far from his forte. The couple's daughter glares at him, but her misty eyes betray the scorn she is trying to channel. James stares back, a self-satisfying grin growing on his lips. The girl sniffles.

"Just ignore him," I say.

The girl gives me a weak smile, then turns her face away from the two of us. She clutches her doll with one hand, using the other to wipe away a tear from her cheek.

Dammit, James! Give him the most disappointed head shake I can muster. He responds by sticking his tongue out.

It's one thing to harass me, but to insult the girl—intended or not—is beyond inappropriate. James is always a bit of a handful, but tonight, over-the-line seems a generous descriptor. He needs a stiff scolding. Something to squeeze this malicious over-confidence out of him.

Any tongue-wiping by me, though, he'll just laugh off, somehow twist such that I'll end up blamed for the entire mess.

Locked in a conversation started before we boarded, the girl's parents show no notice of their daughter's distress. There is no way, though, that Mom will ignore this indiscretion.

Alas, she just brushes her hand at James. "Scoot," she says.

James protests, but cuts himself short. Even he isn't foolish enough to further cross Mom tonight. With a huff, he pushes hard off the side of the compartment and slides across the seat. Hard enough that he propels into my side. My right forearm crushes painfully against the opposite side of the compartment.

Work my arm free and arc toward him, ready to deal a shove in reply, save a death glare from Mom. Opt to rub the soreness from my arm instead. James sits with a smug smile on his face. *Paybacks, buddy—just you wait.*

Everyone seated, Mr. Tosetti makes an expedient work of closing up the carriage and taking his position at the reins. With a small snap of the leather and a *chit, chit*, the landau glides forward. He leads the horses along the right side of an unpaved two-track. Similar to the walkway, gas-feed lamps serve as a divider between the two directions of the track. As on our walk, there are many animals to hear, but few to see—other than squirrels, which keep darting in front of the horses as if playing a game of chicken. The horses troll along, incurious of the rodents.

The wife's belly being plump with child, Mom engrosses herself with the couple. She rattles off a million questions, few of which she waits for an actual response. When are they due? Have they found out the sex? No, well, what are they hoping for? A boy… the perfect nuclear family—so classic. Girls… so huggable when they are babies; nothing but frustration as teens. Self-absorbed, no respect for their elders. But they'll get to experience that all themselves in the not too far future, notching her head toward their preteen daughter.

And on and on she babbles.

Each of the pair manages the occasional "*Ah-ha*" or "*I see*" in the brief moments Mom takes a breath. Whether Mom cares, the two don't seem receptive to her insights, yet that doesn't prevent her from rolling along. The entire episode is more entertaining than anything I've ever witnessed from Mom. Not that she is one to be demure—in fact, quite the opposite—but never so buoyant and wordy.

Silence dominates our side of the cart. The couple's daughter stares outward, ignoring the rest of us. To miss an opportunity to learn about someone new is disappointing, but I cannot blame the girl. She isn't the only one trying to ignore James. Though he holds his tongue, he jams me into the side of the carriage three times as it rolls over each of three bumps. I steel my elbow—the cart bounces—and jerk it left.

"Blah." James rubs his side. At the next pothole, he doesn't move a centimeter in my direction.

The green carriage maintains a twenty-five meters lead. The older couple, sitting such that they face us, huddle together, deep in discussion. Twice in the next several minutes they scan their riding mate, then huddle back together in talk. Though they are far from subtle, their companion pays them no notice. She gazes off to the left, watching for what is hard to say. The forest conceals everything beyond the pathway and the gas lamps are too weak to pierce into the bush. They do nothing more than blind me every ten meters.

We bounce another half kilometer before the trees thin out, revealing the Matters' house at an angle off to the left. *House* being a bit of an understatement. *Mansion* is closer, but between the stone masonry, tall spires, and wooden main entrance that appear a drawbridge from our distance, *castle* fit best. The abode is distant enough, the sky dark enough, that totaling the number of windows incising the building is impossible. Count twenty-three lit ones on the two sides visible from the carriage.

"I see why you need an assistant," I say. "Imagine several."

"Huh?" Mom glares at me, me having interrupted whatever knowledge she is imparting to the pregnant couple.

"Their house," I say, "it's gigantic!"

Mom glances to the left and back again. The couple look over their own shoulders before turning toward Mom, each wearing a face of confusion. Mom flushes. "Ah—yes—quiet impressive." Her glower, though, could not have been more clear: there'd be no follow up.

How could I've been so naïve? The last thing she wants to be tonight is an employee.

I make to mouth an apology, but Mom drops her thesis on the origins of today's ill-mannered youth upon the pair. I turn my attention elsewhere; the castle is not the only impressive structure ahead of us.

A half kilometer to the right of the house, the pavilion shines with an inviting yellowish glow. The pavilion, though, is only one of several single-story outbuildings, tents, and a large stage forming the hexagonal parameter around the party. A solid murmur of many mixed voices carries across the distance. We are running behind, but didn't expect to be part of the "fashionably late" clique.

As we close upon the pavilion, the couple's daughter comes back to life. She re-arranges her doll so they can both watch the oncoming destination then, pointing at each noteworthy feature, whisper an eager observation to the doll. Seems an excellent opportunity to check that James caused no permanent damage. "It's fantastic, isn't it?"

The girl flips around, her eyes bright, an excited smile on her face. Thank the Universe! "I've seen nothing like it." Her doll bounces atop her legs. "I'm so excited!"

"Me too. I've never been to anything like this before."

"Really?"

"Really."

Even as baffling as the day has been... I *am* rather excited! I've been to nothing even close to this before, worn nothing as elegant as the dress decorating my body. Or have my makeup painted by an expert. *Make the most of this magical moment, girl!* I know not if the butterflies fluttering about my stomach dance with hunger, nerves, or anticipation. More like a mix of all three. "Look, we're getting close!"

The green carriage makes a definitive turn toward the pavilion. The rainbow haired lady, though, keeps her eyes married to the house, absorbing the gentle flow of golf cart-like vehicles shuttling between there and the party. Only when the carriage stops at the platform does her interest shift to on-goings of the party. The couple disembark first, the male of the two gawking back at their fellow passenger. His mate slaps him upside the head. He makes some comment, but she just shakes her head and drags him off the platform. Their riding-mate ignores the pair's antics, once more glancing at the house before departing the carriage herself. As she lowers down on the platform, the old man's fascination sparkles forth.

The woman is stunning, even from the distance we've still to cover. She wears a spaghetti-strapped, turquoise sequin mini-dress that wraps her modest hourglass curves tighter than water when stepping naked into the ocean. The dress' side splits from upper hip to hem, the opening laced

together with a thin black ribbon. A pair of narrow cuffs in the same material as the dress wrap around the wrist and biceps of each of her arms.
Strings of reflective beads connect to each pair. A black choker wraps
around her neck. At the end of her muscle-lined legs, tall, thin stemmed
heels in the same color as the dress decorate her feet. As she walks off the
platform, the many lights of the pavilion shine off her dress in a mixture
of greens, blues, and purples.

Ah… thus the hair!

As much of a standout as the woman is, by the time our carriage pulls
alongside the platform, she's blended into the stylish crowd packed into
the hexagon. Opposite the platform, the stage hosts a large wooden dance
floor and a ten-piece string ensemble. Northwest, the golf-carts dart back
and forth between the largest of the buildings. Workers flit between the
structure and the various sized cabanas that make up the rest of the border.
Each hut is one of a beverage cantina or food bar offering appetizers and
other edible goods. The latter calls to my stomach.

Mr. Tosetti steps down from his perch on my side of the carriage, it
being shored up against the platform. He releases a step stool, and with a
click, opens the compartment's door. "Ladies," he says with a small bow.

Before James says something even more rude, I tilt my hand toward the
opening for the young girl. She no more stands when her father grabs her
arm. "Let them go first."

"Oh, that is so polite of you," Mom says.

The wife gives her a weak smile of acknowledgment. The husband offers no comment, his eyes instead locking on the party.

"Well," Mom says, "get moving!"

"Sorry," I say to the girl. "Have fun."

"You too," she replies, that big smile still on her face.

With Mr. Tosetti's help, I gingerly—heedful to not have my dress ride
up and I moon everyone—scoot from the carriage and step over to the
side. James bounces free of the cart. I pluck his hand before he can cause
any commotion, which he tries to pull away. Mom joins us a second thereafter. She edges up next to me.

"I need you to do me a favor," she breathes into my ear, "and watch
James for a bit. Do you think you can do that?"

This is a surprise: the asking, not the watching. Many an evening or
weekend—Dad working late—she'd *tell* me I am watching one or both of

my younger brothers while she goes out to do, well, whatever it is she does without us kids. Never Dewey. Always me. Even if I'm half out the door with my own plans and he's sitting right there on his butt in front of the projectratron. From where's this new graciousness? Perhaps that car ride quality time turned a new page in the story of Mom and me? Please, be so… "Yeah, I can do that."

"Perfect. James?" James stops pulling and turns toward her. "Your sister's in charge. Stay with her."

My ears have to be mishearing. Did Mom assign me authority over James?

"But I don't wanna…"

"Enough! No sass, young man. Listen to your sister. Understand me?"

James drops his chin and kicks at a stone that doesn't exist with a groan. "Yes, Mom."

Mom moves in front of James and lifts his head back up. "Trust me, you'll have a lot more fun with her."

"Doubt it," he says.

Mom smiles and kisses his forehead, then swaggers to and down the steps to the grounds. As she disappears into the crowd, the first alcoholic beverage within reach magnetizes to her hand.

"Come on," I say. With James about to stiffen his stance, I add in haste, "Let's get some food!"

Sure, it's a ploy to get him to succumb to my will, but that makes it no less sincere. He loves to eat anything and everything, and the too long-lived cavity in my midsection has become twisted and achy. James' stomach must concur; he doesn't resist as I lead him through the crowd to a nearby hors d'oeuvre tent.

We leave the waiters working the tent unhappy with us. Though they say nothing of the disorganized mess we create, irritation and disgust make it clear we best not return for seconds. James is a bottomless pit when eating, but the heaping plate of shrimp, crab toast, fried olives, and croquettes in my hand can satisfy my hunger.

At the nearest open table, the two of us dig into our respective piles. I more reserved—against the complaints of my insides—than James. He's a quarter of his plate already stuffed into his mouth, chewing away like a horse, before much of a dent appears in my stack. The food's quality is like none that has ever graced my tongue. Every bite bursts with flavor, paints with textures that tickle the palate. Toy with the pleasure centers of the brain. It is only appropriate—almost a requirement—to eat with patience, savoring every delicious morsel. With each bit that flows over my tongue and down into my belly, every part of my body thanks me.

Survey the crowd as we eat.

To no wonder adults dominate the party. A kid pops into view every so often, but no one who is familiar. The pregnant couple and their daughter pass by. The girl waves, that big smile still on her face. Return the wave. James sighs, rolling his eyes in as exaggerated a manner as possible.

"Oh, just—just—bury your face in your food!" I say.

"Whatever," he says before devouring the ham and cheese sandwich he's made of two canapés.

Spend the next fifteen minutes filling our bellies and searching the crowd. No one recognizable jumps out, inclusive of Papa. *Where can he be?* The last I saw of him was Thursday morning, rushing out the door without even sharing breakfast with me. Though he often worked extra hours or even the occasional weekend, prior to yesterday, one hand could more than count the number of times he missed our breakfast. Now he missed two in a row. Nor did he come to wish me sweet dreams last night. He *always* does that, no matter the late hour. Papa M.I.A… Mom's dual personalities in a matter of hours… James being more Jamesy than ever…

By the stars, what is going on?!

"Oh, my goodness! Girlfriend! Is that, for real, you?"

James sighs. "Oh, great."

Flick my hand at him as I pop from my seat and flip around. "Geli!"

My best friend rushes at me, the skirt of her sleeveless, rose patterned dress fluttering in pursuit. She barrels into my open arms, wrapping her own tight around my shoulders. She snuggles her face into my neck and squeezes. Although not a ditto of Papa's bear hugs, it's a hug much needed. I squeeze back, soaking in the sweet jasmine of her perfume. At last, a friendly face! "It's so great to see you," I whisper into her ear.

Angelica loosens her grip, but still holds me close. She tilts her head such that all of her face draws full into view. Her gracious, walnut-colored eyes lock with my own, but only for the briefest of moments before her cheeks go pink. She slants her head to the side. A deep breath later, she turns back. Her pupils widen. The galaxy within my charm radiates within them. Though *reflection* is not the right word. The image doesn't rest on her eyes, but is breaking out from somewhere deep within. The galaxy floating in each eye brightens. Angelica again leans in, gliding the tip of her tongue across the canary-red, fleshy exit of her mouth.

She raises to her toes and, in a tone as if sharing a secret, breathes, "It's so great…" She plants a small kiss on my left cheek. "to see…" Repeats the gesture on the right. "you too!" Her moistened lips plant themselves against mine, which tingle as an airy mix of honey and fruit drift past. A curious ardor blooms in my core, only to have it stymie by the salmon pâté-flavored saliva flushing from my mouth.

Oh no! I have fish breath! Wait! What am I thinking?!

I wrench my head away, breaking the kiss. Angelica seems indifferent to the sudden change, taking but a single step backward, a joyous smile between her apricot cheeks. Next to us, a half-eaten cracker drops out of James' gaping mouth. Angelica looks with bugged eyes at him and his expression, then giggles.

James goes red and blurts out, "Well—I saw her boobies!"

"James!"

Not missing a beat, Angelica cups the underside of my breasts and bounces what of them there are in her hands. "And they're *marvelous*!"

"Angelica!"

Has everyone's mind evaporated?

Push Angelica's hands away and cross my arms over my chest. "You two," I look from Angelica to James, then back, "I feel so—so violated."

James sits with a blend of eagerness and confusion on his face, likely waiting to see what outrageous thing is going to happen next. He's stockpiling ammunition for our next disagreement without doubt. Can't even imagine what Mom's gonna to say about this.

Angelica ignores my protest, as if I never made it. Her singular reply: she takes my hands in hers, takes a small step back, and surveys me. "You are gorgeous. DeVoe, right? And that amulet"—she leans in for a better study—"is that *moving*? How amazing!"

"Ah, no, it's an illusion." Lift the charm into view and watch as the spiral arms seem to rotate around the sphere of the galactic core. "Well, I guess." Let the charm fall back to my chest. "I *love* your dress too—how the leaves are mixed in with the roses. Cute little belt too."

Angelica clasps her hands together at her waist and sways side-to-side like she just won a prize. The folds of the dress' skirt follow along in a smooth wave. The dress is cute, its empire style fitting her narrow, petite build well. Its bodice has a firm shape which gathers at the waist under a thin brown belt. From there, the skirt flares out down to mid-calf. Printed across the entire outfit are enormous pink and purple roses blended into its off-white base color. Her presentation finishes with a pair of short-heeled peep-toe pumps in the base color of the dress and a pink rose weaved into the left side of her black-brown hair.

"Wait—stop trying to sidetrack me. What was that?"

She bats her eyes as an *I-don't-know-what-you-are-talking-about* grin settles upon her face. "What was what?" She says, coyness in her voice and still swaying.

"That kiss—what in the stars was that about?"

Angelica stops swaying, seriousness crossing her face. "I didn't kiss you," she says in a flat tone.

Huh?! "Look, Geli—you know I love you to death and all—but you, for certain, planted one square on my lips."

"I did no such thing." The defiance on her face whisks away in perkiness. "Spin for me."

"What?"

"Spin. Your dress," she says. "Don't you see it?"

Oh, no, did I spill something? Examine the front of the dress for food stuffs. Did I sit on something? No matter how I stretch, cannot take in the skirt's full rear.

Angelica laughs. "You're so silly. Just spin already!"

"Fine." I stick my tongue out at her. *But don't think I'm just letting this kissing thing go.*

I twist in slow quarter turns. The skirt of my dress adopts a slight lift, the gem flecks sparkling even more so under the artificial light.

"Faster," Angelica urges.

Double my speed, causing the hem of the dress to ride higher as the skirt flares out. The sparkles jive over the dress. The randomness of the gem groupings dissipates and morphs into structured, wavelike patterns.

"Faster."

"I'm getting dizzy!"

"Just a little more," Angelica says.

A little more… until what?

Though my stomach feels queasy, do my best to increase my circular momentum. Close my eyes to keep from overwhelming my sight. The cool breeze tickling at my thighs, I hesitate to turn any faster. Nothing good will come of showing off what is—or, perhaps more accurately, what isn't—under my dress. Anyone who takes notice is already getting well enough of a show. Besides, my legs are gumming up; stumble.

"Stop!" Angelica calls out.

My feet obey, but the rest of my body doesn't. Or, at least, it seems to tip over. Dare not open my eyes as all within my belly petitions for a return trip. I reach my hands out into the blackness to find anything to brace myself against. Angelica clamps on and steadies me. Only then does the murmur of nearby voices settle in my ears.

"You've got to see this," Angelica comments.

Still holding tight to Angelica, crack my eyes open enough to let in a sliver of light. A moment later, further. The sense of rotation subsiding, release my grip on Angelica. Blink twice, then open wide. A broad-eyed Angelica slowly steps back from me. To our left, a small crowd has gathered in a half-circle; everyone stares at me. "What?"

"Just look," Angelica says, pointing to the skirt of my dress.

Two well-formed spirals of gem flecks extend out in long, glistening arms from the now radiant bodice that wraps my upper half. In a gradual motion, the spirals swivel along the skirt, though the dress itself no longer rotates. Open the skirt wide so I can get a better view.

Mind-boggling.

My dress is the Milky Way come alive, with me at the center: Papa's shining galactic princess.

The gathered crowd buzzes, several people wide-eyed frozen. Others whisper among themselves. A mix of *wows* and *amazings* rises above the general buzz. One person quizzes a neighbor, "How did she do that?" Someone claps, and within seconds, a moderate smacking of palms fills the air. Not so loud as to be obnoxious, but enough that those further away glance over, wondering what they have missed. "Do it again!" a youthful-voiced girl calls out. Several *yeahs* second the request.

The whole of my face heats as if sunburned, not expecting to be part of the evening's entertainment. Give the crowd a small wave and say, "Ah, maybe soon." The spinning fades, both on the dress and in my head, but my stomach is still unwinding the knot it's become. Stand for a moment watching the crowd disperse—some with a disappointed look, but most just moving on to seek the next item of interest, whatever that will be. I turn back toward Angelica; we both bust out in giggles.

"How'd you know the dress would do that?" my mouth manages a half-a-minute later.

A mask of contemplation overtakes Angelica's giggles. "Your charm; that spinning galaxy engulfed my mind's eye and then, well, I just knew."

Without a mirror, I don't know which of the two of us wear our empuzzled face better. Angelica's expression begins confused, then transforms into concern. About to say something—anything to break the moment—she bubbles, "You're gonna come hang with us, right? We're near the dance floor. Susan's here, and Oralee, Tyra, Jason, Anthony…"

"I—ah…"

"You'll come," she insists, then teases, "*Abraham* is here. He keeps talking about you."

"Me?"

"Oh, come on, like that's a surprise. You know he's a crush on you."

"That's not here or there," I blurt out. My face grows hot again. "I promised Mom I'd watch…" Twist toward the table, now deserted, save two empty plates. "James," fades from my mouth. "Geli! Where'd he go?"

"Does it matter? Kid's just a nuisance anyhow."

"Come on, he's not that bad," I say. Angelica huffs in disbelief. "Anyhow, that's not the point. Mom and me, we'd a genuine moment on the way here. I don't wanna spoil that."

"A *genuine* moment, huh?" Angelica does nothing to damper the doubt in her voice. "Have you met your mother? I'm thinkin' you done got played. That maybe you're doing her dirty work?"

"It wasn't like that."

"Well, all I know is that there *is* a play area she could have left him in."

I wipe away a tear before it can form in full. Angelica isn't one to downplay facts, no matter their destination, a trait I do value. But it stings—no fault of hers. So long I've been at odds with Mom, so drained is my emotional well-being, that every affection-hungry part of me succumbs to the primal compulsion to make more out of our time in the car than may otherwise be reality. The hunger lurks in the most vulnerable part of my heart, along with the more realistic truth.

"Can you just help me—*please*?"

Angelica's watery eyes make it hard to choke back my desperate tears. She steps forward and wraps her arms around me once again. "I'm sorry. I shouldn't have mocked you like that. You're my best friend and love you beyond question."

"I love you too, Geli. I just so need..."

Angelic squeezes us tight together. "I know."

A sparkle of green and blue grabs at the corner of my eye as we break our embrace. Her back to me is the mystery woman from the green carriage. She is loitering near the southern corner of the staging building, her eyes pinned to the Matters' mansion. Against her hip, she taps her finger with a discrete pulse, pausing here-and-there in a random pattern. One-pause. One-two-pause. One-two-three-four-pause. She folds open a small handbag just long enough to pull something indiscernible from its insides, which she presses upon the tip of the pointer finger of her right hand. She moves next to the "Employees Only" entrance on the southeastern side of the building.

The door opens.

Out steps a college-aged girl wearing the bright white tuxedo shirt with western-style tie and black pants of the wait staff. She carries a small tablet in her left hand.

The fancy-dressed woman engages the waitress, who injects little as the taller woman—even without the heels—carries on. The woman points to her left. At what is hard to say, given all the people milling about. A half-minute later, their conversation ends as the waitress's blonde twisted-top-knot bobs up and down in agreement while she types something into the tablet.

Moving back to the "Employees Only" door, the waitress enters a code into the keypad at its mid-right. The door opens, and she steps past its threshold. The woman shadows the waitress by only a meter and a half. She pins the toe of her shoe in the bottom corner of the frame just before the door reseals. She reaches for the handle, pauses for a moment, then lets herself into the building.

"Ow!" Rub my arm where Angelica pinched it. "What's that for?"

"*Hello!* Did you not hear me?" Angelica says.

"Sorry, what?"

"For the *third* time," she puts extra stress on the count, "your brother... he's by that food tent."

James has one overflowing plate in his hand and is attempting to fill a second, sampling without care as he moves from food item to food item. To their credit, the workers say nothing as they follow his progress, re-straightening the displays he ravages. James tips a bowl, and half of its contents end up on the ground. The worker there rolls his eyes and shakes his head in what appears frustrated disbelief. Before James can make any more of a scene, I start in his direction… then stop and sneak a glance at the "Employees Only" door.

"You okay?" Angelica asks.

"Ah, yeah," I say. "Can you do me a big favor?"

"Forever and always, you can depend upon me."

"I, um, just remembered that I—ah—told Mom I'd pick up a work thing for her. Would you object to running James over to that play area for me?"

"You'll come join us?"

"Ah—sure." I say.

"Good." Angelica bounces her way toward James, calling back, "I'm gonna make sure you have some real fun tonight!"

Like him or not, Angelica will be sure to keep James safe. She always comes through for me, no questions asked, no complaints. She is everything and more that you want in your closest friend. In recent years, friction has dominated so much of my home life. Angelica is always there to bring stability and calm. Someone who lets me be the real me, yet also challenges me to be a better me. She is what family should be.

My stomach knots up at misleading her, but something is drawing me to the rainbow haired woman. An odd familiarity that my mind can't quite figure out. Something deeper than casual recognition, as if she is someone I already know, even though we've not yet met.

CHAPTER SEVEN

DESPITE THE APPLE, MY STOMACH begs for more. What energy reserves we each had, long drained in maneuvering Paul's makeshift stretcher through the caves. By the time we reached the escapees' camp, our clothes were pasted to us as if we walked through a downpour. Mahoney professes that the effort took at least twice as long—over forty-five minutes—as normal to return.

Two hours later, still in clingy clothes and draped in blankets, we've yet to freshen up or eat anything substantial. Though the camp is a distance from the laboratory, Mariana forbids doing anything that may draw attention. That means a single lantern we all huddle around. For certain, no fire, thus no heated bathing water, and no warm meal. I'll settle for another apple, but Mariana claims the little fruit they've left she's reserving for tomorrow's breakfast. At least she shares what fresh water there is.

The entire group sits on edge. Paterson remained behind to keep tabs on the guards. Perchance they find the tunnel entrance, his advanced warning will keep the team safe. Mahoney told me that Paterson could draw the guards through the tunnels and away from the group—a technique that once ended with a pod of guards getting so turned around that they ended up as corpses.

It's disturbing: those poor people lost, panicked, and starved to death.

But then, after less than a half of a day, I appreciate the extremes to which a person will go to stay alive. To be free.

And I'm still a long way from being free.

Mr. Vasquez speaks up over the small talk germinating within the group. "Twenty more minutes. If Paterson isn't back by then, Tozan and I will scout out the situation." His words seem intended more to calm his wife rather than anything else. She's grown fidgety and anxious over the last hour.

Tozan Balci nods and sets about checking over his weapons—two pistols and a shotgun. He's petite for a man, a meter and a half tall, but built solid. What skin he exposes—just his hands and face, the rest being covered in green fatigues—is a light tan. Though he sports both a mustache and beard, unlike his peers, he keeps his trimmed close and kempt. His eyebrows—bushy and wide—come to a tapering arch around the outside of each eye. His most prominent feature, though, is his plump nose, which doesn't seem to fit his otherwise thin physique.

He was the first of the team's balance, for eleven total, that we encountered as we arrived. He was mid-shift as the afternoon lookout, one of many duties each adult member of the team fills. Mahoney explained that though the team considers Tozan their mechanics wizard, there are too few hands to focus on specialties. Everyone takes part in the basic needs and oversight of the camp—from trash disposal to equipment repair. One of few exceptions: meals. Post two consecutive food-borne illnesses, the team concurred that cooking was best left to those with a proclivity to the task.

With no objections to his plan, Mr. Vasquez wraps his right arm around his wife's shoulders and gives a firm squeeze. She responds with a small kiss and lays her head against his chest. With a sigh, she closes her eyes, seeming to resign herself to the wait.

Just as my stomach gives up on a decent meal erelong, the less-than-discrete strides of a petite, wiry young woman pierce the group. Mariana sits bolt upright, her husband jumping up along with Tozan and two others.

"Sir," the girl addresses Mr. Vasquez, "a light approaches."

Everything about her is narrow. Her hips, her shoulders, even her head has a narrow, elongated egg shape. The tight tee shirt she wears is doing its best to make the most of her petite figure. The lantern's yellow-orange glow makes her cockscomb-styled coppery hair look like flames atop her head, as if underscoring the urgency of her message.

That hair… that's the—

"Tozan, Ma and I will check this out," Mr. Vasquez says. "The rest of you take your positions."

Several *Yes, Sirs* echo from the circle of people. Anyone still seated jumps up and moves to various parts of the main chamber, checking their weapons as they scatter. Mahoney, having bound to his feet from his seat next to me at the sight of the woman's approach, reaches down, grabs my right biceps, and plucks me from my seat. "You're with me."

His grip is gentle, but his voice is all-business. He leads me west of the gathering area to a misshapen collection of cubicles that serve as the team's dormitory. The few I peek into boast nothing more than a bed and a small, drawered cabinet for personal effects. Each occupies an area only two-and-a-half meters to a side.

Mahoney places us at the corner of an exception: a unit with double the furnishings, double the size. He maneuvers me behind and to his side, allowing the kitchen behind us to taunt my stomach. He focuses on the cavern entrance, gun drawn, though it'll be a challenge to hit anything in such low light.

A silvery-yellow gleam passing by the kitchen catches my eye: Mariana's own drawn weapon. She rushes toward the western part of the camp, without doubt toward her daughter, whom is busy administering to Paul's overheated condition. "I thought Mariana was with her husband?" I say.

"Huh?" Mahoney says, not looking away from the entrance.

"She's behind us, but Kaden—Mr. Vasquez, I mean—he said that he, Tozan, and *Ma* would go check out who was coming. But Mariana just dashed by, behind us."

Mahoney looks at me, his eyebrows in a knit. His eyes float off to the side in a blank stare. An instant later, the stiffness is his body dissipates. "Oh…" He chuckles. "'Ma' isn't for Mariana. The redhead, that's MissyAnn, but we call her 'Ma'."

"Oh." Shake my head. "Guess I thought 'ma', mom—you know?"

Mahoney chuckles again. "No worries. Ma's great, but keep your wits about you around that one."

"Why's that?"

"Competitive as a spotted hyena, she is. Sets her sights on something, or someone, she'll do *whatever,*" the word stretches from his mouth, "it takes to acquire it."

"I see," I say, then tease, "So, you've first-hand experience being acquired?"

Can't believe I asked that! Mom'd be so disappointed.

Before an apology can make it to my lips, Mahoney laughs. "Seems Ma's not the only one who puts it all out there."

"I shouldn't have—"

"Ah, think nothing of it. Life's a powder flash. A little straightforward talk saves everyone time… and the answer is no. Not that she hasn't offered, at least"—watch his head bounce as he tallies—"six times now. Not my type. One helluva cook, though; woman can make a steak of a rat."

Yeaks! *That* did sound of firsthand experience!

Mahoney turns back to the camp's entrance, sparing my stomach in having to ask. Try to scoot around his bulk for a better view, but he corrals me against the wall. No option otherwise, stare deep into the kitchen.

The dining portion comprises two parallel benched tables, three meters long each. The kitchen proper boasts a pair of steel sinks, likely boosted from the laboratory, backed against the leftmost of a long southwestern wall. A makeshift stove and generous pile of wood between the two is to the rightmost of the same wall. In the center of the kitchen sits a square table layered with various bowls, plates, and kitchen utensils. Along the western wall stands a series of sparsely populated shelves. Perhaps their pantry?

Mariana steps into view and stops at the edge that curves into the western part of the cavern. A pair of night-vision goggles covers her eyes. She takes no interest in us; like Mahoney, she dedicates her focus on the entrance. She seems stiff, breathes hard. Reminds me of a rookie I once saw on the verge of a panic attack. I want to run to her, give her a big hug like those Papa used to soothe me with.

I don't.

She seems poised to shoot anything rushing toward her.

"It's Paterson," Mahoney says as, in the same second, Mariana's body relaxes. "Come on." Without asking, he takes hold of my left hand and moves us toward the gathering area. I can hear Mariana jogging not far behind.

The group of us, now with Paterson, enter the gathering space all at once. Ma is fawning over Paterson—more exacting, the blood streaking down his right arm. He brushes her away, though not with much resolve. "It's nothing—just a scratch or two."

"Crickets, 'it's nothing'," Ma says as they take seats.

The Vasquez pair exchange brief, whispered Spanish, then Mr. Vasquez motions for us all to sit. Mariana, meanwhile, booms, "Lights up. Claudia, some water, the salve, and a wrap, please!" She shoos Ma to the side and sits between the two as she picks up Paterson's arm and surveys the damage.

Most of his lower arm has a thin layer of red over it. None gush forth, but several spots seep fresh blood. Mariana brightens the lantern and surveys the wound again. Mr. Vasquez, on the contrary, has no interest in the injury. "He's fine," he tells his wife, who ignores him, then prompts, "So Paterson?"

"Well, the good news is that they didn't find our passageway and, at least for now, have gone."

"The bad news?" Mahoney asks.

"They'll be back first light, with some specialized tracking device."

A blanket of concern races across both Mariana's and Ma's faces. Tozan shifts where he sits, grunts, shifts again. Next to me, under his breath, Mahoney says, "Shit."

Just then, a short, pale-skinned preteen joins us. She carries a metal water bucket, a porcelain jar about the size of a sugar bowl, and a handful of clothes. Has to be Claudia, the Vasquez's daughter. Between her shoulder-length blonde hair and icy blue eyes, however, she lacks any parental resemblance. Add the oddity to my ever-expanding mental *Need-to-Ask-Mahoney* list.

Without comment, the girl places the items next to her mother and scurries back from where she came. Mariana dips one cloth in the water and wipes away the blood from Paterson's arm with delicate strokes.

"Let's not get ahead of ourselves here," Mr. Vasquez says. "Paterson, walk us through the past couple of hours."

"Sure boss. When I returned to the staircase, all was quiet. Presumed they gave up and left, so I moved across the hall into an office—ow!" Paterson cringes, Mariana finding the source of the blood. Paterson gives her a scornful glance, but otherwise continues, "um, checked out a window and they were at the boathouse. Eight of 'em total. They'd wheeled from it a torch."

"Smart," Tozan interrupts. "Melt their way through the door."

"Actually, the locks—they knew right where they were, cut a perfect arc right around the mechanism."

A *hmmm* escapes Mahoney, drawing my attention. Lost in some thought, he doesn't notice my inquisitive glimpse at first, but when he does, he just nudges his head toward Paterson before shifting his own attention back to the story.

"… to the stairs intending to bolt for it," Paterson says. "The second door grated open as I reached the bottom. Hey! Not so tight!"

Mariana yanks tight the knot she put in the cloth around Paterson's forearm. "Stop being such a baby," she says, her lips tracing a crooked smile. It seems she's less than pleased by his remaining behind.

Paterson pulls his arm away and says, "Once the noise of the door died away, I heard them debating how many people they were pursuing. They knew the two, for sures." Paterson flicks his pointer finger in my direction. "But all the footprints on the beach confused them."

"Sol's fury!" Mr. Vasquez says. He looks at me, irritation lacing his words. "That incident on the beach threw me off. We forgot to cover our tracks."

"We did," Paterson says, "so I stuck around to see what else we may have overlooked."

"And?" Ma's tone sings with a genuine enthrallment of his story. I stare at her, wondering if that had been her, why'd she run like that?

"And nothing," Paterson says. Ma slouches, the edginess of the story drained. "Spent the next hour trailing them through what of the complex they could access. Using the torch, they got through two locked doors before the device's propane expired. By the time they searched the offices, they thought they were chasing ghosts. The guy in charge—a sergeant Mater or Matter, Matters. (Why does that name sound familiar?) Only heard the name once. Anyway, this sergeant surmised the footsteps weren't recent."

Paterson shifts his focus to me, his face pains in anger or disappointment. I'm not sure which. Ma follows his glare, a look of confused jealousy settling upon her face. I stare back, lost. Out of the corner of my eye, Mahoney scoots two centimeters closer.

"I thought," Paterson begins, "they resigned themselves to having found nothing and would leave. Until they entered the laboratory." Paterson pauses, seeming to wait for me to catch up to some secret that only he and I share. His point registers in seconds.

"Crud," is all my mouth offers to the beam of anticipation focused on me.

With a *chit*, Paterson shoots a finger pistol in my direction.

"I never cleaned up the lab," I manage in explanation to the confused others.

"Right'o," Paterson says, addressing the group again. "Blood, water, and broken glass everywhere." He looks at me again, puzzled. "A destroyed HVAC fan?" When I don't explain, he goes on. "Anyhow, they'd their confirmation that they were in the right place. The sergeant ordered the team to split into pairs and do another, more thorough search of the facility. Anywhere they couldn't get into, they plan to return to tomorrow. At that point, I took my leave."

The Vasquez pair exchange concerned looks. Though unable to put my finger on why—how could I've ever known I'd put these people in danger?—a belief from deep within me insists an apology is appropriate. Make to stand and do so when Ma sidetracks the opportunity.

"What about your cuts?" Ma pipes up, the story's twist seeming to pique her interest again.

Paterson lifts his now bandaged arm. "Stupidity. In my rush to get back, I mis-stepped through that mossy section and wiped out."

"Oh." Ma slouches her shoulders again.

Mr. Vasquez rises to his feet. "Well, this is a disappointing turn of events." He surveys the group. "Tozan, time to activate your diversions. You and I will cover that."

"Yes, Sir."

"Mahoney, get the kitchen going. Paterson, you help. I want everyone to have a good meal tonight in the event we need to abandon camp."

"Sir."

"*Mi Amor*, can you organize the others to pack our critical supplies?"

"For sures," the female Vasquez replies, shifting into all-business mode.

"Ma, help our guest find some proper clothing and a shower. Then head topside and see what our contact knows. Be cautious; they've not been this eager to find an escapee in a long while."

"And take these." Mariana hands Ma the jar of medicine and unused clothes, then nods at me. "Help her re-bandage that cut on her thigh."

An excited grin falls upon me. "My pleasure, Ma'am." Ma steps over to Paterson, plants a solid kiss square on his lips. It lingers as she reaches around to his behind with her free hand and squeezes. "And I'll be seeing *you* later," she says as she releases him.

Paterson reddens, though no one but me seems put off by the overt PDA. Save Mahoney, everyone else has already dispersed. "Ignore her," he whispers. "She's marking her territory, so to speak."

"Unnecessary," I whisper back.

Mahoney chuckles as he moves toward the kitchen area. "Paterson," he calls over his shoulder, "stop flirtin' around and let's get to work."

Paterson gives me a weak, apologetic smile as he passes. Ma bounces in right behind him, carrying the lantern by its handle. She surveys me, dismay apparent in her eyes. "Okay, girlfriend, let's get you cleaned up."

I'm *not* your girlfriend.

MissyAnn grabs my hand and pulls me toward the still darkened western part of the cave. She half skips, half bounces along.

Who gets this excited over drab military gear?

For certain, there will be no silk blouses or flowing skirts awaiting us. No flowery sundresses, decorative hair ribbons, peep-toed booties… always fun to go clothes shopping—*Wait! You liked to shop?! For clothes?*—to wear all those colorful, joyful outfits. To troll the stores and wade through the racks in search of the next unique surprise.

Never alone, though.

With a friend… my best friend. A bit of a fashionista, she is. Goading me to try on the craziest of outfits. Stuff Mom never lets me wear. Perky, happy, always forward looking. Without fail, makes me feel good, even in the worst of moments. I remember!

"Who's Angelica?"

"Huh?"

Ma stops us and turns sideways, facing me. "You just whispered 'Angelica'—with quite fondness, I might note. Sister… close friend… *lover,* perhaps?"

"Huh? What? No. No, she isn't my *lover.* She's, ah—" Like it's any of your business!

A shadow plays across a thin curtain to our right.

"I need to check on Paul," I deflect, wasting not a moment in heading toward the door analog.

Unlike the dormitory's cubicles, the room within which Claudia cares for Paul is a natural outcropping in the cavern, its only visible structure a wooden wall extending about a meter out from the rocky wall. The cloth that is the door slides to the side with ease.

"Any change?" my heart hopes.

Claudia sits next to Paul. She folds down his blanket and draws a cloth over his chest, absorbing the sweat pooling there. He lays motionless, save the rhythmic up and down of his chest, on the cot we transferred him to upon arrival. The fresh wrappings around his head are still white—A positive sign!—though the unnatural heat radiating from his skin makes a sauna of the small space.

"None," the girl replies.

Mariana warned there wasn't much she could do for Paul. Close to nothing other than keeping his dressings fresh. They have few medical supplies, let alone anyone with formal medical training. Though she is the unofficial "doctor" for the team, what Mariana knows comes from experimentation. The minimal time I've spent assisting in the Facility's medical ward makes me more qualified than any of the others.

That isn't saying much, though. My presence or not, for this group, a serious wound is a death sentence.

"Though at one point," Claudia's voice wisps with excitement, "he called out for someone, but I couldn't make out who."

Katherine. For certain, he'd call to her. Should have let him—them— be. The poor man has both a broken head and a broken heart because of me. The former I promised myself to do all possible to help heal. Whatever it takes. The latter, from which I'll never escape culpability, there's no way for me to mend. "When?" I say.

"An hour ago. Otherwise, he's been like this."

"I see. If he does that again, please come get me, okay?"

"Sure." The girl rinses the cloth, yawns wide.

"I appreciate you watching over him like this," my heart speaks.

The girl's forehead furrows as she grunts. "Not as if I've much of a choice; Mom insisted I 'do my part.'"

"Speaking of which," Ma chimes in, "we've our own assignments."

Ma latches my hand and directs me back into the cavern proper, closing the curtain behind us. Her tour carries on as we move deeper into the cave, but my ears aren't listening. Paul's unresponsive slumber digs at my heart. So want to turn back, take him in my arms, let him know how regretful I am. How none of this should have happened. For him to hug me and tell me not to worry, that he's going to be alright.

"Will they leave him behind?" blurts from my lips.

"Sorry?"

"The Vasquezes—if we abandon camp, will they leave Paul behind?"

Ma stops. "They can be… decisive. But the Vasquezes are moral leaders. Good people. Care with a genuine zeal about people. Take Claudia, for instance."

"How do you mean?" Ma looks at me like it should be obvious. "Newbie, remember."

"Right," she says as we resume our lazy walk. "For sures, you noticed the lack of a family resemblance?"

"I didn't want to bring it up. You know, avoid any unnecessary pot stirring."

Ma chuckles. "Oh, jeez, there's no pot to stir. Claudia was only six when they rescued her. I'd escaped not a week before, so Mariana assigned me to oversee our camp—another smaller camp—while the others undertook a supply raid. They ended up bringing her back instead.

"Poor girl was paunchy and bloated, by a good seventy kilos, maybe more. Couldn't walk on her own. We struggled to keep her hydrated; for a long while, she wouldn't eat. She was sick *all* the time. No more get over one illness and the next one would set in."

"Sounds like she was malnourished."

"No doubt. Mariana found pin pricks all over the girl's body. Never a good sign, given Mariana's background."

"Huh?"

"She's a biologist by trade."

Astounding! "A biologist… for *real*?"

"Yep." Her words flow with an odd excitement, as if some deep burden lifted. "Says they told her she'd be spearheading the study of microbes or microorganisms or," Ma's hand flings through the air, "such, discovered here on the island. Turns out they started the research long before her invitation. In actuality, they recruited her to help them past a roadblock with the last stage: human drug trials."

"Human drug trials are not abnormal?"

MissyAnn shrugs. "I don't have the brain for that. All I know, whatever they had her doing, it sickened Mariana. She spoke up only to face an ultimatum: do the work, or else." Ma glances at me as if I've intimate knowledge of all the Facility's goings-on.

Student punishments are tough, but fair. Loss of a meal for speaking out-of-line. A night in solitary for unsanctioned brawling. The most effective disciplines, though, are those imposed unofficially by one's peers. A bruise or two, a racoon's eye for greater offenses. Vague death threats, though, that doesn't sound right. They just fire employees. *Right?*

"Anyhow," Ma carries on, "she uncovers the trial notes; exotic tests on some unnamed child. The experiment had gone awry in the most horrible way. Troubles Mariana so deeply. The night she and Mr. Vasquez fled, they vowed to help anyone they could get away from this place.

"When they later find Claudia, Mariana pieces one-and-one together. We spent the next six months trying to get into any records we could, to figure out what they did to her." Ma stops, staring for a moment back toward the curtain. "To no avail."

She takes a deep breath. "The Vasquezes adopted Claudia as their own. Nursed her back to health, have taken care of her since. Mariana protects her from as much of the crap as possible with the vigilance of orangutans." Ma waves her lanterned hand across the space before us. "This is far from a normal life, but they try to make it as regular for Claudia as possible.

"Now that she's older, though, everyone struggles with this stance that she remains so sheltered. The girl's a brilliant mind; she knows this is far from normal. Asks more questions every day, many of which Mariana chastises us for answering honestly." Ma shrugs. "I ignore her. Claudia's as much involved as any of the rest of us. She deserves more than to be stuck here all the time. She wants to be a difference maker too. Mariana struggles with that: balancing Claudia's safety against preparing her for the risks we face."

Hmm… so that's why she argued to leave Paul behind?

MissyAnn's shoulders droop as a somberness befalls her stance. "Claudia was by far the youngest we'd ever seen." Ma looks to the ground, shaking her head. "Not so true anymore."

"Whaddya mean? I've seen no one that young."

"Trust me, they're there. There's a segregated part of the complex—a toddler ward. They keep 'em there until they're preteens, then integrate them with the rest of the Facility."

"That's... that's..."

"I know..." Ma's voice trails away.

My guide stands silent, glaring into the darkness, lips pursed, shaking her head. Whatever movie is playing in her mind's eye, she doesn't share. She lets go of my hand to wipe away a tear. "Let's not dwell on that." She quick-shakes her head side-to-side, then steps forward again.

A wide wooden wall emerges ahead of us. Ma edges to the left and lights an oil lamp next to passageway's narrow entrance. "Showers are through there." A bit of her perkiness returns. "But first, some new threads."

She moves along the wall to an opening at its center and steps through; me close behind. She turns to her left, lights another oil lamp just inside the doorway.

The room is large but not big. Most of the space is unused, broken by the occasional shelf or pile of boxes. The right wall calls to me. It houses several shelves of clothing—men's to the right, women's to the left—divided by two racks of various shoes, boots, and other footwear. Ma waves at the open space. "Our stocks are a little lean, but we've a variety of outfits."

Peruse the many colors and styles of blouses, skirts, shorts, jeans and leggings. There're even shawls and hair ribbons! A bright blue dress overlaid with a transparent black mesh imprinted with large off-white flowers and vines finds my hands. Hold it against me and turn toward Ma. How long it has been since a proper dress draped my body. "Whaddya think?"

"The very definition of cute." A big smile crossed her face. "Can't wait to see you in it."

Secure a shirt, a pair of pants. "I didn't expect this. Thought my choices would be fatigues, fatigues, or fatigues."

"You'll need those too." Ma points to a single shelf near the doorway. "You're welcome to all the clothes you want, though most aren't ideal around here."

"Oh."

"Oh no, don't misunderstand." MissyAnn plucks at her own camos. "None of us wear these things all the time. Most wear normal digs when home. Occasionally, I'll host a special dinner or game night and the team will dress up. You know, anytime we need a reminder of the gentler, normal side of being a human."

"That's great of you," I say. Then out of some unknown place, "I love to dress up!"

"Perfect! I could use an ally convincing this group they need to class things up every so often." She chuckles. "In fact, you and Mahoney seem to be quick friends. Perhaps you can get the guy to put on a shirt that has actual sleeves—maybe even one with buttons."

"We just met. I don't think I'd have any influence—"

"Well crickets, girl! Have you paid any attention to the attention he's givin' you?"

"I guess I, ah…"

"Guy's stickin' to you like glue between two sheets of paper, as if he's your bodyguard. And all those demure glances…" Ma steps over to the fatigues shelf to her left. "I've been trying to bend that guy to my will since he got here."

Yeah, so he mentioned.

Ma spends less than a minute rifling through the shelf before joining me with an armful of clothing. "Have two sets for you. I've a talent for eying sizes. Medium-tall sound right?"

"I'm sure they'll be fine."

"Good." Ma layers the fatigues on top of those outfits already draped over my left arm; a third set she keeps. "You needn't get everything now. You'll not have much space in your room. I'd suggest only a pair of outfits for the moment. You can come back and swap 'em out whenever you want. Everyone does."

"I see," I say. "Just need some shoes and one other thing."

MissyAnn offers to grab my footwear—a pair of laced jackboots for daily use along with blue strappy heels that complement the flower dress—while I troll for undergarments. They organized the clothing well, making it quick to find the right sizes. Grab two utilitarian sets: one an off-white, one a dark beige. Also, a pink and purple lacy bikini brief and balconette coupling that I cannot pass up. It'll be so nice to feel feminine again.

New clothes in hand, we head for the earlier passageway leading to the showers. The corridor rises with a noticeable but undemanding incline. A few meters in, Ma lights a lamp attached to the wall.

"So," I say, "I get how you could swipe the general necessities from the Facility stores, but how'd you build that library of clothing?"

"You don't remember—at least, not yet—but when you arrived, they swapped your clothes for Class Standards. Happens to everyone. Even the staff must trade for standard uniforms, no exceptions. Creates a healthy collection of clothing that was just being incinerated."

"Guess I never thought about it."

"Why would you, after they stole our memories and all? I intercepted my first batch by chance years ago now. Back then we'd not much more than what we escaped with and a few drab odds and ends. Couldn't resist hijacking an outfit with a more colorful flare. Everyone wanted the same once they saw what I'd snatched, so started grabbing garments anytime we'd scout into the Facility. Mariana worried my efforts were a distraction though, so Kaden organized clothing runs to build up our stocks—not only for ourselves, but for those we pledge ourselves to help free. Thus, you've the benefit of choice."

We stop at a ninety-degree leftward split in the passageway. Ma lights another lamp, then points at the rough-carved upward stairway shaping the hall there. "Solarium and greenhouses are that way. No time for that today, but perhaps tomorrow."

I follow Ma as she hurries along our original path, lighting a third lamp after another ten meters. Ten meters further, the tunnel adopts a greater incline as it curves right. Ma extinguishes the lantern as we bend around. There is no need for it any longer; the end of the path is bright.

"Is that…"

"Sunlight!" Ma completes.

Already in the short time I've spent in the cave system, a whole different appreciation for the sun has settled in my bones. Guess for someone like MissyAnn, having spent years living like this, any time in the sun is time cherished. The welcoming joy in how she speaks the word, the renewed bounce in her step, suggests just that. Ma's exuberance propels us into a small vestibule that marks the end of the passageway and entrance to the showers. She speeds what clothing she carries onto a small wooden bench, the footwear on the ground beneath. She points toward a shelf near the bench. "Soaps, shampoos, towels… whatever you need, you'll find there. If you don't, just ask."

As quick as the words are out of her mouth, Ma peels her tee shirt off. Two bug-eyed, burgundy-color areolas stare me down. "Ah…" I clench the clothes in my arms against my chest. "What are you doing?"

MissyAnn bends down, undoes and steps out of her boots. "I need to wash up, too." Her pants waste no time following. Oh crud! They aren't the only thing commando about her.

"I, um"—try averting my eyes toward the ceiling—"thought I'd be alone in the shower."

Ma belly laughs, her nipples jiggling like squiggle eyes on a puppet. As much as I don't need to see this, I can't turn away. Almost burst out laughing. *Keep it together! This is serious.*

"Alone? Here!?" Ma laughs again. "Girlfriend, privacy isn't something this place is in abundance of. Here or there you might get some—maybe in the dunny if it's not too soon after a meal—but most of this camp is a community space, full of eyes and ears. The showers are no exception: co-occupant and co-ed. Same as the barracks."

Umm… Not exactly. Though the Facility's barracks possess communal showers, privacy stalls are not only fitted throughout but are maintained sexually homogeneous with stringent oversight. "You mean the men shower at the *same* time as us?" Discomfort scurries over my skin.

"Sure," she proclaims with a whimsical nod, "them with us, us with them."

My stomach turns. "Even with Claudia?"

"Oh, crickets, no! Vasquez would have your hide!" To which of the two Ma refers, I suspect doesn't matter. Her voice droops as she nods back down the hallway. "That lamp at the solarium cutoff, you ever see a yellow cloth hanging there, means Claudia's up here. Mariana permits no one"— her eyes darken—"and I mean *no one*, save herself, anywhere near here."

Thank the stars! They've some sense of civility.

Just as expedient as her serious demeanor come, it goes. "Otherwise though…" She shrugs her shoulders as her face reads *it-is-what-it-is*.

Okay, showering with the women… that I can adjust to. But the men too?!

Ma laughs. "Don't look so worried. Close to never happens." She punts her clothes to the side of the bench. "We've only four shower heads, so everyone's adopted an unofficial shower schedule. The men take the morning, leaving the early evening—and, in their always gracious way, the day's sun-warmed water—for us ladies. Even when we're off schedule, they give us our space when at all possible. Pretty sure I'm the only woman that's joined them by choice." Boy, there's a shocker. "But when schedules are tight, modesty and inhibitions get set aside. So you might as well trivialize whatever body image issues you have while it's just me around."

"I don't have any 'body image issues'," my mouth protests. "Just because I'm modest doesn't mean I'm not confident in who I am."

"Tell that to the mortified look all over your face." Ma cups her breasts. "My perky rubellites alone seem to have petrified you!"

Just when the day seems as nutty as it can get, MissyAnn shoots her arms into the air and shimmies her chest like an exuberant burlesque dancer. At least, what I think one to look like.

This cannot be happening!

A rumble of laughter bursts from deep within my stomach and out into the open. Ma gyrates around in some oafish dance, which releases a series of gut wrenches from my abdomen. Tears come from a place of long overdue joy. As with so many things discovered of late, a hearty laugh is yet another the Facility robbed of me.

She comes to a smiling stop. "See—awkward only if you let it be. Now strip and get in here."

Ma grabs a towel and soaps and steps into the shower room. The validity of her point aside, my body remains frozen, my mind challenged in absorbing the wanton display just seen. Assert it as she may, there emanates no obvious lack of self-confidence from the girl.

You jealous?

"No."

From the adjoining alcove, Ma calls out, "Hurry up. A hot dinner's only served for so long." Her voice raises over a sudden *twang* of water against rock. "Cooks try to keep the wood burning for as short a time as possible. Don't want the smoke broadcasting our location."

A much overdue hot meal trumping any bashfulness, I pile my clothes on the ground next to MissyAnn's. "On my way," I say as I grab necessities and move through the rough archway separating one room from the other.

Just inside the showers, several wooden pegs stick out of the stone wall to the right. Using Ma's example as a guide, I hang my towel a peg away from her own. To the left, Ma releases a thin chain, cutting the flow from the shower head above. Droplets run down her flat backside, twinkling in the sunlight weaving through the ceiling. The "ceiling" being a large mesh tarp—dyed an array of browns, yellows, and oranges—braced like a circus tent by two thick-diametered poles set upon the imaginary line that marks the center of the room.

"Do a girlfriend a favor," Ma says, "and wash my back. You owe me, after all."

I freeze just inside the entrance. "Owe you, for what?"

"Saving you from those guards."

"That *was* you! But you didn't save me. You took off."

She turns at me, again showing off way more than I need to see. "You found that crevice, didn't ya? And how'd you think that boyfriend of yours found that vent, or even that penlight?"

"He's *not* my boyfriend."

Ma's eyebrows lift. "Hmmm… good to know. Now stop dawdling and come wash my back." She twists around again, the soap perched on her left shoulder.

Okay, this is not a big deal. Just two ladies washing up; an innocent shower.

I place my belongings upon the small table next to a shower head opposite MissyAnn's and step over. I take the soap and run it in side-to-side strokes down to what seems her waistline. Pause there for a moment, unsure how much further to go. A heated tingle fills my cheeks. There lacks a clear border between upper and lower. One of the more obvious ways in which the two of us shine opposites.

Ma glances over her shoulder. "No need to be shy there, Cherry-cheeks!"

Cherry-cheeks.

The epithet beats with affection through my veins. A warm, but distant memory tries to focus in my head. *Robust laughter. A shared inside joke with a friend. A new friend whose widespread, pale pomegranate lips emerge from the fogginess of the memory. Whose metallic eyes sparkle with an indigo iridescence as she giggles. No, this person is more than a friend. She is new, yet familiar—as if we've known each other all our lives. Someone with whom—despite a reasonable explanation—I share a mutual, unequivocal trust.* Her porcelain toned, petite face flashes into my mind. Her name reaches out to my consciousness—only to cast back into the deep vault from which it is trying to emerge.

"They're not gonna wash themselves." Ma gives what there is of her rear end a small jiggle.

"I'm sure you can reach your own behind—and don't call me 'Cherry-cheeks.'"

MissyAnn jerks her hands from her chest—an area she's spent more time than necessary slathering in soap—to her hips. Her right knee flexes, her body drops in the direction. "Fine!" bullets disappointment from her lips.

She yanks at the chain.

Lukewarm water pours out and over the two of us, sending a shiver across my skin. Scuttle out of the flow. Ma, meanwhile, turns side-to-side—twice each—rinsing the soap from her body. A flash later, she grabs her towel and tears from the room.

No comment.

No look in my direction.

The nerve!

She's the inappropriate one. Flaunting about as if this is some nudist community. Scratch. *Flirting and carrying on with a blatant disregard for how her display may make you feel.* Scratch. Scratch. *A person she'd just met! Spent no time probing what makes you, you.* Scratch. Scratch. *To explore your interests.* Scratch. *Dare to comport as if yours is the atypical behavior to disconcert over.* Scratch. Scratch. Scratch.

"Ugh! Why am I so itchy?" My arms are flaming where my nails have dug in. A couple of spots bleed. Scratch. Scratch. Scra—my skin tightens over my muscles; my hip dips. "Crud-it-all…"

You can't let Ma leave like this.

"Hey!"

No response.

"Hello?"

I peek through the archway; her stack of clean clothing—along with both our dirties—gone. In the seconds since she flew from the room, Ma cannot have dressed?! Had she or not didn't change that she isn't there.

Saunter to the shower nearest my belongings and pull its cord. The shower head spits forth its tepid water. I can't tell from where or how. Don't care. I stand for a long tick, eyes closed, letting what scant warmth there is bathe my being, outer and inner. Pass the soap up my arms, across my chest and torso, down my hips and legs. The various cuts and scrapes covering my skin sting, but grow easy to ignore the more cleansed my body becomes.

Ah… so nice to be clean again!

The dirtiness of the day likewise scrubs away from my thoughts. Even if for only a brief pause, put to bed the many questions ricocheting about my noggin.

Relax.

So much so, the intense quiet spooks me.

Aside from the clamor of liquid on stone, the chamber is otherwise mute. Expected to shower in private, but not in silence. Her extremism aside, a part of me wishes Ma is still here, chatting away at me from the antechamber. In the barracks' showers, more often than not, someone else is using the room, creating noise. And in the chance there isn't, the buzz of a squad or two running drills out in the courtyards is there to infiltrate your head. With no such drills to plague the ears here, start whistling some tune whose name escapes my mind.

As much as the quiet is comforting, it is eerie at the same time.

CHAPTER EIGHT

COUNTER TO THE HUBBUB OUTSIDE, an eerie silence pulses through the building's innards. Too silent considering both the sequin-dressed woman and the waitress precede me by only a triad of minutes. Yet neither is about. Don't quibble over their absence, though. My excuse for being inside won't hold up if challenged.

I about gave up getting in. Flooded the keypad with a myriad of combinations: each brother's birthday, parent's anniversary, her divorce, any date of significance to Mom. None worked. Not to mention the continual negative *beep, beep* of the keypad having drawn some unwanted attention as I hovered about the door. On the verge of walking away to rejoin Angelica, I keyed one more date on a whim.

The LED on the keypad flashed green; the door opened with a *click*.

Shocked. Stunned. Astonished. Any of those would have fit my state of mind at that moment. Of all dates, Mom's passcode is *my* birth date—as in that specific date my lungs filled with their first breath of air. For a crisp moment, a sense of honor flooded into my heart before the truth struck me. *"Seven years ago to the date and still as red as the day I bought them,"* Mom boasted from a distant memory. My seventh birthday party and she spent it bludgeoning the mothers of my guests with how much she so adores those damn shoes.

Unbelievable alright!

As mute are the reverberations of the party, so is the light illuminating the interior. The immediate area—a section segregated off from the rest of the building's innards by a long reception desk, the likes of a sign-in desk at a doctor's office—is lit by what artificial exterior light seeps through the single, shade-covered window embedded within the left wall. To the right and past the reception area, the interior opens into a vast storage space lit by a weak orange-yellow glow. The glow emanates along the border and various mid-sections of the ceiling, but from no distinct source.

Centered under the window of the left wall are a trio of chairs bookended by two small, magazine-layered tables. *Printed* magazines are a rarity. Subscription rates are well out of the budget for most folks. The most well-to-do can turn ownership of a complete series into a lucrative collectible on the auction circuit. The expense of even an individual issue gives most people serious pause. With digital copies a significant fraction of the cost, one has to be desperate to impress their peers to commit to a showoff piece. So many of the periodicals laid out that free and casual… both impressive and insulting at the same time.

I glimpse over the top of the reception desk. Bunch of standard office effects. Nothing of interest, save a thin tablet device askew among the other well-organized items. The waitress's? Circle around the end of the desk and pick up the device. The back radiates with the warmth of recent use. Tap my finger on the screen.

The device flicks on with a bluish-white glow, blinding me. Once my vision resets, the screen has filled with the beginnings of an *Incident Report*. Its summary highlights a guest reporting that there is a girl who vomited in the southwest ladies' room.

"Yikes! Glad I don't need to go right now."

Crud—I do!

There has to be a restroom in a building like this, right?

Search past the reception desk. A series of shelves run parallel with and for most of the length of the room's southeastern wall. Various party supplies lay in sections on each shelf. At the far end of the shelves, the orange-yellow light of the room bounces off a glass door angling north. Place the tablet back on the desk face down, allowing my eyes to re-acclimate to the lack of luminescence. Stamped on the top third of the door, the word *Manager* emerges. Not what I'm looking for.

Follow along the reception desk and encounter another glass door a meter past the desk's end. Similar to the entrance, two shaded windows light the inner room. The other side of the glass are two well-padded armchairs divided by a small table—also covered in a (Wow! For serious?!) handful of magazines. A couch rests under the nearer of the two windows and, filling the center of the room, two round tables, each with four chairs. Along the back wall, a vending machine, refrigerator, and the beginnings of a countertop. The depth of the room, combined with metallic lockers resting against the same wall as the door, blocks the rest of the view: a bathroom this room isn't.

Continue on, a last door still awaiting further down that same wall.

To my right, the shelves give way to various stacks of boxes, big and small. Most of the boxes are unmarked, though a few wear a large, block style, double I. The Roman numeral two, except this time the letters reference Papa's employer: Interstellar Industries, and probable origin of the grandiose party. The little Mom talks about her work, the Matters' come off flamboyant in how they spend their abundant wealth, but never did she mention events at this scale. Had even a minute emerged over the past couple of days to connect with Papa, he'd have mentioned why this event is so exceptional.

No time to dwell on that. My bladder presses for my full attention.

Thank the star, the last door is marked with the half-woman/half-man figurine of a unisex restroom. Twist the door's knob and push. Bracing the door with my left foot, I scurry my right hand along the inside wall. Come on! My index finger butts against the bottom of the light switch and makes to flick upward.

Click—click, click—click echoes across the room from behind.

No—no—no! My bladder protests as I drop my hand and ease my foot away. The door's hinges don't make a single squeak as it re-closes.

I twist toward the clicking noise.

The stacks of boxes block most of her, but there is no mistaking the rainbow-hair—the blonder strands copper-tinted from the lighting—of the sequin-dressed woman backing out the manager's office door. Short of sealing the darkened room, she pauses and pokes her head back through. A delay, then she retracts and closes the door.

My mouth opens, ready to challenge her, but my voice hesitates. Her motives being sinister or innocuous, this woman's behavior is odd, so where does this yearning to engage her come from? What advantage is there to drawing her attention? And where's the waitress… where could she have gone so quickly?

The office perhaps, though now's no time to dwell on the question. The woman scans the room as she arches toward the reception desk. I squat below the nearest stack of boxes, counting on the low light to mask my presence. Dam my bladder's mouth with my thighs. My chest constricts. Hold my breath.

Ten long seconds pass without a sound.

Click. Pause. *Click. Click.* Pause.

Draw a fresh, quiet breath. The ping of steps carries throughout the room. Nearer they come. My heart *thumps,* as if trying to break free of my chest. Crouch tighter against the boxes.

Click—click. Click—click.

Closer the woman comes. Beads of sweat pop out on my forehead, down my chest and arms. *Please, Universe, let it only be…* Sweat clings to my inner thighs; they pinch at each other. Cringe at the irritation, but dare not move. Even louder, nearer, the clicking comes. *Tha-thump, tha-thump* my heart booms with each of the woman's nearing steps. She pops out from the aisle separating the shelving from the box stacks as a drip of sweat drops into my left eye. Crud that burns! Whisk away the salty water, only to have my hand smack into the box with a *thud.*

She freezes, about to step into the reception area. One quick glance toward the back of the room and the woman will spot me. I scuttle around the corner of the box. Expect she'll come rushing toward my hiding place, but if she has seen me, there is no immediate sign.

Each second that passes expands the balloon my heart has become; each breath that escapes my lungs in need of a muffler. When the *click* of her shoes resumes, each is a slight bit quieter.

Shew.

Risk a peek around the box.

As the woman moves toward the reception desk, both her dress and stilettos flicker with greens and browns in the unusual lighting. Her smooth, round curves are so familiar, yet unplaceable at the same time. *Just who are you? And what is happening here?*

She picks up the waitress's tablet. With a touch, it again comes alive. She swipes the incident report aside and spreads her fingers over the device's face. With the distance between us, can't tell for what she is looking, but her precise finger work suggests she well knows within which apps she'll find the information she seeks. For certain, nothing good can come of the behavior. And the waitress… "What did you do to her?" I say under my breath.

Glance at the office. Are there answers there?

Shift back out of view and slip my shoes off. They're a much wider heel than the pointed shoes of the woman, but don't want to take any chances on the tiled floor. Crouch below the rim of the boxes and move guardedly to the opposite side of the room. Almost lose my footing two meters on, a louder than desirable *puff* racing uncontrolled past my lips as I fight from ending up in the splits. My stockings offer neither much warmth nor much grip against the cool, smooth floor. Pause and peep over the stack's top box. Engrossed in the digital device, the woman thankfully hasn't noticed my follies.

I recover my footing and move gingerly to the last stack of the row. Stop. To my immediate left is a set of large wooden doors, both closed. They span the floor to ceiling in height and cover almost three meters in width. Each has a large cast-iron handle. In contrast, to the right—maybe fifteen meters down—is the standard-sized glass door of the manager's office. Its small, single round metal knob calls to me. I curve around the end stack of boxes and survey the route.

From my current position, the box stacks are sporadic, not a seamless offering of cover. Squatting as low as my bladder allows, I dart to the front of the next row, about two meters closer to my destination. Hold here for half a second, then rush to the next row. Check over the lip of the box stack.

I have but a partial view of the woman from the angle, but catch the glow of the tablet disappear. The *click-click* of her shoes echoes about the room again.

Crud!

I dive low.

Four clicks, a long pause, then a handful more, though more muted. A trio of breaths thereafter, a tinny *clink* pricks at my ears. And then another.

I stand just enough to listen over the boxes. *Clink.* A pause. *Clink.* Softer than the first pair, from the break room.

Don't waste this chance.

I scurry toward the office, this time taking advantage of my stockinged feet to slide the last meters. Come to a stop in front of the door and cup my hands to the glass. The heels of the t-straps dangling from my fingers reverberate against the glass. I whip my head in the break room's direction. The nearby shelving blocks most of the door, but another *clink* from within suggests my gaffe has gone unnoticed.

Roll my eyes and shake my head. *What are you doing? You're not one to get mixed up in something like this.* The rainbow-haired woman distracted, there's no more ideal an opportunity to head for the exit and leave whatever is happening in here, here. Go find my friends and have the fun evening that Angelica pledged. Then homeward to a nice warm shower and bed. Wake up tomorrow refreshed, with no one—in particular, mom—any the wiser to the distraction. And yet, can't help but turn back to my cupped hands.

What limited light pierces into the enclosure reveals little more than the rough outline of a desk, a trash can to its side. Behind, some cabinets border to the right by a large, tree-like plant. Not far past where the door will swing open, the square side of a couch comes into focus. Something hanging off its front twitches. "What in the stars…"

Draw my head back. Wipe the fresh sweat rolling down my forehead from my eyes. Blink twice quick, then refocus through the door.

The twitch *had* been from a hand. Follow the arm to which it's attached up to the couch's seat where a large blanket-covered lump sprawls upon its surface. At the far side of the lounger, a tight, light-colored bun—the answer to at least one of the many questions exploding in my mind—peeks out from under the covering. The waitress's hand twitches again.

With my free hand, twist the door's knob. Its latch loosens with a *ch'trik.* With a gentle push, I open it just far enough to squeeze through. Hold it open with my foot and sit my shoes atop a small table inside, then soothe the door back closed. I ease the latch back in place, then hustle over to the waitress. Fight my bladder into a crouch near her head.

"Miss," I say is a hushed voice. "Miss." No response. I give the woman's shoulders a terse shake. "Miss!" Again, no response. Hold my hand out above her mouth. A frail current trickles through my fingers. "What *did* she do to you?"

Glass rattles from the break room's direction. Expect the sharp clicks of the mystery woman's heels to follow. Instead, a set of dull clunks comes, growing nearer by the second.

Clunk—clunk. Clunk—clunk.

Position behind the far side of the couch; watch over the waitress's forehead and out through the office door.

Clunk—clunk. Clunk—clunk.

My bladder screams at me, but I dare not move. The shoes gain on my position in seconds. For a moment, there is nothing, then—*clunk, clunk, clunk*—a pair of low-heeled Mary Jane pumps appear. Stepping past the door is not the fancy-dressed, long-haired blonde, but a uniformed waitress whose dark hair—a rich, almost black, brown—drapes to her shoulders. Slung over her right shoulder is a dark-colored, medium-sized bag that appears a mix between a duffel and a backpack.

The lady pauses, glances at the office, then shuffles through the bag. Out comes the tablet device. She taps the screen, bathing herself in a bluish hue. Lack of long hair and a change of clothes aside, the tablet's glow circumscribes her familiar hourglass shape. For whatever purpose the rainbow woman is trying to impersonate a waitress, nothing good can come of the behavior.

Urg.

Almost jump, a drop or two freeing from my bladder. The waitress moans again. Crap! Through the glass door bites a pair of sliver eyes that sparkle with a tint of blue from the tablet.

My muscles calcify. I huddle close to the passed-out waitress. In this dark, there's no way those eyes can distinguish between the two of us. Brace against the stress that is ready to explode from my thighs. The more engaged we stay, the more her gaze burns into my retinas. I want to sink below the couch's end, but know any movement translates to my discovery.

My thoughts grow hazy; not a puffy white or even gray, but sooty black. And not clouds, but smoke and flashes of fire. Glimpses of friends mix with unrecognizable, yet somehow familiar, people. Each intertwines with compassion and love, but also grief, loss, death.

The woman's glare digs deeper.

Visions of my youth blaze past my mind's eye, churn in my stomach. Though the memories are mine, most are fuzzy. For a fraction of a second, one or two slow and focus, playing a lively movie in my head. My first steps… my first training day… first Gold gymnastics medal. My youth speeds into the joys and pains of middle school, the shocks of puberty, to high school. Much to my chagrin, the show slows as each degrading interaction with Katie plays by and stabs at my insides, opening old wounds afresh.

Get out of my head!

The woman's eyes don't let go and, a blink later, the movie of this day flickers forth. Relive the fear, the embarrassment of being trapped in the locker room. The long, cold, wet walk home… the burn of mom's disdain. The hunger burning in my gut, and not just for edible substance. Every muscle in my body tenses. Fight back at everything wreathing away within me.

I want to scream out.

The pain dissipates. A dreaded car ride turned sweet. Mom's smile, her makeup lesson complete. The milky green eyes of our gracious porter. That amazing hug from Angelica… and that fluky kiss… Whatever that was! The sweetness of her breath still licks across my lips. The rainbow-haired woman comes into focus—and with her, not angst or despair, but comfort, security. Strain seeps away from my body. Limbs ease. Muscles loosen.

Loosen too much.

Warm wetness spills along my legs.

I reach for the wastebasket and vault on top of it. A long sigh escapes my mouth as the pressure on my abdomen fades as the more liquid it expels. Don't mind how the cold of the metal on my inner thighs sends a small shiver through my legs. Don't care how the sizzling impact of two distinctly opposed materials reverberates throughout the room. I can't worry how disturbing the entire scene could appear to a random passerby.

Okay, maybe a little on this last one.

By far, this is the most unladylike thing I've ever done. I would most displease Mom.

Shit! For certain, the mysterious woman has seen me now! The space beyond the glass, though, is empty. Finished, I pull the door open and step out. The faux waitress has vaporized, but one of the wooden doors ahead wisps shut.

"You're not escaping me!"

I hurry forward and yank on the large metal handle of the left of the two doors. It's solid, heavy wood doesn't move. Lock both hands around the stem and tug again. The beast yields to the extra force and swings wider under its own momentum. Once there's space enough, contort my body through the gap and step into a flood of light.

The woman has stopped a dozen meters forward. She places her small handbag into a larger one, then presses something onto the tip of her right-hand point finger, as she'd done before engaging the waitress. Half the distance beyond her leans a burly guard against the wall, staring off toward the Matters' manor, his back to the both of us. Whatever the lady put on her finger, I suspect it is responsible for the condition of the young woman in the office.

"Stop that woman!"

The guard jerks at my command and slides a quarter meter down the wall before recovering his footing. He twists to face us, his hand upon the grip of his sidearm, bewilderment layering his forehead.

"Stop her!" I yell out again, though it's too late.

From my first word, the mystery woman reacts, though not with the shocked perplexity of the guard. Instead, she drops her bag and thrusts forward without a single glance back. The guard, seeming to realize where the danger lies, fumbles with his sidearm, bringing it level just as the woman reaches him. She swings hard with the backside of her left fist against his locked wrists. The pistol—a TASER—crackles as two small metal contacts embed themselves in the wall he'd been leaning against.

She brings a balled right fist across her eye-line and—*Crack!*—connects with the left of the guard's chin. His head jerks toward his weapon and smacks against the cinder block. He rocks on his feet, but doesn't fall. Momentum at her advantage, the woman quick steps around in a half twist, left leg raising. The ball of her foot contacts with his left hip. The man and his head smack against the wall a second time. Half supported by the surface, he slouches to the ground, otherwise motionless.

Forget needing answers!

I twist on my heels, ready to scurry from the building.

"Stop right there!" The woman says from behind me. "You're not getting out of this."

My mind races out the door, but my legs fail to follow. Lack of righteous judgment landed me in this mess. Where it might lead now frightens me to my core. Is it too late to play dumb? *Perhaps you can plead for mercy?* I pivot around to face my fate.

The woman strolls toward me, no urgency in her steps. Her eyes remain locked on me, other than to reach down and retrieve her bag as she arrives at its position. She stops there and waves her hand—"Well, come on."—with a *let's go* motion. "You created this mess. Least you can do is help clean it up."

I created this mess! *Me!* Is she blind, or just dumb?

"Neither," the woman remarks.

"'Neither' what?" hesitates from my mouth.

"Neither blind nor dumb, as you asked."

Did I say that out loud? Am certain I hadn't. Either way, this woman will not manipulate me, intimidate me. I take several steps forward. "I'm not helping you clean up anything. I didn't do this." Bolster what there is of my chest as reinforcement, despite the nervous heat cycling through my veins.

The woman glares at me with a strong skepticism. "Hate to break it to you there, Cherry Cheeks, but I'd everything under control until you busted in."

"Don't call me that!" I blurt out, ignoring the vivid, poetic red the whole of my face and chest glow. I step forward again. "And what do you mean 'everything was under control'?" Stop with about two-and-a-half meters left between us. Not that any distance within twenty meters will matter, considering this woman's apparent agility.

The false waitress holds the inside of her pointed finger out to me. The same one she fiddled with both times earlier. At first, there seems nothing to make out against her pale skin. I lean forward. A yellow dot, just over half a centimeter in diameter, emerges from its surroundings.

"What is that?"

She flips her finger around and stares at it. Two seconds and an elongated huff later, she says, "That's not important. More relevant, this could have avoided the unfortunate fate of our friend back down the way." The woman removes a small piece of paper from her pants pocket and affixes the dot to it. As she slips the paper back into her small handbag, she gives me an exasperated look. "Had you not interrupted, that is."

Ignore the poke; instead, peek around the woman. "Is he—dead?"

The woman angles toward the pile of male bulk. He droops to the floor, unmoving, his head hanging low to one side. A dark liquid gleams within his hair.

"No, just knocked out." She focuses back on me. "Though he'll have quite the concussion. Haven't had to put someone out like that in ages."

What the frick does that mean?! "You'll not get away with this!"

The woman chuckles, a grin coming to her lips. "Oh, C.C., I'm most certain that I will."

My legs back me up. Slow, small steps. Perhaps she'll not notice.

"You did something to that waitress," I say, taking another couple of steps back. "She's still alive. She'll remember you and whatever you did to her."

The woman's smile grows wider as she shakes her head from side to side in a small arc. "Friendly girl," the false waitress says. "Most helpful." She pats the side of her bag. "Though she'll not remember anything. Well, more exactly, not me. Best she'll be able to recall, she indulged in too much of the guests' beverages and went into that office to sleep it off. If she values her job, she'll not be sharing that explanation with her employer."

I take a big step back. Though she makes no motion to stop me, the woman must be dense to not notice the distance between us growing. *Dense* not being a descriptor fitting of this woman. Her behavior suggests she doesn't care if I leave. Though my mind knows better, my tongue presses my luck.

"I'm finding Security." Toughen my expression despite no clue where Security is. If there even is a *Security* to find.

"Do what you have to C.C.," her voice grows serious, "but know I'll not hurt you." Her silver eyes reach out to my own. Not as a threat, but with sincerity. "I'd *never* hurt you. Quite the opposite."

My mind screams to run from this craziness, to get into the safety of a crowd. To find a responsible adult who can help, yet I cannot peel away from her amicable gaze. Stop where I am. I may have even taken two steps forward again. The woman is a puzzle within a puzzle. An inexplicable curiosity continues to dominate my actions, evermore drawing me in. "How so?"

"Well, Cherry Cheeks," a smile returns to the woman's face as the epithet left her lips, "my commission is acting as your—what's the right word?

I guess guardian—no, that's a little too strong. Perhaps custodian is better."

She cannot be serious!

"I need no bodyguard, no chaperone—whatever you want to call it. Least of all from someone like you!"

"Ninety percent true," she concedes. "You've always been capable and courageous, even against those forces beyond your knowledge that are trying to bat you down." The woman glances to the side, concern, along with a hint of distress, settling on her face. As fast as it comes, it fades. "So let's agree on 'guiding' you… no matter what we call it, for those things you need to fill your head with, you need me."

The woman is confusing.

Forces beyond my knowledge?

Things I need to fill my head with?

What kind of babble is this?

As if she knows who I am from what, an odd ten minute conversation? Enough of this woman!

Before even one question can leave my lips, she says, "You've a unique spark." She moves toward the guard. "Liked that inventive little trick you pulled on Denise this morning." A chuckle leaves the woman's mouth. "Katie was furious with her."

Huh? Wait… what?! My mouth falls open, but nothing comes out.

The woman carries on, an excitement growing in her words. "That spark…" She twists to face me. "I'm gonna help you turn it into fireworks!"

Just gawk at her as she returns to the guard's slumped body. How'd she know? What's she talking about—a spark? Fireworks? A good half minute passes before I regain control of my body.

"Hey!" I rush forward. "How d'ya know about that?" Then at last, the question eating away at me comes out. "Who are you?!"

No answer comes: the false waitress instead focuses on the guard. She slides him flat as I join her. She removes two liquids from her small handbag, both of which look like perfume samples. The first she spurts on the side of the man's forehead, along the centimeters long gash running from temple to ear. What blood was flowing from the cut turns a dark reddish and gums up in an instant. The second she sprays on the wall where the man's blood was forming a stain. Within seconds, the wetness disappears, as if never there.

Still squatted next to the man, she at last turns her attention to me. "Come on C.C., certainly a bright girl such as yourself already knows? But I'll give you a hint anyway: midnight brown is far from my natural hair color."

I saw her but seconds the first time. Yet the manner in which her turquoise mini-dress enveloped her curves with such precision so mimics a vision that seared into my memory banks earlier in the day. The connection made no sense when first occurring to me—not sure it still makes any sense—but it's also the only logical conclusion. "You're that frosted blonde from the locker room."

The woman smiles at me, her lips recline with satisfaction.

"But how? You look so old."

The woman laughs. "If you only knew."

My face puffs with radiation. "I mean," I clarify, "just, in your dress tonight, well… you're a stunning *woman*." I wave my hands along my body. "For certain, you're no high-schooler."

The woman chuckles again. "Oh, Cherry Cheeks, beauty's not defined by age." She rises and takes my hands within her own. Our eyes lock and sink into the other's. "Make no mistake, you're already a lovely, impressive girl, inside and out. Have been your entire life. And not too long from now, long before you're my age, you're going to be more spectacular than I ever could be."

Impressive my whole life. More spectacular than she? More illogical, out-of-place comments. Papa says as much to me. But that is just Papa being Papa. This woman, though—haven't we just met?

How could she know what I've been like, what I am like? And what about *"well before you're my age"*… just how old does she think I am? How old is she? Sure, there's an age difference between us, but there's no way the separation is all that significant. This woman can't be any more than in her early twenties. Mid-twenties on the outside chance.

A haziness tugs at my thoughts. I break her gaze before she edges any further into my thoughts. "How do you do that?"

"Part of my job is to blend in. Glad to hear, though, that I'm doing it so well."

Not what I meant!

Another more pressing question pops into mind. "Wait a minute… who do you work for?"

"'Work for' is a bit of a misnomer," she says. "I haven't worked for him in years. We've been partners for a long time now."

"You're not answering the question."

The woman hesitates, her pupils lost to the sky. A few seconds later, they return. "Let's say the two of us have an intimate interest in your well-being."

"We don't even know each other. Why would you have any interest in my well-being?"

"Look," the woman goes on before I can press further, "no doubt there are hundreds of questions bouncing around your head right now." That's a bit of an understatement! "I'll answer each of them as best I can in time. But at this moment," she points at the guard, "we need to take care of this and get a move on." The woman glances toward the house. "We've only minutes before the next wave of shuttle carts gets back." She leans down, straddles the man's head, reaches under his shoulders and grips his pits. "If you'll just grab his legs."

CHAPTER NINE

"COME ON NOW," MAHONEY TEASES, "just grab the legs and pull them off!"

The meaty carcass on my plate looks of a rodent, but that doesn't mean that's what it is. Right? My stomach doesn't care.

Split the creature's rear legs away from its torso, creating two tiny drumsticks. As Paterson—sitting across from me—did a moment before, I place the thicker end between my teeth and pull the leg bone forward. Cringe as the muscle peels right off. What'd I just…? The meat is tender and, risking the cliché, tastes of chicken, thanks in part to Mahoney's garlicky butter glaze.

"Good, isn't it?" Paterson asks.

My stomach concurs. Before my mouth finishes its first bite—ignoring the utensils before me, along with any manners—rip a chuck of flesh from the body and stuff the prize into my mouth. Mahoney laughs, tosses his fork down, and does the same. Shrugging his shoulders, Paterson fists his own hulk like he's eating a turkey leg and tears a huge portion of meat off it with his teeth. Part of the meat hangs from the side of his mouth. He edges it in with his tongue.

Paterson ravishes another serving, juices spilling from his mouth and onto the chest of his shirt. I swallow and peel another portion free with more grace than he. No idea what the morning will bring, opted to embrace my inner womanhood and donned the blue dress and strap heels for dinner. Hesitated with the heels, they being taller and thinner stemmed than anything that'd ever been on my feet (in what memories my mind holds, at least). Not even sure if I've worn heels before, but in less than half a dozen steps I rode that bike: once you learn, you never forget. Even took an extra second to stop by the storage room and find a matching blue ribbon to tie back my hair into a ponytail. I'd set out to just keep the wet hair—no way to dry it—from dropping over my face; but the ribbon turned into a welcomed addition to the outfit's cuteness factor.

A quiet laugh escapes my mouth between bites. No doubt James will have told me to stop being so girly.

"You okay there, Jane?"

"Ah—oh" Another piece of meat dangles from my hand, just shy of my mouth. "Sorry, what?"

Mahoney chuckles. "Do you want some water to wash down that meat? Glad to see you like it so much."

"Ah, yeah, that would be great." I tip the meat out. "This is delicious. More so than I expected."

"Good." Mahoney takes the pitcher to his right and tilts it over the glass next to my plate. "Wanted to make you something special. At least, as special as I could do with what we had."

With my free hand, I grab the glass and take a long draw. The extra coolness of the liquid is unexpected but refreshing, causing a small shiver to race through my shoulders and an "Ooo" that sounds more sensual than it should to escape my mouth. Thankfully, everyone's too engrossed in their meals to notice, most unlike before I took my seat.

Ma had said everyone dressed up for special dinners, and what may be our last such meal for how long seemed to qualify. My apparel choice, though, was nothing less than a boulder thrown into a puddle. The wonderment that shot into Claudia's face as I passed the makeshift infirmary still makes me wonder if MissyAnn was toying with me. The family of stunned looks that flew my way as I stepped into the dining area seemed to confirm as much. I didn't care. It was an ego boost I shouldn't have craved, but did.

Paterson's reaction tickled my self-esteem the most. He stood engrossed by my approaching steps, his mouth gaping wider and wider. Six seconds passed that way before Mahoney realized he'd lost his kitchen helper and why. He thwacked Paterson alongside the head, breaking the man's trance, then gave me a big smile and a nod of approval. Perhaps Ma hadn't deceived me?

I glance at Paterson chomping away at his food. *You got off easy. If MissyAnn had been around to see that…* Though, I can't blame the man in full for his behavior. The longer they gawked, the more accentuated was the sway of my hips and the jut of my breasts. All subconscious, of course. I must admit, a callous part of me had wanted Ma to be here; to rub in our differences. Sure: self-serving, petty, most superficial—Mom would have chastised me to no end—but my soul didn't realize the attention it needed until all those eyes were stuck on me.

Such self-absorption now faded, I'm glad MissyAnn wasn't here to see the display. Albeit the distinctions between us are wide, I've this inexplicable affinity toward her that would have been a shame to sabotage in such a blatant manner. I promise to start afresh when she returns. For now, though, Mahoney saddles my attention.

"One of the best things about this place," he says, holding his glass out. "There's a small spring close by. Tozan worked his magic and—abracadabra—fresh, cold water on demand. Good to have, as the surface temperature keeps rising." He guzzles his own glass, then refills both.

"Spekin' oof fings eat'n up," Paterson's stuffed mouth spits out.

"Come on, Paterson." Mahoney brushes a fleck of half mashed potatoes off his arm and back toward its originator.

"'Arry." Paterson quick chews and swallows hard, craning his neck as if in need of the Heimlich. He, instead, greases the load with a small sip of water, then says to me, "What's with MissyAnn?"

"What d'ya mean?" I take another swig of water to fend off the heat rising in my cheeks. Paterson doesn't seem to notice and carries on.

"She's never been so crabby." He shakes his head from side-to-side. "Came bustin' through here mumbling under her breath, naked as a jaybird. Not unusual for her, the naked part, but the irritability of her manner. I kept my distance, I'll tell ya that!" Paterson stuffs another hand of potato chunks into his mouth.

I shrug. "Not sure what to tell ya." I dare not even peek at Mahoney, my face melting as it is. Sense the dubiety radiating from his spot.

Stoking the fire already burning in my cheeks, Mahoney says, "A *little jiggle* more water, Miss Doe?" Guess from the jab that he's insider experience.

"Please!" Continue to avoid his gaze. "You—ah—were saying something about things getting hotter?"

Mahoney laughs. "So it seems!"

I slap his leg. Nothing that can hurt him. "Stop it," I half whisper, popping my chin in Paterson's direction. Paterson can't be naïve enough to not know about his girlfriend's—or whatever their relationship—flirtatious side, but it's impolite to jest about it like this.

Mahoney laughs again.

"What's so 'unny?" Paterson says between chews.

"Nothing!" Mahoney and I say in unison, his laced with a chuckle, mine with a hint of disquiet.

Paterson looks between the two of us, then flaps his hand in the air. "Yeah, whatever." He stands, stuffing what little remains of his meal into his pudgy cheeks, grabs his now empty plate and dinnerware, and rambles toward the kitchen area. His shoulders droop as he walks.

"Crud, I've upset him too." My chin drops to my chest.

Mahoney leans in. "Hey," he gives me a slight body bump and, alas, wins over my gaze, "Paterson'll be fine. He's no dummy. He knows what it means to be tied in with MissyAnn. Trust me, within ten minutes of her getting back, this little chat will be a gone memory."

"But how can she do that to him?"

A big smile encompasses Mahoney's cheeks. "Ma is fantastic. Fun, sincere, a *fierce* ally; I trust her with my life. Sure, she's a bit socially generous..." My eyebrows shoot up. "*Fine*," he rolls his eyes, "blatantly promiscuous. But don't feel bad for Paterson. Their relationship is far from one sided. Believe me, he's not the one being taken advantage of."

I glance toward Paterson, who is helping Mariana wash the dinner's pots and pans, then at our fellow diners. Considering his limited options, I suppose it natural that he take advantage of Ma's—how'd Mahoney phrase it?—"generous" nature. Besides, after all my inappropriate behavior with Paul, is it not hypocritical of me to be so judgmental? If you're happy and not hurting anyone, well, go be happy!

"Pretty sure they're into each other anyhow," Mahoney says. "She's been attached to his hip for weeks now, though no less promiscuous toward us guys. Seems now *you* ladies too." I glower at him, which he shrugs off with another wide smile and adds, "My guess is she's afraid to admit she's in a monogamous relationship that she wants to be in."

Funny, no matter how we get there, seems we all gravitate toward the one that knows us better than we know ourselves.

"Enough of those two," Mahoney says. "Finish up so we can find you a cube."

Not five minutes later, Mahoney grabs my boots in one hand and offers his other arm as we leave for the dormitory. Tuck my unworn clothes under my right arm and slip the other through his. For an otherwise rough-cut cave, the floor is smooth and well kept, clear of debris. Still, appreciate the extra support each time my heels catch a random divot.

"Mariana mentioned you were a sailor?" I say as we walk.

"Sailor is a bit of a stretch, but yes, I worked on a boat. Not for long, as I'm sure she apprised you?"

"Yeah… a prank gone awry?"

"I suppose that *is* one way to put it. Why do you ask?"

"Well, umm," my tongue stumbles, "I mean, sounds like you're an excellent navigator… and seeing as you're the only one who's been off this island… I'm hoping you might tell me where we are?"

"I see." A handful more steps pass before the man responds further. "My sense of direction is strong, but I'm afraid I don't quite know myself."

"Oh," I murmur, making no attempt to suppress my disappointment.

Mahoney shifts his arm and gives my hand a gentle squeeze. "We *all* want that answer. The captain made the staff stay below deck, especially at night. Only a few of the most trusted crew knew where we were, much less our destination." His steps cease. "Here we are."

Mahoney pulls aside the curtain before us. As MissyAnn advised, there is close to nothing in the space: a plain bed and small table, no drawers. A glass lantern sits unlit on the table. That is all. At least in the Facility's barracks, we get dressers and a mirror.

"Though they start barren, you're welcome to decorate as you like."

"Decorate!" I snicker. "With what?"

"The finery one encounters here would amaze you."

"For real?"

Mahoney chuckles.

"You're teasing me, aren't you?"

"Just a little." He pinches his thumb and first finger together like he was holding a pea between the two. "We encounter the odd trinket or curiosity here and there that let us bring some individuality to our spaces." He waves my boots toward the cube. "So, should we consider this yours?"

The room seems larger than Ma implied, but suffers from unusable floor space because of its triangular perimeter. Plus, its "door" opens with a direct view of the dining area. Privacy may be a rarity here, but there has to be another space with more than this. "Well, Sir, while I appreciate how in-demand your units are, I'm aiming for something less, shall we say, alfresco."

"Hmm. Our units *are* going quick," Mahoney says with a small laugh, "but we've a couple others available."

We move past the first row to the opposite side of the cube we hid behind earlier. Turning the corner, Mahoney stops again. "These two to the left are doubles. Ava and Eric, the twin brunettes eating at the other table, occupy the far one. Tozan is alone in the other one. He'd welcome a roommate."

"Ah… I, um…"

"Yeah, I figured as much. Just noting all your options." He points right toward an angled wall. At its center, a pink curtain covered in hand-painted honeybees. "That's MissyAnn's, which means the last option is at the end here."

Mahoney leads me past the pale blue curtain that serves as Ava and Eric's door to the end of the row, where it turns ninety degrees left. On the back wall, right at the corner, is a gray curtain already half opened. I complete the curtain's collapse and step inside. The room is better shaped than the first, but the uneven walls make it somewhat smaller than either of the previous two. All the same, besides the requisite bed and drawerless table, someone fit a small chest-of-drawers overhanging with a mirror into the room.

"I'll take it!" blurts from me.

"Thought you would," Mahoney says, having already put my boots down next to the doorway. "Hope you don't mind that I had Leo, my bald compadre, grab the drawers and mirror for you."

I toss my clothes toward the end of the bed, then wrap my arms as tight as possible around Mahoney's broad shoulders. "Thank you so much," I whisper into his ear.

Perhaps stunned by my actions, Mahoney stands motionless for a second before returning the hug. "Ah… you're most welcome."

Hold the embrace for a couple seconds more before stepping back just enough that my right hand still rests in his left. I give the muscular hand a warmhearted squeeze. "How is it you are so nice to me? You don't even know me."

Mahoney shuffles to his feet, but holds my gaze. Though his dark skin hides any flushness, his cheeks swell all the same. "I've an eye for good people," he says with a gentle tone, "and you are for sures good people."

The raw sincerity of his words soothes into my heart, race into my memories. Papa flickers forth. He is tucking me into bed after a harder than normal day with Katie, not too long after starting seventh grade. Back then, over half of my day I spent in the high school taking honors classes—all with Katie, who used every avenue available that second part of the day to make up for being unable to torment me all morning. *"Be patient, my princess,"* Papa's words echo in my mind. *"You are good people… and know that the elite among them always find each other."* Within Mahoney's benevolent eyes, there is not only compassion, but tenderness, honesty, respect.

Indeed, Papa, the best of them find each other.

Edge closer and place a small kiss on Mahoney's still warm cheek. "As are you."

Though my heart wants to hold the moment forever, too long of a stay will turn it awkward, misunderstood. I desire neither between Mahoney and me; ease away from him and focus on reclaiming the clothes scattered about the end of the bed.

"So," he says after a long silence, "Leo is your immediate neighbor other side of this wall." Mahoney points to the wall against which the bed and dresser rest. "I'm past him, around the corner to the right. You need *anything*, let me know."

"I will." Try popping the words from my lips as casual as possible. I step over to the mini-dresser and open the top of three drawers. Place my new undergarments inside.

"Good. Let's see, Paterson is next to me as you go back up the next row over. If I'm not around for whatever reason, he can help you."

"Okay." Move on to the next drawer, the new home for the shirts wrangled from the storage area.

"Indigo is at the end of that row, back near where we started. She was the one giving you the stink eye when you were walking to dinner, if you noticed."

With the last drawer open midway, stop. *Is there anyone you didn't offend?!*

Plop down on the bed, the pants still in my hands falling to the mattress. "I hadn't." Attempt to sound aloof.

"No worries; she gets jealous real easy. You presented," Mahoney pauses, coaxing me back to my feet for a more fitting view, "—present—classically stunning. You have *nothing* to be bashful over." His head gives a little shake, a *shoo* escaping his lips before a chuckle takes over. "Besides," he says with a smirk, "she's a vegetarian. More certain, our mealtime manners offended her more than your marvelous entrance."

As true as that may be, my brain storms. On one hand, is it my fault the dress fits my curves in an *everyone-look-at-me* manner? Am I to suppress who I am at the long odds of putting someone off? But then, what does twice offending Indigo say about my overall behavior? I would most displease Mom. My left hand pinches the wrist of the right. Dig a nail into my skin. As a newcomer, I should have known the situation called for a more reserved demeanor, to first assimilate with this group so welcoming of a stranger.

"I have to go apologize."

Mahoney steps between the door and me before I can. "Never apologize for being you." He eases me to the side, then grabs the pants and stores them in the last drawer. As he closes the drawer, he says, "The South Pacific."

My face crunches. "Umm, I'm sorry. The South Pacific… what?"

"You asked if I knew where we are. My take is somewhere in the South Pacific. A vague answer, at best."

"Are you kidding? That's better than the absolutely-no-clue answer I assumed you meant."

"Well, the South Pacific is enormous; I've no usable coordinates."

"I beg to differ. My dad once told me, '*You first need to understand where you are to understand where next you need to go.*'"

Wow! From where'd that come?

"Wise words," Mahoney says. "Between my familiarity with the stars and Mariana's expertize—she's an astrobiologist by trade—"

Confused, I stay quiet. She's an *astro*biologist? What was it Ma had said? Mariana objected to "exotic" testing being done. What did that mean? What exotic testing?

Mahoney touches my arm. "Jane? You with me?"

"Yeah—sorry." Gather myself. "Yes. MissyAnn had mentioned that."

"We suspect we're somewhere east of Australia. Near the southern islands of French Polynesia, in rough terms."

I sit back on the bed, unsure which of this added information to contemplate first. As momentous a discovery as extraterrestrial microbes is, push the thought to the back of my mind. Getting off this rock is more important. Even a generic idea of where we are is something. If we can just commandeer the proper vessel…

Droop my head. The last ship to visit the island, at least for the now, had embarked on its return trip. "Mahoney," my voice weeps, "do you expect my parents have given up on finding me?"

Mahoney sits next to me and wraps his arm around my shoulders. With his free hand, he lifts my chin and turns my face to his. "Sweetheart," he soothes, "if I was your father, I'd *never* give up searching for you."

My heart both swells and aches. I lean into his upper arm and close my eyes, do nothing to fight the tears that drip from my cheeks. Mahoney, likewise, makes no sign of wanting to break our embrace. Though he'd say otherwise, saddling the man with my mixed bag of emotions is an exploitation of his kindness. After what is a good five, maybe even ten, minutes, I lift myself erect again.

"Thank you." I brush away the tear trails from my cheeks. "If you don't mind, I'd like to rest."

Mahoney smiles and clasps my shoulder, then stands up. "Good idea. Could be an intense day tomorrow. Plus, not to be too curt, but with MissyAnn not being around, it may be the best rest you get." He steps through the door, but before pulling my curtain shut, says, "Tomorrow, we must find you earplugs."

A chuckle liberates from my mouth. "Perhaps I should have taken you up on your first unit!"

Laughing, Mahoney sticks his head in again. "Wouldn't matter," he whispers and pops his head back out.

Oh, brother!

As his boots thump away, slip my own shoes off and place them next to the jackboots. Turn to the bed and pull the corner of the blanket and top sheet to the side. Lift the skirt of my frock, but drop it back in place. "I would forget to grab nightclothes."

Consider swapping the dress for the olive tee-shirt MissyAnn grabbed as part of my fatigues, but that is likely to get frequent use over the next few days. Alternative is bra and panties—maybe even panties only—though, after that whole beach fiasco. As great as Mahoney is, and really everyone, the camp isn't home yet. Too worn to debate options further, collapse to the bed as is and pull the coverings over me. Close my eyes and sink into the plush mattress. That's a welcomed surprise!

Thump, thump Mahoney's boots fade. Slide my feet across the velvety sheets. *Thump. Thump. Thump.*

Ugh! What's that noise?

I was sleeping so well. Such pleasant dreams. Lounging ocean side with my love. Soaking in the sun, sipping fruity cocktails. Not a worry in the world. Until this annoying thumping.

Thumping doesn't belong on a beach.

"Dear," I say, groggy. Slide my arm to his side of the bed. There's nobody there. The sheets are chilled.

Sit upright. "Dear?" Wipe the sleep from my eyes. Glance left. The bathroom is dark.

A weak flash of light catches my eye from the living room.

"Hello?"

The thumping stops, then rushes. Throw the blanket off and jump from bed.

Although the night is warm, a chill runs across my body. It'd been much warmer under the bedding. Search for my robe, the lace-trimmed camisole and knicker pajamas on my body providing little insulation. A squeak echoes from the other room. Abandon my hunt and shuffle to our bedroom door. "Paul?" Peer out.

Across the living room, in the breakfast nook, three human silhouettes stand out against the ambient light of the night's half moon. Two of the three, their muscles bulging under dark uniforms, work a limp body through the doorway to the garage. But not just any limp body, the limp body of my husband!

"Paul!"

Rush forward, but traverse not two full steps. The feminine curves of the third silhouette twists from overseeing her teammates' work. A gun rises.

Bang!

To my right, chest level, the door frame cracks apart. Splinters of wood dig into my bare shoulder.

Duck and draw back into the bedroom. My upper arm stings. Dark steams of wetness race along my biceps. No time to patch the injury. I need to find a weapon, quick! The thumping grows louder, closer.

Dash to Paul's side of the bed and reach under with my good arm. Thump. Thump. *Watch the doorway as my hand seeks.* Thump. Thump. *Reach. Skid my hand along the floor. Nothing.* THUMP. *Reach again. Swipe back and forth.* THUMP! *Still Nothing!*

Crud! Where is it?!

Lean forward on my elbow and peek underneath the bed. The wrapped handle is a centimeter from my fingers. Stretch and lock onto the bat, the warmth of my hand seeping into the coolness of the metal. Hurry the makeshift club from its resting place, but not quick enough. Return my focus to the doorway to see it filled with the bulk of one of the male kidnappers.

"Little girl, you should've stayed in bed."

Hovering over me, the kidnapper suddenly latches onto my high ponytail and yanks upward.

My temples burn. Giant tears shoot from my eyes. Every part of my body yields to the force and works to get me upright as quick as possible. Beg my shaking legs to help in the effort. Fight to keep everything from just going limp, especially my hand, still grasping tight to the bat.

We lock eyes as I rise. His soulless pair are all that exposes through the mask he wears. A snap *pops at right side of the man's waist. A glint of moonlight shines off the Bowie knife he unsheathes. He wretches my head so my ear is near his mouth. Mercilessness oozes from the man. "Time for you to die," he slithers.*

"Not today, asshole!" *I clench the bat's grip and swing with my full potential.*

Lingering by my ear half a second too long, too late does the man realize my intentions. He arches his knifed hand toward the bat but—CRACK!—his head snaps to his left, his body following in a backwards twist. His right hand flies out to the side. The knife flings from his grip and pierces the hollow core of the bedroom door with a thud.

Still latched onto my hair, his momentum jerks my head right. Lose my footing as he tugs me back and down toward the bed. My grasp on the bat fails, which reverberates with a clang *as it hits the hardwood floor, then rolls toward the bathroom. My damaged shoulder lands square on the corner of the mattress, burrowing the wood embedded in my flesh deeper. I swallow the pain and collapse to the floor, leaving a streak of red from the upper edge of the bedspread hanging over the mattress' edge to the bed skirt. I take two deep breaths to quell my shaking body. Instead, a fresh pump of adrenaline races through my veins.* Paul needs me!

I spring from the floor. The man is sprawled motionless, cater-corner on my bed. Only one of the three stuffed animals—my elephant, Lucky—remains on the bed, the others knocked to the floor by the man's impact. His head lay on my "Dreaming of Gymnastics" embroidered pillow, a pool of his blood leaving it to read "Dreamnastics".

Ignoring the burn in my arm, move over to and brace the bedroom door with my left foot. Wrap my hands around the handle of the blade—its butt embossed with a rose encircled by tiny golden stars—and dislodge it. Move into the living room, then into an empty breakfast nook. Hurry over and press my ear against the door to the garage.

A woman's commanding voice vibrates in my ear. She's goading her companion to get their quarry loaded quicker.

Twist the knob and edge the door open.

Light blinds me. Slam my eyes shut. Wait a moment, then creep them apart.

Two figures at the far end of the rocky passageway, maybe forty meters away, hover at a van. The male is within its rear hold, half crouched as he works the body in. The woman stands to the side, barking orders. Both wear full-body black outfits, masks, and boots… save the woman's bright red soles.

I swing the door the rest of the way open and rush forward. Thirty-five meters to go, mold and wetness choke at my lungs. Thirty meters to go, sweat and tears are indistinguishable. Twenty-five meters to go, enough blood has splattered from my shoulder onto the ruffled skirt of my sky-blue nightdress that several of its imprinted white dogs have turned ruby red. Twenty meters to go, legs burning, lungs burning, arm burning, dig deep… the body is close to loaded. Fifteen meters to go, the man jumps from the van, ready to seal its doors.

"You're not taking Papa!" Mid-stride I heave the knife.

Whoosh! Whoosh! Whoosh! SMACK!

All but the hilt of the knife embeds into the man's upper right thigh. He collapses and grabs at the handle, but the serrated top of the blade keeps it in place. He reaches for the woman, her gun again aiming my way, pulling her askew. The shot she intends for me instead pierces into the rocky ceiling. Still off balance, she cocks her pistol again and screams, "Kilford, you idiot!" She bores a bullet into the man's forehead, shattering part of his skull. Several tufts of curly light brown hair peek out from under his shredded mask. His body goes slack.

Before she can fire a third shot, brace my good shoulder and slam her into one of the rear doors of the van. With a huff, *the air in her lungs flies out. The gun pops from her hand and skids underneath the vehicle. She keels over and grabs the van's floorboard as she struggles to find oxygen.*

The impact flings my body sideways and my feet tangle in the downed kidnapper. Fall hard to my behind, scraping my back along the wall. Everything is a brownish-gray.

Close my eyes and shoo the disorientation away, then open them to see Papa bolt upright and grab the woman's hair through her mask. He heaves her upper body into the van. She screams, at least as much as her air-deprived lungs will allow, and tries clawing his hand away. "Run, Princess!" Blood surfaces with each of her scratches, but he holds her there. "Run now!"

I get to my hands and knees. A wave of dizziness takes me, but I shake it away. The woman struggles harder, digging her nails deeper into Papa's hand. He cringes with each attack, panic building in his eyes. I reach forward as if I can magically erase the space between us. "Papa..."

"Sweetie," he says, "you've got to go now. She's too," he moans, another dig into his skin, "strong. She'll kill you!"

The woman jerks forward, but cannot break Papa's grasp. With the scream of a crazed hyena, she jerks harder and, sacrificing her skull, rips her hair from her head. As her hood flies off, rivers of red fall across her face. She wipes them away from her eyes, but I recognize her regardless.

"Mom?"

"You little rat!" she screams and lunges at me.

I launch myself to my feet and to the side, avoiding her flailing hands. She, instead, slams into the wall with a moan. Start toward Papa.

"No!" He yells. "Run!"

Despite her damage, Mom is already shaking off the collision. I take one last look at Papa, who mouths: Please go, *then turn and rush back along the hall.*

"That's right missy," Mom calls out from behind me, "run away. Run, run, run... but you'll never be able to hide! Do you hear me?! Run like the frightened fawn you are!" So disturbed is the woman, her words flow with a hurried excitement. "Just a panicked little doe with nowhere to go," she sings. "Little Miss Doe and nowhere to go! Little Miss Doe. Nowhere to go!"

Try to fight off her words, not let them sink into my heart, yet my body trembles unrestrained. "Little Miss Doe..." echoes in my ears over and over. "L'tle Miss Doe" Slam the garage door shut behind me, but her voice is as loud as ever. "Miss Doe?"

My legs give out and I fall flat to the ground with an uncontrollable shake. "Miss Doe?!"

"Huh?"

"Miss Doe," a soft, but excited, voice says, "you need to wake up!" A pair of bright ice-blue eyes greet my own.

"Claudia?" Sit up and rub my eyes free of sleep. "What's the hour?"

"Ah, maybe like eleven, eleven thirty. But Miss Doe—"

"Eleven-thirty! Crud, I've been asleep for over six hours!"

Claudia seems unsure what to say. Whatever she wants to share has nothing to do with how long I've been sleeping. "I'm sorry," I say. "What is it, Claudia?"

A broad smile fills her face. "Miss Doe, it's your boyfriend. He's awake!"

"He's not—oh, forget it! Wait! What?"

"Mr. Paul, his fever broke. He's woken up, Miss Doe, and he's asking for you!"

"Paul's awake!"

Bolt from the bed and from my room. Claudia calls out, but what she says, my ears lose. Was that rude? Eh, she's old enough to understand. I dash past and around the double cubes, wishing I'd taken residence in the first Mahoney showed me. Ignore the pebbles digging into my bare soles as my legs carry me from the gathering to the dining areas. As the western part of the cavern approaches, Paul's welcoming baritone laugh hits my ears.

Speed up, ready to whip his curtain open and encase him in the biggest of hugs.

Then stop, meters short of the room. "No, you must be ladylike."

Take a second to catch my breath, straighten my dress. Retie the ribbon holding my hair in place, it woefully loosened. So could use a mirror! Tuck my sweat dampened bangs behind my ears, then wipe the sweat from my forehead with the back of my hand. *You would run over here!* Straighten my dress, again.

"You look beautiful." Turn to find Claudia standing behind me. She lifts her right arm, my heels dangling from her hand. "Thought you might want these," she says in a hushed voice.

I grin and take the shoes from her. "Thank you," I whisper back. "That's so charitable of you. Sorry I took off like that. I've been—"

"It's okay, Miss Doe." A big, knowing smile sits upon Claudia's face.

Using her shoulder for support, brush away what earth stuck to the bottom of each foot and slip the heels on. With one of the long sleeves of her shirt, Claudia cleans what of the remaining liquid buds from my temples. She pulls two thin strands of my bangs out from my ears and hangs them along each cheek. I take a step away from her and whisper, "So?"

She grins wide and whispers back, "You are *so* beautiful."

If only. I reach forward and give her a big hug. "You're darn cute yourself."

"Mere flattery," she says, yet clasps tighter. "But thank you."

As we release, I give Claudia another smile, then we walk hand-in-hand toward Paul's room. From behind the curtain, Mariana's voice plays out, "What do you recall of the last several hours?" I stop us and stretch my ears toward the door.

"Not much," Paul's voice responds. "Several offbeat dreams." *You and me both!* "Thought I was dying once or twice, save this golden haloed angel over-watching me."

I arc toward Claudia and giggle, then in a low voice say, "See, I told you—he's talking about you."

She shakes her head and mouths *no*, but her attempt to hide her rose-flushed cheeks behind her golden blonde locks suggests she desires otherwise. I giggle again, then turn back to the discussion inside, to hear Paul ending, "… think she'll be here?"

"I'm sure any minute now. In fact…" Mariana raises her voice, "Are you going to stand out there the entire night?"

Oh crud!

Claudia releases my hand. "Well, go!"

Take a deep breath, erase what space remains, and slide the curtain open.

Paul looks good. *Real* good. He's sitting up in the bed, bare chested. His skin has a rich, healthy sheen to it. Far from the sweat-drenched paleness that plagued it only hours earlier. His face is bright with life. As he turns to me, there's a sparkle in his eyes that hasn't been there since we first met.

"Little Miss," he sputters, "Spunky?" With each breath, his pecks sharpen, quicken. "Wow! You look…"

Swallow hard, my mouth awash with saliva.

"Oh, screw it!" I bullet forward. Angle onto his bed and wrap my arms tight around him. Nestle against the side of his head, careful to avoid the bandages protecting the injury still there. "I thought I was going to lose you."

He returns the solidity of our embrace. "It's far from that easy to get rid of me."

Forever passes before an *Um-Hum* from Mariana parts us. Our cheeks brush past one another. Noses edge alongside the other, their peaks millimeters apart. Our eyes lock, his pupils aglow with an impassioned fire. A vague memory of only one other ever looking at me like that tickles my mind. My lips part, the need for a deep breath overwhelming me. His brawny scent floods over me; his touch sparks across my skin as our fingers linger upon each other's arms. My head leans right, his goes left. Close my eyes the closer our breaths come to being the same.

"Claudia," Mrs. Vasquez interrupts, "It's time for you to shower and get to bed, and for us to allow these two to catch up."

Just shy of our lips meeting, I pull back and angle my face demurely toward the wall, afraid to reveal my embarrassment.

"Yes, Mom," Claudia says, disappointment lacing the words. Not sure because of what didn't just happen, or what did.

Mariana takes my hand and eases me from Paul's bed in a manner that I can avoid his direct gaze. Not that I don't sooo want to fall into his eyes again. My body aches to wear his skin, to press against him, to have him press against me. Yet these impulses are so unrefined—unrestrained—so much not me.

Or, at least, who I thought was me.

Mariana leads me a meter outside Paul's room, stops, and embraces my cheeks. She angles my face toward her own and holds it there. In a voice that's both tender and authoritative, she says, "He's not ready for that— and I'm certain neither are you." *We aren't. I'm not.* "Oh, erase that disbelief from your face. I'm far from a newborn, sweetheart." She removes her hands from my face, solidifying her own. "A half hour only—*just* talking. He still needs much rest. Do you understand me?"

I glance at the ground, feeling as if I'm six and having just broke a priceless vase. Brush my left foot against the ground. "Yes, ma'am."

Mariana lifts my chin up such that our eyes meet again. Her apprehension diminishes, and with a genuine concern, she says, "Sweetie, please be careful with this one."

I want to ask her what she means, but she turns and heads toward the showers, Claudia having already disappeared through the archway.

Return to Paul's room and draw the curtain. Sit in the chair Mariana, and before her, Claudia, had occupied. I scoot it back from the bed a slight amount, just because. He watches my antics with a goofy grin on this face, but says nothing. If he heard Mariana, I can't tell. I scan the room twice, avoiding his eyes.

"So," Paul breaks the silence first, "*Jane*, eh?"

"Ah, yeah." I feign interest in the dinner plate Claudia left laying on a table next to the chair. "Mr. Vasquez said it would be easier that way, at least until my memories return."

"I see. I still prefer 'Little Miss Spunky'."

"No one here wants to call me that." I fiddle with the lantern that is lighting the room. End up darkening it to a soft, dreamy glow. Not my intention.

"I imagine so…" Paul's voice trails off in a manner that I can't help but make sure he's okay. Alas, he's fine, an even bigger and goofier smile resting on his face at having won back my attention. He pats the bed where I first planted myself. "I won't bite." He chuckles. "Well, unless you'd enjoy that."

I try giving him a dirty look, but end up shifting uncomfortably in the chair. *What is it about this guy?!* Try brightening the lantern again, with no luck.

An idea hits me.

Lock eyes with him—*Now don't let him suck you back in*—and send what I hope is a *come-hither* glare his way. "Maybe," I say with a sultry whisper. Well, at least what I think a sultry whisper sounds like. I have no experience doing this. "*I* want to do the biting." Even before the words emerge, they sound ridiculous. I fight to hold the glare and not, instead, just laugh. Who talks this way?

"Touché!" A brief laugh escapes Paul. I reply in kind and, that easy, the tension disappears. "So," he says as if we were two people who bumped into each other on the street, "what'cha been doing?"

Spend the next twenty-five minutes telling him just that, what I learned of our rescuers, and Mahoney's estimate of where are. Even share my idea of commandeering a vessel, should any return. He glows at the prospect of new, clean clothes, which I offered to help him select in the morning, and almost cries with joy at the thought of a shower.

My mind MissyAnn's and I almost suggest that I help lather his body, but bat the proposal away before it spills out. As alluring as his musk started, after half-an-hour in the tight space of his room, he reeks. That first shower, he'll be on his own.

A light bounces along the face of the curtain, ending the sharing. I peek past its side to see a smiling Mariana and Claudia returning from the showers. The two are engaged in a nice mother-daughter chat. I smile, yet flush with envy. Then flinch, the reflections of my dream surfacing. I search my memories for any resemblance of my mother, my mother-daughter chats, to find nothing but emptiness.

Patience. The memories will come.

"You okay?" Paul asks.

"I—ah—yeah, I'm okay," I murmur.

"*That's* convincing," he drawls.

Ignore the jab. Though I'm not sleepy, the day has run me down; I hunger for a fresh day to arrive. Not to mention Mariana's advice plays over and over in the back of my mind. Scanning Paul and those inviting eyes, my heart begs to stay. I force my head to take charge. "It's late, and you need sleep." Rise to my feet and move to the curtain.

"Don't go," Paul stammers.

"I need to." I avoid any direct eye contact, my heart screaming for a different answer.

"Come on, Miss Spunky." From the corner of my eye, Paul's hand pats my spot on the bed. "Just two adults taking comfort in each other's presence for a restful night of sleep."

My heart yanks my eyes to his. "Just *sleep.*"

"Just sleep," Paul echoes, that goofy smile on his face again. "Scout's honor." He crosses his heart and flings his left hand up with a peace sign.

"Wrong sign, you goofball."

Don't care why I know that. Step over to the lantern and turn down the wick. What remains of its light goes dark. I pause for my eyes to adjust, then free my hair from the pony and move over to the bed. Paul pulls the covers back. Toe off my shoes and sit in my spot. Paul's hand settles at my waist's side, ready to lock me into place once laid flat. I take a long breath, allowing an unexpected realization to soothe my mind, and stand.

"Everything okay?" slumbers from Paul's tongue.

"Perfect." Free my body from my dress. Seconds later, Paul's arm rests firm across my hips and midriff. The heat exchange between our flesh stirs my insides, but brings with it a strong calm. I lay my arm over his and run my fingers between his. His head shifts. His gentle breaths caress my ear. Take a deep breath of my own, smile, and close my eyes. Never, in what memories I possess, am I more secure and at home.

CHAPTER TEN

NEVER, IN WHAT OF THE fifteen years of memories I possess, have I been less secure, less at home than now.

Here I am barreling toward my nemesis' home, with the passed out and beaten body of a guard bumping around in the vehicle's storage space, courtesy of the sibylline woman next to me in the driver's seat, a million questions bouncing between my ears. Despite her commitment otherwise, the woman has yet answered a drip of them.

There have, however, been few opportunities to ask.

No more did we load the guard when a fresh wave of the golf cart-like mini-trucks arrived from the mansion, erasing any chance to extract me unnoticed. Didn't matter, though; there'd be no answers had I stayed back, the woman a danger or not.

Expected she'd shoo me away, but my companion instead joyed *"Excellent"*, then hurried to disguise me. Adorned in the waitress's uniform, she blends in, but my party dress stands out as most suspect. Time short, she wrapped a white tablecloth over me. Not to pass me off as part of the help—as the wrapping looks ridiculous and must appear even more suspicious should anyone garner more than a quick glance—but to offer anonymity. Or so she insists, my dress being, in her words, "a unique piece of art". Before anyone could take more than casual notice of us, she shot us forward and out of the building.

Managed one answer: Xiomara. Her name. "Zee, for short," she tells me her closest friends call her. A pleasurable sentiment, but a leap; I've no history with this woman, nor does consorting together in questionable acts make us "close friends".

She seems to believe otherwise, spewing off a disconcerting number of finer details about my gymnastics performances, academic achievements, and my family as some kind of proof. Fact is, anyone can garner as much from a well-worded INTERNET search (there must be at least half dozen articles about me after winning State last year). A zealous fan—sure. Stalker—perhaps.

She reeling off not only my full name, but why Papa selected as he had, that's concerning. He dabbles in linguistics, and per Zee, my birth name is far from random. Anyone who overhears Dad brag about his princess will know my first name. Nothing noteworthy about that. Knowing my middle name though—last popular in the late 1800s, well over a century and a half ago—that's impressive, yet creepy. Stalker—probably.

Spelled out, many often presume the name's origin is Latin or Spanish, when in actuality it originates from my family's Germanic heritage. Yet this woman's lips rattle off its obscure meaning—*Protector*—as if it's old news. Shocking—for certain. Stalker—the very meaning.

Or perhaps just a lucky guess?

I suspect not. I pick at my legs. *You need to get out of this cart—now!*

Still, knowing all that, she persists in calling me *C.C.* Supposedly for *"my protection"* should things go awry. "Consider it a pseudonym," she says, "to keep you as anonymous as possible."

Why in the world do I need a pseudonym?!

And so double the questions buzzing in my head.

The flow of vehicles guides us just short of an underground garage that mimics the one from which we departed. Zee veers the cart off the main paved pathway along a narrower gravel lane that wraps the back of the manor to the right. She slows, silencing the chatter of the stones under the cart's wheels.

"We still have this business to take care of," she says, flicking her head back toward the rear of the vehicle.

"What do you intend for him?" The guy's condition is none of my do-ing.

Zee glances back and forth between the rear of the house and the land stretching downhill to our right. "Poor fella's gonna have lost control of this here buggy." She jerks the cart cockeyed to the path and stops facing a small grove of trees. "Time for you to get out."

"Mm—okay." I don't move from my seat. I've not come this far to have her abandon me.

"Don't worry, I'll be but a minute." She points to a glass-windowed door twenty meters diagonal the cart. "Wait near the door there—and try your best to stay off the grass, obscure any signs of our presence."

"Right, stay off the grass." Extracting myself from the cart, I'm careful to stay on the pebble path as I walk to its front.

My companion, meanwhile, leaves her own seat and peers into the cargo hold as she moves along the cart's side. She reaches the rear of the vehicle, takes a deep breath, and drops its gate. She climbs into the bed and shuffles around to grab underneath the guard's shoulders, then works him counterclockwise until his head rests at the end of the storage space. Wiping her forehead with her sleeve, she glances my way. "You want to do this?" A slight irritation wrinkles her brow.

"No!" I hurry my attention to the door and beam-walk the thin line between the stone lane and grass as best I can. The periodic pebble that traps under my bare soles digs into my skin as if broken glass. I'd prefer the full of the grass, it's much softer—and quicker—but too revealing; per Zee's instructions, I advance with soft feet.

Behind me flows a series of grunts, then a heavy crunch of rocks. *EERRRG!* comes Zee's groans, intermixed with the irregular crackle of gravel as if two fat branches are being dragged through it. *EERRRG! Crackle, crackle. Crackle—RRRR!—Crackle.* "Oh, shit!" echoes in my ears, followed by a heavy crunch of rocks. "OW!"

Just before the juncture where the path turns toward the door, I stop and twist. Zee is back flat to the path, the bulk of the guard overlaying the lower two-thirds of her body.

"You okay?" I ask, half muted.

"No!" She tries wiggling her body out from under the guard.

"Do you need help?"

"No," comes a brusque reply.

None of this funny, yet a laugh escapes my body. Zee's contortions pause and a scowl flashes at me. While grossly inappropriate, I point at her and laugh even more.

She growls. "Oh, shut up!" she says, yet her shoulders shake with a giggle.

Not thirty seconds later, Xiomara is not only free of the man's mass, but has him seated—as best that you can seat the rubbery architecture of an unconscious body—behind the wheel of the cart. She fiddles near his feet, then reaches across his body to grab her bag. She slings the bag over each shoulder, positioning it as if it's a backpack. With one last look over her work, she latches the outside of the driver's compartment, tucks her right leg up onto what of the seat there is available and, in a half crouch, reaches out to the cart's accelerator with the other.

The cart pulses forward.

Straightaway the unnatural distribution of weight rocks the vehicle, but it otherwise maintains on route toward the grove. Within seconds, the bulk of the cart's body disappears below the curve of the lawn. The rest, along with what remains of Zee, sinks a moment later.

I return to my journey. Don't even jump when the crash reverberates up the hill. *That's it?* Driving over a large plastic trash can would be more dramatic. The pulse of the party dominating the air, there's no way anyone at the pavilion, or even in the mansion, heard the collision.

At the door, I rub my sore feet for an entire minute. My shoes are still back in the manager's office. Slipped my mind to grab them in my rush to confront Zee; a minor price to pay for actual answers. *If you can get any answers out of her!*

Spend another minute pacing in a small circle. Where is she? I consider retracing my steps, just to check. Eh—too impractical. Could be hazardous to work my way back along the path and not scar the bottoms of my feet—a potential ender for a gymnast—then still needing to cross the lawn while generating no trace of my presence. And what then? If something is wrong, we'll need help. Help that, quick thereafter, could demand of my tongue explanations still foreign to my mind, let alone conveyable to someone else.

But it's now been three minutes. I no more step at the hill, not caring how things might play out, and Zee's head pops over the top. I sigh. "Thank the stars."

Xiomara uses the tracks left from the cart's wheels as a makeshift pathway back to the gravel, then scoots along the path to me. As she turns the corner, she works off her backpack. Her advance slows as she shuffles through its contents. Out comes the sparkling green stilettos she wore earlier. "You're gonna need these," she says, holding the shoes out as we rejoin.

I snatch them right away. Sure, they don't match my dress, but I'm not one to complain. Even if they don't fit well, I'll not mind, yet they slip onto my feet as if belonging there. Thin-tipped heels though… merely a couple hours ago did my feet don raised heels for the first time. Heels neither so thin nor so tall. No sooner do I put pressure on them and the shoes dig into the walkway's pebbles. "Not sure," my ankles rock with erratic twitches over the marbles under my feet, "I can walk in these."

Half squatted at the door's passcode entry pad, Zee pries at the pad's shell with a thick nail file she extracted from where I didn't see. "Don't worry", she says without taking her eye off the task, "Wearing heels is the same as riding a bike: once you find your balance, you'll be zooming." The metal side she is working bends out but doesn't giveaway. "A gymnast of your caliber—" A grunt stretches past her lips. "should have no problem. Just—ah—" And another.

TWANG!

"Ow!" Xiomara shakes her hand, the nail file having broke loose of the casing and flinging against her fingers. She stands and looks at me, rubbing one hand with the other. "Start with small steps," she says, then turns her attention back to the contents of her bag.

The keypad looks the same as the one for the preparation building. *What are the chances?* I risk a sequence of timid steps around Zee and press the keypad's buttons.

Click!

"How did you…?"

"Inside source," I beam.

Zee smiles. "Knew you'd be valuable to have here." She edges the door open, takes a quick look in. "Come on, we've work to do." She toggles a switch right inside the doorway as she passes over the small step delineating the home's border. Centered overhead, a pair of parallel tube lights blink on, filling the room in a bright bluish-white hue. I follow, placing my left shoe inside the mudroom. Lift upward with my left leg, freeing the right shoe from the ground.

Wobble.

A lot.

Oh crud!

I grab Zee's arm to keep from planting a kiss on the firmer flooring of the room. She chuckles, but otherwise helps steady my footing.

"Thanks." I adjust my center of balance and release her arm.

"Remember," she says, "small steps."

As instructed, pass with ginger steps a set of lockers first inside the doorway, their backs to the same wall as the door. The left wall houses a double sink and shelving, the lowest two empty and the rest stacked with canisters and liquid-filled bottles. Most have labels too worn to read, if not outright missing. The right wall bears a large, framed cork board, void of any postings, and a small computer screen with a keyboard folded underneath the device. The screen is dark, a thin layer of dust sleeping on its face.

"What are we doing here?"

"Spying," a flat response comes. Able to move quicker than me, Zee doesn't give any of the room's contents a glance and proceeds straight for the far wall. A spiral staircase and an elevator door await there. She stops, retrieves the waitress's tablet from her bag, and again works its screen.

"Pardon? Did you—" Although the tile flooring better accommodates a good balance, still trip. I clutch the side of the electronic display to keep from falling. "—say '*spying*'?"

"Hiding listening devices, to be exact," she clarifies. "You know, electronic bugs. Couldn't pass over the opportunity—most of the staff is engaged with the party, leaving this place near empty." She pauses, seeming to have found something of interest upon the device. Her fingers work faster. After a moment, she says, "You're here to watch and learn. Your first lesson, so to speak."

"My first lesson? I don't want to be a spy!"

She grunts. "You're not." She then looks up from the tablet and laughs.

Whatever mix of befuddlement and disbelief my face wears, it must be a good one.

"Come on... after everything you've seen since following me into that building back there," Xiomara points toward the party, "you think we're on a tour?"

The question is rhetorical, yet still stammer, "Well—no."

"For sures, you must be curious what secrets that nemesis of yours is hiding?"

Didn't consider what it is we are doing in here. I seek answers, yet my head only swims with endless questions. Speaking of which... "Wait a minute! You knew I was following you the whole time?"

"Ah—spy." Xiomara flicks her thumbs at herself. "Or, at least, that's one of my specialties. But yes."

"*One* of your specialties. Do I want to be privy to the others?"

"No," she says in no uncertain terms. "Look, no judgment on what you do or don't do with this opportunity, but one thing we need to work on is your skill at staying inconspicuous." She fans out her arms as if revealing a won prize. "Alas, here starts your first lesson." She pushes the button to call the elevator.

"Inconspicuous! Is that what you call that dress of yours?" The sarcasm oozes uncontrolled from my mouth.

Can't believe I said that!

The elevator door opens. Zee steps in and spins on her heel. A smile spans her cheeks. "Good," she says, "You're feisty." Her hand braces the door. "You coming or not?"

My shoes click forward and into the lift. As the door shuts, Zee presses the square button next to the *2*. The compartment rises.

"Sorry," I say after a momentary silence.

"No worries—inconspicuous doesn't mean hidden; to go unnoticed, you need to blend. For instance..." She cycles her hands along the outfit adorning her figure, then leans into me and in a hushed voice says, "Truth be told, that dress' purpose is to shock... besides, too few are there excuses to deck oneself out, so I went for gold." I can't figure who she thinks can overhear.

Zee wraps her arm around my shoulders and squeezes. "Regardless of what the world may think," she says, "never hesitate to celebrate your inner womanhood." She squeezes again while laying a gentle kiss on my forehead. Her grip releases only as the elevator stops and its door reopens.

The short hall before us opens into a foyer much different from that we left. A warm, yellowish glow bathes everything. Plush carpet patterned in various shades of blue layers the floor. Rich-stained oak trims both bottom and top of white painted walls. The one door, of the same colored oak, visible from the lift faces straight on from us.

"Hold the door." Zee steps onto the carpeted floor and takes several steps forward before stopping short of where the right wall arches open into another room. She peeps around the corner.

With pressure on the square "Open" button, glance around the vestibule. To the left, a circular staircase cuts right and up. To the right and diagonal from the lift is a second oak door. Through the railings surrounding the hollow center of the vestibule sits, on the floor lower, a small wooden table with the ivory-colored bust of a young woman. The lines of its face play in my mind, seeming more and more familiar. Tilt my head to get a better view.

For serious! Is that—

Zee cuts across the view. "You can let go," she says as she edges past me. As the door closes, she grabs me by the waist and twists me to the side. Her fingers work at the zipper of my dress.

Try batting her away. "What are you doing?!"

"Stop moving! You're going to ruin the dress."

The upper half of the gown pops loose. "What the!" I cup my breasts.

"It's not gonna fall off." Xiomara moves counterclockwise around me, unwrapping the jeweled bodice from what turns out to be an under layer that makes up the base of the dress. In a similar manner, she removes the mesh skirt cover and stuffs both in her bag, leaving me in nothing but the purple-sheened, black velvet skater-cut underdress. She tightens the cross straps spanning the back of the altered outfit, then rotates me faceward and looks along my height.

"One more thing," she says, pulling a small spray can from her bag. She gives the can a good shake. "Close your eyes."

A clump of my hair lifts off my left shoulder. *Tssshhh.*

From the right. *Tssshhh.*

The remaining rear. *Tssshhh.*

"Nice," sizzles from Xiomara, beckoning my eyes again open. Her cheeks beam.

"What did you…" Lift my hand, intending to run my fingers through my hair, but Zee latches my wrist first.

"Not yet. Needs another second or two."

"What does?"

"Your green highlights, to match your shoes."

Throw my arms up in confusion. "But my dress—how did you—why?"

"Trust me," Xiomara says, "your dress will be fine. It's designed to do this. Besides, Jeffery can mend any garment I befoul. Universe knows, this isn't the first time."

Stand there, not sure how long before realizing my mouth has dropped open. "You know Jeffery *DeVoe*? Personally?"

"Yeah, an old friend." Xiomara flings her hand through the air. "We went to grade school together." What? DeVoe's got to be in his mid-sixties! "He tailors my clothes," she says. "But that's not here or there. Me staying inconspicuous calls for a distraction." Her finger shoots at me. "Namely you."

"Excuse me?"

"This is part of the lesson, C.C.," Xiomara instructs. "If you can neither avoid nor blend in, you distract. And, in this moment, you're my distraction." She hits the button to open the door of the lift. "That said, can't have you be too recognizable. Remember that whole anonymity goal?"

"Well, sure, but what am I supposed to be doing? How will I find you again?"

"I'll find you," Xiomara says. "And keep it natural. Don't get tripped up with a complex lie."

"Lie! I don't lie!"

A low laugh rumbles from Zee as she twists me. With a slap on my bottom, she nudges me from the compartment. "I believe you just did."

I stumble forward as my ankles struggle with a new surface. Make to move back into the lift and protest, but Xiomara calls out a loud "Hello?" and lets the door close on me. I turn at the shuffles approaching from the arch. A guard—younger, taller, and more muscular than the earlier one we encountered—steps through.

"Miss," he says in a gruff, commanding voice, "you cannot be up here."

"I—ah—" Consider bolting for the stairs. A distraction it'd be, though guess not the one Zee intends. My left ankle wobbles, a reminder such a choice will not end well for me anyhow. *Yikes! If mom finds out what you're doing right now!* I fight the urge to pick at my exposed arms and force a demure smile on my face. "I—ah—sorry, I'm, um, twisted around right now."

The guard grunts, uninterested in my coyness. "Miss, you know there are no guests allowed within the house proper tonight." He moves closer, placing me within grabbing distance.

"I do, but, ah…" The pretentious bust a floor below jumps into my mind. "Katie asked me to meet her here," rushes from my mouth.

The guard shuffles back half a step. He glares at me, doubt lacing his face. His eyes fixed on me, he pulls a small tablet—mimicking that which Xiomara liberated from the waitress—from the belt around his waist and taps at it.

"Which of Ms. Matters' personal guests are you?" he asks, his finger hovering over the pad.

Crap! I'd not seen Katie at the party. No idea if she is even here, let alone with whom she'll be hanging. Suspect he'll recognize her close friends. Who besides her closest friends can even make such a list? *Dummy, you've no practical answer!* Posing the distraction is not my forte.

"Miss, your name?" the guard prompts again.

"I'm, um…" Had I just minded my business, not followed Xiomara into that building… Wait… the preparation building!

I pinch my thighs together, hands cupped in front of my abdomen, and sway at the hips. I shuffle my feet. Force my cheeks flush—no simple task when you must. Focus on my earlier discomfort. "This is embarrassing," I say, "but I've urgent need of a washroom."

The guard rolls his eyes, but his shoulders slacken. He places the tablet back at his side. "Washroom's this way."

He leads me through the oak door that is diagonal to the lift. It opens into another hall, windows facing into the yard on the left and a series of similar oak doors on the right. We proceed to its end, where the passage intersects a second, wider hall in a T shape. The guard turns left and points.

"Door at the end of the hall," he says.

"Thanks," I reply with a small smile. Hurry as best as my shoes allow through the brief passage and into the lavatory. Flip on the light. Close then—*click*—lock the door.

How am I ever going to get out of this?

I rest my hands upon the pedestal sink. The mirror above reflects not the school girl so often seen, but a young woman I'd not realized is within me. Cheeks blush with a temperate rosy plumpness. Big, dramatic lashes surround eyes shadowed in a slight black. Lips full of red deliciousness. Each contour accents to show off its most defining line. Each applied in a manner that compliments the natural tint of my skin.

Regardless of whatever else she is, Mom is a true facial artist.

My amulet likewise echoes in the mirror. The swirling arms of the galaxy within leisure around its center, pulsing with an enticing glow. Every so often, an individual star blasts alive, as if going supernova.

How can it look so real?

The gravity of the massive black hole at its center yanks at my mind's eye. The galaxy grows bigger, closer, fills the bottom third of the mirror, then the whole of the mirror liquefies in dust clouds accented with pinpricks of light. Grows again. Envelopes the mirrored wall, the ceiling and surrounding walls. Within seconds, the bathroom disappears into a nursery of stars… giant fiery blues, dim dwarf reds, life-giving yellows. Each with accretion disks full of planets birthing forth. Several pass by the tips of my fingers. Yet the warmth they radiate doesn't burn, but is comforting, inviting.

"Come to us," a sugary voice sounds from no particular direction.

"Yes, come to us," begs another from my right.

"Please, come," eight times over from each compass direction.

"Where," I call out, "where are you?"

The stars pulse and spit, huge flares bursting from their skins. Close to indiscernible at first, they move, each in a different direction, but each in a sphere with me at its center. In a blink, they gain speed, becoming blurry streaks of colors—where they cross, blending into a kaleidoscope of color as if oil on water. Faster they orbit, then faster still into a solid globe of ever brightening white light.

With a flash, the white disappears. Above me, a single bright yellow illuminates an occasional white wisp of cloud, breaking an otherwise uniform light blue. Far below, little jewels of light rays dance off an ocean full of dark blue waves. Closer and closer the waves come. Small specks of browns and greens emerge from amid the water. Hundreds of islands turned into thousands.

One brown comes closer, grows bigger. A second later, its parameter looms before me. As fast, the edge of the island transforms into a bay. A sign of humanity—a mix of walls protrude from a rocky backing—materialize. The building sports few windows; a single glass door decorating its front. The cliffs of the bay shoot up around me as my body bullets for the ground. A meter from impact, a pocket of air embraces me as if I'm in a comforting hand. As my feet cushion onto the beach, a small puff of dust cycles into the air.

"Come to us," the sugary voice calls. *"Come help us, save us!"*

"Save me," says the voice to my right.

"Save me," says the child at my left.

"Save us," calls a jumbled chorus that pains my head.

Spin on my heels. "Who are you?" The yard is empty. The building at its back is dark, lifeless. "Where are you?!"

"My Princess," a too familiar baritone whispers from the building, as if his mouth is next to my ear, *"save me."*

Run forward, tears streaming from my eyes.

Papa!

The ground rumbles. The building bulges. A mix of red, orange, and yellow ooze like molasses from its few windows.

Kaaaa-boooooooommmmmmm!

A shock wave rips through its walls, tossing me ten meters and crashing upon my rear end. What structures remain flash blinding white. Puffs of gray and black rise into the sky.

"Help us!" the voices scream out, fewer each second.

Kaa-booommm! another explosion reverberates off the cliffs, sending rocks and boulders plummeting everywhere.

Clouds of soot pollute the air as if blackened ghosts haunting the skies, their shadows darkening the beach. Blisters bubble along my arms as the air boils around me. Flesh melts from my legs. Collapse to my knees, unable to scream.

"Please help us!" the voices call out, ever fading.

"Help me," I murmur back. Close my water filled eyes. Shake my head.

Ka-boom!

Wait… that wasn't an explosion.

Shake my head again.

Boom! Boom!

"Miss," a muffled voice asks, "are you okay? It's been a good ten minutes."

Open my eyes, which pain back from the mirror before me. "I—ah…" My body shakes in a cool breeze that doesn't exist. Several strands of my hairdo loosen and fall across the view. Finger brush them behind my ears. "Yes, I'm okay."

Streams of black streak the curves of my soaked cheeks. Grab a tissue from a box on the small table next to the sink and dab at the mess. What was that?! Glance at the amulet's reflection: the galaxy within is gray, its arms unmoving.

"Roberts here," the muffled voice says, pulling me away from dwelling on the matter.

"I'm sorry?" I ask.

"But, Sir," the guard continues, "I'm watching—" Feet shuffle outside the door. "Yes, Sir. I understand, Sir." The guard mumbles something, followed by a languid knock.

"Yes?" I ask.

"I have to step away," the guard says. "Far side of the hall, you'll find Ms. Matters' sitting room."

A sitting room—for serious?! "Ah, okay," I say. "And thank you!"

There's no reply. Press my ear to the door. Silence. I relieve the lock and edge the door open. The hall is empty.

Thank the stars.

Turn back to the mirror. The job of clearing the black lines from my face is not complete. I fold a fresh tissue and dab away. With no supplies to replenish my look, not that I can match Mom's artistry even if I did, my cheeks take on a gray sheen that mimics the amulet. I dab my lips several times, their buoyant shine dominating the deadened palette now living upon my face.

"Good enough," I assure my mirrored self. "Time to get outta here!"

Finish opening the door, its squeaky hinges complaining through the last third of the arc. A squeakier, backbone chilling, laugh echoes from the leg of the T-shaped hall.

Oh, no!

I flick the washroom light off and blend into what shadows appear. Dare not shut the door. Even if the opportunity exists, any motion a dead giveaway to my presence. Half crouch to the side of the toilet, watching out through the wide open entry.

From the hall's leg comes… Katie?

Her French-braided, lemonade-red hair aside, there is nothing before me that is recognizable as the girl. Unlike her mainstay of flesh revealing outfits, a floor-length, scoop neck gown covers most of her body. Even over her exposed arms—the dress being sleeveless—she wears a translucent shawl in the same emerald green of the dress. *You can't deny, for once, she looks a principled lady.*

Her companion, not so much so.

Karen Shaw—Katie's closest friend, subsequent Denise—looks a belly dancer in her plum-colored dress. The bodice, what there *is* of it, composes of a V-shaped plunge neck top and open mid-section outlined by a three centimeter oval band that arches from its vertex at the center of the bikini-styled top to each co-vertex just above the hips. At first glance, the dress' skirt deceives conservative. While it drops near to the floor, two long slits running along the front from its hem to upper thigh flash the full length of her bare legs with each step.

"Shame Denise couldn't make it tonight," Karen says, though her tone contains no discontent at being the sole awardee of Katie's attention.

Katie wheels around, red-faced, and flings her right pointer finger into Karen's face. "Don't say that name."

Karen throws her hands into the air as if being arrested. "Fine!" She stands that way as Katie twists away and moves toward the far side of the hall, to her room. Karen trolls after her a second later. "So, when are you gonna get 'em done?"

Only when at her door does Katie again face Karen. "No time soon." Irritation floods from her words. "DNA manipulation regulations are stringent, in particular for cosmetic reasons."

"Buy your way in," Karen says. "You've the money. Or just go old-school with implants and call it done."

Katie shakes a finger at her companion. "*No* fakes; It's *au naturel* or noway. Besides, my parents won't sign the consent."

"Screw that! Pile a wad of cash on the next unscrupulous doc you find, forge the consent, and before long, you're off bra shopping. Hell, I'll sign it for you. Or your boyfriend. I'm sure he'd be more than happy to sign for you."

Katie's face falls bleak, floods with red. Her voice begrudges, "He's not noticed."

"Come off it," Karen says. "How could he not know?"

"He just doesn't!"

Karen slouches, then goes stiff a second later. "Wait a minute," she says as if she discovered a secret treasure, "are you saying the two of you haven't yet—well you know…" She pumps her hips.

"Don't be ridiculous," Katie says, "And stop that." Karen locks her hips back in place. "Not that it's any of your business, but let's just say I've not yet let the girls out to play."

Karen laughs. "Men are idiots," she says. "Can't believe he keeps falling for that mound of padding."

Katie rolls her eyes. "Forget it, okay. Shouldn't have even told you." Katie clenches Karen by the arm, bringing a premature end to her giggle. "And if I find out you've told *anyone*…" Katie draws a finger across her own throat. "Got it!"

Karen rips her arm from Katie's grip. "Yeah, I 'got it'." Fear and hurt echo in her words.

"Besides," Katie says in a tone as if she never made the threat, "we've more urgent things to discuss. Dad says this weekend's a go, and as Junior Lieutenant of our squad, it's my responsibility to be sure we're prepared."

What did she say?! I lean forward, careful to not fall into the yellow rays blazing through the opening.

Katie's mouth opens, only to shut with an abrupt huff. She arches past Karen's shoulder; her eyes squint into the washroom.

Crap!

The amulet sways at my chest, just shy of the hall's exposing light. Dare not grab at it. *Please don't see it. Please don't see it.*

Karen angles her body sideways, her eyes joining Katie's in searching this end of the hall. "What?"

Both girls peer into the washroom. Half expect Katie to rush at me, but she instead shakes her head. "This stress! I swear it has me seeing things."

"Hmm," Karen says. She shrugs, grabs Katie's hand, and turns them both toward the bedroom door. "Let's share a cup of tea and, as you said, focus on the tasks at hand."

Katie glances back over her shoulder, but otherwise agrees to Karen's suggestion. Four steps later, the two pass through the oak door that delineates Katie's sitting room from the rest of the house and move out of sight. Shoo… that could have been a disaster.

Still, Katie's comments plague my mind. Was *"Junior Lieutenant"* a field hockey thing? Any team I've been on, we only had a team captain, maybe two. And for what might her dad need her to prepare a "squad" to do?

Curiosity yanks at me; prudence, though, wins the moment… in case they peek out from the door. Count off forty-five apples, then another fifteen, to be sure, before moving a muscle. I safeguard the amulet under my dress and scoot from the washroom. With the carpet to absorb my presence, cover the distance to Katie's room straightaway. The best that carries through the door, though, is nothing more than mumbles. Cup my hands between the wood and my ear.

"… couldn't say when," Katie's voice reverberates. The volume grows and fades, as if she's turning in a circle. "… go in… ready to deploy… notice."

Karen asks a question hidden to my ears by a brief but regular *clink*, metal on china.

"For now," Katie answers, "we do nothing different…"—*Clink. Clink. Clink*—"back to the… get suspicious…"

My ears hear nothing more that's coherent. Seconds later, the pair's voices fade altogether.

Wait ten seconds, then twenty, which becomes forty. Another full minute passes. Huh. Pull away from the door. Guess I should—

A boisterous laugh escapes Karen. Crunch my cupped ear again against the wood. What tidbits the door doesn't otherwise absorb evade a cohesive connection to one another. Save one obvious commonality that emerges in a hurry: there's much more to Katie and her friends than mere high school bullies. In what way, though, the thickness of the door doesn't publish.

"… have the plans in my room," Karen's voice pounds into my ear. "I'll get them," she says, each word growing louder as it came forth.

Launch from the door a step and a half when my right heel snags on the carpet. Stagger and twist clockwise. My left shoulder—"OWW!"—smacks into the wall but I otherwise maintain my footing. *Squeak* opens the door just beyond my right shoulder.

"Who in the Universe are you?"

Jerk my head toward Karen's voice, where she stands in the doorframe not a meter away. Her chin has fallen from her face, the spoils of surprise mine to take. Rather than flee, my feet hold firm as a strength greater than I've ever experienced surges through my body. The charm atop my cleavage bursts alive with a radiant glow, forcing Karen to mask her eyes. As if an instinct, ball my left hand, spin upon the balls of my feet in the same clockwise direction my body flung, and—*Crack!*—connect knuckles to right cheek.

Karen's face snaps to her left; blood flings onto the outer surface of the door she just opened. Her body flows along, as if slicing through gelatin. Off balance, she catches her left foot in the front panel of her dress and falls into the side of a chair just inside the room. She bounces off its cushioned arm, half rolls, and smacks back first onto the floor. An audible *whoosh* escapes her mouth.

Glance at my still balled hand, then back to Karen. She gasps for oxygen.

What have I done?!

Never have my hands acted in that way. Through my brothers' devious antics (and there were many!), through my mother's perplexing mix of despotic oversight and emotional detachment, and even through every taunt, browbeating, and insult Katie tried laying on me, never has such extreme aggression burst from me. From where that came, I fear knowing. Yet the deepest part of my being comforts in the assurance that when it needed done, I'll get it done. An act any less could have been futile... as if signaling surrender before the war even began.

"Karen?"

Katie's figure steps into my peripheral view, overshadowing my stomach's consternation with a more immediate concern. If this is a war, my run-in with Karen is but the first battle. Overcome with an abrupt fatigue, my well-being cannot bear another so soon. The closer she comes, the more my muscles shake. Wipe away tears that, for how long, I didn't even realize where there.

Katie rushes to her friend's side. "Karen!"

How has she not seen me?! Of the questions tormenting my brain though, that's one my curiosity need not have answered. As if an exclamation point on the opportunity, my mind screams, *"Run! Now!"* And so obeys every conscious and unconscious neuron that sparks within me. Clear the leg of the T hall within seconds.

"Who the—GUARDS!" Katie howls.

Xiomara, where are you?!

I round the corner with a singular focus: get past the door twelve meters down the hall. Three meters in, I haste past the first of the three windows now on my right, the dark oak doors to my left. Care not what's happening beyond either. Halfway to my destination, Katie again shouts for the guards. The scream is fainter, a comfort that she isn't gum stuck to my heels. Three meters to go, reach my right hand out, ready to grab the handle and yank the door open.

Instead, the door opens in greeting.

I know it is too optimistic to believe Katie's pleas will go unanswered. Though his face sparks familiar, the guard blocking my escape is shorter, less bulky than the original I encountered, yet still overall bigger than I. Drive my treads hard into the floor, tip my left shoulder, and aim for his chest. Crud if I'm getting trapped with Katie at the other end!

I slam full speed into the man… who pivots, translating the blow into a brushing glance across his right pectoral and into his upper arm. He staggers as he sidesteps, creating gap enough along the left wall.

Or so my ambitions perceive.

My already aching shoulder smacks the guard's biceps. A shock wave of C4 bursts into my arm and across my chest. Instead of pivoting around the guard, end up bouncing off the wall and sideways right into his arms. He wastes no time locking me in place with a grunt. "Miss Rogers, wait!"

Twist clockwise to break his grasp, to no success. Try shimmying an arm free, but the man's grip holds firm. I raise my left foot, ready to spring the stiletto's spike into the roof of his own shoe.

"Miss Rogers," the guard says again, "I'm here to help." He pulls me around to face him, forcing my foot back to the floor unsprung. "Zee sent me."

The milky green of his eyes… the freckles peppered across his neck and face… "You're the porter. Ah… Adrian, wasn't it?"

The man releases his grip and half smiles. "Close—Adrian's my twin. I'm Marcus." Marcus glances at the storm pouring from the hall, concern flashing into his eyes. "I need you to come with me now."

"You! Guard!" Katie rages from the far end of the hall. "Stop that woman!" She rushes forward. Fast.

Marcus is faster.

"Not today, you louse!" He yanks the door shut. A small can appears from nowhere within his right hand—*Where do these people keep getting these magic liquids from?*—with which he sprays the door's lever. Seconds later, he tosses the can aside, grabs my left and ushers me around the banister toward the elevator. "That should hold her for a minute or two."

"What will?"

"The spray," he says, taking us past the elevator and up the staircase. "It'll cement the handle mechanism in place, at least long enough for us to get out of here."

"GUARDS!" Katie's voice screams from the other side of the blockage, now muffled. *Boom! Boom! Boom!* the door reverberates.

I stop three steps up and pull at Marcus' arm back toward the elevator. "Don't we need to go downstairs?"

"We do," he says, yanking back, "but not that way. Doesn't take us where we need to go."

"GUARDS!"

Jerk at Katie's shrill outburst. Unfriendlies are sure to investigate the commotion before long. The intricacies of the mansion's layout a mystery, the only logical choice is to take Marcus' escape route. Still, have to make out as if there's a choice. I'm no lemming.

"Where then?" I protest.

"Back to the party, of course," he titters.

Dah… where else would the man take you, Miss Paranoid? Then again, in the short time you've dealt with Xiomara, look where you've ended up—what you're doing!

Whether that extends to her colleagues, sense I'm about to find out.

"GUARDS!" Katie yelps.

From below us, "Yes Sir, we're checking now." The *clunk, clunk, clunk* of rubber-heeled boots against ceramic tiles carry up to the landing.

"We've got to go," Marcus urges. He doesn't wait for my concession.

We spend next to no time on the next floor, a mimic of the floor below except for the green patterned carpet. A chambermaid pushing a housekeeping cart along the landing gasps as we whip by, but Marcus has us around the banner and climbing the next set of stairs before she can react further.

As we crest the final staircase, Marcus pauses, a smile befallen his face. The door pounding two floors below has stopped, replaced with vociferous attempts at communication. Part of his plan or not, his magic spray confounds the guards in their efforts to free Katie from her makeshift prison.

Marcus puts his pointer finger against his lips and whispers, "This way."

From the stairs, we move through a small, plain antechamber into a larger lounge. Carpet again overlays the floor, but with a pale brown utilitarian thread. Two groups of couches and recliners, one set in an arc facing a low-budget projectratron, occupy most of the lounge. The rest contains a card table and four upright chairs. A handful of generic photos—a grab bag of outdoor nature scenes—break up the wood-paneled walls. Bless the stars, the room is empty. Marcus leads us past the furniture and through an off-white door at the far end.

In the shape of an L, a short, gloomy hall extends out ahead of us—a second, likewise dim, longer hall to our immediate left. Align the right side of the latter, the third of four doors is open. Bright light and classical music emanate from its interior. Hold my breath as a shadow passes in front of the light, then again twice more. When no one steps out, I mutter, "Where are we?"

"Servants' quarters," Marcus whispers. "This way." Marcus juts his chin toward the shorter hall.

The hall ends in a U-shaped collection of five closed doors. Marcus ignores those, instead choosing to lower us the two steps at our right and into another corridor. Save the slivers of moonlight piercing two small windows along the outer wall, the hall's unlit. Unfazed by the relative darkness, Marcus says, "Come on," then struts to the third of the three doors along the inner wall.

I pursue, taking care to not let my heels resound against the hardwood floor, the carpet having ended at the U. Before I even pass the first door—a faded brass plate reading *Storage A* on its face—Marcus arrives at, opens, and steps through the third door. As *Storage B* comes and goes, low grunts and shuffles exude from that last room. A handful of steps later, pass into *Storage C* and ease the door half shut when a whiff of mildew raids my nose.

AH-CHEW!

Marcus shoots an alarmed look my way, pausing in his effort to shuffle a queen mattress away from an empty bookcase.

"Sorry," I mouth.

"Hello?" a man's voice carries from the hall's entrance. "Is someone there?"

Marcus' eyes bulge. "Grab hold," he instructs as he moves to the far end of the mattress. The unsupported half wavers back and forth.

I rush to the loose end as what has to be the squeaky hinges of *Storage A* echo the length of the hall.

"Move it against those boxes," Marcus says as he juts his chin at a stack a couple meters our right.

With no time to spare, we slide the mattress aside in seconds. Marcus returns to the bookcase. He kneels and shuffles his hand along the rear underside of the second shelf from the bottom.

Click.

He stands and angles the bookcase open in the manner of a hinged door. At that same moment, the footsteps of our curious guest abound from the wall shared with *Storage B.*

"Quick," Marcus says. He guides me through the half-height opening hidden behind the bookcase before shuffling through himself. He then pulls the case shut until there's another small *click*, extinguishing what little light there was. "You can stand," he whispers, "but don't move."

A second after closing the door, complete darkness gives way to rough outlines. A second later, understand why Marcus doesn't want me to move. Not half a meter from us, a tight spiral staircase rushes downward. Next to me, Marcus' shape sharpens. He works a slender tube from a thigh pocket: a penlight.

How is this so vivid?!

I shield my eyes from the sting of sudden brightness. Marcus' mass slithers past me and steps downward to the first stair. "Hold my shoulder."

I move my free hand to his right shoulder. He lowers another stair and pauses; presume to be sure I'm matching him. I take the first stair, then together we take the next and the one after that, falling in-sync with one another. Ten steps along, my eyes adjust to the penlight. The framing of the stairway crystallizes before me, as if the miniature light is bathing the passage in sunlight. Though I no longer need Marcus' shoulder, my hand remains in place; my ankles appreciate the extra stability of his mass given the narrow, triangular steps.

We circle clockwise, deeper and deeper. Just as my strained feet think we'll never stop descending, the staircase ends in a miniature vestibule similar to the one from which we started. Marcus focuses his light two-thirds of a meter from the floor. There, in plain sight, is a small red push button. He raises his booted left foot and depresses the toggle.

Click.

The wall before us loosens. Marcus tempers it open, fluorescent light flooding over us the wider the gap grows. He side-squeezes through just as it grows wide enough. Free of the passage, he turns back, "Wait here," then shrinks the opening all but the final centimeter. A minute later, the portal widens again. As if exiting our limo again, Marcus' outstretched hand beckons me into a waiting cart. He takes a moment to *click* the false door shut before boarding the vehicle himself. He depresses the accelerator and brakes us from the mansion's sub-garage and onto the path leading to the preparation building.

"Do you think anyone saw us?" I ask.

"No worries; the garage was empty," Marcus says, though hesitation intertwined his words. "I'll have you back at the party before anyone pieces your side jaunt together."

I sneak a glance behind us. "I'm not worried." Turn back to find Marcus smiling at me.

"Good," he says, chuckling. His left hand digs into another of his pockets. "Here, from Xiomara." A tiny, sealed vial of a bright bluish liquid is in his hand. "Use it to wash the die from your hair."

I accept the container from him. "What magic is this stuff?"

"Ah… *shampoo.*"

"Oh." Sure… your commonplace tiny unmarked bottle of florescent liquid… that'd be obvious to anyone.

"I'll drop you behind the prep building." Marcus points ahead, the building growing before us. "Circle to the outside, right." His finger arcs in the direction. "There's a woman's restroom that side of the building where you can wash out the die."

My torso twists at the house. "But Xiomara?"

"She's done and left. Wanted me to apologize on her behalf and said to let you know she'll reach out before the weekend's over."

"Oh." Don't hide my disappointment. Am I ever going to get my questions answered?

"One other thing," Marcus says. "Here." He hands me a small paper folded in thirds, its two flaps secured by a metallic sticker: a rose encircled by tiny golden stars.

"What's this?"

"Open it, memorize it, eat it."

"Pardon me?"

"Time's short." Marcus slows the cart. The preparation building looms large. "We'll get you a transponder soon. For now, if there's any trouble, hit four-one-one on any phone or communicator. When prompted, recite the code.

"But," he continues, "you need to memorize it—now—then eat the paper. We can't have that falling into the wrong hands."

"Wrong hands? What wrong hands?" This guy's as confusing as Zee!

Marcus stops us mere meters from the cart port and turns full attention to me. "Different circumstances, I'd be happy to explain, but I'm working way outside my directive for the night. For now, I need you to memorize that code, eat the record, and let me get you to safety."

The man hasn't failed my blind trust as yet. The sincerity of his words reflecting in his eyes, my fingers pull at the paper's halves. Try as I may, though, the sticker doesn't release.

"Sorry," Marcus says, "press with your left thumb."

Do so. The label dissolves as if having never been there. How'd these people manage that?! Fold out the flaps and read *Jay-N-oh-four-four-nine*. Look up at Marcus. "That's my—"

"Don't tell me," he blurts out. "That's not for me to know. Now eat it, please."

Pop the note into my mouth and chew. As with the label, the paper dissolves quicker than snowflakes falling upon a campfire. Leaves a slight strawberry taste in my mouth.

"Thank you," Marcus utters, slumping back in the seat. "You should get to the restroom and rinse your hair, then go enjoy the rest of the night with your friends, as if nothing happened. I'll calm things back at the house."

But so much *has* happened. So much I need to talk through with *someone*. A million questions want to hurtle from my mouth, but several voices pop from the loading dock of the preparation building: "… claims she was only going to have one," one voice carries on, "but they were so good, she couldn't stop drinking."

Even with the waves of turmoil in my skull, can't help but chuckle at the report. Unbelievable!

Marcus tenses. "Go!"

He's right; once again, any opportunity for enlightenment has expired.

"Thank *you*." I lean in and place a small kiss on his cheek, then twist out of the cart, intending to head straight for the side of the building. The exigency of avoiding discovery aside, my hand holds firm to the frame. "Please," I ask, turning back toward him, "tell me why Xiomara… you… why so much interest in *me*? I'm a nobody."

Shock flashes across Marcus' face. "Didn't she tell you?" he puzzles, then rolls his eyes. "Of course she didn't tell you," he says, more to himself than anyone else. He leans across the seat. "Ask Xiomara. Answering that isn't my place."

I drop my hands, droop my head. Choke back any further plea. Fight at the water filling my vision. "Forget it," I murmur. "Just go."

Though it should, the cart doesn't move.

"But…" Marcus pauses until he regains my eyes. "I can say with the whole of my heart—with undeniable certainty—that, of anyone, you are the most polar opposite of a nobody."

CHAPTER ELEVEN

WE'RE GONNA DO NOTHING! I shoot up the rest of the stairs. "You can't let them execute her as if she's a nobody!"

"What the—!" MissyAnn bucks up from the bench upon which she is sitting and draws her pistol. Points it dead at my chest.

"*¿Quien diablos?*" Mariana half-shouts, but otherwise remains in her seat.

No one else is about, as it's still early in the morning. Maybe between three and four, though I've no way to know. As no one was awake when I headed to the toilets, I expected the same on my return.

"Lower your weapon," Mariana instructs Ma, then to me in a quiet but authoritative tone, "Why are you awake? What did you hear?"

My ears expected to hear nothing. The gibberish of their hissed whispers—two snakes engaged in more than a causal conversion—hit them halfway up the stairway. I stopped there, unsure what to do. Between the low-wicked lanterns along the corridor and, where none are, being able to see well enough without one, I carried no light with which to broadcast my presence. Bounced between clearing my throat or forcing a cough, then decided it was best to walk past as if there was nothing abnormal about the situation. A girl's allowed to pee, right? With each step closer to the exit, the exchange became more vivid—MissyAnn was reporting out—and I couldn't avoid but to hear.

Two meters from emerging, of whom they spoke registered with my ears.

Katherine.

She's still alive! I halted, unable to avoid listening as Ma confirmed the fact again—but only for the night! I couldn't just stand there and not take action!

"Earth to Jane? Are you there, *Jane*?!" MissyAnn says, lips pursed, eyes narrowed at me.

"Uh… sorry," I say, coming back to the moment at hand.

"Jane," Mariana commands my attention, "how long have you been there?"

"Long enough. How can you talk about Katherine like she's inconsequential?"

"Who?" the two say in unison.

"*Katherine*—Paul's fiancé."

"Sweetie," Mariana starts, "we don't know…"

"It *is* her."

"Rumor is that the prisoner is a recent deserter," Ma says, a hint of support in her words.

Mariana looks at us. "The timing suggests as much," she says after a moment of what seems introspection. "All the more reason for us to not get involved. It's a lure to draw us," she angles toward me, "you in particular, out. I won't allow that to happen." A sternness settles on her face. "There's nothing we can do."

I stomp at her. "I guess I was told wrong." From the corner of my eye, Ma's gun twitches but remains pointed at the dirt floor. "You only care about yourself and this," I wave my arms out as if showing off a grandiose display, "this little world you've cocooned yourself within."

Ma's mouth drops open. I sicken as soon as the words seep from me. I've known the woman less than twenty-four hours, all of which she's been nothing but giving, caring. Stern, but always from a place of heartfelt concern.

A mom.

All the same, there's my commitment to Paul and Katherine. I'll do anything for even the slightest chance of reuniting the pair. Can't live with myself, let alone even look at Paul, squandering such a chance. I stand my ground, doing my best to hide my regret at playing so dirty. "I thought this team was about helping escapees, or is that all for show?"

Mariana dips her chin, shakes her head side-to-side, sighs.

Ma's eyes, though, shoot a burning disapproval through me. She rocks toward me, possibly intending to jump me right here, to rip me to shreds. Mariana positions herself between us, her focus on Ma. "MissyAnn," she commands, "you're dismissed. Go get some sleep. We'll finish in the morning."

Ma releases her stare down and snaps to. "Yes, ma'am." She salutes, turns on her booted heels, and heads for the dormitory. My ears think she mumbles something about *tomorrow being too late*, but if she did, Mariana hasn't noticed. The female Vasquez watches after Ma until she blends into the darkness, then focuses her attention on me.

Half expect a browbeating—I've been harsh—yet it's sympathy, not anger, written on her face. She pats the bench next to her. "Please sit."

My brain tells my legs to hold firm, but my ashamed heart compels me otherwise. "I'm sorry," I say as I sit. "You took us in on faith and have only been kind since. I shouldn't have said—"

Mariana grasps my left hand with her right and gives it a squeeze. "It's okay, dear. You've bold words," my eyes drop from her own, "but," she pauses until they again look at her, "they're laced with truth."

Huh?!

The woman's head shakes in a small arch. "You're not mistaken. I *am* protective of 'this little world' in the interest of self-preservation. But not to cower away. So that, for as long as I'm still breathing, I can provide a haven for those who need it the most."

My heart wants to erase my outburst. Still… "We can't just let them kill her," I insist, though the words come out with more desperation than inflexibility.

Mariana squeezes my hand again. "We can." A tear races down her cheek. "Keeping us safe has demanded more tough decisions than I'd burden anyone with. This, perhaps, is one of the toughest. I'm sorry, my dear, the answer is no."

"But Paul…," my resolve stammers, "I promised…"

Mariana takes me in her arms and squeezes, our tears mixing on our adjoined cheeks. Several seconds of silence pass as we hold together in mutual sorrow. "The unfortunate part of promises," her voice whispers into my ear, "is that, for circumstances beyond our control, they sometimes break."

I push back from the embrace. "Not mine. I'm going for her, with or without you!"

Mariana smiles small and, with the cuff of her long sleeve nightgown, dabs the tears from my cheeks. "Sweetie, I've no doubts about your confidence and boldness. In fact, I admire them! But don't let the combination make you flush with blind courage. Work past your emotions and focus on the facts. In all the time you've spent in that place, was there ever a public execution? Did you ever even *hear* about one?"

I shake my head side-to-side with reluctance. Not that I desire to answer otherwise, just don't want to concede her point.

"I thought not," Mariana says, "because there's never been one. So why now, after all the time you've been here—heck, after *all* the time I've been here—would they make such a spectacle? Perhaps there's been a policy change, or someone in charge wants to make a point… but I think not." She looks deep into my eyes. "I know you think not too."

Any resolve in my shoulders falls away. My head follows. "You're right," I say, "it all seems suspicious."

She smiles, not broad with satisfaction but narrow, with only the slightest uptick at the corners. The smile of someone who doesn't want to be right.

"When we first met," Mariana says, "I told you I was choosing to trust you. At this moment, I'm again choosing to trust you. To trust that, as hard as this is, you *will* let it drop. I'd hate to post a guard outside your room. Can I trust that you'll not pursue this?"

My heart breaks into a thousand pieces as a devastated Paul consumes my thoughts. Every soulful part of me urges my lips to defy Mariana, to say, regardless of her misgivings, that I'm still going to fight. The mindful part of me pushes back. Without Mariana's—and the team's—help, going it alone will land me a prisoner or even in a grave. In either event, the outcome for Katherine will not change. My head bobs up and down as fresh tears flow down my cheeks. "I need to be the one to tell Paul."

He'll never forgive me.

"I understand," Mariana says. She squeezes my hands in unison. "Let's get some sleep. I suspect tomorrow to prove demanding of us all."

She stands, lifting me with her. We hug again.

"I am so sorry," I murmur into her ear.

"Me too." She pecks my forehead with her lips. "Now, off to *your* bed."

I break our embrace and step toward the western part of the cavern. From behind me comes a disapproving "*Um-hmm.*"

"Oh, crud," I utter. *Does she know? Stupid question…* of course *she knows! You're in his shirt and not much else!*

I flash turn on my right heel and head for the dormitory and my actual room. Sneak not a glance back the entire way to the perimeter of the cubicles. I sense Mariana's eyes overseeing the entire trek, though she has to have lost sight of me not far along. At that hour, the camp boasts only a few lit lamps too scattered to overcome the dark distance between us.

I turn the corner toward my room, relieved to be out of her line of sight. To my right, MissyAnn's cubicle is dark and silent.

Thank the Universe; I can't deal with her wrath right now.

I make haste down the passageway and yank my fabric door to the side. Notice the light first, then her upright outline at the foot of my bed, half a second too late. She whips the high beam at my face, a sound tactic. I shield my eyes with my right hand and bring my left arm across my abdomen to deflect any low blows. Shift my weight left toward my dresser, scrambling to put some distance between us while my vision adjusts.

MissyAnn sighs. "What in the stars are you doing?"

I blink twice, then lift my hand up to see Ma staring at me, confused. "I don't wanna fight you," blurts from my lips.

"Fight you!" A laugh busts from Ma. "I'm not here to fight you, you scraighead."

"But, back with Mariana… I thought you were about to jump me."

Ma again giggles as she bends at the small table at the end of my bed and sets the lantern there to cast a low light about the room. She flips her flashlight off, then squeezes past me. "It'd crossed my mind; you were quite disparaging of Mariana." She pulls the fatigues from the lowest drawer of the dresser. "Your hostile approach aside," she opens the shirt drawer, "you weren't wrong to insist we help. Before you butted in, I was making the same appeal." She tosses the full uniform onto my bed and moves to the topmost drawer.

"I'm sorry, what?" I plop down on the bed, bouncing once. MissyAnn tosses the dark beige underclothes I selected earlier into my lap. "What are you doing?"

She ignores my question and instead says, "You didn't grab that shirt." Her eyes grow quizzical. I turn my face to the side, cheeks afire. "Wait a second," she excites, "you little minx… so?"

"*So…* what?"

"Don't go tryin' to play all coy with me." MissyAnn plops down next to me, an eagerness aflame in her eyes. "Don't look at me like you don't know what I'm talking about," she said. "I'm not fallin' for the whole little-miss-innocence act anymore. Details, girl!"

My brow furrows. "Details?"

Ma flips her eyes at the ceiling, throws her hands into the air. "By the stars, do I have to spell it out? Was he as energetic as I keep imagining he'd be?!"

My cheeks crunch into my nose. *As energetic as she keeps imagining…?* "Oh, frick!" Jump from the bed and back into the far wall, as if Ma's contagious with some disease. As if putting literal distance between us will shield me from her implication.

"Wow!" Ma says. "That fun, huh?" She sticks out her bottom lip and shakes her head up and down. Then she freezes. "Or," her face flashes concern, "was he *that* bad?"

"What! No. It wasn't bad." A smile spreads across Ma's lips. "No. It wasn't good either. Well—it *was* good, but not like that. We're not like that. I mean, we didn't—*Ugh*! Nothing happened!"

Ma's head droops. "Ah, sure. Pretend 'nothing happened' all you want, but know I *will* get the details out of you. For now, though…" She leans over and picks up from the floor the bra and underwear where they landed. She tosses them at me. "Hurry and change. Our window of opportunity is closing." MissyAnn pushes up from the bed and ogles at me with the eagerness of a dog waiting for a treat.

I scowl back. Two seconds pass that way when it registers, "You changed." Ma not only changed camos from a green/brown mix to black/gray since Mariana's dismissal, but she enhanced her on-person arsenal. Her shoulders support the straps of a thin backpack. Her left hip boasts a second pistol. Around her waist, a couple of grenades and distended snap-flap pouches. She sports an ivory-handled blade strapped along the side of her right calf. She decorated each wrist with a watch, the left of which she peeks at.

"Well," she says, "get changed already!" She eyes me up and down with a desirous smirk.

I tug down on Paul's shirt to stretch what limited discreetness it provides. "I'm not changing in front of you!"

"For serious? I just saw you as raw as the day you were born not hours ago," she protests. I reply with a death glare. "Crickets," she balks, but turns around all the same.

"Eyes," I bark. Does she think I don't see her peeking in the mirror?

Ma huffs but closes her eyes. All the same, turn my back toward her. As I fast swap panties, she hums. Draw my arms and the utilitarian brassiere inside. Unclasp the lacy version and let it fall to the floor over its relative. Securing the hooks of the replacement, realize I've been humming along—something familiar about the tune snagging at a memory I can't quiet place. I part my lips to ask when the humming stops mid-measure.

"By the way, how's that gash on your leg?" Ma asks.

"Well," my mouth replies, my mind engrossed by the song. As the question registers, realize I don't know. The cut has quieted since I redressed it after showering. In fact, other than the slight tightness of the wrapping, notice no pain or discomfort. I turn to the side, lift my right foot to the tabletop, and peel the cloth from my thigh.

"Huh."

"'Huh' what?"

Drop my foot back to the floor and toss the wrapping on the table. Other than a light discoloring of my normal warm beige tone, the cut has disappeared. "Mariana's salve is effective."

"I suppose so," MissyAnn dismisses my observation. "Does a decent job of reducing pain. Keeps infection at bay, of course."

Wow! That's an underwhelming testimonial.

I flick the worn undergarments to the corner with my foot and tiptoe to the bed to grab the rest of the clothes. As I bend forward to retrieve the pants, the thing about Ma's tune hits me. I'd whistled the same in the showers. "What song was that?"

MissyAnn jerks to the side with a gasp. "Jeez you're a sneaky one tonight. Good thing, seeing as what we're about to do."

I slide the pants on. "That song you were humming, what is it?"

"Mahoney hums it when he thinks no one is listening." I start to take Paul's shirt off. "Musta worn off on me." She brushes aside a strand of hair fallen over her eyes. I hesitate a tick to ensure she isn't sneaking a peek. "Some ancient song. He told me the lyrics once." Her eyes remain shut. Scurry Paul's shirt off and toss it to the corner, fit the other over my body. "Something about when all else feels lost, love is always in us, eager to bloom forth like a flower."

I sit on the bed. "Hand me my boots, please?"

"Ah, so now I may view Your Highness?"

It's a sarcastic question, and though the words hit my ears, I don't hear them. Instead, the song hums over and over in my head. Then, in a flash, the hums turn to lyrics—and Papa. "'The Rose'," tenders from my mouth. "It's the song's title. Papa would sing it to me."

"That's nice," Ma says, but only with impatience, no empathy. She shakes the boots before my face. I snatch the offering and toss them on the bed to my right, then hurry my socks on. For serious, give a girl a minute! The boots are on and laced twenty seconds later.

"About time," Ma says. "Now let's go."

With that, she scurries out of my room and to the right. I pursue. We pass by Leo's room—he snoring with a soft whistle—and right again at the next corner. The short hall ends with a white-curtained room on our left. A large, masculine-oozing shadow dances across the semi-transparent cloth. No debate, its owner Mahoney.

Ma slips through the cloth door without hesitation. I lemming the maneuver.

"Thought you mighta changed your mind," Mahoney says to MissyAnn as we enter.

Her hair tosses back in my direction. "Had to wait on this one."

Mahoney waves the justification away. "No worries; she's not here yet anyhow."

He no more speaks the words when the room fills with an earnest *knock, knock, knock* from behind a large wooden dresser placed against the right wall. I jerk away from the furniture and bump into Ma, who giggles. "Speaking of which…"

Mahoney steps to the dresser's side and reaches around its upper back. *Click.* The cabinet raises just off the floor, wheels popping into view at each of its four corners. He no more glides the furniture to the side when a slender body darts from the half-height entryway.

Claudia?!

It's her, but also not her. At least, not the first-impression of her reflecting within my head.

The girl has her hair pulled into a tight double dutch braid, over which a pair of vintage welding goggles in an antique gold tone rest. Her upper half she layered first with a white pleated tunic whose sleeves end just below the elbows. Over that, a black and brown stripped leather corset-like vest with narrow shoulder straps and metallic gold front-clasps. A chestnut-brown guard overlays her left wrist. The lower half bears midnight black leggings with a leather-like sheen. Short-heeled chestnut-brown boots, laced with gold-tinted ribbon, run the length of her calves. Separating the two at her waist, a wide brown leather belt with a small, single-hand crossbow attached at one hip and a quiver of bolts at the other. Another quiver, this one full of faux-feathered arrows in various colors, slings across her back at a diagonal, a hard maple and black fiberglass armed recursive bow perpendicular to the arrows.

The look's appealing; the implication, not so much. To MissyAnn I say, "She's not going."

Claudia's excitement flashes away. "What?" She looks between the three of us, resting with Mahoney.

In a flat, undebatable tone, Ma says, "We need her." She too focuses on Mahoney. "Mahoney?"

The man looks between the two, then at me. "She's ready."

Out of the corner of my eye, Claudia regains composure, a big smile returning to her face. Even discounting the ironic role reversal, it breaks my heart to break the girl's heart. "Ready or not, there is no way she goes," I retort. "I'm already well onto Vasquez' crap list. She'll kill me—us—if we take her."

"She's gonna kill us for doing this anyhow," Ma says, only half under her breath.

Mahoney gives Ma a disapproving glance. She sticks her tongue out at him. He ignores the gesture and focuses on me. "This mission depends on stealth," his familiar *all business* voice says, "and Claudia's a natural with a bow. She's part of the team or there is no team—your choice." The gravity of his words sends a chill up my back.

Ma mouths *She's ready* as my vision shifts from Mahoney, past her, and to Claudia, whose eyes steel for the ultimate word on the matter.

My ultimate word.

Every part of my fiber wants to acquiesce, to lift the burden my heart has carried since Katherine's capture. But to risk the life of this youth just to appease my guilt is to only replace one burden with another. And should anything happen to her… *Mariana would skin you alive!*

"Your mother's bound to check on you," I say.

"Already did, before I left," Claudia responds. "Found her precious girl sound asleep. She won't check again tonight."

We stare at each other, unblinking. Confidence radiates from her, but its hard not to see the child beneath.

Our eyes engage. I try to look past her powder blue irises, past the child, as Mariana's words reverberate between my ears: "*Work past your emotions and focus on the facts.*" She presents well-prepared and ready, but anyone can appear a fighter on the surface. I sink into her, beyond more than just a gut feeling; almost as if I am her, as if I lived her experiences. She's a solid, well-trained warrior, born from the demands of survival, with the potential to be more potent than anything the Facility could ever hope to produce.

I smile widely. "So, what's our plan?"

"Excellent choice." Mahoney beckons us to a large table opposite the dresser. On its top are many maps and diagrams. He reaches over them to grab a half sheet of paper, crude sketches on its surface. "This," Mahoney says as we gathered at the table, "is the Building C holding block. The guards Ma milked say your friend"—Mahoney glances up at me—"is being held here. You familiar with this building?"

"In a manner of speaking. A teammate once was a runner for a top commander with an office there. Said he passed through three checkpoints before he'd much access to the bulk of the building. Even at that, a guard chaperoned him the entire time."

"Well, crap," MissyAnn pipes up. "Our guy also knew nothing."

"Oh, I know stuff," I clarify. Three pairs of confused eyes stare at me. "I'm not allowed inside, but I've spent a fair bit of time there. Or, rather, the ventilation ducts. Those into the holding cells are too narrow, but just outside the cells there's a guard station"—grab the paper from Mahoney and rotate it ninety degrees, jab my finger tip against the page about four centimeters from its edge—"about here, fed by a larger vent. This time of the night, there'll be one guard on watch and another roaming the floor. Duties rotate every twenty minutes."

"That sounds promising." Mahoney gives me a nod of approval. "Where can we get into the ducts?"

"You've a map of the complex?"

"Sure." Mahoney pages through the maps on his table, pulling from the stack a sheet fifteen deep. The sheet is a professional rendering of the eastern part of the upper courtyard, with *Building C* and its adjoining buildings well marked. I point to the smaller and only one of the three to the left of the principal building.

"The HVAC system here interconnects all these buildings." Circle *Building C* and its children with my finger. "We get in there, we get into the holding area."

Claudia joins the discussion. "That seems too easy. All that security inside the building, yet the ventilation is just *open* like that?"

"Fair point. The vents only go so far before they're blocked with thick grating. They also secured the more sensitive areas with what might be motion sensors. Haven't wanted to press my luck to find out.

"In our case, though, someone cut through a handful of the grating, including those leading to the holding cells. No idea who did it or why, but they have done us a big favor. Outside a blowtorch, I haven't yet figured a way past the sealed grates, let alone the sensors."

"Let's keep this basic. There should be a tunnel…" Mahoney shuffles through his maps again, bringing one not too deep to the pile's top. "Yes, yes… this is perfect… right here." The hand-drawn map shows a passage ending in the maintenance room. "Haven't used that tunnel in some time, but it should be passable." He double-points at the spot. "I'll get us there; Jane, you get us through the vents. Once at the guard station, we strike a minute after the shift change. Incapacitate the one guard, free the captive—"

"Katherine," I say.

"Yes—free Katherine, then back the way we came." Mahoney looks between the three of us. "All sures?"

MissyAnn shakes her head side-to-side. "The *maybe* fifteen minutes we'll have before the roamer returns will not be enough. He'll raise an alarm as soon as he finds his partner." She looks at me. "Jane, how long to get through the venting?"

I shrug my shoulders. "Silently, at least a half-hour. Forgetting that, ten minutes—but we'd be making a racket."

"Right," Ma says, "which means we need to take that second guard out as well. That'd give us at least a couple of hours."

"We'll be back here before they even know she's gone," Claudia adds.

"For sures." Ma winks at the insightful youth.

"Then we take out both guards," Mahoney concurs with a nod of his head. "We'll jump the second at the shift change."

"No kills though." Three pairs of confused eyes again stare at me. Claudia appears more so anxious than confused though, as if my words are her first realization someone could die.

A second of silence passes, then Ma chuckles. "You're a funny one."

"For serious." I look between her and Mahoney. "No one dies."

Ma bounces upon her toes, her mouth dropping open. Mahoney, though, vocalizes first. "Sweetheart, no matter how covert we are, there are many factors that could force us to act. Given your training, you know that."

I gruff, "My training is why no one need die."

Mahoney throws his hands up in surrender. "Your mission, your parameters: we do this non-lethal."

Ma rolls her eyes and turns from the table. "What a pile of scrag," she says with her not-so-subtle under-the-breath voice.

Mahoney shakes his head as he turns his attention to Claudia. "Did you find everything?"

"Yes, Sir. Everything is at the junction."

"Perfect! Let's move out." Mahoney grabs the lantern from the map table and shuffles to the cave entrance. "Claudia follows behind me," he instructs as he pauses there, "Ma, you bring up the rear." He then ducks into the portal, his light fading.

Claudia pulls her goggles over her eyes, gives the lenses a small twist, and follows Mahoney. Ma, meanwhile, flips the flashlight in her right hand on and sweeps the left out before her. "After you, *princess*."

Papa! Only he's allowed to call me that! Make to say as much, but Ma mumbles on about me kidding myself if I think Mahoney won't bend to my will. Any protest on either account will only fall upon deaf ears. I bend at the hips to navigate the opening. Ma's flashlight casts my shadow ahead like a stretched stick man.

"Bringin' up the rear," Ma says from behind me, "just the way I like it!" She pinches my buttocks!

"Ow!" I jerk upright; my head smashes against the low ceiling. "OW!" I'd no choice but to put up with my brothers' continual goading. Now I do, and I'm not putting up with your antics! I half twist back to look at Ma, but just blind myself in the light.

"You're welcome," Ma says.

"Huh?" Memories of my younger brothers burst before my overexposed eyes. Some good, like an afternoon of intense hide-and-seek at the park. They never found me that day! But most are a sampling of the irritating, vindictive pranks they'd pull that were, somehow, always *my* fault. As if Mom's precious baby James could ever do anything wrong!

"I said 'you're welcome'." Ma comes into focus again. She crouches down, ready to enter the tunnel herself, a big smile on her face.

"*Excuse* me!"

"I've seen that look on escapees before, when tidbits of the past come back. So, you're welcome; I'm happy to have helped jolt a memory back." The smile on her face dims, replaces with a look of anticipation. "So, what'd you remember?"

I shake my head. "This is not the time." As much as my heart desires to explore the memories, a literal life-or-death task is at hand. Besides, enough is enough. "And dammit, Missy, you've gotta cut that flirting shit out! I'm not attracted to you."

The light beam flips to the ceiling as she throws her hands up as if in surrender. "Okay—okay," she says, then with little conviction, "I'll stop." The light beam drops and her free hand shoots onto what she has of a right hip. "But know, I've a keen ability to read people, to see them for whom they really are." I believe she believes it is an indubitable claim. "One week tops, the true you will crave to be in my bed."

Being honest with myself, having spent so long as only an ID number, the attention's appealing—not just from MissyAnn, but Mahoney and all the others. Though misplaced and wholly inappropriate, Ma's flirts tickle at me in a way I didn't know I desired.

Don't you dare admit that to her!

"That will *not* happen," I say. "I'm not interested, and you've a committed boyfriend." Despite my insistence, the self-gratifying look on her face does not diminish.

"Eh… he's a causal companion, free to explore his options."

"Easy to say when you're his only option." My throbbing head done with the topic, I turn and start again down the corridor. "Well, until I arrived, that is," I call over my shoulder as the ceiling rises to the point I can stand again. I shouldn't have said that. Why did I say that? My eyes adjust to the low light and, within seconds, I make out the residual glow of Mahoney's lantern. Paterson's even less my type than Ma. *Plus, aren't you supposed to be starting your friendship over, starting right, with her?* I pick up my pace, half ashamed, half having no interest in whatever retort Ma has queued.

I follow the slight curvature of the pathway to the right. Mahoney and Claudia have stopped several meters ahead. Claudia points left, then disappears in the direction. As I draw near the two, find that the passageway breaks off in the direction Claudia stepped. She's standing just inside, next to a small pile of equipment, Mahoney addressing her.

"You found all four?"

"Along with extra batteries."

"Good," Mahoney says to Claudia, then turns his attention to me. "There you are. Let's get you equipped." He peeks past my shoulder. "Ma, move it!"

Several meters back, MissyAnn's beam bounces along the walls of the cave. I turn to Claudia, who hands me a sheathed carbon fiber handled blade they must have swiped from the Facility's weapons store. "Ma just secured this yesterday. Designed to strap to your calf."

"Nice." I reach down to do so, angling my behind away from the arriving, winded MissyAnn.

"Pulse rifle," Claudia says of the next item she hands me. Logical choice given it's a device with which I've trained. "And this," she hands me a mid-sleeved leather jacket, "I picked out special, from me, to you." The jacket is deer-fur brown, paler than her own vest, with black trim inlaid with antique copper dome studs. Two black ribs with similar studs run the length of the front from waist to shoulder. The shoulders are each covered in a hard black leather plate. Slip my arms in, finding the coat lighter and cooler than expected.

"It's a perfect fit!" Say it not to humor her: the jacket hugs me as if tailored for my shape. The right side curves similar to a thin, elongated S— the left side a mirror of the right—over the outer third of my breast and inward to my waist before flaring out again at my upper hips.

Claudia smiles big. "Let me help with the buckles." She brings the lower half of the jacket together and weaves each of the four bands there through their corresponding clasps. When the girl finishes, she steps back, beaming. "So?"

I bring each arm across my chest, then stretch them overhead. The jacket's snug, but comfortable and non-restrictive. "This is great!"

"Good look," Mahoney comments as he turns to MissyAnn. "You've that spare chronometer?"

"Right here." She removes the watch from her right arm and hands it to me. "It's wound full." The device is a combination timepiece and stopwatch, with classic hour, minute and second hands. Three twenty-three, ante meridiem. At last! The Facility's schedule is so ridged, not knowing the actual time is mentally awkward.

"Headlamps and goggles," Claudia announces, giving a set to each of us. Am certain I can get by without, but that's not the moment to broach the topic.

"Where did you get all this?" I ask.

Claudia angles sideways and points down the side passage. "From The Safe."

"'The Safe?'" Don't remember seeing anything like this in there? "Is that what you call the storeroom?"

MissyAnn answers first, a slight irritation in her voice. "The Safe is next to the storeroom. The Vasquezes keep our weapons and other equipment locked up inside, behind steel doors we salvaged from that lab you were in."

Claudia lights up. "Mom thinks she keeps the key hidden, but I found it about a year ago."

"These caves are our emergency escapes," Ma says. "Once Claudia found the key, we started using them to meet up for training."

"Ladies," Mahoney breaks in, "hate to break up the tea party, but time's not our friend this morning." He taps at his watch to emphasize the point.

All three of us reply, unplanned, in unison. "Sir, yes Sir." Ma snaps upright and salutes Mahoney. Claudia gives him a drawn out, sarcastic, "*Sooorrrrryyy,*" which blends with my own satirical, "*Sorry* we're keeping you". We look at each other and laugh.

Mahoney shakes his head, then flips on his headlamp and moves further into the caves. We all trail after him, still laughing.

Half an hour along, not only has the giggling long faded—navigating at Mahoney's pace is breath sapping—but the seriousness of our mission has set in. Not to mention, I'm turned about, and turned again. Drop my pace and space out from the leaders.

"How's he navigate these tunnels so fast?" I ask over my shoulder in a low voice. "My sense of direction is in knots!"

Ma chuckles. "He's spent *a lot* of time on those maps. Imagine they plague his dreams." She takes a deep breath, the passageway's incline being steep. As we level off again two dozen seconds later, she continues, "For those parts he can't remember, he'll follow the markers."

"Those designations written on the maps?"

"That's right. A compass direction, relative distance from the Facility, and depth. We mark them about ten centimeters from the floor at each end of each hall—in fact, there's a set." Ma angles her headlamp toward the floor of the corridor we are about to pass out of. Discreetly chiseled into the wall, S14-9 sits on top of SW16-11. "The top value marks the start of the tunnel and the bottom where it ends," she said. "The smaller the numbers, the closer to the Facility you are getting."

"So, where's camp then?"

"The main entrance starts at south-southwest nineteen, fourteen. Our old camp was much closer, west-southwest seven, five. We'll pass by the artery that leads there in another ten minutes at this hurried pace." For certain, our leader has us on no casual stroll.

"You know," I say, "he's very fond of you. Mahoney, that is."

"He's a friend," comes a nonchalant reply. I glimpse over my shoulder, catching Ma's eye. "What?" Whatever innocence she's trying to fabricate, I'm not buying. Swivel around on my heel, stopping us both. "What are you doing?!" she asks.

Scratch my jaw. "'He's a friend'," the dry challenge leaves my mouth.

Ma shifts her eyes past my shoulder. "We're falling behind." She tries edging around me, but I block her path.

She shuffles her feet, huffs, huffs again. "Oh, crickets!" She glances past my shoulder again, then back to me, surrender in her expression. "Fine! Mahoney is not just a friend. He's my *best* friend, a trusted confidant." She takes a deep breath. "I love him and, well, I'd do anything for him." A fierce seriousness flashes on her face. "And don't you dare tell anyone I said that, especially him!" Despite her stern words, behind her eyes there appears relief. At last, a glimpse of the real MissyAnn—the compassionate person Mahoney says is there—shining through.

"I swear, by the stars," I say, though am certain Mahoney already knows.

"Good. Now can we go? They're way ahead."

Turn around to find Mahoney and Claudia several meters ahead. Their lights fade to the left along the curve of the hall. We double time our pace until they're within eyesight again.

Neither being back instep with our teammates, nor knowing how they mark the cave system, leaves me any less disoriented. We weave down many passages that, after about ten minutes (as Ma has predicted), take us past the turnoff to the team's previous camp. Had Ma not pointed it out, I'd miss the cleft, not much wider than that which I hid from the guards less than—hard to believe—twenty-four hours prior, marking the entrance. In the sixteen minutes that pass thereafter, we go from W5-4 to NW4-3 back to W5-5 and—after several minutes of twists and turns that seem as if we are circling upon ourselves—end at a split in the passage, one leg of which starts E2-1. A low mechanical rumble echoes from the far end of the leg.

Mahoney stops our group here.

"Another fifteen meters that way," he points up E2-1, "should be the cave entrance. Make no assumptions. They monitor everything. We move with deliberate motives and, should I determine our plan's gone awry, we abandon the mission." Mahoney focuses on me. "*No* exceptions. Are we clear?"

Three simultaneous "Yes, Sirs" fill the tunnel. No giggling follows.

Mahoney nods, and our group begins the fifteen meters down the passageway.

Not two meters in, we bat our way past a thick mesh of cobwebs. While the deeper caves flip between the smell of course, over-stale bread and a wet, mud-covered dog, the cutoff tastes humid, but not stale. Rather, it boasts a complex mixture of viridity and rot interlaced with an acrid undercurrent of charred oil. Four meters further, mushrooms and other fungi appear on the walls. A grab bag of millipedes scatter before the beam of my headlamp. The closer the passage's end comes, the thicker the vegetation and variety of critters. Too, the stronger the stench of burnt oil, the louder the machinery running beyond. Mahoney stops us two meters from the end.

"Wait here, while I get the door open."

The three of us spread out across the width of the tunnel, me furthest left, Ma two steps back to my immediate right, and Claudia to the far right, in line with Ma. Mahoney, meanwhile, moves to the end of the passage and feels along the left side of what the sheen from our lights suggest is the back of a metal cabinet. A narrow smile plays at Mahoney's lips as his hand finds its goal.

An almost silent *click* follows.

Mahoney weaves his hands into two grooves about two-thirds of the way up the right side. He yanks. Nothing moves. He yanks again, his muscles ballooning under the skin of his arms. All at once, a metallic *pop!* rings past us as a fluorescent glow engulfs the passageway. Propelled by his own force, Mahoney's grip fails, and he flies backward, stumbles over his own feet, and slams back first into the wall. A distinctive *OOFFHH* of air shoots out his mouth as he falls to the ground.

"Oh, shit!" Ma's whispered words mimic those which cycle unspoken through my head.

I make to rush to his side—a repeat of Paul's injury haunting me—but MissyAnn speeds past me, throwing enough of a hip-check to knock me off balance. Brace my left arm against the wall to stay upright.

Rather than offer an apology, Ma kneels by Mahoney's side, turns off his headlamp, then pulls it from his head. She lowers the intensity of her own beam—I presume to not blind him—and surveys his scalp. Seeming to find nothing, she lifts his face to her own and studies his eyes. "Are you dizzy?"

I don't hear his answer, for Claudia's urgent voice grabs my attention. "Ah, *guys*..." She removes her bow and points its top tip toward the doorway. For all Mahoney's effort, the exit is open only two-thirds of its full width, but—with a couple steps to the right—the guard stepping through the room's proper door twenty-some-odd meters away is in full view, as are we to him. He turns and startles; a bewildered expression overtakes his face. For the moment, his pistol stays holstered at his hip, his pulse rifle slung over his shoulder. Engrained with the Facility's training, I know his weapons will not stay so for long.

Grab at Claudia to pull her into the relative safety of what of the door remains closed, but she steps forward out of my immediate reach. She nocks a blue feathered arrow into her bow.

"Claudia, no!"

My no-kill directive aside, she'll find no gratification in her actions. Your first kill haunts your subliminal thoughts day-in and day-out, often seeping to the forefront as a sober reminder of the inhuman darkness present in each of us. A darkness that will overtake one's essence if left to fester.

The arrow releases… and misses its target (Thank the stars!), instead burrowing into a small control panel mere centimeters to the guard's right. He glances at the now sparking panel, then back at us as he pulls his pulse rifle forward.

I turn again to Claudia before she can let loose another arrow to find her bow at her side. She looks at me. The reflective glow of the fluorescent lights against the side of her pale face intensifies. She flips off her headlamp. The lights flicker and buzz, pop out with a *PAUH!* I flip off my headlamp in understanding. *PAUH—PAUH—PAUH* three more go dark. With one left, Claudia pulls down her goggles, a big grin on her face… confirmation her arrow indeed found its intended target.

I drop my goggles to the ground. The glimmer of Ma's headgear combined with the half shine of the moon through the skylight is all my eyes need. Grab Claudia's biceps and edge her behind the door's protection. Ma shuffles at the opening. "No", I say, "Stay here! All of you."

With no time for protests, I bolt through the opening and at the guard. His trigger finger is at the ready, but the weapon itself still dips toward the floor. He, instead, peers at the ceiling. His vision, however, drops in my direction as the clunk of my boots overtakes the grumble of the machines. He squints, an uncertainty plants on his face. Too late, he raises the gun.

I bat—*POOMB!*—the rifle to the side with my left wrist. Its shock wave crushes with an ear-ringing boom into a metal cabinet in that direction. Swing my balled up right hand across his left chin. His head snaps likewise, which half spins the man. I twist and kick out sideways with my right foot, connecting with his rear and fling his midsection into the door. His forehead follows half a second behind, hitting the metal door with a decisive *crack!* His body slumps to the floor.

To his misfortune, they always assign newbies to the crud jobs.

CRRUUNCH!

A spasm shoots from my left shoulder down the same arm and my chest, but no pain follows. I smell the garlicky breath of his partner only in time to shift counterclockwise enough to deflect what will have otherwise been a blow to the side of my face. I teeter between the motion and the strike, but hold my footing, and arc my still balled up right toward the man.

He grunts as I connect with his chest, then gasps for air, wheezing several times. His weapon dips to his side. I grab its scope and yank forward. Slam my knee into his pudgy waist. He doubles over as the rifle loosens from his grip. I whip the butt around and slam it across his face. His head jerks to the side, then he collapses to the floor, unconscious.

"Flipping scraigs! What was that?!"

I switch on my headlamp—normal brightness—and rotate to find MissyAnn stopped about halfway between the cave and the downed guards. I ignore that she's ignored my instructions. "Training. Like it or not, I'm a product of this place."

Also ignoring my instructions, Claudia trails Ma by a handful of steps. At her side, Mahoney stands off-kilter, her shoulder his crutch. Claudia's torso dips toward their common center. I'm pretty sure she'll crack in half if he leans any further into her.

"Not what I meant." Ma holds out my goggles in her right hand and flicks a free finger toward the slouched guards. "You've no goggles, so how *did* you do that?" Her voice seems laced with both confusion and concern.

I shrug. "I don't know; I'm just able to see."

Ma stiffens. A wariness befalls her face.

"You can see in the dark!" Claudia says as Mahoney and she join Ma.

"Just outlines and shades," I clarify, "but, yes. Sometimes finer details if there's enough ambient light."

"That's amazing!" Claudia says. MissyAnn radiates none of Claudia's enthusiasm. She seems both hurt and put off by my confirmation. "What else can you do?"

Before I can answer, Mahoney says, "*That's* a question for later." He glances to MissyAnn. "Ma, bandage their heads and get them bound."

"Yes, Sir." Her expression relaxes a slight bit as she slips back into mission mode. Still, she approaches me with reserved steps.

"So, Jane," Mahoney says, "where is this vent of yours?"

I orient myself to the room, a second later pointing to a pathway between two sets of shelves on the right about two-thirds of the distance from me to my teammates. "Should be around the corner there, far wall." I tramp in their direction as Mahoney and Claudia follow several paces behind Ma in mine. Smile at Ma as we two cross paths. She doesn't reply in kind, but passes by as if I'm not even there. Want to explain, but, despite being encumbered, Claudia and Mahoney are already near the shelves' ends. Hurry to them.

"You okay?" Mahoney says as I rejoin the pair.

Presume he means the altercation, and not Ma's sudden distaste for me. "Shoulder's gonna be sore, but yes, I'm fine—thanks to Claudia's gift!" The girl wears a wide smile.

"Good." He turns to Claudia. "Go help MissyAnn, please. Jane should be able to assist me from here."

"Sure," Claudia says, a bounce in both her voice and step.

Mahoney braces himself on my healthy shoulder, and the two of us watch Claudia go in silence. When she advances about three meters, he nudges me down the pathway between the shelves. "We need to talk." His words speak with an irritation I've not heard from him before. An urge to apologize hits me. For what in particular, I don't know. I was straight with MissyAnn—I've no clue how I can see in the dark.

"I should call this mission right now," isn't what I expected to hear next out of his mouth.

"Sorry, what?"

"That mess back there," he nods in the rough direction of the fallen guards, "does not scream stealth."

"I, ah—"

"No worries; you did what you had to, given the circumstances. I'd expect nothing less." A cringe sets on Mahoney's face as he takes a deep breath. "It's my right ribs. They're bruised pretty bad, if not fractured."

I stop. "Oh, crud! We need—"

Mahoney holds up his free hand in a hold-on-a-minute way. "I'll be fine, at least for the time you ladies need. But my role in this mission ends here. I'm putting MissyAnn in charge for the rest of the rescue."

For real?! Didn't he already brand this *my* mission?

"Don't let her reaction put you off," Mahoney says, misreading my confusion. "You caught her off guard, but I assure you, she's focused." We connect eyes, his own flush with assurance. "She *will* come through for you."

"I know," I capitulate. Not that I've the history to know she will. Crud, we met not even a full day ago. But Mahoney's solid, and that's enough for me to have confidence that she will. Though I've known him only hours longer than Ma, there's an immediate, implicit trust between us. From where it comes is as much a mystery to me as being able to see in the dark, but so natural is our connection that his genuine nature already endears a special portion of my heart.

Although taken aback by Ma's sudden change in demeanor, Mahoney's impression weighs of lead over me. Even if the gentleman within him gives no such sign otherwise, my actions must have caught him by surprise. Maybe even offended him, unintentionally or not, that I've not confessed my ability before now. Have I violated his trust? Do I owe him an apology?

Before the words can leave my mouth, he says, "Worry not—everything always works out as it's meant to." He pins a small kiss on my forehead, then restarts us down the walkway. "Now, let's find that grate."

CHAPTER TWELVE

"SEEMS THINGS ALWAYS WORK OUT as they're meant to."

I glimpse up from the sink, the mirror above confirming the smug grin behind me. Not that I need it to: her grating voice being one of those maddening, overplayed songs my mind lacks any wherewithal to shake.

"Leave me alone, Denise."

Shut off the water and twist to face her. Two girls—neither I recognize—stand on each side of her. The three have on identical knee-length, party dresses in a Rainbow Sherbet mix of colors, with coordinated handbags and open-toed heels. Denise, in the juicy orange, swaggers toward me.

"Hmmm…" She gives me a once-over. "I don't think so." She fingers the dry half of my hair, the die not yet washed out. Water from the wet half runs down my back. My body shivers from the chill—or, perhaps, nerves. She flicks her left hand at the sink, several bunches of shampoo suds still present within. "What's this about?" A fiendish annotation laces her words.

I bat her fingers out of my hair. "That's my business."

"Ooh… a little feisty, are we?" She fades half a step, then quick locks a clump of my hair and jerks backward. My body follows and smacks my hips against the side of the sink at an awkward angle. "Wrong answer, Sewer Rat. *I* belong here, *you* don't." She yanks further, forcing my weight to my toes and my behind part way up the sink's edge. Slivers of stress cut from my toes to gut as the pain trickles down my cheeks.

"Denise!" The most petite of the three—in red raspberry—advances, mouth gaped, eyebrows crunched. Seems this isn't the restroom visit she expected.

Denise flings a grunt over her shoulder. "Stow it, Sloane!" She releases her grip, retreats a meter, and surveys me again. "Gotta hand it to you, Rat, you clean up well." Her tone carries no graciousness. "Never imagined I'd see you wear something so…" Her pupils lift to the ceiling as if someone has printed the right adjective there. "Un-granny-like." Her brown eyes again latch onto me.

"Screw you!" Whoa—did that just pass my lips? Mom would not approve of the slur. Then again, as one to not mince words, at least when she addresses me, my aggression might impress her. "As if you have any clue who I am." As if I want you to! Shuffle toward the exit.

"Where do you think you're going?"

I step twice more. *You need to get out before this worsens.* "I don't have to put up with you. I'm leaving."

Denise snickers. "Yeah, I don't think so." She snaps her fingers at her companions. The bulkier of the two—lime—slides in front of the door and blocks the only exit.

I continue toward the door. *Don't let Denise spook you; she's harmless… and perchance not…* With the right distraction, I can plow past the brute. "What are *you* doing here? After that lipstick incident, I'm amazed Katie would invite you to come."

Too late, my mind registers my mouth's mistake. Not so for Denise, whose eyes pop. "You *were* in the locker room." Her voice drops into a growl. "You planted that lipstick!"

The situation is worse, but not beyond escape. Shrug, then dart for the doorway. About to pass the brute, my right foot slides across a damp spot. My leg collapses toward the brute, who knees my thigh. I fall to the floor with an immediate cramp.

"Pick her up!"

The brute hauls me to my feet, keeping one hand braced upon my shoulder while the other binds my wrists behind my back. Wiggle, but her grip just tightens.

The situation is much more than worse, my attempt to rattle Denise having backfired. She rushes over and stuffs her pudgy face only a handful of centimeters from my own. "You little bitch! Do you know how long I've been friends with Katie Matters?"

My injured thigh twitches, the restrained arm likewise. "Years?" I offer, though from her tone, presume she didn't expect an actual answer.

"You bet your ass years!" A fleck of her spittle lands on my cheek. "Best friends since we were two. And what happens when that lipstick turns up in my bag? 'We're done' she says! Just like that. No chance to defend myself. Like all that time means nothing. 'We're done' and she walks away."

"Hmmm," my loose lips prick at her, "seems you're the sewer rat now."

SMACK!

Sloane gasps as my face wrenches to the side. A tinny wetness teases my tongue before dripping down and off my chin. The ring on Denise's finger has done some damage.

Across from me, Sloane seems near hyperventilation. She looks at me, then touches Denise's arm. "Denise, she's a minor. I don't think—"

"SHUT UP, SLOANE!" Denise turns and walks deeper into the room, shaking her head. "That the two of you are siblings is beyond me."

Of course!

"DEWEY!"

He's with Denise tonight; he'll be just outside the door waiting, given the short leash she keeps him on.

Denise flips back around. "What the—?"

"DEWEY! HELP ME!" We aren't the closest of siblings, but he'll not let Denise do this to me. Right?

"Shut her up!"

Lime moves her hand from my shoulder to my mouth. *Bite her finger!* The girl's smart. She clasps both the bottom of my chin and the bridge of my nose such that my mouth can't open.

"He's not here." Denise's face glazes over as if she's lost her puppy.

How can that be? Mom said, *"having dinner with his girlfriend's family."* I'm sure. Unless… Oh crud!

Denise paces in a small circle, her brows in a tight scowl, for a full minute. When she stops, she stares at me with deep disgust. "Yell again and my friend will knock free your pearly whites—"

"Denise!"

Denise gives Sloane a death glare, from which the girl cowers back, before her eye return to me. "Am I clear?"

I raise and lower my head as best I can, considering the brute's grasp. Denise nods her chin, and my mouth loosens. I take a deep breath.

"Why do you think your brother's here?" Denise's words drip with suspicion.

He's gonna hate you forever. "He's having dinner with you." Denise rubs her neck, grimacing as she does. *But you need the distraction.* "Is that *not* the case?" I poke the bear.

Denise shuffles at me until the tips of our noses are about to touch. "B.S." The spit she includes latches onto my chin. Garlic and tuna seep into my nose. As unstable as Denise is, I try not to cringe; I've no desire to know what she'll do if I do.

"Honest," I say. "My mother said he was with you tonight."

Denise leans back, though keeps her eyes affixed to my own. "Huh." She tramps back toward her pacing circle. Her body dips as she walks. Three laps in, she goes erect. "That slut!" She flips around and looks past me to Lime. "That floozy Samantha Collins… she's gonna feel my wrath." Denise shifts her focus again to me. "But tonight, I start my revenge on your scum of a family, beginning with you." She retrieves her digicell, rose-gold with diamond trim, from her purse and taps the device's screen. "Remember this?" She angles the display in my direction.

The silliness aside, why is she showing me my spinning dress? "Yeah, so?"

A broad smile sets Denise's cheeks. She bounces atop her toes and brings the device near her lips. "Reset, fifty percent playback." She shoves the device forward such that it fills most of my vision. "Look close."

On screen, the skirt of my dress climbs half-speed into the air—higher, then higher again. "*Just a little more,*" Angelica's voice reverberates between my ears. How she conned me into that stunt… "*More,*" her voice echoes again, and again the dress's trim rises—*Oh, shit!*

I peek over the digicell. "Denise, don't you dare…"

The girl glows, her trap sprung. "Oh, dear," she mocks innocence, "seems someone forgot her undies today."

"Denise, *please.*" My tense muscles ache. There is a wetness around the hang nail I'm picking at.

"I admire the boldness—you've more than I do." Denise's wide smile goes wider. "But, Rat, you made this so darn easy; this *is* getting posted!"

She rocks her head up and down, her bottom lip pushes out. "With certain elements highlighted, of course."

I twist left and right, then left again. My arms burn but will not release from Lime's solid grip.

"You've been full of surprises today, Rat. I'd never have pegged you as a maverick." Denise manipulates the digicell. "For instance…" The screen fills with Angelica when earlier approaching James and I. "What's that annoying little girlfriend of yours named? Angie… Angel…"

"Angelica," I grunt, not needing the live-action fresher.

"Whatever." Denise flaps her hand in the air as if batting away a fly. "She'd love to see that passionate kiss on-line, don't you agree?" I twist back and forth again, to no avail. "I've the perfect caption: 'Love's first kiss'" Denise's feet dance. "Or was that not the first? Maybe, 'Sweet Love-birds'? Whadda you think?"

"Leave her out of this! It's not like that!"

Denise's laugh cannot be heartier. Lime's grip loosens—though not enough—as she too chuckles. Sloane cowers near the door, seeming unsure what to do.

"Amazes me how individuals like you are so very knowledgeable, Rat, yet so very clueless. That girl's hot for you and you're oblivious to all her passing glances in the halls. The way she lights up every time she sees you turn a corner? Goodness knows what she's like when you two are alone."

It'd never crossed my mind we are anything more than best friends. Best friends should be excited to see each other. Right? Sure, I love her and she me—we often tell each other as much—but it's all platonic. Isn't it? Friends can hold hands, snuggle while watching a movie, share a little *hello* peck here or there… *or… or…* "Crap, we're a couple."

"Ya think?" Denise mocks.

I'd no intention of saying that out loud. "Anything. Whatever you want, as long as you delete those videos!"

"Wow!" Denise grins. "*Anything* you say." She looks between her cohort. "That was easy."

And so reveals the truth of her harassment. "So what is it? What do you want?"

"Not one," she flings a V into the air with her fingers, "two. For two videos, you owe me two things."

"Fine." Ignore my gut's growing concern over what I'm agreeing to. "Two videos, two things." I try suppressing the desperation in my voice. "So…?"

"First, you're gonna record a video for me, admitting to fiddling with Katie's lipstick. You cost me *my* best friend. You're earning her back."

Not so bad. "Deal."

"Not so fast." Denise looks around the restroom, her view settling on the far stall. "You apologize on your hands and knees, in that puddle of toilet water." She pauses, perhaps awaiting my protest. As disgusting as her request is, those videos must go away. As I don't respond, she continues, "I delete the videos *only* after Katie takes me back."

Wow! Talk about infatuation!

"Still a deal, and that's your two things."

"Oh, no, Rat," Denise replies, "all that's just the first."

"No, it's two."

"Given the circumstances, I'd think you'd not be debating with me." Denise stops pacing and locks her eyes on my chest. "I want that necklace."

I gaze down. The amulet hangs outside my dress, shaken out by my struggling. The gentle glow of the galaxy within has returned. "Not a chance."

"Now Rat, you said 'anything' and that necklace is *something*. Are you reneging on your offer?"

Firm my tone. "The necklace is off limits."

"Here's the thing, Rat… no matter how this goes, that amulet will be mine." Her finger hovers over her digital device. "Last chance for civility."

"You call this civil?"

"Fine, we do this the hard way." Her finger doesn't depress; instead, she slips the device into her purse. "Chloe."

The brute's hand moves from my shoulder and works the necklace's clasp. I feel her grip on my wrists give. I twist hard and pull toward the door.

"Hold still!" Chloe snatches the upper back of my dress. "I wouldn't mind the chance to separate you from your teeth."

Her other hand re-tightens in proof any further resistance will be fruitless. Whoever this Chloe is, I've a distinct impression this isn't the first time she's restrained someone. Locked in place as I am, Denise is right about one thing: she's about to get my necklace. Instead of returning to the jewelry, though, the brute picks at the rim of my dress' bodice.

"Denise," she says, "she's wearing a DeVoe!"

"Doubtful," Denise dismisses the information. "A fake for certain."

"No, this *is* one—the tag looks the real deal."

Denise steps around to my left. Chloe yanks the lip of the dress in Denise's direction. After a moment, Denise backs up to her pacing spot. "Is this for real, Rat?"

I nod, Chloe's vice grip such that I can't reply otherwise.

"Who'd you steal this from?"

"No one." I squeak. Chloe's hand lets loose. I suck at the air.

"There's no way the salary of a glorified maid paid for that."

Lungs again oxygen enriched, I shoot back, "My mom's not a 'glorified maid'—she runs this household! She's amazing and underpaid for all the work she does." I don't know her salary or task load, but carry on in her defense. "Without her, the Matters would be an unorganized mess."

Denise rolls her eyes. "Think what you will, Rat, but in the end, she's the one cleaning the shit out of someone else's toilet. With her access to this place, she musta swiped that dress from one of Katie's closets?"

"She didn't steal it! It's a gift from my dad!"

"Yeah, sure, like he could afford a DeVoe on his weak paycheck. He's nothing more than a two-bit—"

Beads of sweat drip off my forehead, one stream leaking into the cut at my lip. Ignore the irritation and focus on a whole different irritation. "Don't you *dare* talk about Papa that way!"

"Oooo, seems I've found a sore spot." Denise says to her peers. Only Chloe acknowledges her with a small laugh. Denise glares at me. "Or what, Rat? You're not in any position to be making demands. In fact," she rubs her hands together, "I've a costume idea for our apology video." Denise opens her purse and retrieves a pearl handled switchblade. She twirls it between her fingers twice before gripping the instrument proper. "This dress seems *way* too nice for a sewer rat, wouldn't you say, ladies?"

The blade pops out with a snappy *click*. Denise's eyes flame with a perverted excitement as the polished metal glistens in the light.

Before I can object, Sloane speaks up. "I can't be part of this." The words quiver from her, but with defiance. "We're here to crash a party, not harass some teenybopper." *Teenybopper! For real?! Okay, now is not the time to quibble.* "This isn't right."

Denise turns toward Sloane. "Get outta here you wus—and if you tell anyone about any of this…" Denise twists her knife such that its reflected light dances across Sloane's eyes.

My eyes beseech Sloane's. "Help me… *please.*"

Conflict races over Sloane's face. *You almost have her.* "Sloane, you can stop this."

"SHUT UP!" Chloe yanks my head back by my hair. "One more word and I *will* knock more than your teeth out!"

I try spitting in her face as it hovers above mine, but my mouth's too dry to muster anything meaningful. A devilish grin forms upon Chloe's lips. She puckers up and lets a lazy trail of saliva drip onto my mouth. Though I hold mine shut tight, I still taste the aftermath of crab cakes.

"I'm sorry," Sloane says. To which of us she's directing her apology, I can't tell. Consider yelling when she opens the door to exit, but the booming music beyond makes doing so pointless.

"We're dumping her," Denise says as the door shut. "But, first, we've a dress to restyle."

"This will be fun," Chloe says, each word oozing pleasure. She releases my hair and clicks open her own handbag. A second later, it clicks shut. "And when we're done with the dress," her voice leeches into my ear, "looks like you're due a hair trim, too." She positions her free hand atop my shoulder, near the same ear.

Click opens what can only be a mimic of Denise's switchblade.

A glint of light reflects into the corner of my eye. As it disappears, the cool, smooth surface of metal runs down the back of my shoulder and across to my spine. She eases its side down the middle of my back until it slides just below the rim of the dress. The flat side twists just enough that its sharpness depresses my skin, my pulse racing against the blade.

"Don't make me have to cut you," Chloe coos into my ear. Is that a threat or concern? The slight hesitation in her voice makes it hard to tell, though her behavior suggests the latter.

Denise skips to us, leans forward, and pulls my skirt away from my legs. "As you enjoy being on display…" She flips her knife around to a stabbing position and drives it through the fabric. The cloth offers no resistance as she yanks crosswise from the top of my right thigh to the lower inside of my left. She then jabs the knife into the loose lower flap and—*Rrrripppp!*—slices to the opposite angle. The free triangle falls to the floor, leaving a jagged beach sarong that will make protecting my womanhood from even the slightest of breezes a challenge.

Denise stands erect to admire her handiwork, but her eyes lock on my chest. "What in the..."

The glow of the amulet intensifies and dims, then again, pulsing ever quicker and brighter the more it matches my racing heart.

Chloe shifts. "What is it?" Her breath tickles across my neck as she loosens her grip to peek to my right.

Denise half steps back and stares at the amulet for a second before reaching forward to pluck it from my neck.

Tzzzzzz!

Denise jumps back and drops her knife to the floor as she grasps one hand with the other. *"AAOOWWW!"* The air reeks of burnt flesh. Denise rushes to the sink I vacated, twists the cold water on high, and buries her hand under the stream.

"What'd you do to her?" Chloe asks, a mix of confusion and unease filling her words.

It's now or never!

Every muscle that my right leg possesses slams heel first into the top of Chloe's foot. Multiple toes crack.

Screaming, Chloe releases my wrists, but jerks up with her knifed hand. The blade slices into my skin and across my shoulder with a sting. A stream of wetness that can only be blood races down my back under the dress. I twist away as adrenaline saturates my veins. So rapid is my heartbeat, the amulet adopts a steady golden radiance.

Chloe tips forward and grabs for her foot. A small pool of blood settles under her smashed big toe. She gags. Her knees buckle. As she falls, I buck my left knee skyward, nailing her solid in the face. Her body jolts up and back. She rocks on her feet again, then collapses—*Crunch!*—onto her tail bone. She rolls to her side, one hand seeking her behind while the other seems torn between nursing her toe or pinching her bleeding nose.

I rotate a quarter turn. Denise is still nursing her own wound, otherwise oblivious to the goings on behind her. Her purse strap lays diagonal her back, the bag itself angles onto her right buttock. I dip to the floor and retrieve her knife, then rush at her.

"UGH!" she blurts as I pin her against the sink. I slide the knife under the strap near the bag and saw. The sharp blade makes quick of the faux leather. By the time Denise registers my intent, the purse is already in my hand. I back away from her.

"You're making a big mistake, Rat." She turns to face me, but sticks upon Chloe rocking and moaning on the floor. The surety worn on her face fades.

I continue backing up, keeping Denise in view and the knife at the ready. "Seems circumstances have changed. How about a new deal?"

"You—!" Denise moves toward me.

I give the knife a small shake and say, "It's my turn to talk. This is what's gonna happen: I'm walking away with the videos." I tilt my chin at Chloe. "In trade, I don't do that to you."

It's an empty threat. I've no chance one-on-one against Denise. She glances again at Chloe, seems to second guess whatever she's thinking, and stops. The bluff works. The advantage in my favor, I back another step, my sole goal to depart the restroom in haste.

"I'm gonna beat the crap out of you!" Chloe screams. She tries lifting to her hands and knees, but ends up reaching for her tail bone with a moan. I wide step around her, avoiding a weak attempt to kick me with her good foot.

Two more steps backward, my butt finds the door. I reach right. The handle is there! I wrap three fingers around the cool metal, the remaining two working to maintain a grasp on the broken strap of Denise's purse. Denise dares a step forward. "I'm gonna make your everyday unbearable!"

A laugh escapes me. As if you already haven't! I glare back at her. "I'll take my chances" After all, what worse could she do? I yank the door open, twist past its edge, and break out into the party.

"YOU, BITCH!"

The door clanks shut on Denise's outburst. The nearby guests studied me for only seconds before they return to their established conversations. All the better than someone take an inquisitive notice of my exposed condition, or the knife glinting in my hand. I collapse the blade and slip the weapon into the bandeau between my modest cleavage. The blade's grip is an ice cube against my heated skin. Cringe, several drips of sweat leeching into the cut on my back. Ignore the sting as best I can and prop up onto my toes. *You need a hiding place quick!*

Nowhere stands out, though it's hard to see through the thick crowd. Wait! That's it!

As Xiomara said: when you can't avoid, blend in.

I make to sprint straight ahead for the thickest of the crowd, when a breeze teases at my torn skirt and flashes much more than just the tops of my stockings. Slap the flap down, thankful no one seems to notice, though my dress is an impediment. Instead, turn left and scurry toward the dance floor. *If there's anyone that can do something about this…*

The restroom door crashes open with me only a couple of meters into the crowd. I shuffle through a group of five locked in debate over the latest tariffs on fresh water as a middle-aged woman bumps past me in the opposite direction. Given the distress buckling her face, not sure what she'll think of what awaits her within the commode. I cut left around one ball gown, only to tangle with another. Juke right and bounce off a man strolling hand-in-hand with his wife, or girlfriend, or whatever relation she is. "What the…?" he says.

I turn to apologize, but trip over the train of a red-wine Bariano full maxi. "Hey, are you okay?" the dress's wearer asks. Ignore the inquiry and move deeper into the crowd. A murmur of questions follows not far behind me. "Did you *see* that dress?" one woman asks of another. "Is that girl okay?" asks another. "Is her lip bleeding?" a man's voice hits my ear. I wipe the half-dried stream from my face, leaving the back of my hand smeared red.

"Help!" The middle-aged woman seems to have reached the restroom. The piercing howl shifts everyone's attention. "Someone's attacked a girl!"

Against my better judgment, I glance over my shoulder. The crowd pulls apart not far behind me. "Get the fuck out of the way!" Denise's voice is close.

I ricochet off of a portly gentleman and half twist my left foot. I cannot compensate with the right and tumble to the side, recoiling off another party goer. "Watch out!" the woman says. One heel catches on the other and collapses me flat to the ground.

"OOWW!"

"Look Mommy—that's the girl we rode in the carriage with!" The pink-polka-dotted girl points at me from a couple of meters away.

"What dear?" Her mother rotates in my direction. Her eyes bug out. "Oh, my!" She closes the distance between us as quick as her pregnant belly allows. "Are you okay, dear?" She reaches out, only to stop mid-distance. "Oh, gosh… your back! Philip," she calls to her husband, "get some help!"

"I'm fine," I lie. Forsake her half-offered hand and rise onto my knees. My show fresher than the commotion back at the restroom, the crowd shuffles into a rough six meter diameter circle, all eyes focus on me and the bulging woman at its center. *So, how are you gonna get up without flashing everyone?*

Innocent of the display before her, the polka-dotted girl steps forward with Denise's purse outstretched in her free hand. "You dropped this," she says, a smile of proving useful on her face.

"Thief!" Denise busts through the parameter of the circle and stops. "That's mine!" Her bellow kills the crowd's whispers. "That girl is a thief!"

The polka-dotted girl drops the purse and scurries behind her mother, thinking Denise is referring to her. Use the distraction to jump to my feet with as much discretion as possible. The gasps to my right suggest I've not been so on at least one of those counts. Mrs. Polka-Dot rebounds with my sudden rise, confusion and fear racing across her face.

"It's not what it seems." Why did I feel the need to say that?

I grab the purse from the ground and bolt for the edge of the circle one-hundred and eighty degrees from Denise, only to have my route blocked by one of the waitstaff and an officer. Philip stands just behind the pair. The officer snatches my arm before I can sidestep the trio, halting me in place. "Hold on there, young lady."

"She's a thief!" Denise steps at us, but another officer pops through that side of the circle and secures her wrist before she makes it two paces. "She beat up my friend—jumped us in the restroom."

A gasp circulates through the growing crowd.

"Help me, please," I beg of the officer restraining me. "She's lying. She's the one who jumped me."

The officer yanks the purse from my hand. "So, this is yours?"

Stare at him, unsure what to say. Denise isn't wrong: I'm not innocent, though not in the manner in which she's portraying me.

The waitress saves me from having to answer. "This girl needs some medical care, and out of this crowd before we create even more of a scene."

The gossip around the circle exceeds a mild rumble. Several digicells pop out, no doubt their recorders set for ultra-definition capture.

The officer glances around as if only having just then noticed the increasing commotion. He looks across the circle to his counterpart. "Let's go." The officer opposite nods his head and guides Denise, despite her protests, from the circle. "Please come with us," he asks as if there's an option, his grip no looser than when first placed. "Patch her in the office," he says to the waitress as we move across the circle in the same direction as his peer.

Denise is unlikely to try anything with the officers around, but being forced into any office with her will not end well for me. Can't appeal to the waitress, who breaks away to go get a medical kit. Mrs. Polka-Dot latches onto her sobbing daughter and retreats to her husband. The *how-could-you* glare she shoots my way as we pass shuts the door on any help from her. The crowd bears no familiar face. I've no option but to comply.

"Stop right there!"

Thank the stars!

Never have I so welcomed Mom's voice. The crowd parts to my left as she steps through. She's latched onto James with her right hand, he trailing the length of their combined arms. The fury in her step, the irritability on her face… This guard is going to get demolished. She barrels past the edge of the circle. My shoes—the ones that coordinate with my dress, or rather, what of it remains—dangles from her other hand.

Oh, crap!

"Let her go!" *Yes! She* is *here to help you!* I twist at her with renewed optimism. She glowers in return. "*I'll* take care of this one." *Err, perhaps not.*

The officer glimpses between the two of us, ending on Mom. "Yes, ma'am." He releases my arm and disappears into the crowd in haste.

Mom saddles to my side a second later as she scoffs at all the eyes hyperfocused on us. "Go back to your own worlds!" The command of her voice sends several guests turning away, though a handful continue to peek over their shoulders.

Before she can yank me away to wherever she intends to lie into me, I try getting ahead of her anger. A heartfelt "Thank you" rushes from my mouth.

"Thank you!" She hoots. "Girl, you've some nerve! What was the one thing I asked you to do for me tonight?"

Dip my head. Seems we're going to do this with an audience. "Watch after James," I croak.

"Look at me when I am talking to you." As Mom demands, so I do. "Just that one simple request," she goes on, "and what happens instead? My half naked son comes busting into the middle of a conversation I'm having with some Elites, his chest covered in whipped cream and jelly!" A touch of grape I'd not at first noticed smears out from the top of James' shirt. Fight with everything I have to keep from busting out with a laugh. "… one of my staff in chase, blood dripping from his arm where your brother bit the poor man." James pops his chest out with satisfaction. "What do you have to say, young lady?"

"I, ah, well, I just needed—"

"I don't care what you needed!" Mom restrains the yell, but only in part. More guests gaze our way. "You commit to something, you follow through. Understand me?"

"Yes, ma'am."

"Then in the middle of cleaning your brother," Mom continues as if I said nothing, "I'm notified one of my staff got drunk and passed out in an office. And to top it off, she pees in a trash can! Something *I* have to explain to my employer! Do you comprehend how incompetent that makes *me* appear?! Do you?!"

I say nothing. Err on the side of it being a rhetorical question. Mom continues on a scant breath later.

"Imagine my utmost surprise to find these," she holds up the shoes, "in that same office. 'For certain,' I told myself, 'those cannot be whose I think they are?' Yet, they're one-of-a-kind; only one person possesses them. 'So how did they end up here' I asked myself." I go to say something, but the disgust layering Mom's face chokes the words in my throat. "Was it a trade… booze for your shoes? Or did you manipulate May to let you into that building so the two of you could get drunk together? Huh? Which is it?"

"Neither," I say. "I was—" A breeze brushes across my exposed thigh. My hand cannot respond fast enough.

"For the love of…" Mom's hands shoot into the air. "What in Sol's fury happened to your dress?" Given the volume of her voice, she doesn't seem to care—or, perhaps, notice—most of the crowd staring again. "I do you the favor of allowing you to come to this party—a *paramount* night for me. Work extra shifts to scrap together enough credit to buy you that beautiful gown. Do you know how much I spent on that?" You bought it? What? "Do you?!"

"But didn't Dad—"

"Now look at it!" she carries on, ignoring my interjection. "It's—it's—I don't have a clue what it is, other than a skimpy rag! And those shoes… where did you get those?! These"—she holds up my shoes again—"weren't feminine enough for you?"

"I love those shoes! It's just that—"

"You just couldn't keep it classy, could you? Dressing like a floozy… stealing from people…" Oh, crap! The purse! "And did I hear right? You beat down some poor girl? What is wrong with you?!"

"It's not like that." Despite any consequences, she needs to hear the truth. "I'm so very sorry, Mom," my candid words flow. "After you left, James and I—"

"You know what," Mom cuts in, "I've no interest in your continued fabrications. You're out of control, missy, and I'm done coddling you!" She rotates on her heels and breaks back through the circle the way she came, James again in tow. He flashes his tongue in my direction as they leave.

"Dammit!" my heart screams, no longer able to hold back my frustration or my tears. "For once, *you* listen to me!"

Mom stiffens. Her back raises and lowers as she takes in and releases a deep breath. Every eye around glued to her, she pivots to face me. A *you're-so-naïve* smile befalls her lips.

"Dear girl," she says in a softened tone, as if correcting a toddler, "I do everything for you." For me! What?! A double-take later, make sure she isn't instead talking to James. "Just one favor I ask, and this," she runs her hand up and down in my direction, "is how you thank me." She pauses, perhaps trying to emphasize her words. "I should have known better." She turns and proceeds along the artificial path before her.

We've not been close in years, but my heart breaks a thousand times over anyhow. "Do you love me?" I cry out.

She stops in her tracks and rotates. "What?"

"You heard me. Do you love me?"

She stuffs my shoes into James' hands and pushes back through the circle of guests. She draws tight alongside me, her lips a mere centimeter from my ear.

"Love you?" She chuckles. "I can't believe you even have to ask."

"Do you?" my voice manages between a gasp and sniffle.

"No." The icy answer shivers off my eardrum and chills into my core. Mom twists away, but there's a question that nags at my heart. One my soul has long feared to utter, but it can avoid the answer no longer.

"Did you ever?"

Disdain emanates from the woman as she leans in again, but the darkness that exudes her eyes speaks volumes. Triumph interweaves the malicious "No" that leaves her lips.

"You lie."

"Oh, do I?" she says only for my ears. "And what makes you say that?"

"Earlier…" I say through a sob, "in the town car—your eyes—they glistened with love, for me… your daughter."

She leans in even closer, her typical move to make certain that every word she's about to say I well understand. "And there," comes her whisper, "is the crux of it all… you've *never* been my daughter."

Desperate for a truth that doesn't exist, my desires fight against the anguish flooding my chest. My nails dig into a pinch of skin on my inside forearm. "You lie…" falls from my lips like a feather fighting to stay upright in a hurricane.

Her demonic voice smiles as she says, "and you *never* will be."

CHAPTER THIRTEEN

A HIGH-PITCH CACKLE RICOCHETS past us.

"So she starts at me—*as if* the woman could take me—and I say, 'Fact is, you never will be.' She flips me off as if it's *my* fault she's too short and storms away." Our trio creeps closer to the vent. "Anyhow, where was I? Oh, yes, all doors confirmed sealed and secure. Philips is covering checkpoint one and that pig—Yants or Youst, something like that—he's at two. Can you believe the goon hit on me *again*? Third time just tonight!"

Neither the speech giver nor her companion have I met, but his name flashes into my mind as he responds. "Give a guy some points for persistence," Walters says.

Ma signals to extinguish our headlamps as we arrive at the edge of the vent.

"Persistence! Try annoyance," the female huffs. "Guy doesn't register 'no' for an answer. What the frick does he think we'd do anyhow? Go dancing at the local bar?!"

Ma moves to the opposite side of the grate as Walter's meaty laugh resonates from below. She waves Claudia closer, and the two study the scene playing outside the vent.

"You *are* rather fetching," Walters says. MissyAnn cringes, suggesting otherwise. "Perhaps he's looking for a hook-up?"

"Can it, you baboon! Like I need to deal with *that* headache." The woman's words soften. "How's the detainee?"

"Still dead to the world." MissyAnn's eyes roll at the response's poor comedic undertone. Though we're near to changing Katherine's fate, my stomach churns, considering the near reality of his jest.

"Come on, Walters, you had to go there?"

"Eh," is Walters' sole response. Picture him shrugging with a *hey-one-of-us-had-to-say-it* expression on his face.

"Just go do rounds." Exasperation leaks from the woman's words.

Two pairs of boots clunk their way past each other, followed by a whir, a *beep* and the swoosh of a door sliding open. "Oh," Walters says, "I might be off schedule this time. Tonight's burrito dinner isn't sitting too well."

"Thanks for sharing," the woman says, the response drowning with annoyance.

A *swoosh* and an airy *furish* of what has to be the door sealing shut cuts Walters' hearty laugh short. In the same moment, the squeak of a chair bearing weight anew carries into the duct. The *click-click-click* of keyboard keystrokes follows, only to pause ten seconds later as the chair squeaks again. "I need to find a new assignment," the woman says. She sounds drained. "That guy's a jackass."

Claudia slams a hand to her mouth, fighting to extinguish a laugh. She snorts instead. Ma bites her lip, clenches her fists. Claudia looks between us, her eyes big with a mix of panic and apology. Below us, the keyboard continues to click at a feverish pace. I give Claudia's arm a *no-harm-done* squeeze.

Past her, Ma taps her watch—our fifteen minute window having started. To Claudia, she makes a fist with her right hand and blows into it, then tilts her head onto her overlaid palms, eyes closed. When Ma reopens her eyes, Claudia gives her a thumbs up and opens a thin pouch along the side of her left thigh. From it, she retrieves two wooden rods, twenty centimeters long each. She places the end of one over the other and locks them together with a twist. From a vest pouch, the girl pulls a small, yellow-feathered dart and stuffs it into the end of the tube. With delicate hands, she threads the open end past the vent cover slats, takes a deep breath, and blows.

With an almost inaudible *whoop*, the projectile shoots out. "Ow!" the woman below calls out. Ma holds three fingers up and closes one. "What the..." She closes the second. The chair below squeals. Ma's last finger drops. The keyboard crashes as if we dropped a dictionary upon it.

"She's out," MissyAnn says at normal volume. She hands Claudia her backpack and shifts to releasing the clasps holding the vent closed. Claudia, meanwhile, extracts a climber's rope, several metal tubes and a box about the size of a brick and attached with a series of pulleys. Claudia holds the items in wait as Ma gives the loosened cover a push with her boot. It swings open on its hinge. Over the fresh opening, the two erect a pyramid to the height of the ductwork with the box at its top. Ma hastens the rope through the pulleys, then has Claudia hand me the bulk of the line.

Three minutes spent.

"Without Mahoney," Ma says, "you'll be our anchor." I want to protest, but Ma carries on before there can be any debate. "The locking mechanism on the pulleys will do most of the work. In that bag," Ma nods to Claudia, who passes me the backpack, "are gloves so you don't burn your hands and spikes for your boots to prevent you from slipping."

Ma turns to Claudia, assigning her the tasks of retrieving the dart and anything useful from the guard station. "I'll go for Katherine," she says. The course forward in motion, I retrieve the two remaining items from the otherwise empty bag and gear up, spikes first.

As I slip the second glove on, MissyAnn sits on the edge of the vent and locks her foot into a loop. She flips a switch on the box, which clanks against the top of the venting. A small green light twinkles on its face. "Electromagnet," she answers before my question emerges. She nods at me to grab my end of the rope. "Nice and easy."

The rope goes taut as she slips her behind off the edge. Between her diminutive shape and the pulleys, I don't even break a sweat lowering her to the floor. Do a quick reset, then lower Claudia using but a single hand.

Guess you just wait now.

Five minutes consumed, shift to the edge and peer through the gap.

Ma, having pushed the guard to the side, is typing feverously at the computer terminal. "No," she half says. *Click, click.* "No." *Click, click, click.*

Claudia, meanwhile, leans the guard's drooping head sideways, plucks the dart from her neck, and returns it to a small pouch at the left waist of her vest. The woman's hair falls from her face, revealing a series of deep pinkish pockmarks, temple to cheek. Care not to know the cause of such a scar.

"No." *Click, click, click.* "Scraig it." Ma rubs the back of her neck.

I shuffle to the other side of the opening. No matter the angle, though, can't get a distinct look at the screen.

Click, click. "No." *Click.* "Wait a minute…" her voice perks up. "Cameras. Not surprising." *Click—click—click, click.* "And that turns those off. Now for the doors."

The guard's pockets exhausted, Claudia turns her attention to the desk's only drawer. Onto the desk's top, she places a couple of pens, a stapler, a box of paper clips.

Check my watch.

Another two minutes have ticked away.

"Well, crickets," Ma says. "Doors won't open without an authorization code. Looks like a manual job." She abandons the computer and steps around the shorter leg of the desk's L-shaped countertop. "I'll be back."

"Sure," Claudia says as she sinks her arm deeper into the drawer. From it she scoops a handful of odds and ends and spreads them over the desk's surface. Being of no value, most she just swats back to the drawer. As she moves on to a small, blank paper pad, the girl jars upright.

"Claudia," I ask, "everything alright?"

The girl holds up a *give-me-a-second* finger, tosses the pad into the drawer, and hurries back to the guard.

"What?" I ask, but remain ignored while Claudia scuttles back with a small folded paper.

"I think…" she undoes its crease and runs a finger along the contents of the page, "it's a list of pass codes." She looks up at me. "You don't suppose…?"

I go to agree, but she types away at the computer terminal before the words leave my mouth. The visible part of the paper's face contains six sets of four numbers each. The first failing, Claudia hits ENTER on the second. *Beep.* "Darn." She keys the third and receives another *beep* of failure. *Click, click, click, click*—ENTER. *Beep—beep—beep.*

Burrrr—Clank!

"What in the stars!" MissyAnn's voice echoes from another room.

"Yes!" Claudia hustles around the end of the counter and disappears in the same direction Ma left.

More than half of our window is now history.

"Watch your—!" Ma's voice again echoes.

"Ow!" Claudia cries out.

"What happened?!" I try not to scream, yet still need my voice to carry.

Ten seconds with nothing, then MissyAnn's mumbles reach my ears. Can't gather exact words, but her frustrated undertone suggests phrases sure to burn Claudia's ears.

"Let me help," says a third, feminine voice.

My heart skips a beat! *Katherine!* I smile. *Paul will be so happy!*

We're far from mission accomplished, though, and our time continues to tick away. "Ladies," I say louder, with more panic than intended, "we've maybe six minutes."

"I know!" Ma's tone is tight, dripping with annoyance.

Thirty seconds later, she steps into view, supporting Claudia from one side. An unkempt mess of coppery-red holds Claudia from the other.

"How are you?" my lips blurt.

What a stupid question! The sudden shot from MissyAnn confirms as much.

The other woman looks at me, revealing a dated scar on the right side of her temple. Her cheeks have a slight droop—presume from being woken up in the most unexpected of ways—but she manages a timid smile.

"We can get reacquainted later," Ma acrimoniously instructs. "Right now, we need to get moving. We've only four minutes before that guard gets back." Ma looks at Claudia. Gauze wraps across the girl's forehead and around her braids. The material over the left temple seeps red. "You okay?"

Claudia gives a thumbs up.

"Good. You first up…" Ma glances at Katherine, "and then you, Red." Ma shifts her gaze between Katherine and I. "The three of you head back. I'll wait here for the other guard."

"Who's gonna haul you up?" I ask.

"Just drop the gloves and both ends of the rope; I can lift myself."

"Oh." I inspect the pulley system. Why am I stuck up here then?

"Jane!" Ma's demand jerks at my attention. "You ready?"

"Ah, yeah, sorry."

Claudia has a foot already secured in the line. I finger the rope and re-trieve the girl in no time. She flashes me a tight smile as I help her into the vent. Her head cloth bears a much larger spot of blood than it had when she was waiting below.

"What happened?"

Claudia's cheeks go as red as her head wrap. She opens her mouth to reply, but Ma ends the explanation before it even starts. "Jane, rope!"

For crud sake! What is with the attitude?!

I hurry the line back to the floor. As Ma helps secure her foot, Katherine says, "Thanks"—her tone weary. Ma nods her head and gives the rope a small tug.

My biceps balloon as I heave, Katherine being of a similar Spartan build to me. Sweat leaches from my forehead by the third yank, the pulley's help debatable. *Uurrrggg.* Closer, albeit near a snail's pace, her red hair comes. Tug and tug until, on the tenth tug, enough of her pops through the opening that Claudia can grab a hand and help complete Katherine's ascent. Secure in the vent, she twists onto her behind and slips the loop from her foot. She flashes me another half smile, but her face otherwise screams duress. For me, saying the last twenty-four hours have been overwhelming is a weak comparison. Being mere hours from execution, I dare not compare my emotional state to the roller coaster Katherine is trying to absorb.

"Come on." Claudia flips her headlamp on and begins scooting back through the ductwork the way we came. Katherine rush-mouths a *thank you* in my direction, flips to hands and knees, and dutifully follows. Check my watch—fourteen minutes exhausted—then down the hole.

Ma stares back and says, "Don't look so worried. We've freed your girlfriend and we'll be safe back at camp in no time. Just lower the loop and go. I'll be mere minutes behind—I promise."

I should stay—now having hauled Katherine up, understand why Ma left me behind: lifting oneself, even a petite oneself, will be no small chore. Whether via the certainty in her voice or the impish smile (*Or perhaps the combination?*), sense she's moved beyond whatever angst she felt since finding out I can see in the dark. Thus, I hold my tongue and just lower the rope along with the gloves. Return the spikes to the backpack, move across the hole, and scurry after Claudia and Katherine. The two are well ahead of me.

Guess Mahoney's not the sole speedster among us.

I make the midpoint of the venting as the pair reaches the ascension shaft. Claudia's light dims as she stands and starts her climb to the level above. Katherine scoots under the shaft, then sneaks a glance over her shoulder. Despite what of the faint glow from the former's headlamp remains, the latter's disconcertment stops me.

What's she so unsettled about?

Katherine disappears up the shaft, along with the last residual glimmer from Claudia's light. My nauseated stomach begs me to rush forward and ask, but Claudia's words hold me in place. *"That seems too easy,"* she said of our plan.

Sure, someone removed all the grates along our path, but they've been so for months. The shaft to the cells was pre-strung with a climber's rope, yet such examples exist throughout the vents. Few guards around to challenge us, except we chose a time that'd be the case.

The rescue was easy because we kept the plan simple by intent. Still...

Have we played into the very lure Mariana foreshadowed?

Jane, stop that! The mission's been far from uneventful: two injuries, the maintenance room run-in, Ma's mixed personalities... MA!

I listen... to silence.

My head imprinted with Katherine's foreboding face, haste as best I can without creating a clamor back to the grate. Stop just shy of the hole and listen...

Nothing.

I lean forward and peek through the opening.

Where is she... and where's the guard—the chair?!

Brace my arms against the legs of the artificial pyramid and poke my head through the opening. "MissyAnn?"

An *Eeek—eek!* speeds from a hall beyond desk. "Ma?"

Still nothing.

The corners of my vision haze. Blink and jerk my head side-to-side, trying to shake it, to no avail. Push back and upright, pumping my blood back into all the proper places. I shake my head again to clear the residual dizziness.

Eeek—Clank!

Crud!

Plop to my butt and dangle my legs out through the opening. I pull at the rope. Stuff my right foot into the rising loop, then shuffle myself off the edge.

The metal of the vent calls out with an angry *twang* that makes me think it's about to give out, but holds firm against the sudden challenge. My muscles balloon and burn, my arms concurring. Ease my grip, allowing the counter rope to flow. Though the pulleys help, the fibers grab at my skin, heating my palms. The floor seems kilometers away.

Wish I still had those gloves!

Shift my palms one below the other, over and over, my wishing fruitless.

Half way down… *Swoosh.*

My grip tightens. Jerk to a stop, peeling my palms. Wetness ensues.

"You know, I was thinking…" Walters' thought doesn't complete. He puzzles at me for only a second, then draws his sidearm. "What the frick is this?!"

Dangle, saying nothing.

Walters shuffles further into the room, but not too close. His weapon remains square on me. Behind him, a *swoosh* and subsequent *click* of the door sealing shut.

Like your fate.

"Where's Livingsteen?" Walters' question comes off a demand.

Good question!

I continue to keep silent. My hands slipping, shift each to a higher dry part of the rope.

"Sam?" Walters asks. He circles to my right, still focused on me, save sneaking glances toward the desk. He's a bulk of a guy, Mahoney's doppelgänger in terms of build, though a hair shorter. Gives him a more flabby than muscular look, though his anatomy still echoes the message: *don't mess with me!*

My left hand again slips. Then the right. I grip tighter, freezing out the pain pinging through my arms.

"Lower yourself," Walters says. "Slow-like."

I creep my hands along the counter rope, arguing with my angry palms. Every touch a mark of history stained in red. Every connection a lightning strike to my flesh. My legs jerk with every shock. Sweat zips down my back. My face contorts with a steady cringe. *Ignore the pain!* Down a little more. *Ignore the pain!* A little more. *Can't ignore the pain!* Closer.

Get me to the floor already!

Walters moves to the corner of the counter such that the smaller of its two halves acts as a partial shield—for him. To him, my full body remains unobscured.

Good training.

Half a meter from the floor, I loosen my grip one last time. My free foot touches the ground, at last! I bend to free the loop from the other, then stand.

She catches the corner of my eye. Ma, that is. Behind Walters, she creeps from the passageway that leads to the cells. Before I can react, she puts a finger to her lips. Her left hand clenches around a thin white tube. Shift my focus back to Walters, hoping he'll not notice the derivation.

He seems about to ask me something, but a realization flashes across his face instead.

Crap! I gave her away!

"You're that runaway," Walters says. *Huh?* "We had to spend hours looking for you in those damn, dank-ass caves," irritation fills his voice, "'specially after we found what you did to Zanzibar and Luis." *Who?!* "Man, was the Captain pissed!" He nods toward the knife at my ankle. "See ya kept Z's blade as a trophy." His tone switches, becoming quizzical. "Makes me wonder what in the Universe you're doing here?"

I don't have an answer to share, and an answer isn't what I need, anyway. *Be the distraction*—Ma slithered closer—*just a hint longer.*

"Doesn't matter." He moves a finger to a button on the communicator attached near his left shoulder. "Think I best alert the Commander."

"NO!"

Ma's sudden bolt forward catches me off guard; however, not Walters, perhaps given his training, along with my inadvertent forewarning. He flicks toward Ma, bringing the pistol around with him. Half a second before the gun trains on her, she leaps forward and stabs the tube at his chest. He deflects the attempt. Both slam into the countertop.

Walters' gun flies over and falls with a *clank* to the backside of the counter, over the computer monitor and comes to a rest to the right of the keyboard. The tube drops with a *tang, tang-tang, tang* to the floor as Ma staggers and collapses to her knees. She gasps, struggling to get air back into her lungs.

Walters grabs Ma by her lapels and yanks her back to her feet. "You stuuupid girl."

With a grunt, he heaves her across the room. Ma slams back-first into the far wall, opposite the desk area. What air she restored to her lungs shoots out with a gasp. Her body tips in a sluggish arch face-forward to the floor and remains otherwise motionless.

"MISSYANN!"

Tossing MissyAnn leaves Walters unprotected by the counter, his back straight on to me. I blitz at him with two wide strides, leap into the air, and latch onto his back. He staggers, but doesn't fall. I grip his hips with my thighs and squeeze my heels into his stomach, just below the ribs.

His lungs fight against my grasp.

Wrap my right arm around his neck and grab onto its wrist with my left hand. I want to scream, pain exploding from my raw palm, but push the agony to the back of my mind. Pull tighter.

Walters gurgles and slams me backward toward the counter. Lift myself just in time that I end up sitting atop its surface. I lean backward, using my body weight to strengthen the hold.

Walters gurgles again, struggling for any air he can catch. He latches onto my forearm and yanks, but the attempt does little. His nails scrape at the leather of my jacket—likewise, to no avail. His struggles, though, loosen my bloodied grip enough that he can suck in fresh oxygen.

With renewed energy, Walters switches from my arms to my legs. He balls his hands and pounds at my thighs, his fists bricks. My legs struggle to hold as he connects with my still healing injury. Although its surface signs faded, his punches pinch at the damage still beneath. My right leg jerks free against my will. He whips left and pulls me from my perch. I throw my weight left, tipping us. His left knee buckles with the extra inertia and we collapse together to the floor.

Walters' own weight pins my still wrapped left leg between him and the floor. He rolls right, trying to keep me locked to the ground. Use the motion to lock his Adam's Apple into my elbow pit. Shift my left hand up to my right forearm and yank again. He gasps and wheezes as air fights to get past the dam I create. Walters weakens. His roll falters, and he instead falls back to the left. With a weak *oof*, his body goes limp. I hold my grip two seconds longer, just to be sure.

Missy!

With what limit of my strength remains, liberate my leg from Walters' body and push to my knees. Check his pulse. Weak, but there. I scurry to Ma and roll her onto her back. A small stream of blood runs from her nose. "Missy?" Give her body a small shake.

No response.

Crap!

Check her pulse. It's also weak, as are small breaths passing in and out of her mouth. Thank the stars!

Ruby red droplets trail my hands everywhere they hover. With ginger fingers, I search Ma's various pockets for the gauze she used for Claudia. I find it and an already half bloodied cloth on the fourth try. Sit the cloth to the side and pinch the end of the gauze between my thumb and first finger, then wrap the palm of my left hand. No simple task, given the liquid dripping from my right. With the knife from my ankle, slice through the material. I repeat the process using the other hand.

Ma tilts to her left side with a weak but audible moan and reaches along her leg.

"Don't move." I eased her again flat.

"But the guard…"

I glance toward Walters. "Taken care of…" Though incapacitated, the up and down of his chest is growing stronger. I focus back on Ma. "How are you?"

She sniggers. "Feel like he slammed me against a wall." Her injuries are no joke, yet can't keep the corners of my lips from turning up. "My back is killing me," she says, her tone more sober. "Having some difficulty breathing, and my nose aches."

Fetch the cloth and dab at the corner of her nose with the clean half.

"Ow!"

I pull the cloth away. "Sorry." To my relief, the blood's already coagulating. Ma raises to her elbows, her face skewing with discomfort. "I said to stay still!"

"We need to get moving," she says. I go to protest, but as if on cue, Walters moans. Ma peers at me, then us both at him. "Thought you said he was out?"

Walters moans again and twists from one side to the other. His breaths are strengthening.

"Here." Ma reaches for one pocket along her pants, about mid-thigh. She rips its Velcro flap open and pulls another round, white tube, it about a centimeter in diameter and three long. A thin black line runs the circumference about a centimeter from one end. "Pull the cap"—she places the tube in my hand—"and depress into his neck."

"What is it?"

"Something that's gonna keep him sleeping a lot longer than whatever you did." Her facial cringe deepens as Ma sits up to her behind.

"No killing," I insist.

"No killing," Ma mocks as she shakes her head, "just a deep sleep."

Walters pushes up on to his side with a grunt.

I rush over and pull the cap off of the device. With no hesitation, slam the open end against the base of his neck. He collapses back onto the floor, gentle streams of air cycling from his mouth.

Turn back toward MissyAnn to find her struggling to her feet. "For scraigs sake," I say, "slow down and let me help you!"

Hurry to her, stuffing the recapped device into one of my own pockets. I crouch to her height so as to not strain her back all the more, then wrap her arm around my shoulder. Plod her to the edge of the countertop nearest the rope. Nod toward the opening in the ceiling. "Can you hold on long enough for me to get you up?"

"No problem," Ma says, though the slight buckling of her knees claim otherwise. The slight green of her face hints at something else altogether.

"You sure?"

Ma's cheeks burst with a deep pink and she growls, though not without a wince. "If I say I'm ready, I'm ready." With that, she pushes off the desk, steps to the rope, and slips her foot into the loop. That done, she stands upright and takes hold of the cord just above her head. "Well, lift."

Forsaking the instruction, I step forward and wrap my arms around her. "I'm so glad you are okay."

Ma's arms encircle around me. She nuzzles into my chest, mumbling an "Ouch" as her nose catches on my jacket, yet she doesn't release me. Her body collapses into my own, and there we stand, fasten tight, no need to verbalize our reconciliation.

I want to hold her forever, but such moments don't exist in a practical world. There's always a point where you pull back to reality. For me, that's about half a minute into our embrace. MissyAnn is right—we need to get a move on. Though we gained a good chuck of time in knocking out both guards, the early morning is waning, meaning the overnight shift is near its end. Given the team's amassed injuries, we're gonna need every second before they discover Katherine's escape.

Ma seems to realize the same, and we release each other. I snap up the gloves and slip them on, then grasp the rope and tug down. At first, Ma does indeed seem fine. A third of the way, though, her looped leg takes on a shake—at first subtle, then with a blatant twitch the higher her body rises. Two-thirds of the way, her eyes shut and she goes—for a hint of a moment—limp. She—Thank the Universe!—catches herself before losing her grip. Pull quicker. A couple of seconds later, to my relief, she works her way into the vent.

"Your turn," she says. "Let me manage the counter rope."

"I don't think—"

"Frick it all, Jane—when are you going to trust me?"

"It's your health I'm concerned with," I shoot back—and am. It's not a question of trust, though I can't be sure that it isn't. Not that I don't trust Ma, but also can't assert that I do. There's an unmistakable, albeit peculiar, magnetism flourishing between us. Unlike the natural fit I share with Mahoney, her companionship is as enticing as it is off-putting. Yet the connection seems as likewise inevitable. *Opposites attract* so many say. Do I care about her well-being? For certain. Trust though…

"For the last time," Ma says, "I'm fine!"

Debatable… she's not seen herself on the rope; the pain radiating from my hands, though, makes my predicament no better. Neither the wrappings nor gloves provided much cushioning, but at least she's now in the vent. I remove the gloves to find the wrappings well bloodied through. Just holding onto the rope is going to be hard enough, let alone act as a self-anchor. There's no avoiding the situation's truth: we need each other.

I release the rope. "You're right." Not that she's fine, but that she has to manage the counter rope. The distinction doesn't seem to matter to her, though.

"You bet I am!"

Once Ma readies with the spikes, I toss her the gloves. She slips them on, then resets the rope. I lock my foot into place as she backs a couple of paces deeper into the vent and out of my sight. "Ready?" she asks.

I cinch my palms around the ascension rope. A reluctant, "Ready," leaves my lips.

The rope tightens, and I dangle the first couple of centimeters off the floor a blink later. The vent fights against the effort.

"Eerrrggg!" Ma's struggles echo from above as she pulls me five centimeters higher. More grunts as centimeters six and seven disappear. An

"ERRR!" bellows from the vent as six centimeters more disappear. Three more grunts get me lifted past the first quarter of the height to the vent.

Shy halfway, the flow remains smooth, but progress drops to two centimeters with each pull. I tilt my head toward the hole. "You okay?"

"Can't—*errrggg*—talk!"

Three-fourths to the top, the ascension rope jerks down. "Aarrggg!" MissyAnn's voice complains. The vent cries out as she digs the spikes into the casing. The metal at the feet of two of the pyramid legs pits with a loud *twang!*

"Missy!"

"Almost—*errr*—there!"

The lip of the hole is less than a meter away. The box's green light fades for a moment, then blinks with aggression.

With pained groans from above, another of the pyramid's legs deforms the metal.

The grunts and groans that are MissyAnn's growing struggles boil from the grate's opening. The green exasperates in brisk alert as I jerk upward.

Twang! goes the metal again.

The green blackens. The box lets loose the vent's top.

Shoot my hands up, gripping the edge of the air vent just as the rope goes limp. "Ooowww!" Tears streaming from my eyes, I pull up into the encasing. Collapse stomach first on to the cool metal and roll to my side. I look across the gap at Ma. She's sitting up, arms droop to the side, pale and spent. Her legs shake, muscles pulsate. Regardless of what her physique may advertise, that's one damn tough woman!

Ma glances up and offers me a gentle smile. "Piece of cake," she says with a deep inhale.

Chuckle and hold out my hands. "We're a frickin' mess!"

Ma dislodges the spikes from the metal, a *twang* echoing around us. "Stealthy," she says, before letting free a round of gut bursts.

Unable to help myself, a laugh busts from my belly. "Guess we should have rung the concierge for help!"

Ma spreads her thumb and index fingers to their extremes and holds them to the side of her head. "My dear man," she acts the snob, "we could use a hand!"

And so we carry on for a good minute before Ma brings her laughter under control. "Okay", she says, "I'll pack this stuff up," she waves a hand at the now defunct pyramid, "and see what I can do to fix the damage here. You go catch up with Claudia, as per your original orders."

What!? "Seriously!" I protest. "Had I not—"

"Jane!" A wide smile dimples Ma's cheeks. "Thank you," she says with more sincerity than anything I've heard leave her mouth, "for saving my life."

"We saved each other."

"Indeed, we did." She half smiles again. "But don't make it a habit of ignoring my orders."

Regardless of any other feelings I harbor toward her, Mahoney was right… She came through.

I smile back. "Yes, ma'am."

Without hesitation, rotate onto my hands and knees and shuffle forward. Although the cool venting is a mild comfort on my palms, am still glad to arrive at the ascension shaft where I can stand. Angle my face upward.

Huh…? There's a faint but notable afterglow. "They should be further along than that."

Using more fingers than palms, take hold of a rung and follow. Make the top of the shaft to catch the pair—well, a glimmer of Claudia's head-lamp—turning left a corner well ahead of me. Crawl forward. About three-fourths of the way to the corner, what residual rays of her headlamp that are repeating across the metal fade to nothingness. Flip my headlamp on low, my sight blinding for several seconds.

Dummy… you do that every time!

Seconds later, my vision resets enough to move on. I scuttle past a handful of shafts ascending to the right and three spaced out, gated cutoffs to the left.

"Wait, that's not right." I stop just short of the next corner and turn back. Pass the first of the three cutoffs now on my right, pausing at the second. "This wasn't open before?"

A glint reflects off the far wall of the cutoff. Frick it! They went the wrong way. "Claudia," I call out, firm but not too loud. "Katherine."

I proceed after them.

The passageway—stretching the opposite direction we need to go—ends in a T.

I glance right, but there's no sign of them; the prong radiates nothing but darkness. Shake my head. "Crud! We should be outta here by now."

I peer left. A weak yellowish-orange glow bends around yet another corner several meters ahead.

Where are they going?!

"Claudia!" Use more force than the last time. No response, though the glow holds steady. I hurry in the direction to catch them before they set off again. Ten meters to go… nine… eight. "Ladies?" Six… five. "Are you there?" No change in the glow. Three meters. Two. "You're going the wrong—"

Clunk!

"What the frick!"

The metal below gives way.

The floor rushes forward.

Though I twist enough so that my side absorbs the impact, a thousand needles still race throughout my core. "Son of a—!" Roll to my back, willing the sensation away. My headlamp reflects off the dangling hatch cover that my lack of focus caused me to miss. *Damn, you always pay more attention than that!* I lay there for several minutes, my arm and shoulder throbbing. Not so much, though, to suggest I've broken anything. After a moment more, sit upright and scope the headlamp around the room.

The corner of a solid wood desk not more than a meter from where I landed catches my attention. I stand and turn on the lamp that's upon its top, then douse my light.

In all my time at the Facility, I've been in only a few offices, this one now the nicest of them. Faux leather couch and chairs. Wooden cabinetry. The desk is large, yet bare laden: the lamp, a computer terminal, a small cup holding three pens, framed photo next to a groomed bonsai tree, and phone. A small fish bowl on a table to the side. Out of place, two stacks of file boxes—each against the far wall, about a third stamped with the text: *READY TO BURN* in a bold, bright red.

Look up through the hole—the light and, thus, the ladies gone—then again at the boxes. "Maybe?"

I cross the room and grab the first box. Dust scatters off its lid as it releases from the pile. The cardboard's solid despite its yellowish tint and musty smell. I place it on the ground and sweep away the layer of dust.

Underneath, a printed label: *GGC - Confidential.* Below that, an all too familiar two-letter, four-digit code. *AP1253.* Glance back at the pile.

Is it possible?

I grab another box and wipe away its label: *AU2555.* Rifle through the boxes. *DE0556… FE2956…* a second *FE2956.* "Please, there has to be one here!" Discard another three aside. The next is a *JA.* So close to some answers! I reach for the next box.

MA0560.

"No!"

Check them once more, only to fail at my goal again. Crud! Lumber back to the desk and plop into the owner's plush chair. Toss back, close my eyes, and rub my temples. How could it not be there? Wipe a tear away. My chest heaves up, then down. And again, slower.

After some time, open my eyes to find two women staring at me from the photo. Yellow edged and faded, the picture isn't recent. Unsurprising; the Facility isn't a place that generates picture-worthy memories.

At the side of a dais, the scientists stand together with their arms around each other's shoulders, both brimming with pride. The older of the two—her early forties perhaps—holds up a small vial of blue liquid. The younger—a blonde in her mid to late twenties—holds a glossy-covered, bound report titled: *Project X.* Its font is too small to make out the subtitle, but that doesn't matter. The white lab coats the two wear jiggle one of my earliest memories of the Facility loose.

The report carrying woman is older, maybe by ten years, but for certain she performed my physical when I arrived at the Facility. Recall how intent she was to tend to me—yanked the nurse assigned to me to the side—yet so callous and dispassionate in her treatment. A shadow pain in my right forearm, from her repeated failures in finding a vein from which to draw blood. Could swear she did that on purpose!

An even more familiar aspect of the photo catches my eye. A projection screen fills the bulk of the background, with what has to be the title page of their presentation. In black, near the top of the photo, is the bottom half of their *Project X* title. The subtitle below that, blocked in part by the podium, reads:—*tion of JN0449.* "What the frick!" I grab the photo and tilt it under the light, as if it glows with a magic that will reveal the subtitle's initial phrases.

Shake my head. "What are you doing?!"

I toss the frame back on the desk. It slides across the polished surface and pings to a stop against the phone base. Chuckle. Guess we should have rung the concierge for help. I set the frame right, catching the subtitle again—*JN0449*—then glance back at the phone. Is it possible?

Lift the receiver to my ear. *Zzzzzz*… Take a guess. Hit nine. *Beep, Beep*— *Zzzzzz*… Four-one-one.

Brinng. Brinng. Brinng. Brinng.

"Crud."

I arch the receiver towards its perch when "Code?" faints from the ear-piece.

"Huh!" I smack the headset to my ear, almost pinching it. "Hello?"

"Your code, please," a pleasant, almost boyish voice chimes.

Is this for real going to work?! "Jay-N-oh-four-four-nine."

A gasp carries through the line, then the voice says with urgency, "I'm sorry, say again."

"Jay-N-oh—"

"Drop the receiver and place your hands atop your head. Now!"

My eyeballs boil from the sudden brightness filling the room. I slam them shut and drop the phone, which clunks onto the surface of the desk. *How had you not seen him? Not heard the door open?*

Raise my hands into the air and sit them on to my temples. *"Hello?"* the phone asks.

"Move to the front of the desk." The bass' command makes it clear I dare not debate otherwise.

Do as told and lift from the chair, but as if crippled, in order to give my eyes time to adjust. *"Hello?"* Reach a hand to the edge of the desk as a guide and slide forward. Stop at the front edge, my eyes at last able to open.

A tall, hulking brute stands in the doorway, at least two meters from sole to top, his pulse rifle trained on me. *Youst*, his name tape reads.

"Youst! Just the guy I'm looking for…" press my luck, "Livingsteen asked me—"

"Wrong!" The guard shifts into the room, but not too close. "I don't know who you are, but Livingsteen wouldn't be sending anyone in *here* for anything."

"For sures, not with you here!" The words just fall out.

Youst's mouth flinches back. His brows crinkle, but only for a moment before the phone's faint buzz brings him back to the moment. He nods toward the device. "Warning went off as soon as that left the cradle. Once I brought up the cameras and saw those curves"—his pupils ogle my breasts—"I knew you weren't the Doc."

So Mahoney warned—of the cameras, not juvenile guards.

The annoyance nudges the tip of his weapon toward the door. "Let's go. And make one wrong move, I shoot. Got me? Be a shame to damage such a fine package."

Livingsteen was right, you *are* a pig! "I do." I whisk past the man and through the door into the hall.

Youst follows behind several paces. Not so close that I can strike at him, not so far that I can dodge away. He's perhaps an idiot when inter-acting with women, but not his job.

Several meters along, the hall cuts right. "Through those," Youst says of the glass doors at the end of the passage, "and to the left." I shuffle forward until, *swoosh,* the doors split. Walk two paces and turn to the left, as instructed. A moment later, Youst moves through and they swoosh shut again. "To the elevator at the end," he says.

As careful as you've been, me in an enclosed space will be your mistake!

"Phillips…" Youst says, "you there?"

A reply buzzes from Youst's earpiece, but I can't discern the content.

"I have a breach here," the one-sided conversation continues. "Can you bring the cuffs?"

Another buzz in acknowledgment. Crud—seems you are careful.

"Youst out."

As we continue forward, rack my mind for any advantage. The two solid doors on each side of the passage in the direction we head are bio-secured. I manage a quick glance in the other direction, which ends with a security checkpoint that seals us off from the dark lobby beyond. The hall contains nothing, not even so much as a trash can.

"Stop and spread your legs," Youst says with more zeal than the situa-tion merits. "Time for a pat-down."

I halt, but do nothing more. A growl springs from deep within me. "You're not touching me."

"Guess again, Sweet Chee—"

From behind, a door opens with a *turrissh* and the air fills with a *whoosh, whoosh, WHOP!*

Youst's body collapses against me. I thrust him off, and he hits the floor like a large sandbag. The back center of his head seeps crimson. Sticks out a bowie knife, its butt embossed with a rose encircle by tiny golden stars.

What the…!

I turn. Down the hall, he stands with his throwing arm still extended. "The lady said no, asshole."

As thankful as I am to see him… "Dammit Mahoney, no fatalities!"

To his left, Katherine braces MissyAnn. Claudia hovers half out-of-sight behind the trio with her head drooped toward the floor.

"Sorry, Sweetheart"—Mahoney nods his head to his right—"her mission, her parameters." An irate Mariana steps out from behind the group.

I open my mouth to explain, but catch a faint shake of Ma's head. *Not now*, she mouths.

Without peeling her eyes off of me and a with voice layered in blatant animosity and disappointment, Mariana says to Mahoney, "Get that mess cleaned up."

CHAPTER FOURTEEN

THE MIRROR REFLECTS A COMPLETE mess.

Frazzled, half green-tinted hair. Dark, wary eyes. Scalp burned like someone has ripped out half my hair.

My wrists are black and blue and sore, as is my thigh. Three bandages line the inside of my right forearm, two on my left. A million hornets sting my right shoulder blade. Edge the neck of my gown to the left. The blade there is a dark bluish-black too.

My heart's shredded, my soul shattered. The eyes staring at me seem ready to shower the sink at any moment.

What happened to you?

The girl in that mirror is no one recognizable, least of all as me.

"You should try—"

"Oh, jeez!" Jerk around one-hundred and eighty degrees.

"Sorry," the soft voice says, "didn't mean to scare you."

I flash her a weak smile. "No, I'm sorry. Didn't mean to wake you." I didn't, though the distraction is nice; I've had more than enough of this reflection.

"How are you?" her words worry.

"I don't know." Beyond the obvious… *confused… uncertain… amiss.* "Sore and bruised. Every part of me just throbs."

She rushes forward, tears ballooning from her eyes, and wraps her arms around me. "I'm so sorry! I've always known she was icy, but to leave you like that—how could *any* mother ever do that?"

I don't reply, for there is no acceptable answer. Besides, at this moment, just having her there is all I need. Wrap my arms over her shoulders and squeeze.

"I love you too," Angelica purrs, "but not so tight."

I ease my hold, but don't let go. Despite being tender, my arms are firm, more so than my gymnastics training produced. Likewise, my legs, torso, core—the whole of me. In fact… "Did you shrink?"

Geli's body reverberates against my own with a chuckle. "Goodness— I hope not!"

But then this means… "I—I think I'm *taller?*"

Angelica tightens her grip. "Must be," she says in a tone that makes it seem she's only half listening.

I run a hand over the outer edge of my right breast. "And my boobs…," I say in a low tone, meant more for me than her, "they're—*bigger?*"

Angelica half smiles and shrugs. "Lucky you."

I drop my arms. "Geli, I'm serious—my body's different."

Angelica hesitates, but too releases her arms and backs away a couple of paces with a deep sigh. A second later, her hand shoots along her scalp in a deep press. She peeps at my chest, then hurries her vision to the floor. "I don't know," she blurts.

"Oh, stop that—we both have 'em."

Angelica puzzles at me. "Okay, who are you, and *what* did you do with my best friend?"

I giggle—Oh, that feels so good!—then, feigning smugness, say, "I'm embracing my inner womanhood." As the words emerge, realize I mean them a lot more than my tone conveys.

Geli's doubt gives way to a chuckle. "In that case," she looks me up and down, "I guess you're taller, a touch," she glances at my breasts, her cheeks pinking again, "bigger." She shrugs her shoulders. "Regardless, nothing of mine could fit you anyhow, so I grabbed one of Jackie's night-gowns."

My toes curl. Glance at the bandages on my forearms. "Ah—Geli, who undressed me?"

"Mom," she says, as if any other answer is absurd to even consider.

No… no. "Geli…" I twist my forearms out toward her. Her eyebrows crunch together, then she throws her hand over her mouth as she gasps. "Your mom knows now," I say, "doesn't she?"

Angelica's face greens. She swallows hard. "When I found you, your dress…" she shudders, "that cut on your back, took us forever to stop the bleeding. I mean—well—" She points at the mirror, tears falling from her eyes. "You just saw yourself. I didn't even think about those. I don't know what Mom thinks they are."

I can't be mad at her. I neither meant for her to carry my burden, nor is it her who spilled the secret. "Oh, Geli…" I pull her into a tight hug. Her lungs expand against my core, telegraphing her racing heartbeat against my skin.

"When I found you like that," she says through her tears, "I was so scared for you. If only I—"

"No," I say as I separate us. "Don't traverse that dead-end. You're responsible for none of this."

"But your condition," she stammers. "I'll tell Mom that you—"

I wipe her tears away with my hands. "Geli, I don't want you lying for me. You've done more for me than anyone would expect, even from a best friend. And if there is anyone else who I'd want to know, it's your mom."

"Okay," Angelica says, but her eyes swirl with turmoil. "What *did* happen to you?"

"I, ah,…" always share everything with Angelica, but my tongue numbs. Even a single detail could drive her to confront Denise, who might spill truths that'd devastate our friendship. Now is not the time to confront those feelings. Besides Papa, Geli's the only other genuine person in my life. *You can't lose her!*

"No pressure," Angelica says. "I'm sure you're still sorting everything out." She takes my hands. "Share when you're ready. Besides, it's still early *and* a Saturday; we should go back to bed."

I give her a cottony clench back. "I promise I'll tell you everything once—"

"I know." She chuckles, then releases my hands.

She's so good to me, so gracious and understanding. Maybe we're destined to… No! Focus! "I need to get home and talk to Papa." He'll not deny me actual answers.

Angelica's head shakes. "I can't believe you'd be in the same house as *that* woman right now." She lifts to her toes and latches onto my biceps. "Stay with me a couple more hours. Daybreak's not far off and I'm sure Mom will be happy to make French toast!"

I chuckle. "That's inviting, but I need to talk to Papa as soon as possible. I've not seen him in a couple of days and—"

Angelica's smile slacks.

My heart pauses. *If anyone knows how important Papa is to you…* "Geli, what's wrong?"

Her knees weaken. "I'm sure, given the dense crowd, it's nothing…" her cheeks go translucent, "but Mom, she looked everywhere at the party. She couldn't find him."

"He's been busy," my lips dismiss her concern, "dealing with all kinds of issues as of late. They probably called him into the office." My heart notes Angelica shift sideways and twist the lilac inlaid platinum ring on her right pointer.

"Mom's been busy at work, too. She thought the same at first. Then she started talking to their coworkers…" She plops onto the toilet seat, hiding her face behind her hands.

Angelica isn't one to avoid truths. "Geli?"

A deep breath and tearful cheeks greet me. "Thing is, *no one* she talked to saw him at the party or at the lab yesterday."

The room turns into a deep-freeze. I rock with dizziness. "Huh?"

"Your dad, he's… disappeared," the blunt confirmation comes.

I collapse, or so my mind recalls many minutes later. End up sitting on Angelica's bed, my head resting on her shoulder.

Wait, you know where he is!

I sit upright with a jolt. "He sometimes has to work on special projects." Angelica doesn't reply. She may think I'm delusional. I don't care. "I'm sure he'll be home by now." I stand up and search the room.

"What are you doing?"

"Where's my stuff? I need to change and get home."

Angelica stands and grabs my arms, stopping me, face disbelieving. As if her reaction should be obvious, she says, "Your dress—well, that rag—was trash."

"Oh," I say. Of course it was. "Crap. I've nothing to wear."

Angelica points toward the bathroom she shares with her sister. "Jackie's got a ton of clothes she's not worn since going to University. Take whatever you want; she'll know no different."

I smile. "Thank you." I give her a small peck on the cheek, rush through the bathroom, and into Jackie's room.

In her dresser, there's a tee and, buried under several cheekies, a pair of respectable shorts. From the top drawer, withdraw the sole Plain-Jane brassiere and cotton undies there. The bra's not my size… *though, what now is your size?* Slip my arms through the straps, letting the cups meld over my breasts. Unbelievable… a perfect fit. Step into the underwear and hurry on the shirt and shorts, then slide open the door of Jackie's shoe closet.

"When did you get these?" Look back to find Geli, already dressed, examining the heels Xiomara lent me.

"Long story, and I'll stick with these today." I slip on a low-heeled pair of open-toed, tan sandals. Like the rest of the clothes, they are a perfect fit despite being a size larger than what I wear. *Or rather, used to wear… yesterday!*

"So breakfast then? Yummy French toast…"

Geli's playing dirty, trying to work through my grumbling stomach. *Your favorite breakfast is French toast.* Still…

"Thanks so much for everything, Geli." At least, what of everything that isn't a blur. "Not sure of all you did for me, but thank you."

"I'd do anything for you."

Smile. "I know, but I've this gut feeling I need to get home."

"I thought you'd say as much, so I'm going with you. I'm *not* leaving you alone with that *witch*!"

I'm sure I'll be fine with Papa at home, but don't argue. Besides, the company will be nice. "I'd have it no other way." Nod at the heels as I walk toward her. "Best those stay here, though." Dare not trigger Mom again. "Can I borrow a couple of dollars for the bus?"

"No need; I already called us a taxi. Mom linked her account to my Digicell."

"I can't ask you to do that!"

"Nonsense." Angelica flicks her hand through the air. "She won't mind."

Wow, do we ever have different mothers! "I *will* pay her back."

"Fair enough," Geli says, though we both know even if I come up with the money, she won't accept it. "Against my better judgment, I'll let you leave without breakfast, but *not* with that thorny bush of hair!" She pulls me into the bathroom.

For ten painful—*"Ow! Don't tug so hard!"*… *"Would you rather I cut them out?"*… *"No."*—minutes she works my hair, not only removing each snarl and kink, but washing away all but faint bits of the green dye. Still, she blocks the exit, insisting I scrub my face. I huff and puff, but concur the act is medicinal—as if mopping away all that stale makeup mops away the night's angst with it.

"Just a touch of concealer for your cheek." Angelica covers the one physical mark Denise left on me, other than the corner of my lip where her ring connected; graciously, the spot has swollen little. "Need be, pawn that off as a cold sore. Otherwise, though, beautiful as always." She smiles big at me.

My cheeks warm. "You're too kind," I demur. Now knowing her compliments come from a much different place than born of innocent friendship, want to be sure to not lead her on. Ugh! Our friendship shouldn't have to be like this! That sensitive conversion—Please, please don't let it ruin us—seems inevitable sooner than later.

Not, though, in the immediate. "Shouldn't we go?" The taxi must be waiting by now.

"We should," Angelica says with more cheer than anyone should have this early in the morning. She grabs a thin-strapped pocket purse from her dresser, then leads us into the hall. With a skip, she propels us past the rooms of her sleeping parents, down the staircase, and into the home's foyer. Through the front door's glass side window, the beginnings of the morning sunshine twinkle through.

The headlights of what has to be our taxi burst into the otherwise dark house. Throw my free hand up in front of my eyes. "Guess we timed that right."

"Yep," Angelica says as if she's pre-planned everything with such precision. "I should leave Mom a note. I'll be right back." She proceeds down the short hall leading to the kitchen, the glow of the taxi's still moving lights tailing her. A sparkle catches the corner of my eye. I angle in the direction.

Against the wall of the staircase is a small table, a decorative ceramic bowl resting on its top. Next to the bowl, Angelica's Mom's purse. Clipped to its shoulder strap is her security badge.

I step over and palm the badge. Mrs. Woo's smiling photo dominates its surface, her face so much like Geli's that it warms my heart. I run my thumb over the border of miniature double block "I"s, the unmistakable tag of Interstellar Industries, surrounding the photo. Bet this gets her into a lot of places.

Last week, Interstellar promoted Geli's mother into a senior manager role. Though she works in a division separate from Papa, their projects cross here and there. Enough so our two families have a causal acquaintanceship. Happily, my personal relationship with the Woo family is much deeper.

The group of them are fantastic, though—after Angelica—I gravitate toward Mrs. Woo the most. She's the mom I often deceive myself into believing that I have, a fallacy I struggle to maintain in recent years.

No matter how demanding their professional lives, the Woos always find time to stay in touch with Angelica and her sister. Sometimes brief notes of encouragement in a lunch bag or a quick *how's-your-day-going* call after school. Other times, grand, love-infused, home-cooked meals—courtesy of Mr. Woo—full of lively debates; everyone's opinion given its fair due. Long ago, I lost track of all the hours Mrs. Woo helped us with homework, even those nights the stresses of the day beat her down.

From the first time Angelica brought me home, they were giving individuals. Over the years, the greater their generosity and concern for my well-being grew. I now spend so much time with them, Mrs. Woo often teases her husband that I'm her "secret love child". Geli never utters as much, but I know Mrs. Woo works through her to make sure I always have that which my home fails in providing, both the tangible and the intangible. I'm careful to never abuse that.

She'll understand. I unclip the badge from her purse and slip it into my back pocket.

"Shall we?"

I jerk around for the second time that morning to face Angelica.

Geli giggles. "What is with you?"

Glide my hand away from my pocket. "Nothing."

She cocks her head, one eyebrow raises, but otherwise offers no challenge. No doubt she'd say something if she saw me pocket the badge. Instead, she moves past me with a shrug and an "Okay," and places her thumb against the door's lock. It clicks, then edges open. Geli takes hold of the handle and arches it wide. "Let's go then." She waits as I pass through, then pulls the door shut and uses a similar thumb pad on its exterior to relock the door.

The tip of the sun breaks over the horizon as we approach the taxi. I open the door for Geli, who shuffles in. I follow right behind.

"You're paying for my wait time," the taxi driver says no sooner than I close the door. Indeed, he already has the meter tallying. *$10.25* and counting. I make to protest, but Angelica accedes before I can.

"Of course," her nonchalant reply comes. She twists on the seat and tucks one leg under the thigh of the other. "So?" Her stare down makes it clear she's no longer willing to be left in the dark.

Xiomara said nothing of keeping our adventure private… yet, for an inexplicable reason, confessing the night's activities, even to Geli, is premature. Besides, a good chunk of the night's a blur. First, I need some clarity.

I sigh. "Geli, what happened after—" I glance at the driver, whom seems preoccupied with the directions his navigator mapped out. "Well, you know, after Mom?"

The brief sign of letdown in her expression overwrites with consternation. "You remember nothing?"

"There's this movie of surreal scenes playing in my head. I can't tell which clips are real and which my subconscious is making up."

This isn't a hundred percent accurate.

Not that I'm lying. *I'll never do that to Geli. Well, okay, a white lie here or there, but never anything meaningful.* Many aspects of the night are quite sharp in my head, though clarity makes them no less surreal. And everything after Mom stranded me among that crowd of onlookers is an honest haze.

My mind struggles to piece together how I ended up at the Woo's.

Angelica cringes. "Doubt I'll be helpful." Whether she's more disappointed to be giving, rather than getting, answers isn't clear. "I dropped James at the play area, then went to hang with the gang and wait for *you.*" Her tongue pokes into her cheek as a long breath sucks past her lips. "Anyhow, five minutes passed, then ten. By fifteen, you had me concerned."

She wipes a tear from her cheek.

"The group of us split into pairs and scoured the party. Half an hour later, still no you—though your dress was still a wave of excitement traversing the crowd. Tyra said she'd seen your mother nearby. No other option, I sought her out.

"Of course,"—Angelica snorts—"that proved fruitless. We've been friends for how long and she can't even remember who I am. Not that I'd the chance to ask her anything meaningful before your brother comes running past—no shirt, smeared in whipped cream and purple goo—"

"Grape jelly," I clarify.

The reds and oranges of the morning fading, catch Geli's head flinch back, her eyebrows two merging speed-bumps. She shakes her head. "Anyhow, what little of your mom's attention I had your brother sucked away."

"That's my every day," I sympathize.

"I don't know how you can stand it." A sigh escapes her mouth. "So, I found one of the waitstaff who directed me to a security office. Argued with them for, must've been twenty minutes, that I'd not 'overlooked' you in the crowd. They took a report, but I'm sure just to get rid of me." Few things anger Geli like being minimized.

"I'm sorry you had to go through all that."

Her expression softens. "Water under the bridge. More interesting, as I was finishing up, an officer walked in with none other than—you will not believe this—Denise Brightford!" *Oh no! How much* does *she know?* "She was carrying on about how they had better get her Digicell back. I caught little of her rant, though, before they closed her into another room.

"Then, maybe twenty seconds later, another officer comes in with her cell, talking about how the mother of the 'other girl' upstaged him. I knew there could be but one mother of whom he was talking. I bolted from the office to find you.

"By the time I did, your mother was nowhere near. You"—she shivers—"had collapsed to your knees, crying, this absent look on your face…" Angelica wipes another tear from her cheek. "Swollen, bloodied cheek…" The words struggle to escape her mouth. "Did *she*," her voice shakes, "do that to you? 'Cause if she did…"

Ants chew at my heart, my sidebar having hurt Geli so. "No, nothing like that."

"When I find out who…" Angelica's voice fades into her thoughts. *Yea… keeping the details of your run-in with Denise to yourself is imperative—for now.* A long second passes. She snaps to and resumes, "Got you to your feet and walking. I did my best to shield you but your dress was—well—I mean, the night had turned breezy and," the corner's of Geli's cheeks dips, "and all these people—adults!—just stood there watching…" She wipes another tear from her cheek. "Some even had their 'cells out…"

Her pupils burst with anger and disgust, finishing what her mouth cannot. My stomach twists, driving an acidic taste into my throat. I swallow hard. "You did everything you could."

"This young girl volunteered this adorable pink polka-dotted shawl to help cover you," gusts from Angelica. Her nose wrinkles. "You remember none of this?"

I shake my head. "Bits and pieces, but nothing cohesive."

"Huh." Angelica says, then turns away and stares out the window. She's gonna need a couple of minutes, time to extract what logic she can from the illogical.

I peer out my window.

We've traveled out of the well-to-do neighborhoods, weaving through what remains of the middle-class. "*The ever shrinking masses between the 'Have' and the 'Have Nots'*", so the article we read last week in our 'The Shapes of Society' class understated. In reality, the middle-class is struggling to hold on, having itself subdivided even further into those that have and those that don't. Angelica's family fits well into the top of the former. Mine's toiling to stay out of the latter; we one of many families left within the new in-between—the so called "middle-middle-class". Those who have just enough to get by, but never enough to do any better.

Angelica, how'd we ever find each other?

The whole of the sun breaks the horizon like a yoke from a shattering egg. Warmth blankets my face. I close my eyes, letting the rays wash away thoughts not worth having. I reach for my amulet.

My necklace! I turn at Angelica. "Where's my necklace?"

She emerges for a moment from whatever thought is consuming her mind to mutter, "I have it," but explains no further. Instead, her fingers drift to a small lump under the center of her chest. "How could no one do anything—think that was right?"

Not sure to which part of it she's referring. Maybe all of it. "I don't know," is all my brain finds to say as it watches her toy with my necklace. I want my gift back. Open my mouth to say as much, but Angelica bursts back into the moment.

"So sorry," she says, "my head was getting twisted. Ah, where was I? Right! So Abraham—"

"Oh, crud! He didn't see—"

"No," Angelica assures me, "I'd you wrapped in the shawl before he found us. He'd actually come searching for me, seeing as I'd not returned. I sent him to get my mom. Unable to find your dad, she decided you'd come home with us for the night." Angelica smiles. "Of course, *I'd* already made that decision."

I wrap my arms around Angelica as best the space allows. "I can always count on you."

The taxi snaps to a stop, jerking us apart. "Your destination, Ladies." The meter reads *$123.45*.

My lips bear into the driver. "That's ridiculous! That couldn't have been over fifteen kilometers. What are you trying to take us for?!"

The driver shrugs his shoulders. "Sorry, Miss—you agreed to the 'Special Destination Fee'."

I glimpse at Angelica—after all, I've not agreed to anything—then back to the driver. "'Special Destination Fee'—what the frick is that?"

"*Ma'am*," the driver's impatience flares, "everyone knows there's a seventy-five dollar surcharge for destinations in—"

"Why don't you go check on your dad," Angelica cuts him off, "and let me take care of this." She nudges me toward the door with her hip.

"Geli, a surcharge for destinations in where?"

"I'll explain in a minute."

I open the door and bust from the vehicle as spit shoots from my lips. "Shit holes, right? Destinations in shit holes."

Out of the corner of my eye, Angelica's mouth drops open. The driver tilts his head to the side with what seems to be a *pretty-much* nod. I twist face-on to Geli. "Don't you pay that." Then to him, "This *place* is my home, asshole."

Angelica gawks at me as I slam the door. Stand outside the car and take a long draw of the cool air. Its briskness clears my head, settles the hurt racing through me.

I take another breath.

Who was that? You never talk that way! Let alone talk to people *that way!*

Afraid to look back, I haste to our porch and up to the door. Go for the key in my purse. *Dummy… you have nothing… not even your own clothes!* I've never knocked on my front door. Unsure my soul can bear another day of firsts, my balled fingers hang in the air.

The door whisks open.

"Oh, my!" Rush my hand to my side.

"Sorry, didn't mean to spook you," his soft baritone cheers. "Thought I'd heard a car pull up."

The man looks good. Real good. Better than I've ever seen him, though I've never seen him in so little before. He opens the door to its full width, the contours of his bare chest sharpening, his biceps plumping. He arcs to the side to make room for me to pass, but my feet don't move as my brain battles to not let my eyes glance at his tight shorts. My heart thumps against my eardrums, my face is on fire.

"Might wanna get that drool," Angelica whispers into my ear. When did she walk up?

I shoot my eyes to his sparkling own. His snowy white teeth peek through a wide smile. "You gonna come in?" he says with a small laugh.

Geli pushes by me with a *huff* and steps into our family room. She twists to face me, the sole of her right shoe bobs with a frantic pace against the floor.

I cross the threshold. He closes the door, then edges past me. His ribbed abdomen brushes against my forearm, sending shivers quaking through my body.

"I'm Angelica." Geli stretches her arm out to him as she throws me a quick look of irritation.

He takes her hand and gives it a gentle shake. "PJ," the man says. "Nice to meet you." He angles back toward me. "I guess: welcome home?"

I swallow hard, still struggling to not glance down.

"She needs to see her dad," Angelica busts in. "Is he up?"

PJ looks at Geli, then back to me. "Sorry, I don't *think* he's here."

"Oh." My heart drops. How can he not be here?

"I was on the couch all night—" PJ points toward the furniture aligned against the far wall. My face heats again. *Oh no, your underwear!* Good fortune on my side, only a pillow and folded blanket rest there. "but it's possible he came in early this morning."

"Oh, please!" Just beyond PJ's shoulder, Angelica's eyes spin in their sockets. "Why are *you* here?" her voice accuses.

"Geli!" It isn't like her to embarrass me like that!

PJ laughs. "No, it's all right," he says to me, then arches at Angelica. "Giselle—er, Mrs. Rogers I should say, was quite distraught over the night's events and, well, with her husband otherwise occupied, called me to relieve her of James for the night." He turns back to me, a comforting smile on his face. "After all, my job is to assist."

Angelica rolls her eyes again. "Yeah, I bet it is." She glares at me. "Are you not going to say anything about this?!"

Before I can speak, PJ breaks in. "I'm not sure what is happening here," he glances between the two of us, "but I was about to make some coffee. Either of you care for a cup?"

"Sure!" *Didn't mean to blurt that…* but my mouth won't listen.

Angelica's arms lock over her chest as she throws me another scowl.

"Good," PJ says as he turns and heads for the kitchen. My eyes slide down his brawny back to his tight behind.

"By the stars!" Angelica clasps my biceps.

"Ow!"

The *squeak* of a cabinet opening carries from the kitchen.

"Cut it out!" she says in an aggressive whisper. "And since when do you drink coffee?!"

Clinks and *clunks* signal the retrieval of mugs.

Yank my arm free. "I have a cup now and again," I say, but the tight line of Angelica's lips knows otherwise. "And cut what out?"

"Come off it," she shoots back, flinging her hand toward the kitchen. "You're ogling him."

"No, I'm not."

"Seriously!" The outer tip of Angelica's brow twitches, as it always does when I'm being so bloody-minded. "You think you're gonna pull that off on me?"

PJ whistles a tune that Papa sings me often.

"Fine." There's no viable option other than to relent. "So, now what? You gonna tell me he's 'too old', 'too mature', for me?" *What is wrong with you? You're never this defensive with Geli!*

"Damn straight he is." As always, Angelica cuts right to the point. "I thought you were into Abraham. Besides," she takes a full breath, from which a calmer tone emerges, "you never know who else might be interested."

I do… with more awareness than you know.

Not now! I twist to face the stairway as someone descends into my peripheral vision. I can't believe my eyes. "What are *you* doing in my house?!"

"Not that it's any of your business…" Denise says as she reaches the bottom of the stairs, "but I felt compelled to remind your brother whom his girlfriend is." She still wears her party dress, though her hair is now unkempt, her makeup only half there.

Denise stops about a meter from me and nudges her chin toward the kitchen—the sink's tap is running. A devious grin sits on her lips. "That's one piece of eye candy we girls wouldn't mind getting a taste of, eh?" She snoops past my shoulder and, faking a whisper, says, "Presuming that's your thing, of course."

Grunt and drop my voice. "Leave it alone."

Denise shakes her shoulders. She brushes past me and over to Angelica, whose hands she takes hold of and fans out. "You are a cute one."

"Don't touch me." Angelica jerks her hands away. Ever one to stand her ground no matter the odds, Geli takes a step forward into Denise's personal space.

Denise angles toward me, a smirk stretching cheek to cheek. "Hope you like 'em feisty!"

An almost imperceptible movement, Angelica's aggressive stance eases just a hair. Her chin dips a centimeter toward the floor. *Crap!* She hurries a peep in my direction, then away as quick, her cheeks flush.

Angelica's not one to embarrass.

I have to stop Denise before her innuendo gains any more of a hold.

As if having read my mind, PJ pokes his head around the wall dividing the kitchen from the family room. "Denise—thought I heard you. Coffee?"

Denise shoots me a *watch-and-learn* sneer and twists toward PJ. "You are such a dear to think of me," she purrs. "A mug would be perfect." She runs her hand through her hair, tilts at the hips.

"My pleasure," he says, a faint hunger in his words. He gives her a not-subtle once over.

Denise waves him away with a giggle. PJ smiles, then disappears behind the wall. "Scrumptious," she hums when he's gone.

"Hypocrite." The disgust in Angelica's voice is plain.

Denise, however, seems unfazed. She angles back to face Geli, the devious smirk back on her face. "At least I'm not hiding who I am," she sniggers.

That's a blatant lie, but Angelica's left me no opportunity to interject. "What's that supposed to mean?" she says, her face blazing red.

Denise chuckles. "From the looks of it," she says to me, "I'd say your little girlfriend knows *precisely* what I mean." She looks back at Angelica and snorts. "Don't you?"

Angelica balls her hands.

"Geli, no!" I reach forward and grab her. "She doesn't know what she's talking about. She's just trying to get a rise out of you!"

"Oh, Rat," Denise says, "I'd have expected last night's lesson to stick with you better than that."

Angelica opens her mouth, but nothing comes out. Her whole manner becomes discombobulated. She shakes in my grasp. She gazes at me for a moment, then pulls herself free and steps back two paces. I've seen her perplexed before, but never so troubled.

"It was her…" Her voice is delicate, desperate, seeming to not want to admit the truth. "That video—you knew?" Seems more a statement than a question.

"Geli?" I take a tiny step toward her, from which she backs away. A tear falls from her cheek.

"Coffee's ready," PJ calls from the kitchen. Behind me, Denise's dress swooshes. I about face, latching onto her arm as I do.

"You—you—" Every inappropriate word I've ever heard races through my head. *No, you're better than her!* "Get out of *my* house!"

"Ladies?" PJ's concerned voice approaches.

Denise rips my hand from her arm. "Yeah," her arrogance squirts forth, "I'm certain that's not your decision." Her eyes flash toward the stairway. Her lips smirks.

I *cannot* deal with Mom right now!

Rotate on my heel to not see Mom, rather the foyer empty, the front door shutting.

No!

I twist with a growl and aim a death glare at Denise. "How could you?!"

"What happened?" PJ's concern struggles to register with my brain.

In a low, calculated voice, her soulless eyes deadlocking with my own, Denise says, "Payback—a friend for a friend."

I don't care which of the two of us she's answering. *You're not worth my time!* I bolt for the door and pull it open. "Angelica?" She isn't on the porch, isn't anywhere to be seen. "Angelica?!"

My plea goes unanswered.

Where did she go so fast?!

"Daddy!" a child's excitement scurries from atop the staircase.

I hurry over the threshold of the door—Mom'll have to deal with the disappointment awaiting James—pulling it shut behind me. Not before, however, Denise coys at the kitchen, "Guess you're stuck with little old me."

Roll my eyes. For certain, PJ'll see right through that.

I ache to go back and make sure he does, but hurt more acutely for Angelica. Pause at the top of the porch's steps. No one to the left. No one to the right.

"*Please*, Geli, where are you?" *I need you…*

Nothing.

I collapse to the stairway and bury my forehead in my hands. Close my eyes and rub my temples, hard. *First Papa. Now Geli. Both gone… when you need them more than ever.*

There's no help for me back in the house. I'm on my own. I rip one bandage off and scratch at the spot below. The wood of the stairs pricks into my right buttocks.

I pop open an eye. That's not wood! And the other. Pull Mrs. Woo's security badge out from my pocket.

"*Any trouble…,*" Marcus said.

"The code!"

Perhaps you're not so alone after all.

CHAPTER FIFTEEN

CAN'T **FIND AN OPPORTUNITY FOR** some time alone with your thoughts? Turns out there's a simple answer: piss off the woman in charge.

Doing so had not been my intent in undertaking Katherine's rescue. Sure, we came back a little worse for wear, but we *all* came back... mission accomplished! Right?

Alas, Mariana spoke not a single word to me the entire way back; forbade Claudia to be in my presence. I figure most of the others to comply with her direction.

Most.

The soft snores of the one exception reverberate from behind me.

"Oh, for the love of...!"

I pop open an eye. Okay, two exceptions. Not that he's allowed a choice. Open the other. "*Hello* to you too Paterson."

A flippant hand flings in my direction. "It's the late afternoon," he says, a harsh squint decorating his face. "Why are you still here?"

"Why wouldn't I be? Though, I do imagine I'll need a pee at some point."

Paterson's green eyes roll at the ceiling as he shakes his head and huffs. "You know what I mean."

I suppose from his perspective, he's a point. Still, I can't pass up some innocent taunting. "Now Paterson, you *understand* why I'm here." Ma snuggles up against me, but otherwise stays hidden behind my larger form. Her squiggly eyes prick through my thin tee. Don't chuckle. Don't chuckle.

"Oh, come off it!" Paterson does nothing to hide his agitation. "She's fine."

"*I'll* be the judge of when she's 'fine'." Ma snakes an arm around my waist and pulls herself in tighter, if that's even possible.

"You're monopolizing her. Besides, I should be the one taking care of her!"

"*Ooo,* he's so cute when he's jealous." Ma's whisper tickles at my ear, sending a shiver along my spine.

"That's ah…"—shake the distraction away—"why I'm still here," I harass him, "because I know how you'd *take care* of her."

Ma's body shakes with a silent giggle. Buried against me as she is, I'm certain she doesn't see Paterson's chest fall.

He isn't wrong; little have we been apart since returning, but not over any genuine concern about how he'd "take care" of her. That wasn't fair for me to say. I imagine he'll do a more doting job of it than I. He's also right that she's fine. With a shower and a good rest behind us, she is back to acting her amorous self. Truth is, given the fallout from Katherine's rescue, I just don't want to be alone.

That, however, isn't on him.

Stealing her all day is greedy. "I'm sorry," I say. "I didn't mean—"

"Yeah, whatever," he says, sounding defeated. I expect him to storm away as he did last night's dinner, but he lingers. "Just tell her it's ready."

Ma pops up. "Thanks Sweetie," she purrs. "You need to be patient only a little longer and then I'm all yours. We're just having some girl time right now."

He opens his mouth to say something, but catches himself. The irk on his face dissolves as an impish spark flares in his eyes. "You two think…" He circles his pointer finger between him and us. "Maybe?"

"No!" Ma and I say in unison. We peek at each other, a blithe laugh braking out between us.

Paterson huffs. "You damn women!" He storms from Ma's room, whipping her honeybee curtain shut.

"What a goofball," Ma says with a tender chuckle.

"You did that on purpose!" I flip to my back, eying her. "Why do you tease him?"

"Eh… harmless fun." She leans into me, the apricot of the scented body wash we found wafting from her, and slides her hand under my shirt. "Though you get a lot more game time playing for both teams."

My eyelids ease shut of their own accord as my body quivers. *You shouldn't like this.*

My libido disagrees.

Her gentle breaths tease over my neck as she slips her hand along my torso. My lungs grab for oxygen. Her fingers linger shy of my right breast.

"No!" I tumble from the bed, landing with an awkward *thud* on my left hand and knee. The other half of me leans against the side of the bed. Close my eyes and suck in a deep breath. Open them to find Ma eying me, her finger sliding across her lower lip.

"You know you want this," steams from her.

Crush me! I so do. Jump to my feet and blabber, "Paterson's *so* in love with you!"

MissyAnn shrugs as she tries to blank out her face.

"And I'm certain you him."

Ma shakes her head. "You're seeing things, Jane."

"You sleep talk, you know—with a lot of passion for one person in particular."

For the first time since we met, Ma seems lost at what to say. She half hides her face in the pillow, blushing like a beet. A good fifteen seconds pass before she lifts back up. A resolved excitement dances in her eyes. "I *am* Jane," a blissful smile says, "I am so madly in love with him."

I smile back, my ears dismayed she admits it. "I'm so happy for you two."

Ma sits up, the sheet—thank the stars—rising with her. We stare at each other, she with a growing eagerness in her eyes. "Ssooo…?" coos from her after several seconds.

"Ah, 'so' what?"

"So," she asks with a mischievous smirk, "now what about you?"

Crud! How do I not crush her? "Look, Missy," I demur, "I like you *a lot*, but you and I—"

"Oh, for cricket's sake!" Ma rolls her eyes. "Not me, though, if you are so inclined…" She pats the surface of the bed.

"Not even if it meant you could teleport me off this rock," I lie. *Ugh!* Why does she affect me like this?

Ma laughs. "Come on, Jane, you know who I mean. You have yet to stop talking about him."

"I, ah…" have no grounds to protest on. "Oh, Missy, I so do like him." I plop down onto the bed. "My brain keeps reminding me he's engaged— to a woman I helped rescue! But my heart…" I lay my head in her lap. "What am I going to do? I want him to be happy, yet I can't stop thinking about him."

Ma weaves her hands through my hair. "Girlfriend," her gentle voice says, "that's precisely what you are going to do… let him—them—be happy. That is who you are." She strokes my hair again. "Then you're gonna focus that attention on your happiness." She smiles. "Perhaps yours is waiting right around the corner."

Close my eyes. "Doubtful; it's not like this is Camp Withermoore."

"I'm sorry," Ma perplexes, "Camp What-er-more?"

"When I was a kid," stumbles from me as my brain tries to absorb the sudden memory. "Um…" shake my head in a tight arc, "Summer camp. Angelica and I would go."

"We couldn't afford camp." A hint of jealousy drips from Ma's comment.

Open my eyes and sit back up. "Me neither," I assure her, a flood of fresh recollections drowning my mind. "Angelica's parents covered the cost—they were always doing things like that… swim lessons, cooking classes…"—chuckle—"even paid for a *Tae Kwon Do* phase Angelica pursued. Lost track of the number of times they insisted I stay with them for our gymnastics tournaments, never letting me pay for anything."

"Think I need to befriend this Angelica of yours," Ma teases.

A gentle smile tweaks my cheeks. "Her parents always talked about how important that us girls be 'well-rounded'. As we already did everything else together, they sent me along too. Gained all kinds of talents over those summers… horseback riding, woodworking, yoga… not to mention skills you'd never think you'd need: archery and firearms… first-aid… wilderness survival…" I chuckle again. "Now look at me!"

"Never know what the Universe has in store for us, do we?"

"Suppose so," I mutter, the memories ending as fast as they started. Oh, Geli… so wish you were here right now.

"Speaking of which," Ma says, "I've heard Mahoney has something special planned for tonight's dinner…" The comment lingers in the air as if some big revelation is about to occur.

"Oh?" I prompt.

Ma smiles in a self-satisfying way. "For you, Jane," she bubbles. "He's making it special for you!"

An unexpected craving smacks me. "Is he making me frozen lemonade? I love frozen lemonade."

"Sorry, no." Apprehension sprinkles over her excitement. "But whatever it is, it's supposedly one big apology for whatever he did to cause you to avoid him."

"I'm not avoiding him." Skepticism races across Missy's face. I deflect, "You've just been my focus."

"And I thank you for that," Ma lays her hand over my own, "but on the walk back, you could have stood a pair of elephants between you two. What happened?"

That damn knife happened!

"You can tell me." Her voice has none of its usual folly, only genuine concern.

"Last night, I—" A sincere friendship is blooming between us; a friendship I never expected, but is MissyAnn the one to be talking to about this? *He's a trusted confidant*, Ma said. It wouldn't be right, Mahoney finding out second hand. *Besides, dreams are meaningless. Right? For certain, you're making way more out of a mere coincidence—*

"Last night, Jane, what about it?" Ma leans forward, bouncing on the bed.

Just great… Ma awaiting confirmation of some secret that she seems to think she already knows. She's gonna keep trying to step through that door if I don't give her something.

"Mahoney and I seemed so in-sync," comes the truth, "but after what he did to that guard…" Likewise true, just not for the reason I'm implying. I don't relish deceiving her, but I'm not sure how she'll take the truth of the troublesome connections racing through my mind.

Ma yanks back the covers and pushes out of bed. "Mahoney's not one to hesitate when it matters." As she steps toward her chest-of-drawers, her peaches and cream skin glimmers an orange-yellow in the low light. "But most of the time, he's just a big teddy bear." She pulls a mint green blouse from the middle of three drawers. "You need to rectify whatever is going on between the two of you," she says as she slips it over her arms, "soon, before you lose the few friends you still have."

"You're right." A day of data points is far from enough to draw any conclusion contrariwise.

"I *am*," MissyAnn says, not the slightest bit of doubt in her voice. From the top of the chest, she takes hold of a hairbrush and begins teasing at her hair.

I shove from the bed. "Let me help you with that."

"Thanks." Ma relinquishes the brush without the slightest protest.

With careful fingers, I separate a tangled, static-laden clump in one of the few spots long enough to snarl. "You sure a party is the right approach?"

"For sures! We should celebrate Katherine's rescue and let everyone see your fun side." Ma's quizzical eyes glare into the mirror. "You have a fun side, yes?" Before I can respond, she carries on, "You need to win folks over before Mariana's newfound reservations pervade them."

Great, a popularity contest. "Do you think she'll forgive me?" I work at a stubborn tangle atop her head.

Ma slumps. "Don't know; what credibility I had evaporated. Couldn't persuade her to let me stay, let alone anyone else. Mahoney petitioned her on our behalves but did no better. From what I've gathered, only after Katherine stepped in did Mariana abdicate."

I pause mid-brush and gawk at her reflection. "A stranger convinced her to let us stay?"

"Don't over-think it, just be grateful that she did." Ma opens the upper drawer and shuffles through its contents. "Though she owed us to try; we saved her life, after all."

Well, sure, but only after I'd gotten her caught to begin with!

The drawer smacks shut. A round, palm-sized cobalt jar rests in Ma's left hand. She twists off its cap and scoops two fingers through a translucent gel, then sits the jar atop the chest. "You finished?"

"Almost." I separate the last knot and back away a couple of paces to her right. "All set."

Ma angles to the side and bends at the waist, such that her hair falls forward. She spreads the gel between her hands and rubs it through her hair, pulling it outward into spikes.

"How'd you get hair gel?"

"Homemade." Ma stands and turns toward the dresser, culling a black handkerchief skirt from the bottommost drawer. "Not everything you learn at camp." She steps into the garment and slips its elastic waistband over her shirt up to her midsection. She plucks her blouse into a loose tuck. From the top of the chest, she picks up an artificial lily and clips it into the right side of her hair with a pair of bobby pins. Its white color glows against her red hair. "So?" She spins to face me.

"Adorable!" Not just the outfit—a pairing I picture myself wearing—but more so the person within. Seems I haven't given Ma's depth of femininity its due. "Aren't you forgetting something?"

She looks at herself from top to bottom. "Dah! Of course." She steps to the bed, kneels, and slides a pair of black pumps from its underside.

"I meant, underwear?"

Ma chuckles. "I didn't forget." She slips into the shoes. "Plenty of time for panties once I go incontinent. Until then, though, I'm staying unencumbered!" She plops onto the bed and nods toward the brush still in my hand. "Your turn."

I tread instead to the foot of the bed and pick my shorts from the floor—"I'd love to…"

"But?" Impending disappointment carries in MissyAnn's voice.

Excise my watch from the shorts' right pocket and confirm my suspicions. "You must have other things to get ready right now." Flash its face toward her.

"Yeeks!" Ma jolts up. "I sure do!" She scuttles to the room's exit. "Sorry! I was looking forward to helping you get ready."

"No worries," I assure her.

Ma pauses at the threshold, pouting. "In your room, I've something special for you, for tonight." She takes an exacerbated breath. "Truth told, Eddy found it—"

"I can only imagine." The words slip out before I can check myself, the freshness of Paterson's ogling trumping my normal restraints.

Ma chuckles. "Don't fret," she says, seeming unfazed by my rudeness, "I was exact about what to find for you."

Not sure that's any better!

I hold up the brush. "Mind if I borrow this?"

"Not at all." She hurries past the bumblebees. "Oh, and be sure to put it on *before* you make up with Mahoney!" The *click, click* of her heels pause. "And don't dawdle—I could use some help."

I shake my head. What in the Universe did she have Paterson get me? I hurry my shorts and boots on, grab a lantern, and quick-step down the hall to my room. In seconds, scoot past its drapery door and glance at my bed. An unexpected, but warming, sense of *déjà vu* overtakes me.

Its trigger, however, eludes me.

I worked with the awkward boxes—their length about twice their width, yet height diminutive—many times in the kitchens. Most contain either foodstuffs or diningware; never anything of personal consequence. Perhaps it's the hand drawn roses and the narrow, deep purple cloth wrapping around each edge and into a bow on the top, doing what they can to mask the dull kraft paper-brown of the cardboard, that triggers my smile? Or maybe my heart knows—without doubt—that something extra special awaits inside.

Set the brush to the side. Loosen the bow and flip open the top flaps. Butcher's paper wraps the gift within. A simple handmade card sits on its top, reading:

Thank you for all your kindness and care.
Eternally yours,
Missy

Under the paper, a striking vintage royal purple greets me. I take hold of its semi-transparent, lacy shoulders and liberate the garment from the box. The dress unfolds, revealing a similar translucent bateau neckline and chiffon bodice flowing into a below-the-knee skirt. Front and back, a mixture of embroidery, beading, and appliques embellish from the shoulders to just below the waistline. Hold it against me and turn to face my mirror.

Alluring while still becoming… "A pleasant surprise coming from you, Ma."

I lay the dress on my bed and return to the box. Also inside, an off-white, strapless slip with built-in shelf bra and a pair of tie wedges in a dark purple. Kick my boots to the side of the door and yank off my shirt. Pluck up the slip. Guide my arms through the bottom and work the bra over my breasts, letting the rest fall down my body. The fit can't be more perfect. I retrieve the brush and move to the mirror. Start liberating the snarls in my hair. *Can find all these nice clothes, yet we can't find a decent conditioner.* A solid fifteen minutes later, fight the last batch out.

I put the brush on the dresser top and stare.

Hair down? *Nah.* With so few bobby pins, I've limited options. *Pony?* "Eh." *Something off your face perhaps…* "Braids?" A near hair-disaster at my first Junior High dance—seventh grade—flashes to mind. "I know!" Run my fingers over each ear, pulling the loose hair back and into even parts. I hold each section just below the base and tie them into a single shoelace knot at the center of my head. Twist the right tail around the knot right. Lock it in place with a couple of bobby pins. Repeat with the left, opposite direction. Add a last pin top and bottom of the resulting bun. Simple yet stylish. *Thank you, Angelica!*

"Hello?"

Twist toward the door. She's unexpected. "Ah—come in."

My dull curtain pushes to the side, and Katherine steps into my room, flashing a kind smile. "Hope I'm not intruding?"

"Not at all—I, ah, just wasn't expecting anyone."

"Me, you mean?" *Never!* I make to clarify, but she continues before the words leave my mouth. "It's okay; Paul and I have been a little busy." Her already rosy cheeks go redder.

I force a smile. Please don't talk to me about him!

Katherine glances toward the bed. "That's a pretty dress."

A quick change of topic… thank the stars! "Yours is so lovely too!"

Katherine smiles wide and twists twice. The outer tulle layer of her dress' skirt, several centimeters shorter than my own, lifts off its matching sand-colored under-liner. "Thanks," she says, shrugging her head to her left. The loose ends of her double-dutch braid pull over the lacy right shoulder strap of her dress, its embroidered floral pattern repeating across the entire fitted top. "I'd have never expected to find something like this here."

I nod toward my dress. "Ditto. Can't figure where the people who brought this stuff thought they were going."

An *I-know-what-you-mean* smirk plays across Katherine's lips. "Me either; though I'm not here to talk about dresses. I wanted…" Her manner demurs. "I couldn't find anything meaningful to show how grateful I am—I mean knowing what it seems to have cost you—that you came for me, and everything I've heard you did for Paul, getting him to safety. It's not much of a thank you…" Her eyes peek toward the small zipper case in her left hand. "And not that I'm surprised that there wasn't much to find, but I was hoping, thinking it would be nice for the party, if I could, ah," she points at her own made-up face, "help you doll-up a little?"

I ignore the fresh shot of inexplicable *déjà vu* teasing at my lack of memories. "Of course!" Step forward and pick up my dress. "Can you help me with this first?"

Katherine zips me into my dress and the two of us sit on the bed, half-twisting toward one another. Katherine isn't kidding about there being little makeup to find. Her case contains only blush, eye shadow, and two tubes of lipstick. I op for the lighter of the two: a pinkish-red only a shade or two bolder than my natural lip color. "I'll save the darker for Ma," Katherine says of the two lipsticks as she works my closed eyelids, "so us girls have a touch of variety. Mariana would only let me use the lighter one on Claudia."

"Surprised she'd let you put anything on her daughter."

Katherine chuckles. "Took some convincing, and a bit of begging on Claudia's part, but Mariana caved." Katherine's voice takes on a stern Hispanic tone. "'*Esto sólo una vez.*'"

"Hah-ha-ha!"

"Stop laughing," Katherine castigates, "you made me smear it!" A wet finger wipes hard against the left side of my left eye.

"Ow!"

"Sorry," she demurs again, "my fault for the joke. Let me just touch that up"—the applicator runs across my left lid again—"and then some blush."

"Nothing too heavy, please."

"For certain not." The soft tips of a wide brush tickle at my left cheek. "I must admit I'm rather jealous: your natural tone is so vibrant. Redheads like Ma and I, our paleness needs the artificial help."

"As if! The two of you are dazzling in your own right."

The brush shifts to the right. "I suppose so." Her tone lacks any genuine belief. "No matter how I pretend, I'll never be as rich as you." The comment lingers in the air for twenty silent seconds before she eases the brush away. "All done!" I open my eyes to find her smiling widely. "Go look." She nods toward the mirror.

I stand and turn.

Don't know the last time I wore any makeup, yet my subconscious tells me the job Katherine did is perfect. The extra color is subtle, just enough to highlight what's already a part of me. "Thank you *so* much."

"No," Katherine says, "thank you." She gasps. "Crap! Is that the time?!"

Turn toward her, lifting my watched arm up. The start of dinner is not far off. "'Fraid so."

Katherine hurries the makeup back into its pouch and jumps up. "Here, in case." She tosses the lighter lipstick on the bed. "Sorry to have to run out on you like this"—she scuttles to the doorway—"but I need to get to Ma before dinner starts. You understand, right?"

"I do; I've a couple of things to do myself anyhow."

"Then I guess we are both off." With that, Katherine disappears.

I do hope we can spend some more time together... "but for the immediate moment, my dear, you've another relationship that needs some focus."

I step into the first of the two wedges, kneeling down to wrap and tie its ankle ribbon. Likewise, secure the second, stand, and rotate to the mirror one last time. "Alright Mr. Mahoney, let's see you try to not forgive this."

Retrieve the lipstick tube and slide it into a small, hidden pocket designed for the purpose. Lower the light of my lantern and depart to the right from my room. At the corner, glance right. A light shines from Mahoney's room. The glow dims, brightens, dims again. Footsteps shuffle about. Good, he's there. Our conversation is not one to have in the kitchen's openness.

I pace across the handful of meters ahead and stop outside his door, take a deep breath, then knock on the wood paneling. The shadow freezes, but gives no response.

I knock again. "Mahoney?" Wait several seconds. Still nothing. Pinch the curtain to the side. "Mahoney, you okay?"

He's facing away from me, shirtless, his slacks hugging tight over his firm buttocks. The slightest dew sparkles as his back shifts with each breath.

My groin tightens. Frick! He looks so good!

"Mind helping me pick out a shirt?"

"I'm sorry—what?"

"A shirt, Jane." Paul twists partway toward me, snapping to a stop about three quarters complete. His eyes bulge as he swallows hard. "Crush me, you are—striking."

Ugh! Can say the same! Need a distraction, quick! "Why didn't you respond?"

Paul puzzles at me as he completes his turn. "I did. Twice."

"No, you—you did?"

"Twice," he confirms. "Something wrong, Jane?"

He did? Shake my head. "Ah, no. I'm fine."

"I'd say so." Paul's eyes scan my profile. "You're always so captivating."

Dammit… don't entice me like that! "You said something about a shirt," races from my lips.

A taunting smile stretches Paul's cheeks as he turns back toward the bed. "Couldn't find one in the stash, so Mahoney said to check his." Paul waves his hand toward the bed, where three un-Mahoney dress shirts lay. "Narrowed it to these."

I stroll toward the bed, taking a moment to check the mirror over Mahoney's dresser.

Oh, crud!

My cheeks look as if a pair of roses that are in full bloom. *So much unexpected happening today!*

I take another deep breath, then hurry on a fresh layer of lipstick. Hoist the bustier under my dress. One more breath, then eliminate what space remains between us. I give him a little nudge to the side with my hip. What more might the Universe have in store?

He bumps me back with a small chuckle.

I examine the shirts, though the answer is obvious. Still… need to be sure. Hold the first against his warm, sturdy chest. Smooth it along his ridges. Repeat with the second. Take a touch longer with the third. "Hmm… let me check…" Reach for the first again, ready to repeat.

Paul chuckles. "Jane?"

"*Huh!*—Fine!" Pluck the middle shirt and throw it against his chest. "This one. Complements your eyes."

"Perfect." His fingers lace my extended forearm, and he turns me face on. Those damn eyes lock me in place before my brain registers to look away. "After they'd found us in the courtyard," he abashes, "I lost any hope of seeing her again." His chin dips, but not his eyes. "But you came into my life with this amazing ability to create hope where there should be none." His Adam's Apple bobs up and down as he swallows hard. "At first, I kept telling myself I was only trying to fill a fresh void"—Where's this going?—"but having her back, I had to admit the genuine connection… the attraction between the two of us." His free hand glides up my other arm, teasing out the tingle of goose pimples. "I can't—I don't want to—deny the feelings."

By the stars, he cannot have just said that?!

I close my mouth, it having fallen half open at some point. I was so depending upon his devotion to help me get past these feelings! How can I do that now?! Knowing *this*! Catch myself biting at my lower lip. *Just when you accepted…*

Paul slides his left hand to my side, then across my back. "Jane," his voice soothes, "please say something." His eyes sparkle with a mash up of anxiety, nervousness, and yearning. I can't imagine what mine are telling him.

"I—I—" know what I want to say… *but if you do…*

He pulls us that much nearer, his other arm wrapping over my right. "It's okay," he purrs.

"I—"

Zzzzzzzziiip.

The bodice of my dress loosens. Paul eases his left hand over my chemise, toward the top of my buttocks. I drop the shirt as he glides us tighter, my arms left with no option but to surround him. His muscles ripple across my fingers. My body electrifies! Despite the layers of cloth between us, his generous manhood pulses against my inner thigh. My nipples stiffen, mouth drops a hair open. The stronger becomes the citrusy air as the centimeters between our lips disappear. Not but a centimeter to go, eyes close.

This is happening!

A sudden rush of air shoots into my mouth. "I've thought about this for years."

"Me t—" *Huh?!* I yank my head back and flip my eyes open.

For a moment, Paul's lips stay pursed until he realizes there's no kiss where there should be one. His eyes open, full of confusion. "Jane?"

I pull my arms back and slip them up his chest. I push him away. "What did you say?"

His grip loosens, but doesn't release; my torso bends at an awkward angle backward. "I said it's okay. It's clear we both have—"

"Not that." I put more pressure against his chest. "You said you've 'thought about this for years.' What did that mean, Paul?"

"I did?" He shakes his head. "Guess I lost my head in the moment." He strokes my arm. "What I meant was for what *feels* like years." He tries pulling me back into him, but I twist to the side, breaking his grasp. Face away from his devastated eyes, the only way to hide my own.

"Zip me please." I wipe away a tear.

"Jane?" Paul again caresses my arm, bringing back the goose pimples. "For real, I'll figure out—"

"No," I blurt. "We can't do this. I can't do this to Katherine, after all she's been through. I cannot be part of breaking her heart..." I take a breath, fighting back the tears of my own shattering heart. "I cannot put you in a position where you have to. Now, please, just zip me."

A long sigh punctures my bare back. "Of course you're right." A second later, my bodice firms back in place. His grip lingers at my waist.

Please... let go.

"Your integrity"—he tries nudging me back to face him—"one trait I so admire about you." I can't bring myself to turn—won't be able to control myself if I do. My mind is near to being overcome by a coup.

He sighs again. "I'm sorry," he says as he let his grasp loosen.

"No, this is my fault." I hurry to the room's door. "Won't happen again."

I yank its curtain shut as I half run through. "What have I done?! First Mariana, then Mahoney, now Katherine..." I'm only half aware of the dirt floor rushing past my feet. *After she'd reached out in such a thoughtful manner, you repay her by flirting with her boyfriend! How'd you let matters get to this point?*

"There you are!"

I stop and look up.

Ma bounces toward me. "That dress is perfect for you!" She wraps her arms around me. I respond in kind to the much needed welcome. When we break, Ma clasps my hands, takes a single step back, and scans me. "Glad to see Katherine caught you. She's almost finished with me."

"More like trying to," Katherine teases from the dining area. None of me dare to even glance her way.

"You've perfect timing," Ma says, ignoring the jest. "Could you please arrange the rest of the plate settings?" She points toward the tables. They are about two-thirds set, a short stack of plates and dinnerware remaining at the stopping point.

Can't I just go hide in my room? "Of course," I say.

Hands locked together, we stroll toward the dining area, and Katherine. "Why so flush?" she asks as we near.

I peep Katherine's way just long enough that I won't seem rude otherwise. "Running behind," I say, details being most inappropriate.

"Speaking of which," Katherine says to Ma, "sit your butt down and let me finish."

I leave MissyAnn with Katherine and continue to the waiting dinnerware. Ma already completed a substantial amount of the preparations. The same butcher paper that wrapped my dress also covers each table—flowers, butterflies, and rainbows hand-drawn in random spots about each. Small bunches of fresh flowers sit in large drinking glasses at the center of each table. I suck in their sweetness. My immediate stresses fade. My soul could use some time within that greenhouse. Spread out the remaining plates and silverware.

As I place the last setting, Ma sounds from my side. "Can you grab some glasses and water pitchers, too?"

Katherine huffs. "Stop moving!"

Isn't how I want to first talk to Mahoney, but options and time are running short. At least there aren't a bunch of people around yet. "Sure, I'll get the water." Turn toward the kitchen—For real?!—only to twist back. "Where's Mahoney?"

Katherine pulls the lipstick back—"You two!"—just as Ma rotates her head my way.

"He and Indigo went to get some fresh herbs," MissyAnn says. "Left Paterson"—she nods in the kitchen's direction—"to watch over the cooking." She smiles, the half-done highlighting making it look as if she has a thick, currant-colored pencil-line for a mouth. "Nothing but the best for you," she jests.

Katherine glimpses my way, grinning. "So *that* is going on, eh?"

"No!" I vociferate. The two lock eyes and giggle. I turn away and whisk toward the kitchen with an emerging empathy for Paterson.

CHAPTER SIXTEEN

I **APPRECIATE** **J**ASPER'S **EMPATHY, BUT** that isn't my aim. Just having the chance to vocalize the oddities of the past day and a half has been therapeutic enough. Still, I lean across the seat and peck his cheek. "Thanks, Jasper, for the ride and—well—everything."

His cheeks go pink. "Now Miss,"—clears his throat—"you needn't be doing that to an old man."

"Why?" As Papa says, *kindness begets kindness.*

"Because your gra—" A hint of grimace crosses his face before it goes stern. "It's not appropriate," his resolute voice says.

I only spent a couple of hours with the man, but how an innocent kiss can rattle someone so seems peculiar? "*Whom* says it's inappropriate?" What are you not telling me?

His head shakes side-to-side. "I shouldn't have let you ride up here." His face puzzles. "Didn't Xiomara explain to you last night?"

"*Explain!* Yeah, right." Whirl at him. "Wait! You know Zee?"

"I've assisted her for years; after all, she's—" Another grimace as he shakes his head again. "Yes," he says, more to himself than me, "for certain, shouldn't have let you ride up here."

Out of the corner of my eye, the Twinkie—perchance from our cross-town rival—pulls away. *Crap!* My opportunity to sneak in diminishing, I'm once again left amassing more questions than answers.

Certain answers, though, are more important than others. I loosen the door's handle, push it open, and launch from the seat.

"Shall I wait?" Jasper shoots out.

Edge down enough to look back through the door. "No, I'll ride home with Dad." Make to close the door, but catch myself and lean back in. "Next time," I only half tease, "I expect some answers."

His reply cuts short as the door shuts—something about no more riding up front. I rush, giggling, around the front of the limo and up the steps to the building's main entrance. Make the one active turnstile as the last student steps through, latch the crossbar awaiting me, and rotate into the lobby.

The area is expansive, but busy with both physical and virtual displays of the corporation's successes. A blatant attempt to impress guests. None of it, though, is as mystifying to me as it once was. Then again, was but ten last Papa brought me. Most of the students seem as tepid, chatting in their various gaggles, oblivious to the surrounding wonders. Only the few loners gawk at the displays.

"Students!" a not wholly feminine, gruff voice calls out from the front of the group. "Everyone *must* have a visitor's badge before we can enter. Our guide, Miss—ah—"

"Williams," says a nearby cheery—very female—voice.

"Yes," Gruffy says, "Miss Williams is distributing them now."

I weave with care between the primary group of thirty and some straggler duos and trios, contrariwise to the guide. Feel my back pocket, confirming the only badge I need is still there.

"Who's that?" a girl half whispers as I pass one pair. I turn away, feigning interest in a nearby display.

Please ignore me.

My ears concentrate, but the mummer of the crowd clouds the pair's continued whispers. Not, though, the wooden heels clunking toward me.

"Excuse me, but—"

"Those of you with your badges," Gruffy—Thank the stars!—interrupts, "please move this way."

I twist. The whisperer is paused mere meters away, glancing toward the teacher's call. Perfect! She doesn't have a badge yet. As her attention shifts back toward me, I flash her a big smile. "That's me!" Before she challenges me further, I merge into the human river flowing from the lobby.

I file into an amphitheater, new since my previous visit. Manage a seat two-thirds to the top at the far end. Whisperer and her companion enter last, leaving them stuck sitting in the front. To my relief, neither attempts to catch sight of me in the brief moments before the lights dim. A video starts, a smooth male narrating.

Prepare for an adventure like none you've ever experienced. From the deepest oceans to the farthest reaches of the Solar System... and beyond... Today you join the elite explorers who have combed realms once unknown. Join the pioneers at the forefront of medicine and genetics. Stand with those who are shaping the world in which you live. Welcome to Interstellar Industries!

For serious, we can do without the sales pitch! Our guide stands to my right, blocking the doors to what has to be our next destination. The EXIT doors all warn of sounding an alarm. With no viable options, I settle into my chair and ease back. Close my eyes. Pick at my outer thigh, just under my shorts. At least the narrator is pleasant to the ears.

... had already completed successful manned missions to all of Mars, Jupiter, and Saturn through the late twenties to mid-thirties when the corporation secured the assets of the China National Space Administration near the end of the Chinese Civil War. This placed Interstellar Industries in ownership, along with the Space X/Bigelow Aerospace conglomerate, of several Lunar colonies...

Yeah, yeah, yeah—and by April of thirty-six they absorbed ISRO, making them the largest space faring organization, etcetera, etcetera... Years ago, Papa had me memorize the history—for what reason, he's never said. Quizzes me at least once a month on some aspect ever since. Interstellar was already the richest corporation worldwide when it made the Indian acquisition. From its inception, the company focused on the Asteroid Belt, establishing several mining outposts that returned a thousandfold on the investment as natural resources on Earth—consumable water most for want—dwindled. *By the stars, this is* so *boring.* Scratch and poke at the irritated spot.

... expanded humanity's access to space... once inconceivable technologies... revolutionary medicines... unlimited opportunities!

Open my eyes. "Sure… for a price," I murmur. The video flickers, darkening the room for half-a-second. According to Papa, Interstellar either all out owns or collects on some portion of everything its resources help facilitate. Not that the company doesn't give back through many humanitarian and social efforts—including sponsoring an undisclosed, but substantial, number of academic scholarships and scientific studies. My nail breaks into my skin. Once they consumed the Space X/Bigelow corporation—and thus all the former NASA assets SpaceX owned—in forty-three, however, Interstellar became the sole option for anyone wanting to do anything in outer space. The screen fills with the growing globe of Mars as the narrator drones on.

At the turn of the year twenty forty-four, the first settlers disembarked the IIS-Pioneer *for their new permanent Martian home. Within two years, similar settlements populated in both the Jovian and Saturnian Systems. Today, a mere twenty years later, Interstellar Industries boasts thirty-three settlements on Luna, five permanent colonies on Mars, and seven others throughout the Solar System that over sixteen point seven million call home.*

A twinge races from my lower thigh into my brain. *What are you doing?!* I can't pick at my legs. My leotard won't cover that! "Ugh! You've gotta stop this already."

The video flickers again as the narration stutters, then mutes. The room goes dark. A barrage of confused voices germinate about the room. As the lights come back up, several nearby students glare my way. *Crap! You said that out loud, didn't you?* The Universe on my side, the guide isn't paying attention. She abandons her post and moves toward the front section of seating.

"I apologize," the girl's frantic voice says, "this has never happened." The frazzled girl peers toward the teacher, who shakes her shoulders. "Ah…" The guide glances toward the students, then back to the teacher. "I guess—" She looks toward her previous post. "—we'll just move on. If you could, please follow me into the museum, one row at a time." She hurries back to the doors and props one open, the first row of students hot on her heels.

I mask behind my neighbors as Whisperer and her friend pass by. Whisperer, though, seems to spot me before I them. She mutters something to her companion, who looks my direction. A big smile flashing to her face, she turns back to Whisperer bouncing upon her toes.

That's not good.

A minute later, I move into the museum—well, the first floor of three, at least as of the last time I'd been inside—with the tail end of the group. The guide reiterates instructions for us stragglers. "Start on either side. We'll regather at the far end in thirty minutes." Whisperer and her friend migrated right to the second display on that side. Both are staring back at the door. The friend flashes me a petite wave. I ignore the greeting and shuffle to the left, which works for me on three counts: avoid the pair, fewer people, and my interest lay to the left anyhow.

The first-floor houses some of Interstellar's most noteworthy technological, medical, and scientific advances. Work my way quick-casual to the nearest display. Examine the large drill head resting there. Not in any detail. I already know what the display will tell me. The drill's not my goal. Let twenty seconds pass and move to the next display, and a step closer to what is.

I spend half that time at that display, then move again. The third is new—the attached press announcement dated yesterday. *Interstellar Industries is proud to announce its latest medical breakthrough: QuickHeal.* "That explains the party." As much as my curiosity begs me to read more, my eyes catch a group of five working their way over. The tour group is dispersing, drawing nearer.

Better breeze past the next two displays.

"Ah, hello?"

"Huh?" I flip around, half shy of the fourth exhibit. Whisperer and her friend close in.

"It *is* her!" the friend joys. "Oh, my—what are you doing here?" She rolls her eyes. "I mean, I don't recall seeing you around school. Do you go to our school now? That'd be *so* fantastic!"

Puzzle at the pair. "I—ah—no." Quake my head. "Sorry, what?"

Whisperer moves half a step closer. "No," she gives her companion a brief glare, "we're sorry. I'm Amanda—well, Mandy. This is Samantha—"

"You can call me Sam," the other girl interjects.

"Yeah—Sam." Mandy flings her thumb in Sam's direction. "She's a big fan."

"The biggest!" Sam says. "Can I get a photo with you?!" She pulls a pink Digicell from her back pocket.

The two have to be confused. Unless—oh no!—the video… "I don't think—"

Sam bumps past Mandy. "Oh, *please?* The girls on the team will never believe me otherwise." Her eyes brighten. "Unless, of course, you're *on* our team?"

"On your team?"

Mandy steps forward again, shaking her head. "Sam, everyone knows people only want to get *in* there. No one ever transfers out." Then to me, "Sorry"—another glare at her friend—"again. Sam's on our school's gymnastics team"—*Aahhhh*—"but you're on the Paris Heights squad, right?"

Smile at the two. "That's right." I angle straight on Sam. "And— sorry—no, I've not transferred schools." Sam's face droops, but only for a second.

"You'll take States again this year, for sures," she glows. "Do you think this time you'll compete at Nationals?"

I shrug, unsure how to answer. The season's not even half over, States, let alone Nationals, a way off yet.

"*Please* say you'll attend Nationals," Sam carries on. "You're the most skilled gymnast ever. I mean, how are you not in the Olympics by now?"

My cheeks burn. Because my family can't afford it. That's none of their concern, though. Smile and say, "You're so kind. Just taking the season one step at a time." The group is tilting in favor of our side of the room, news of the *QuickHeal* display spreading. *Need to get rid of these two.* "You said something about a photo?"

"Oh, please, yes!" Sam can't contain herself. She and Mandy bunch around me, squeezing tight. As nice as they are, several photos and precious minutes later, I'm ready to be done with the pair.

"Nice to meet you both," I say. "Hope you have a good finish to the season." Twist away from them.

"Perhaps," Mandy says, "you'd finish the tour with us?"

Blast it all! I turn back and smile. "I appreciate the offer, but—" Survey the immediate area for any out. "Mmm…" Run my hands down my waist, into my back pockets. My right index finger pricks on Mrs. Woo's security badge. Ah, yes! I move closer to the pair and motion for them to huddle with me. With a hushed voice, I say, "I'm not supposed to be here"—pull Mrs. Woos badge from my pocket, doing my best to cover the bulk of its details with my fingers—"I'm an intern."—flash the badge.

"*Oohhh...*," Mandy drops her voice. The eyes of the two beg for more details.

"I should duck out and get back to work." I nod toward the *Employees Only* door off to my left, behind the fifth exhibit. "I hope you understand."

"Of course," Mandy says while Sam nods her head. "I'd love to work here. I don't suppose you could...?"

I break from the huddle. "I'll see what I can do." Loath lying, though, I'm certain I'll not see the pair again. "Sorry, but I have to go now." Half turn away, then pause. "And be sure to say *nothing* to anyone about this. Right?" Both of the girls nod, Sam flashing a thumbs up.

Complete my turn and stroll to my target. Thank the Universe! The door requires badge access only. Adjust Mrs. Woo's badge so its back surface faces out. *Please work.* Place it against the sensor.

Click! The door edges open several centimeters.

"Thank you, Mrs. Woo," I say for my ears alone. Before pushing through, arch around.

Everyone's attention is engaged elsewhere, save Mandy and Sam. Both stare right at me, big smiles on their faces. *That's not being subtle, ladies!* Shoo at them with my hand. Mandy flicks a thumbs up, but neither turn. I shake my head and step through the door. As it clicks shut, catch the two deep in eager whispers as they continue to stand there.

The hall before me is short, about twenty meters, before angling to the right. I make my way to the junction and the elevator doors there. Press the call button, setting the machine whirring. Three seconds pass before it stops with a *ding* and the doors separate. I step in and hit 6. *Yeeks... you best hope Papa's office hasn't moved.*

The elevator lifts, ticking away the floors on a digital display above the buttons: *01—02—03—* Another quarter minute later before—*Ding*— glows *06*. The doors spread.

I hurry into the maze of cubicles, taking the first left presented. I stop, the lavatory access dead ahead. "Da! Wrong way, silly." Left would be correct from the main elevators, not the maintenance. Turn on my heels as the elevator door shuts, leaving me in darkness. Well, more like quarter moon darkness. Random overhead bulbs cast a weak twilight across the expanse.

Bring up a mental map, I flip it one hundred eighty degrees, and step forward again.

Left.

Right.

Speed past a small break room.

Right again.

Break into a small jog, one more left to go.

Turn the corner.

Forty meters down, the gaps around the fourth door along the right shine. A shadow dims the glow.

"Papa!"

Five meters disappear. Then ten. *There's so much I need to tell you!*

Crash!

"Dammit, Luis," a woman's irritated voice carries from the office, "can't you be more careful?"

I freeze midway through the next ten.

"Well, who leaves a coffee cup *right there?!*" a likewise irritated man replies. Not Papa. "Hand me that trash can, will you?"

"Just leave it," the woman instructs. "It's not here and the Lieutenant's gonna be back any minute."

"Fine by me," Luis says. The light within the office goes out. A flashlight beam pierces the hall. I dive into the nearest cubicle and slide around its narrow wall. Hold my breath.

Two pairs of boots clump into the tiled hallway.

"What a waste," Luis says. "She really thinks he'd leave something like that in his office?"

"Orders are orders." The woman's voice is a touch fainter. Clumps echo down the hall, each a little less distinct than the previous. Hold my breath two seconds more. Peer around the edge of the cubicle wall.

Military?

Far end of the hall, the two step through the gleam of one of the few lit overhead lights. Each wears blue-gray fatigues accessorized with a knife, pistol, rifle, and assorted devices belted at the waist. Just beyond the light, they cut left and disappear.

"What is happening?" I rush forward past Papa's vacant office, through the gleam, pausing at the same corner the soldiers took. Peek around. Ten meters ahead, the two pass through the main elevator lobby. I stay tight against the wall and slide like putty along the corridor after them.

"So, Z," Luis' voice cuts the silence as they move on, "Two Marines are walking down the street when one spots a dog licking himself. He turns to his mate and says—"

"No." The woman's response is definitive.

Luis stops. "Oh, come on Z," he begs.

The woman turns toward him. *Crap!* Press tight into what little of a crevice houses the middle elevator door, the lobby's light otherwise splashing over me. "No," she repeats, "I'm tired of your shitty jokes. Now let's go."

"Fine," Luis says with a sigh. Two pairs of boots again clump against the tiled hallway, fading more with each step.

I dare to peep their direction. Where'd they go? I hurry out of the lobby's light, pass where they paused, and stop short a turn in the hall.

Silence.

Peek around the edge. The short walk ahead ends at a single secured door lit from above by a dim yellow. Large, solid red block letters label the door *Laboratory D*. Finger Mrs. Woo's badge through my shorts' pocket and step forward. Press my ear against the door. Clinking. Metal—or glass. Maybe both. A few indiscernible words, though, speak away from the door. "Well," pull the badge out, "here goes nothing."

Swipe the badge over the scanner, which flashes red and reads *Access Denied.* "Big surprise," I mumble.

Clump—Clump—Clump. I jerk my head back down the path I came.

"How did we not know there was a tour today?" complains an aggressive female voice. "Having to take care of that will put us behind schedule."

Is that—?

Clump—Clump—Clump. "No idea, ma'am," says an approaching squeaky baritone. "We checked the schedule three times."

"No! No! No!" I hurry the card over the sensor again.

I eye the surrounding walls. *You've nowhere to hide!* I rub the card against the cotton of my shorts—as if a magic lamp from which a genie would spring—and then press it against the sensor. "Please," I beg, "let me in."

Beep. Beep. Beep.

The door opens with a soft *turish*. I rush through the portal and into a low-lit anteroom about nine meters square. Opposite the entrance, six tall wooden cabinets. *Clump—Clump.* A back-to-back row of three seats each run down the center of the room. Short of the far-left corner, a thin glowing column—the room's light source—pass through a hinged door, propped ajar. Glass clinks and metal drawers slide open and clank close from the other side.

What are they looking for?

Behind me, several pairs of boots break the bend. No time to dwell on that! I shoot around the right of the bank of chairs as the door reseals, pull open the first cabinet, *Dr. Emilia Foster* on its placard, and stuff my body back-first against the bright yellow polyethylene smock inside. Shuffle my feet between rubber boots. Ease the door shut, but the sliver of these frickin' breasts don't let it fully close. Ugh! So want *my* body back.

The anteroom's door opens again.

"—can explain ma'am?"

"She'd better!" says one of a group of three crossing toward the left door.

I don't believe it!

Be it not for her voice so ingrained in my subconscious, I may not have recognized her otherwise—unfaltering camouflage, unpadded chest (*so you now know!*), no heels, almost an indiscernible layer of makeup. Her demeanor, though, leaving no doubt whom is in charge. *Junior Lieutenant of our squad*, she pointed out to Karen.

Blink my eyes, hoping they are deceiving me.

Would have never imagined *this* is the squad she meant!

The anteroom bursts with brightness. I twist my head sideways to avoid the glare. Three times the extra light dims and brightens, then fades with a gradual steadiness.

Slowly open the cabinet door several centimeters more. The room's vacant, the propped door settling back into place. The activity beyond louder, doubled by the newcomers.

Time to go!

I slide my left hand along the wood, angling the door further open. "Ouch!" Shake the hand. A line of red streaks the side of my index finger. Fallen to the floor, the photo I cut it upon. I bend down and pick up the picture.

It's crisp, rich in color, recent. Two women: a young blonde, in her mid-twenties, with an arm around an older… *Wait!?* "Doctor Fitzpatrick?" I say to myself. My pediatrician?

The two stand next to a dais wearing white lab coats and wide smiles. The blonde holds a glossy-covered, bound report titled Project X in her hand while my pediatrician displays a small vial of blue liquid. A large screen behind them displays their presentation, what of its subtitle not hidden by their bodies reading:—*tion of JN0449*.

"What the frick?"

That's the code Marcus gave you. Not that it's the secret he implied, but why's my birth date the subtitle of some presentation?

I pace in front of the cabinets.

Fitzpatrick's been my doctor since I was born. We've often talked about her work. *Crud, she's why you want to specialize as a pediatric nurse.* She volunteered to write me a letter of recommendation to the nursing academy, to be my mentor while there. Never once, though, has she mentioned me as a subject of her research. I plop down onto a seat and peer at the photo. All those tests, the blood draws—Geli's long insisted they're not normal. *And the things you've told her in confidence. The things she's seen!*

What about me is in that presentation?!

"Ma'am!" I drop the photo and jerk my head toward the door, the masculine voice beyond breaking into my thoughts. "I've got the files!"

"Frick me!" breezes past my lips, I having momentarily forgotten where I am, what I'm doing. I twist out of the seat and into a crouch outside the door. As I do, the nameplate on the leftmost cabinet door catches my eye. Line one: *Dr. L. Fitzpatrick, M.D., Ph.D.* Line two: *Chief Medical Scientist.* By the stars, this is *her* lab!

What about me is behind this door?

I ease over to the crack in the door and peer through.

Thirty degrees to my left, two of the soldiers study the many vials, beakers, and jars atop a U-shaped lab table. Another, further behind, riffles through the drawers of a countertop stretching the length of the right wall. The others are out of my sight, but given the rattling glass and clunking metal hitting my ears, have to be searching other parts of the large laboratory. I scoot a slight bit right and ease the door further open. A fraction of Katie appears. She's standing about halfway down the length of the lab, at the edge of a second U-shaped table, surveying the contents of a manila folder.

"I think I found it!" one of the out-of-sight female soldiers boasts. Katie turns toward the voice and steps out of view.

Dammit!

Shift right and push my hand again against the door. *Squueeak* it calls out.

"Shhiiit," slithers from my lips.

Katie flips around and stares, a puzzled look on her face. "How in the—"

A realization flashes across her face. She flings the folder shut and shoots the pointer finger of her now free left hand forward in my direction. "Grab her!"

I shoot upright. Glance right, expecting one of the nearby soldiers to bolt toward me. Instead, the door flings open. Luis—as the name tape on his fatigues reads—grabs my left arm as I turn in retreat. "Little birdie fly too far from mommy's nest?" he quips. He yanks me into the lab toward a salivating Katie.

"Only mid-morning and already quite the day," Katie says as Luis nudges me in front of her. "You're the last person I expected to see today, Rat."

I grunt. "Could say the same."

Over Katie's shoulder, a petite female soldier rushes the corner ahead, her short pony bouncing as she quick steps toward us. "Ma'am!" She holds up three small vials of blue liquid in her left hand. Katie shoots me a devious grin before turning toward the approaching woman.

"Zanzibar," Katie says as she tosses the folder atop several others on a small table to her right. She accepts one vial and angles it to the light, highlighting its label. Printed in a prominent green is GGC. A date stamp and what seems to be a serial number typed below. Next to that, handwritten— Of course it would be!—JN0449.

I huff. "That's not yours!" Know not why the vial has such a label, or even *what* it contains, but I know at least that much.

"You're both right," Katie places the vial back in Zanzibar's hand, "and wrong." To the soldier, she says, "Box these up—well."

"Yes, ma'am."

"And keep searching..." Katie turns back to face me, dropping her voice, "while I take care of this."

This is bad. As often as I heard that deleterious tone, this time her words drip with a devious excitement. Why, it seems, I've no choice but to find out. Though Luis isn't restraining me per se, his grip holds firm enough on my arm that pulling away will be difficult. Another soldier joins us, flanking the side opposite Luis. Even if I break the grip, I'll not get far.

"Shaw," Katie called out, "bring over some of that tubing."

Oh crap! She *would* be here too! I run my right hand in a causal arc over my earlobe, freeing several clumps of hair to hang my cheek. Tilt my chin left and down at the table as Karen approaches. A small photo of a golden-haired toddler stapled to the folder's cover stares at me. The folder's tab reads *AP2356*.

How many of us has she experimented with?

"Boss," Karen says. A hand holding about a meter of rubber tubing—used with Bunsen Burners—pops into my peripheral vision.

Katie's chin notches forward. "Holder." Karen tosses the tubing to the soldier on my right, then with what seems no interest in me, clumps away. At the same moment, Holder locks my wrist and pulls it to my back. Luis does the same from my left. *Don't fight it.* Not that being bound is a step in the positive, but drawing any of Karen's attention will not help my situation. *Ugh!*—a tight first loop—*If Katie finds out it was you in... Ow!*—then another. An even tighter third burns into my already sore wrists. I try, with no success, to hold back a tear. *Don't—fight—*

"OW!" Can't help myself as Holder yanks another loop in place. I right my head. Karen pauses three meters down the passage between the two U-shaped tables and stares back at me. What of her nose that I'd smashed last night not covered in medical tape is bruised a grayish brown, the undersides of her eyes swollen. She cocks her head as she considers me. *Please don't recognize me.* Her mouth drops open. *No—please—no!*

A firm grasp latches onto my arm and spins me around, leaving me facing a cock smiled Luis. "Ma'am," says Holder, now behind me on my left.

Whom can only be Katie jerks at the makeshift cuffs. My shoulders prick with a thousand pins. An "Ouch!" squeaks out, as does another tear. Luis chuckles.

"Ma'am?"

"Not now, Shaw," Katie pushes at the center of my back, causing me to stumble over the left foot of a still chuckling Luis. "Zanzibar's in charge," Katie calls out, pushing me forward again as I regain my balance.

A gasping breath cuts through the room. "But ma'am—"

"I *said* Zanzibar." Katie's boot slams into my rear, lurching me ahead and smacking shoulder first into the frame of the door to the antechamber. My body twists clockwise, tangling my feet. My balance flounders and I fall backward into the bank of waiting room chairs, knocking them askew with a piercing *squeeeakk*. The end chair's metal arm frame scrapes across my left shoulder blade as my body collapses sideways to the floor. In an instant, a warm wetness sponges into my shirt.

Katie stomps into the room, stopping six centimeters short of my feet. "Aawww…," she says in a baby voice, "did poor whittle Rat have a whittle stumble?"

I tuck my knees tight to my stomach and, ignoring my stinging back, push up on my right elbow. With a small rock, sit close to cross-legged, butted against the end chair, facing Katie's mocking grin. The rubber rips at the hairs on my wrists, leaking a fresh stream of tears over my cheeks.

"Oh, my." Katie raises her eyebrows in fabricated concern and pats her pants' pockets. "Now, I could have sworn I had some tissue here somewhere." She throws her hands up—"Guess not"—then extends her right out toward me. "Let me lend you a hand up." Her devious grin returns. "Least I can do."

"Screw you, you bitch!" I kick out at her.

"Huh—seems someone found her backbone."

Sorry Papa, I know I should feel sorry for her… not let her get to me. Her malicious grin says as much. *She's created so much pain all bottled up inside me.* "Let me loose, and I'll show you how much of a backbone I have!"

Katie laughs. "As if." She steps around me with a nonchalant swagger, yet stays well short of my legs. "Your dad's no backbone," her baby voice teases, "and everyone knows mommy's not gonna fight your battles."

A menacing growl bursts past my lips as I twist my wrists, only to dig the binding in deeper. "I'm going to end your tyranny!" The words spit uncontrolled from my mouth. "You're nothing but a scared bully and a fake. Everything about you is fake!"

Katie shoots at me, digging her knee into my back and forcing my torso bent forward. "Watch yourself there, Rat," she hisses. "One well placed kick and your gymnastics career is over." She digs her thumb into the cut with a little twist. I fight back a scream. She leans into my ear and snarls. "Permanently." She pushes down with her knee once more, then eases back. "Now get up."

Cruel is a generous word for the many ways in which Katie attacked me over the years, but this surpasses the very meaning of the word. *Evil—she's pure evil.* No doubt baiting her any further is only going to make matters worse. I prop onto my knees and, with what support I can garner from the chair frame given my bound hands, struggle back to my feet. No more do I upright when Katie shoves me toward the office area.

"Where are you taking me?"

"There's someone that needs to see you," she shoves again, targeting the cut, "and he will not be happy to find out you've been loitering around."

"'He' who?"

"Daddy—*my* daddy," Katie says as we step out of the anteroom and down the hall.

Why in the stars would Mister Matters care if I was here? What is going on?

As much as I want to ask, I'm certain I'll not get the answer—at least from Katie—and not without the possibility of my circumstance worsening. Remain mute as Katie prods me around the corner, back right, toward the elevator lobby. She moves us to the first on the left, one labeled *Executive Levels.* With her thumbprint, she activates the call button. A whirring grind breaks what has otherwise become silence.

Ding!

Another push, this time into the far corner of the lift. Katie stays near the door, using her thumbprint to access the top floor. *President.* She faces me, hand resting upon her pistol grip, as the door closes. "Don't try—"

"Save the cliche." I ignore her glare—*Don't let her intimidate you!*—and brace into the corner as the elevator lifts. I stare at the wall ahead. *Ignore her and you take her power away.* Still, never have I borne such aggression from Katie, such raw intimidation. My brain struggles to stop the shaking within my fatiguing arms. I pull on one nail with another.

The elevator whirs on.

Out of the corner of my eye, the floor indicator passes into the double digits. *Ow!* The nail rips half off and into the nail bed. A sticky wetness coats the tip of the picking finger.

Katie chuckles as we slip between the twenty-third and fourth floors. "What was your plan, anyhow?" her sarcasm comes. "You're just a weak little girl who's all alone."

I ready a retort—*Don't*—but clasp my mouth shut.

"You tryin' to be some hero?" her taunting continues.

She's baiting you… trying to get a rise out of you. The digital display hurries into the thirties.

"Well, Rat, there're no heroics that can stop this; it's been in motion for *long* before either of us existed."

What is she talking about?!

Katie steps forward, cutting off my view of the indicator as it flips to thirty-eight, and growls. "Look at me when I'm talking to you!" A hand wrenches my face around. "It's all gonna be *mine!*" Katie's eyes drill into my own. Her menacing glare, however, is only a thin layer over the jealousy they hold. "You think you're so much better than us?"

I think *I'm* better? What?! Over Katie's shoulder, the display echoes *SM.*

"You're a nobody," she spits, pinching my cheeks harder. "Forever a sewer rat, no matter what you're entitled to. Daddy's making sure you get none of it!"

I tear my face from her grasp. Her fingernail digs into my chin, but it's no pain I've not felt many times over. No clue what in the Universe you're talkin' about, but I know one thing… if there's something you're so desperate for, for certain… "I don't want any of it!"

Katie's stiffness falls away, and she steps back. Her eyes fill with confusion, quick follows absence as they tilt toward the floor. A second later, she chuckles at me. "Unbelievable," she mutters, then turns away, shaking her head. She shuffles back toward the elevator controls as the display flips to *EM.*

Now! I lean into the corner and crank my right leg toward my chest. *Hard, square the buttocks. That should do—*

"They've never told you…" Katie perplexes, "You've no clue who you are." The elevator slows.

I drop my leg. "What do you mean who I—?"

Ding!

"Who the fuck now?!" Katie agitates. The indicator shines *VP*.

The elevator doors open into a blackened lobby, save the dim glow of a single overhead light above a large, arching welcome desk about six meters straight ahead. Katie draws her gun. She leans to the side, glaring out the portal.

The woman—her form-fitting cat suit leaving no doubt contrariwise—pops out from the right. Katie swings the gun at her, but it's too late. A baton smacks the muzzle toward the ceiling—*BANG!*—sending the shot into the paneling and clinking against the metal beyond. At the same moment, the woman's right elbow flings into Katie's chin, sending her spinning clockwise. Katie slams against the elevator wall, dropping her weapon. She leans against the compartment wall, breathless. Her legs shake.

A sparkle of silver ganders my way, then swivels back to the woman's primary target. Her batoned arm cocks back, then tenses.

Nothing more do I want than Katie out of my life… but not like this. "Don't kill her," I beg.

The woman pauses, arm frozen in the air. A second—maybe two—passes, she unmoving, staying fixed on her prey, struggling to remain standing. She drops her arm to her side, then with a slight bend, places the weapon into a sleeve running down the side of her calf.

Katie bursts upright with a growl, pulling a knife with a vigorous whip from her right waistband. She slashes at the cat woman, slicing across her stomach. The woman bends at the waist, but instead of falling over in pain, balls her right fist and cranks it upward—*CRACK!*—into the left of Katie's face. Katie's head flings sideways, splattering blood across the control panel. She smacks, again, into the wall—hard—and collapses to the floor in a limp mound. Streams of red leak from both her mouth and right temple.

"She won't be a problem anymore," the woman says. "Now," she bends down and snatches Katie's blade, "about you."

Never thought a situation can get worse than Katie. "I—I—" pee myself a little.

The woman laughs as she faces me. "I'm not gonna kill you." A blemish streaks the midsection of her suit, but there's otherwise no sign of Katie's attack.

"How—"

The woman latches onto my shoulder and spins me to face the wall. An all too familiar chill slides between my wrists. "This is for not being there for you last night."

I know that voice!

The tubing falls to the floor. I spin around. "Xiomara!"

The woman peels her black hood off, an enormous smile greeting me from underneath. She tosses the knife to the side and wraps her arms tight around me. "I'm *so* sorry, Cee Cee," she says with a soft whisper, "that this happened to you. I shouldn't have left you alone last night."

Tears stream my cheeks. "I—I—" Tighten my embrace. "How'd you find me?"

Zee breaks us apart. She runs her hands along my arms and into my own. Squeeze. "I have my ways."

"Your stomach," I say, her body again in view, "how are your guts not splatted everywhere?"

Zee releases my right and tries brushing away the discoloration with the hood. "One of many answers I owe you, but right now we're well outnumbered." She twists toward the elevator opening, still holding tight my left hand. "It's time to go." She yanks me from the lift before I can protest, to the right of the desk, and toward the emergency stairway. Moments later, she busts through its door, me in tow.

"Wait!" I grab the frame and yank us to a stop. Free my hand from hers and step back through. *Right where it should be!* I grab the white handle and—as its red lettering instructs—pull down.

A whooping alarm shrieks all around us. Florescent strobes flash everywhere.

Xiomara cups her hands around her mouth as if a megaphone. "Why'd you pull the fire alarm?"

"There's a tour today," Katie had said, *"take care of that."* Not that she's now in any condition to take care of anything, but whatever is happening, the tour doesn't deserve to be mixed up in it. "For Sam and Mandy."

"Who?" Xiomara's face crunches.

I smile. "Sorry, can't answer right now," I tease as I race past her. "It's time to go!"

CHAPTER SEVENTEEN

"… TIME TO GO."

I half bat at the hand prodding me. "Huh?"

"Come on, Jane,"—the hand prods again—"it's time to call it a night."

My mouth is gummy, the corners of my lips stick together. Lift my head, rubbing a kink from the left side of my neck. Open an eye. Ma is sitting almost on top of me, a wide smile on her face.

"Here," she holds out a glass, "some water." I take the glass and guzzle a large swig. "You passed out," she says as she uses a nearby cloth napkin to wipe a pasty wetness—no doubt drool—from my cheek.

"What? How?"

Ma chuckles. "How do you think, silly?" She nods toward my glass, still half full of its reddish-orange liquid. "How many of those did you have?"

"I—" struggle to recall. Not only the drink count, the last several hours. "What's it matter anyhow," I protest, "it's just punch."

Ma shakes her head with a chuckle. "Tozan pulled the same trick on me my first time."

"Your 'first time' what?"

"Girlfriend, that stuff is Tozan's *special* punch." Ma air quotes the word. She pauses, anticipation lighting her eyes as if she presented more of a question than the statement that it is. When I don't reply, she says, "His special *fermented* punch."

"Yeah, I got it from the first 'special'." I'm not *that* naïve! Crunch my face. "But it was so sweet, no bitter alcoholic flavor."

Ma laughs again. "B-I-N-G-O."

I sigh and rub my temples, as if this will somehow defog my memory. "I'd a couple before dinner, and, maybe, a couple more with."

"From what I saw, it was more than a couple," Ma pokes, "and then some after that! Have you ever drank alcohol before?"

"A little. Alcohol's a rarity up top. One guy once made what he claimed was moonshine. Burned like battery acid"—the recollection alone knots my stomach—"well, what I presume battery acid would taste like."

"So a big no, then?" Ma's eyes fill with humor, as if there's some big prank about to spring on me. "*That* explains things—"

"What things?" Wonder if my face mimics the panic in my voice. "Ma, what did I do?!"

Ma's smile grows even wider. "Oh, nothing *too* embarrassing."

My cheeks burn, fearing what miss-no-inhibitions considers '*nothing too embarrassing*'. I survey the room for criticizing glances. Paterson glowers at the two of us from the next table over. In the kitchen, Mahoney washes cookware. Other than that… "Where's everyone?"

"Off to bed, you goof," Ma's voice giggles. "Katherine and your boy-friend retired early—given, well, you know…"

I don't—"Oh, no!"—I do!

Way too many minutes of some heavy fawning bursts to the forefront of my mind.

"I didn't…?"

"Oh, but you did." Ma laughs again. "Don't worry, though, Katherine was so intoxicated she blithely concurred with all your raving about how alluring her fiancé is."

I bury my head in my hands, several clumps of disheveled black falling over my face. What does Paul think of me now? Rub my temples even harder, my pointer nail finding a small lump to dig into.

"Everyone else," Ma carries on as if the distress coursing through me is no big deal, "stuck around for another couple of hours. We're what's left as of ten minutes ago."

I tuck my hair back, unsure what to think, to say. Should I be breaking down in hopeless tears or doubling-over in delirious laughter?

"Oh! I almost forgot…" The excitement in her voice suggests otherwise, "complements from the Vasquezes on your undies!"

Say what! "I did not!"

Ma stands, walks toward Paterson. "Just pullin' your leg," she calls over her shoulder with a laugh. She stops just short of her beau and twists enough to give me a devious grin. "Though…"

"MA! Who'd I flash?!"

Paterson shakes his head as he grips MissyAnn's hand and pulls her toward the dormitory.

I growl. "MissyAnn?!"

"Guess we'll just have to see what gossip the morning brings." She skips forward, swapping the leading role with Paterson in hurrying to their destination.

"Frickin' Tozan!" I'm gonna have a couple of divisive words waiting for your morning! What I can recall of the evening is a lot of banter and prattle, but never the apology I owe Mahoney.

Push up from the bench to plop—my legs well-chewed bubblegum— right back down. Frick me! What *was* in that stuff?! Jiggle each leg to get fresh blood through.

Someone is shuffling up from the bathroom stairway. Maybe Paul? I stand, finger my hair off my face. The steps are closer. I brush out the skirt of my dress, one part having ridden up my thigh. There's a petite foot, a petite hand, a petite body…

"Claudia!"

"Oh!" the girl jerks. "Sorry. Didn't mean to wake you." She shuffles sideways, her pace quickening.

"Claudia?"

She mis-steps, twists back at me.

I take two steps forward, but stop when the girl clenches her hands. I smile. "You enjoy the party?"

Claudia's face allays with a smile. Her mouth parts, seeming about to share a recent recollection, then clamps shut. Her glow evaporates. "I can't talk to you," she deadpans.

"Sure," I say, "I understand." *That your mother's being ridiculous.* "I'm sorry that's the case."

Claudia rocks forward, a sadness emerging in her eyes.

A hug—she needs a hug!

My feet don't move. Instead, Claudia's eyes seize me, draw me in. Deeper I sink, their soft powder solidifying into a cool, hard steel blue. Deeper still, giving way to a dark royal color before everything falls black.

A scream! Brilliant light. Breathe! Cry, howl! Breathe!

Cocoon against her chest, her lively blue eyes absorbing me. A huge smile plants upon her face, her sunny blonde hair a scraggy mess.

Mommy.

A crawl! First steps. Another! Take more! Another!

Curiosity peaks… branch out, eager to learn and explore. A deep laugh erupts from my belly, the dewy grass tickling my toes.

Who's that?

A man! Dark stranger. Run! Call out! Run!

Fear surges throughout my body, scared to look behind. Legs too short, too slow, he yanks me from the ground. Mom shrieks!

"My baby girl!"

She sprints too late! She fades farther and farther from me the faster the strange man moves. Stretch over his shoulder, trying to get back.

A fruitless attempt for a mere toddler.

"AAHHH!!!"

The pain is too much, too intense. Needles, so many needles. Veins flowing blue. Muscles rip from bone, the growth is too erratic.

The food slot opens. Too enfeebled to crawl to the meager broth being passed off as a meal. "AP2356—as you can observe—a complete failure."

Slosh around in urine, struggle for oxygen. Discarded.

I don't deserve to be alive.

Everything falls black.

"Out! Get out!"

A flash of light.

"Get out of my head!"

My legs wobble. I stumble and fall to my knees. Shake my head. *What was that?!* I look up. Claudia's angst burns through me, tears streaming both our cheeks.

"What," the word stammers from her, "what did you do to me?!"

I… I don't know. I reach out to her. "Claudia?"

She backs a step. "I didn't believe it—until tonight." Another step back, her tears plopping to the floor as she does. "Mom was right," she shoots, "you're dangerous." The girl turns—"Stay away from me!"—and races toward her room.

"Claudia!" I fight to my feet and after her. "Wait!" Lengthen my already wider stride, fighting my clouded head. Race within centimeters. *Nooo!* A wave of nausea hits. I collapse just shy of the opening to the western cavern. "Wait...," weakens from my mouth. My stomach churns, twists. I retch, but nothing comes out. My vision fades. What light exists dims.

"Come to us," a sugary voice calls. *"Come help us, save us!"*

I am! I'm coming!

"Yes, come," echoes a child's voice.

"Save me," says a voice to my right.

"Save me," says a voice to my left.

I will—I'm coming to save you!

"Jane! Save me!" a chorus of calls echoes around me.

"And me, Jane, come save me!"

"Me, Jane, Me!"

"Come, Jane!"—"Jane!"—"Jane!"

"Jane!"

Two firm hands yank me to my feet.

"By the stars," Mahoney proclaims, "what's wrong with Claudia?"

Her actual name...

I stumble. Mahoney hefts me into his arms. "You need some water." He carries me to Paterson's not so long ago vacated spot. Sits me down. He sits near, fills a cup, and pushes it into my left hand. "Drink." I pick up the cup, it not having been a request. "Told Tozan to not make that crap tonight." The pinched lines on his head soften. "What happened?"

Drain the cup. "I—I think Claudia is why the Universe brought me here."

"Okay..." Mahoney puzzles.

"My vision, or a memory, or whatever it was..." I say, as if he should just understand my babbling, "I know who Claudia is—or rather, who she was. I know who her parents are."

Skepticism stares back at me, then doubt. "Jane, there's no way—"

"I do!" *AP2356.* Her file again flashes my mind's vision, and the photo of that golden-haired toddler. Her photo, just one atop too large a stack. "And there are others! The files—in that office—we need to get to those, to help these tortured children!"

Mahoney's fingers press into my shoulder. "Don't."

"But they are all alone, unable to defend themselves."

Mahoney's hand slides down my arm. "We can't," he says with a bow of his head.

I jump up. Stagger. Fight a sudden dizziness. "What do you mean 'we can't'?" I protest. "You risk helping me rescue Katherine, but not these abused kids? Mahoney," I wipe a tear away, "I could feel her pain, even now. She wanted to die."

Slam!

The dinnerware around where Mahoney's fist pounded the table rattles.

"Don't you think I want help?!" He dips his head and takes a deep breath. A moment later, he looks up and wraps my hand. "I'm sorry." He gives it a small squeeze, then nudges me to sit again. "What happened to those children makes me as sick as it does you. But Jane, you're relying upon a partial memory and a weak coincidence." There's pain in his words. "Mariana would never approve it."

"So that means we don't even try?"

Mahoney shakes his head. "Of course not." His face washes with sadness. He takes a breath, then gentler, "You don't know what those folders contain, how dated they are. That puts everything good we've been able to do at tremendous risk for answers which are no better than those we already have." His tone is pain, but he believes in what he is says. "Besides, you're assuming there's even anyone to save."

I squeeze his hand back. "I can't explain how, but I guarantee they're still alive, and that there are answers in those files about us all. They need our help."

"I want to believe you," Mahoney says, yet his voice betrays his doubt. His elbows crash to the table, his head plops into his hands. He digs his fingertips into his temples. Seconds later, another deep breath passes his lips. "Claudia," he utters as his hands drop, "you've seen but a drop of all it has taken—all the sacrifices Mariana's made—to keep her protected. The older she gets, the harder that is. Keeps Mariana up night-after-night with worry." He shakes his head. "More children would drive her past her limits."

"But we can all share the responsibility."

Mahoney chuckles, but not in the ha-ha sense, in the *in-the-know* sense. "We would try, but Mariana's nature is to watch over us all… including you, despite her anger right now. Sharing responsibilities, no matter how much, wouldn't allay her concerns."

I reach for his hand again. "We could—"

His lips fold in on themselves. "Sweetheart, our feelings aside, we've nowhere to bunk more people, let alone children. No clothes for them to wear—"

"Solvable problems," my optimism interjects.

Mahoney sighs. "Perhaps, but with yesterday's boat the last supply shipment, we've no way of replenishing our already limited resources. Trust me, if Mariana could help, she would. What makes her an effective leader is that she weighs all aspects of a decision in a fair manner. She carries a heavy burden."

"One she'll need to share," my sincere words come, "I *have* to do this,"—clutch his hand—"even if that means on my own."

Mahoney groans. "No, not alone." He swings his head. Surrender imbues in its motion. "If you're doing this, it's with help and a plan." I bounce in my seat. "A *lot* of help," he tempers his acquiescence, "and a *proper* plan."

"Perfect!" I snatch his face and plant a firm kiss on his lips. Nothing passionate, only appreciative. That's appropriate… right?

Mahoney snaps back, his cheeks puffy, a hint of red piercing his dark tone.

Maybe a touch too much? I stand. "I'll go tell Ma," I say, attempting to ease the sudden awkwardness.

"Ah… no." Mahoney jilts his head. "Not her. Mariana."

He's got to be kidding! "What? But you just said—"

"Jane," he cuts in, "without her on board, everything would be for nil. If there is anyone to help, they'll end up here. She needs to be part of this." He pauses, perhaps to emphasize his point. "Even in your short time here, you for sures recognize that's unavoidable."

"I do," I admit, though I don't want to have to. "So, to Mariana then!"

I make to stand again, but Mahoney locks my arm. "Tomorrow, Jane," says a weary voice. "Right now, you need a solid night of sleep. We all do. Mariana will not be easy to win over. Give me the night to think through this and tomorrow *I* will talk to her. Tomorrow, I promise, I will make this right."

I've no doubts otherwise. "Okay," I consent, "tomorrow."

"Good!" Mahoney offers me his arm as the night before. Wow, already seems so long ago! "Let's go get some rest," he says. "We can finish cleaning up tomorrow."

Survey the area as I swoop my arm through his offering. "Ma did a marvelous job."

"She does put on a delightful party," we start toward the cubicles, "but it's Paterson's artistry that adds the color."

"Wait, he drew all that?"

"Of course," Mahoney surprises back, "Paints and sculpts too. Ma didn't mention it?"

"No," oozes from my mouth. Who'd of figured? An unforeseen admiration surges my heart. So *he* decorated my gift box! I smile. Hope Ma rewards you well tonight.

As we stroll toward the cubicles, though, none of the noises I prepare for emerge. Ma's cube radiates an eerie, silent darkness. Not even Tozan's horn is blowing as we draw to the T between our two rooms. Mahoney pauses. "Goodnight, Jane." He releases my arm and kisses my forehead. "Promise me—" he pulls back—"you do nothing before tomorrow."

Peek at my watch. 12:08 AM. Smile wide.

"*After*," Mahoney clarifies, seeming to know the acknowledgment my mind's preparing, in strict terms, is not a lie, "I talk with Mariana."

I throw up the peace sign. "I promise," I say with a smile.

Mahoney shakes his head. "Have a good night's sleep." He chuckles, then starts the last steps toward his room.

"You too," I half whisper, then turn away and skip ahead. Pass by Tozan's curtain. Perhaps, in some backward way, I owe you thanks. A few skips later, shuffle past my curtain.

Shoes.

I reach down and undo the left ribbon, freeing my ankle. Pull my foot out. I hope Mahoney convinces her. Arch toward and undo the other. He has to convince her. Sit the shoes to the side, next to my boots. Reach around my back with my right hand—*Zzziiipppp*—loosen my dress. *Think positive, Jane...* I let it drop to the floor and step outside its doughnut. He will convince her! Toss the dress on the dirties.

Yikes, my hair!

I know it isn't good, but my mirror proves how much so. Release what bobbies remain, then run my hands through, freeing those tangles that will. I crawl into bed.

And toss five minutes…

And turn five more…

Toss again another five.

"Ugh!" This isn't something to be excited about! Turn. No, not excited—anxious.

Sit up.

Perhaps I could—

"No! You promised Mahoney. Besides, you're exhausted… and borderline drunk!"

I lay back down and suck in two deep breaths. Roll to my side. Close my eyes.

Let go, Jane. Release and relax.

The path ahead is clear. Mahoney will not let me down. He *will* convince her. No matter anything else, that much I'm certain. As certain as I am that—though I recognize none of them—the assuaged faces flooding my cerebral vision feel the end of their suffering nearing. *They know*, my heart soothed, *they know you're coming for them.* My mind eases. My breaths slow. A sense of ease fills my mind as I drift…

SSSNOORRTT!

What the…!

Another snore, then another, from Tozan. Flip to my left, wrapping my pillow around my head. The sudden minefield of snorts explodes against my head.

I grunt. "Dammit, Tozan!"

There's a shuffle from the other wall, then an "Ooo", an "Ahhh". For scraigs, you've got to be kidding! An "Oh, yes!" pierces the thin barrier. Ear plugs! I need ear plugs! The slippery and sloppy sounds of skin-on-skin contact assault my virgin ears.

I bolt up.

"Frick this!" Pull my boots on and start out my door.

Pause.

Might be chilly.

I turn and snatch my jacket from the end of the bed. Hurry down the hall, plugging my ears as best as possible with my fingers—to little success—as I rush past and away from the butterfly curtain. *Just had to slip in one more thank you?!*

Chuckle. *Nice double entendre.*

A flicker from the lookout to the left.

Wave.

Ava half waves back.

Don't envy you. Be they five minutes or five hours, I don't want to be stuck listening to those two.

I race into the dinner area and pass at the artistic table liners. Smile. *I'll forgive you this one time, Paterson.*

Turn into the western part of the cavern.

My grin flips. A faint whimper pins at my ear.

Oh, Claudia… I'm so sorry.

Slant left, only to find the Vasquez's rooms still and dark. I peek at the cubby to my right. A slender yellow-orange outlines the drawn curtain there. A shadow flashes as a feminine giggle breaks past the barrier, then the light disappears.

"Ugh!" Quicken my step.

Now stop it, Jane. Celebrate them—all of them, that they've found humanity's unique gift; one that—one day—you will too.

I enter the shower tunnel and slow. A handful of paces along, I break left and start the climb to the greenhouse.

Not five meters along, a freshness I've not smelt in some time tickles at my nose. Though the climb is steep, a renewed vigor carries me on. The growing viridity of the air encourages my legs another five meters. The cavern dampens, not in the musty rot of the maintenance shaft, but a subtle sweetness—like a freshly cut orange—interlaced with a slight jolt of salt.

Must be close!

I take the steps two at a time, my forehead leaking sweat. Wipe it away to have it no sooner replace. Calves burn. Feels good! I climb five meters more—perhaps six?—when the rock gives way to thick palms, several trees, bushes galore. I prod through the undergrowth another meter, two, three, before the canopy thins. The hardness under my feet sponges at meter four—Are those… stars?!—five…

I erupt from the vegetation.

Freeze.

"By the stars!"

Thousands—no… tens of thousands!—fill the sky from valley's edge to valley's edge. The full moon casts a light over a greenhouse like none I've ever seen.

The plant filled depression sports grasses of various lengths with a mix of ferns, shrubs, and trees tracing three of the outer edges. To my right, a small cultivation pops out from the surrounding growth: *tomatoes.* Next to that, *carrots and… zucchini?* The distant plots hide their contents, but ahead, the fourth edge gives way to a blanket of twinkling moonlight: *the ocean.*

I pull my boots off and slither my bare feet through the cushiony grass. *Aaahhh.*

Lazy further in and find a clear, fleshy spot near a growth of melons. Sit. Listen. No snoring and no—well—MissyAnn. I make a pillow of my jacket, lay back, close my eyes, and let the calming *whoosh* of the waves fill my ears.

Perfect.

My mind erases. My heart slows. Breaths soften…

"Greenhouse?" I jerk upright at the voice. "Seems a bit of a misnomer." Sweep my right leg around and out. "Hey!" He jumps back, just avoiding the strike.

"Paul?!" Haul my leg back.

"Sorry," he says, "didn't mean to frighten you."

"What are you doing here?"

His boxer shorts leave little to the imagination. The tank top he wears is no better.

"Saw you go by; you looked soured." I did? Is my resentment so plain? "Thought I'd check on you."

"Thanks," I mutter. "I'm fine. You can go." *Please don't!*

"If you don't mind," he surveys the area in brief, then looks up to the sky, "I'd like to stick around for a bit."

Yes! Yes! YES! "Ah, sure," fling my hand out to an open spot on my right.

Paul grins and sits. Our hips brush. "So, what part of this is the *house?*"

I shrug. "Maybe there's a building out that way." I point a finger in the sea's direction.

"And all these stars!" Paul glances up again. "I've never paid attention enough to notice them all before."

"I know." A silent second passes. "Paul, I, uh…" He angles at me. His pecks flex. His eyes suck at my own. *Hurry, girl! Say it!* "I'm so sorry about earlier. I'm not—"

He laces his fingers between my own. "No worries," he says with a knowing smile. "Nothing that's not happened before." Paul relaxes to his back and stares up. I match him, resting again on my makeshift pillow. Neither of us release our mutual grip.

A minute passes that way, then two, four, eight. Fingers interlock, doing nothing more than watching the stars twinkle. A meteoroid flashes by.

"You see that?" Paul pumps my hand.

"Yeah," I purr.

No! Wait! What are you doing?! Retrieve my hand and lean to my side, facing Paul. *Damn, how'd you let this happen again?* "Paul, you should—"

His head tilts the slight bit necessary to look back. "It's okay."

"No," I say, though with no more strength than a popsicle stick holding up a brick wall. Why's he so enticing?! "This isn't—"

"Jane"—Paul angles himself as if a mirror image of me—"we both want this." His left hand brushes a tear from my cheek I'd not realized is there. It lingers for a moment, then scoops below my ear and around to the nape of my neck. His eyes sparkle.

"But I've never…" My body quivers with goose pimples. "At least, not other than by myself."

Paul guides us closer. "Slow and tender," he hums as he leans in. A familiar citrus seeps into my nose as our everything draws closer.

Jane, you need to stop this!

So my mind commands, yet my body shows no hesitation in mimicking Paul's lean.

Jane, you know this isn't right!

The tingle growing in my groin disagrees.

Halt, Jane! Halt right now!

An inexplicable energy pulls my lips into a pucker, forces my eyes to close.

Stop now!

A bolt of lightning pierces my lips and caresses over my skin. My muscles shudder with vivacity. Caress my hand along Paul's sculpted side. *This is happening!* Another spark jumps between our lips. A wave of adrenaline cycles from head to toes. I slam my thighs together to keep the blossoming exuberance from escaping.

Ugh! Screw doing the right thing!

I part my lips, sucking in Paul's flavor, his rising energy. Our tongues tease each other as they dance a sultry tango. He eases me back to the ground, edging his firm body over mine. His masculinity ripples across my form. He glides his hand to my shoulder, then down my chest and brushing against my titillated womanhood with the smoothness of silk.

I moan, tighten my crotch all the more. *Can't hold it in!*

An unrecognizable me latches onto Paul's wrist and flings us over. I lock his other wrist to the ground, in line with his ears. Straddle his crotch with my own and thrust down with my hips. "I need you in me!" growls a now unchained animal.

Where'd that come from?!

"I—ah—" What dismay stammers from Paul's mouth, the stiffness teasing at the explosion building between my thighs counters with no such reservations.

"I need you in me *now!*" I fling down Paul's legs. Clutch his shorts and wrench them apart. *How'd you do that?!* His erection springs upright, free of its confinement. I ogle in delight as his enthusiastic beacon pulses in anticipation of being the first to survey a cavern unplumbed.

Who are you right now?!

An unrestrainable force scoots my body forward, allowing the hard flesh to caress my thinly concealed petals. "Mmmmmm!" *Feels so good!* Pitch and dip.

"Thought,"—Paul moans—"this is your first time?"

His neck is rigid, eyes shut, mouth open and panting. I lean forward. "My gift to you," I warm into his ear. Lift my hips up and whisk my panties taut to the side.

I ease down.

Not a centimeter disappears when skin contacts skin, a whole different current pulsating my anatomy.

"Disgraceful!"

I bolt upright, frozen.

"By the stars," Paul begs, "don't stop!"

I boost to my knees, my underpants snapping back. Whisk my head to each side. "Did you hear that?"

He latches my hips. "Don't worry, everyone's dead tonight. No one'll discover us up here." He tries tugging my body back down.

I stay locked in place. "Not them." Stretch my ears. My finger rubs at a mole on the back of my neck.

Paul's hand slithers under my underskirt, across my midsection, and—*Oh, that feels so good!*—over my left breast.

A wetness leaches through my panties.

"Imprudent strumpet!"

I vault to my feet and back. "Mom?!"

A slack-jawed Paul jumps up. "What the—who?!"

I whirl on my tiptoes. "Shush."

Silence, save for the slight rustling of the trees.

I quiver, pull at the skin on my arm. "What have I done?" pleads my heart. "You're engaged!"

Bend for my jacket, but Paul fastens my wrist and draws me to him. "I'm the one responsible."

"No, I—"

He plants his lips against my own.

My everything tingles.

Our tongues flirt, aching my vagina. Against the ninety-nine point nine percent of me that wants to finish what we've started, the faintest of reason fights. I slip my arms between us and nudge his chest, breaking our lip lock.

"This," I so don't want to say, "shouldn't have happened. You need to get back."

"Perhaps." He slips his hand around my back and pulls my hips tight to his own. "But you're whom I want." His renewed manhood messages no doubt of his desires.

"Go," emerges my weak plea, "before"—*She!*—"anyone finds us."

Paul relaxes his grip, but doesn't let me loose. "I suppose you're right," he wavers, weaving his hands into my own as the joints of his mouth tweak up. He leans in.

I twist free before our lips again touch. Had they… I'd not be able to control myself.

"I"—*so, so*—"want to," I say to his now crunched face, "but…" Dip my chin toward the ground.

Paul's posture goes stiff. "I'll talk to her," he says, seeming to know the words that cannot leave my mouth. He glides my face up and locks my eyes. "Later this morning," he purrs. "But for now…" His chin tilts, mouth parting.

I paste my hand against his lips. "No more!"

A pout paints my palm.

"Until after," I allow, smoothing my hand down his chest.

"Twenty minutes more?" he beseeches.

Only a measly twenty?!

"You're unbelievable," I say. "Half that, and you keep," I linger at his unabated erection, "*all* your extremities to yourself."

He faints a curtsy. "As you command, Your Ladyship."

Roll my eyes to the sky. "Universe, so help me!"

CHAPTER EIGHTEEN

EERRGG! HOW'S THIS HELPING ME? I latch Xiomara's wrist as she releases the steering wheel and starts twisting out.

"Papa's here?"

"No. Necessary pit stop." She pops free and out through the opening. "Come on!" she calls as her door reseals. Close to two hours of offering nothing more than idle chit-chat and now we're making a "pit stop". She serious?!

Suck in a deep breath.

Calming breaths. Patience.

Suck another in.

She assured you he's safe. Besides, as versatile as the woman is, I imagine her skills don't encompass being a meteorologist. A freak monsoon in the dead of winter, sure; but in the early fall… not her fault the flooding tripled our drive. We've our ancestral global-warming deniers to thank for that.

You just need to push through this last distraction.

I open and pop my legs through my door. Yank up and out from the low riding vehicle.

Zee jetted us into the center of a half-arch of vehicles. To the right, a rugged, electro-solar Land Rover of a model I've never seen before. To the left, a metallic red BMW roadster sits charging. Both badges a common sight in the school lot. Near one-o'clock the area squares, housing a car lift surrounded on two sides with well-stocked tool benches. A large shelf of boxes and bins extend along the right wall, ending in four towers of tires.

I glance at Xiomara and think, the way you peeled in here, no wonder you need so many of those! I close my door and step around the front of the car, and start hacking. The underground garage appears well kept, but is musty. A little suffocating, on account of the burnt rubber, Zee's newest skid marks almost invisible over the collection already present.

As if it will act as an air filter, cover my mouth with my forearm to no actual effect. Hurry northwest toward the angled wall opposite the work area. Join Zee waiting inside an opened lift. "You must go through a lot of rubbers."

"There's an understatement," a baritone teases from above.

Is that…?

"Best you stop there!" Zee peers upward, McIntosh cheeks radiating her pale skin. "Or Jasper'll be resetting more than just that circuit."

In a caricature of the man, the overhead voice replies butlery, "But uuv coourse, Madam."

I'm pretty sure…

Xiomara shakes her head, rolls her eyes. "You can stop that, too." She rests her hand on a sensor that flashes blue, then green. As she lifts her hand up, the elevator doors close, and the compartment rises.

"Welcome back, ma'am," our digitized companion warmly greets.

Has to be! "You're the presenter, aren't you?" I say into the air.

"The same," the voice replies. "If you would so indulge me, you seemed quite perturbed by my presentation Your Gr—"

"Iain, we'll get to that later."

"Oh, yes. Sorry, ma'am." The voice offers a genuine apology. I look at Xiomara square on.

"How'd he know—"

"That you were in the audience?" she finishes for me. "Without your chip, I'd imagine facial recognition."

"I smelled you first," Iain chimes in.

"What?!" I survey Zee for an explanation, who shrugs.

"The human body does not *smell*," Iain says. My mind sees two stacks of ones and zeros quoting the word. *Freaky!* "Body odor results from bacteria living on the skin that breaks down the proteins secreted in sweat into acid." The lift stops, but the door remains shut. "A person's unique odortype," he goes on, "transmits through these proteins and, thus, iden-tify that individual. As good as a fingerprint, if not better. More scientifically—"

"Thank you, Iain," Zee cuts in.

"Of course, ma'am." The doors slide open.

Xiomara steps out and says, "My home is yours," then cuts left.

"My home…" My feet hesitate to follow. Why'd we come here? I poke my head a hair forward and glance around from the right.

Zee's apartment is an open design, the living space alone much larger than my home's whole first floor. Two Lazy Boy chairs, each siding a small couch that faces a fireplace, outline what one might call a living room. A small oak coffee table sits in the middle of the furniture. I look as close as I can—*Is that genuine wood? Surely not…* Even rarer, a large photo album sits on its top. If she owns a projectratron, she keeps it well hidden.

Past the living room, a gym dominates the bulk of the space. Not the *couple-of-free-weights-and-a-treadmill* showpiece many families sport and never use. *This* is the real deal. On one side, an artificial rock wall climbs close to three stories high, ending in an apparatus of dangling ropes, monkey bars, and other rigging attached to the ceiling. A similar structure emerges from the floor. It houses a disparate mix of punching bags, rope ladders, and other gear whose purpose isn't obvious. Gymnastic mats with ramps, rods, and inclines of varying thicknesses stratify the floor.

An adult's playscape.

I step out of the elevator, only to freeze at once.

What in the Universe… I mystify at the far wall… *have you gotten into?* A library of weaponry—militia to martial—decorate two off-white peg boards: pistols and daggers, many concealable, some far from so; a long-nosed rifle, two semi-automatics, a fencing sword, a Samurai. *A mace!* Nunchaku, batons—some collapsible—an assegai… a mix of other exotic gear and devices—*Is that a Frisbee?*—that seems more toys than armament. *Who—what?!—is this woman?*

She's already told you, in a way.

I twist left, pointing at the display. "What kind of spy are you?"

Xiomara has her back to me, spreading out the contents of a medikit atop an island in the center her kitchen.

"A lethal one," she says with a casual chuckle. "Though to be more exact, I'm an assa—" The spreading hesitates. She turns toward me, a wide smile on her face. "We'll cover that later; let's get your wound clean." She sits, padding the top of a stool near her own.

Ugh! Her varying candor is so confusing! Her inconsistent mix of blunt honesty and coded responses is chaffing to sort through. What can you be so eager to tell me, my mind asks her, yet so reluctant about at the same time? I push my hunger for an answer aside and move in her direction. The adrenaline of our escape having long faded, my back is killing me.

Like the rest of her apartment, Xiomara's kitchen is enormous. Above the island workspace, a host of cast-iron and steel pans hang. Wooden cabinets, granite countertops, and an array of steel appliances—most doubled—line the area. Whoever she is, the woman has lavish tastes. I zero the distance between us and arrange myself on the stool there, facing away from her.

"Turn a touch more, please." Xiomara nudges my right shoulder forward.

I comply, though my shorts stick on the stool and run up. I quickly yank them down before she notices the damage I've done to my thighs. Out of the corner of my eye, Zee reaches for a pair of meat shears from a nearby knife block.

"Those are for…?" I try hiding the unease in my voice.

Zee chuckles. "Your shirt; don't want you ripping that gash any further by having you pull it off." She lifts the back of the shirt and cuts, spawning a pair of ever widening flaps. Four snips later, the neckline gives way, save the fabric clenching my left shoulder.

"This will hurt." Zee yanks the garment free. I swallow the pain. *Don't you dare be weak!* As the shirt slips from my arms, the severity of my injury registers: the bulk of its back is stained crimson. Zee nudges the left strap of my bra to the side. A cool cloth then dabs around the top of my shoulder, working downward. "She did a job on you."

I stay silent, the rawness of my run-in with Katie flashing into focus as a tear streaks my cheek.

Xiomara hands me a kerchief. "She was unexpected, wasn't she?"

Dry my face and nod. "I'd have never thought…" My words fall short.

Zee rubs what unscathed of my back there is. "Me neither, sweetheart," she soothes, then a second later sighs, "I underestimated her." I make to ask what she means, but Zee first says, "Everyone in threes."

I arch around. "Everyone in threes?"

"You need to sit still." Zee angles me back in place and resumes her dabbing. "The person we let others see," she says two dabs in, "the person we think we are, and the person we actually are. Most people spend their entire lives trying to drown the last by the first two." The dabbing stops and a glass clinks and something sloshes, gurgles. "How deep into Katie have you seen?"

The answer hits without hesitation. "The last. She acts as the righteous debutante, plays the masterful bully convincingly, but through all that facade…" *Huh!* That the adjectives are ready at the tip of my tongue is like performing a Hecht transition when having misjudged the high bar. "She's insecure, fragile—anguished."

The gurgling stops. "Why?"

That's the key question. She's twice my bulk, an equal academically, yet there's something else, there has to be. "She seems afraid, almost as if… I'm not sure why. There's something else…"

"Yes?" Zee bubbles with eagerness.

"You've no clue who you actually are." Katie's words cycle through my mind. *"Who you* actually *are."*

An unforeseen truth sweeps over me, which Zee seems to sense. "There's what?" The prompt drips from her mouth.

"The third me," I say. "She's afraid of the third me, the real me."

"In ways she has no clue," Xiomara's blunt assertion comes.

I contort, not letting Zee stop me this time. "What do you mean?"

Xiomara grabs my upper arm and pushes me forward again. "Darn it, now you're bleeding again." The dabbing resumes in haste.

Several seconds of nothing else passes.

"Zee—please?"

She pushes a finger into my lower back. "Don't slouch." Another silent moment passes, then the cloth stalls. Zee sighs. "You've found yourself more emotional of late, right?" Zee's voice is soft and calm, close to a whisper. The cloth pulls away.

I nod, not wanting a verbal response to derail her. Do all I can to not twist at the scrapes and plops that have started behind me.

"But you're physically stronger, more agile?"

I nod again.

"I'd expect as much. Brace for a sting."

I grip the stool and stiffen, more so from anticipation than instruction. At last, some answers! The gel is pasty and cool. *That doesn't*—"Ow!" I flinch, but otherwise hold firm. Within seconds, the coolness of the coating melds to the cut, erasing the sting. Relax my posture.

"Like how you got this." Zee's hand brushes over the patch affixed to my right shoulder blade.

Where is this going? "That's nothing; an accident."

"I see." Zee peels away the bandage before I can protest. "As I thought."

"What?"

Schliikkk. A flash of white tickles my peripheral vision, yanking my head right. Denise's switchblade slides to a stop not more than a quarter meter away. "This your accident?" Zee asks.

"How'd you—"

"Adrian found it partially smashed into the ground around where, well"—her hand goes heavy—"you know. Based upon the stories he heard, says you earned it."

I spin to face Xiomara. This time, she doesn't stop me. "Earned it!" Do nothing to hide my disgust. "I want nothing to do with it."

"Understandable," Zee muses, "but see beyond the weapon. It's a symbol of empowerment. First Denise's, now—by right—yours. A reminder of what you're capable of."

Shake my head. "I was just lucky."

"Luck is an illusion. My guess, you remained calm and waited for an opening, then acted without hesitation. Empowered yourself." She locks eyes with me. "Together, we are going to refine that power. I will teach you how to weld it, how to shape and bend its energy to your needs, whatever those needs.

"That includes teaching you how to defend yourself and, when necessary, how to be the aggressor."

I shake my head again. My left hand slides toward my right arm. I will it to grab the lip of the stool instead. "That's not me. I'm not—"

"Me?" Xiomara runs her left fingers across my cheek, a warm smile stretching her lips wide. "My sweet Cherry Cheeks, you're gonna be so much more than me." Her hand motions around the apartment. "Besides, I imagine you don't want to be locked up here forever. Nor will I always be with you. Though I seem to be quite adept at defying death, Beelzebub will catch me one of these days."

Zee clenches my hands, her face lighting in excitement. "This metamorphosis you're undergoing, this adventure that has started, my obligation is to ensure you're able to walk the path of your destiny, and more."

"My destiny?" *She's a charlatan, just sans the crystal ball. This isn't rig—Oh, shut up! Stop over reacting.* "You—you know what is happening to me?"

"And what will," Zee says, "Better than anyone." She stands before I can say anything more. "I'm sure you're hungry, would like to freshen up?" She points toward a door past what appears to be her office area, near a tight spiral staircase to the second floor. "Washroom's there; everything you'll need inside." She looks me up and down. "And you can throw all that away." She flings a finger at what clothes I still have on. "I've a new outfit for you."

How? Was this all somehow planned?

I stand, then peek at the elevator. Its door is still open.

It's now or never, girl. Run!

My legs will not move.

She's your only link to Papa.

"Well," Zee nudges my arm, "go clean up." She speaks with a kind, but definitive tone. "Then we'll talk. Answers to all the questions you can ask."

Something beyond my control makes me nod, makes my legs advance into the office area, toward the washroom. As I go, Xiomara busies herself in the kitchen.

The top of Zee's desk has little on it, no computer or traditional workplace devices of any type. An orb—maybe eight centimeters in diameter—sits to one side. A pearly mauve globular blob hangs by some unseen force at the center. The mass contorts and twists, discharging a periodic lime tinge.

Huh… seems she's a soothsayer with a crystal ball after all.

On the opposite side, a silver-framed photo sits at an angle in the top corner, fronted by two pale brown folders, each closed with a red tie. Dragging my feet as I near, catch the printed label on the flap of the top folder—*Project: Forgotten Roots.* More arresting, the note scribbled below: *a.k.a. Memory Wipe.*

Peek over my shoulder. Zee's buttocks stick out from the refrigerator. I reach forward and slither the tie loose.

The desk's globe flashes with a bright spark. "That's not yours to peruse."

"Sol's fury!" I jolt my hand from the folder as if it's a burning log.

"What's that, sweetie?" Zee calls from the kitchen.

"Nothing!" I snap the photo up.

A sunny day at a park. Large blanket, weighed down with picnic baskets, plates of food, and a gaggle of smiling people. Xiomara sits at the top of blanket. A thick-bearded, grandfatherly gentleman sits tightly at her side, his arm affectionately around her. *Yikes!* That *is not right!* To their left, rests back a young man in a too small button down that wraps his physique in what appears more his second skin than a shirt. He's rolled the garment's already short sleeves even shorter. Chuckle. *Proud of that mermaid tat are you?* A young, loose-haired blonde in a bright yellow, flared, cami-fit sundress leans into him.

I think that's...

She's younger, and her two appearances can't have been more opposed, but that smile leaves no doubt.

Doctor Foster! With Xiomara?

To the right, a couple in their thirties and their daugh—That cannot be... "AP2356?"

"Sorry?" Zee's stirring something on the gas stove top.

"Mmmm...." I blink long, then study the photo again. No doubt... that golden hair—both the girl's and who could only be her mother's. "This girl," I hold the face of the frame out, "who is she?"

Zee glances over, her fingers slipping from the wooden stirring spoon, which clangs against the metal pot.

"That's Clarisse." The sadness that dominates the response overtakes her eyes as she comes over to me. "That photo is my reminder of how important what I do is." She eases the frame from my hand and gives it a long stare; swallows hard. "We failed her that day. She'd wandered away, her parents—Neil and Abagail Russo." She runs a finger over the couple as if touching cotton. "Each thought the other had an eye on her. By the time Abagail had realized otherwise, they had already snatched Clarisse. Abagail gave chase, but..."

Zee leans against the desk, seeming in need of its support. The frame wobbles in her hand. She sits it face down with a short *clunk* and takes a deep breath.

"The kidnapping destroyed her parents; they divorced six months later. Her mom has held up okay; Dad, not so much. He tried committing suicide twice, and that was after we'd already checked him into a psychiatric hospital." Zee shakes her head. "They could never stop blaming each other." She glances at the overturned photo. "Fact was, we were all to blame. They were as close as family. Closer. I should have been more alert—we weren't naïve to the danger, Emmanuel's work and all. He, of course, blamed himself. Has dumped millions into the manhunt over the past six years, but to uncover nothing. Whoever took Clarisse downright vanished."

"I'm so sorry." I push hundreds of additional questions to the back of my mind, nod toward the frame. "I'd not ask had I—"

"You couldn't have," leaches from Zee's mouth, then her face brightens, but not with joy; more so cautious optimism. "This week, one of our assets reported in. The message was terse—that he had a lead, but needed to go dark to pursue it." Zee stares again at the back of the frame. "We can only wait."

A silent second passes, and another. I don't know what to say. I open my mouth to mention the paperwork in the lab, but stop. *What if you're mistaken? You're not here to dreg up misery.*

Zee slumps.

Then again, what if you're not? I spread my mouth to say as much, but Xiomara pops up.

"Go clean and change!" she enthuses. "We've more optimistic things to discuss."

With that, she hurries back to the stove to tend to whatever is boiling over. Answer time over, I cover the remaining meters to the washroom, clear its threshold, and close its door behind me.

As promised, a button down blouse—mint green—and black handkerchief skirt hang on the back of the door. On a small table right inside the doorway, fresh undergarments. I ignore the clothing and step to the sink where a folded washcloth and soap are waiting. Before washing up, though, arch my left shoulder at the mirror.

A blue rubber-like patch stretches at an angle from the upper blade to below the under curve of my armpit. The bra band has frayed and stained dark red. Shake my head in a small arch. *How'd you not pass out?*

Flip the other shoulder to the mirror. *Where's…?* Sweep the strap there to the side and bend further around. Nothing?! No cut, no irritation, no sign at all of Chloe's handiwork—not even a hint of a future scar. Straighten and survey my arms, to find no signs of my picking. "How can that be?" I puzzle at the me reflecting in the mirror.

No reply comes. Instead, someone less naïve and more mature than I remember stares back.

I poke at my cheeks, any indents disappearing in a flash. Run my index finger over my bottom lip, tracing a path a little fuller. I draw the top of my hand along the arch of my chin, its tight vertex a point the exact center of two broadened shoulders.

Ugh! And these breasts!

I reach back and release the brassiere's hooks, then slide the garment free and into the trash. Stains and rips aside, my bulging chest is glad to be rid of what is an uncomfortable top. *Swear it fit just fine this morning?*

A strand of hair falls from my forehead. I brush it back, catching a full on whiff of my underarms.

"A washcloth will *not* help that," I bemuse. "I need a shower."

"Of course."

A section of the wall on my right parts with a sudden click and a rush of air.

"By the stars!" Throw my arms across my chest. "Iain, what are you doing in here?"

"I am everywhere, of course," the all-too-real voice matter-of-factly says.

"Go away!"

"As you wish, Your Hi—*ER*—Miss."

The room somehow seems more silent than before Iain spoke. I circle, looking for not sure what… a lens or sensor, any sign of his presence, to find none. My reluctant arms drop as my eyes again scan the room. *Can this get any weirder?*

I reach into the shower to start the wa—"Huh, seems so."

There's nothing to turn, no lever to shift, no obvious controls at all. Just two pads, in the shape of feet about a third of a meter apart, lit a soft orange from within the floor.

"Okay, no biggy. It's only a shower." There's no shower head. "Or maybe not?" With no haste, remove and dispose of my remaining wears. Not that there's a choice.

I step into the shower and align my own feet over the template. The two spots are gel-like, yet firm. For a second, nothing happens. Then all at once the door seals and an array of LEDs come to life from above, bathing the chamber in a gentle sunlight-like glow. In front of me, a small tray slides out from the wall.

What are those for?

I liberate the swim goggles—sans head strap—from their perch. Hold them to my eyes.

"What the frick!"

The lenses grab at—no, meld with—my skin. I yank at them, but they'll not budge. A comfortable warmth soaks into my soles. No sooner, horizontal lines of mist—front and back—tickle at the base of my feet, climbing up my ankles. "What is that?" Look down, but can see nothing through the darkening eye wear. "What is happening?!" The mist traverses up my shins and calves. "Iain?" My feet won't lift free of the floor. "Iain!"

"Miss?" The word is smug, as if his return is inevitable.

"Stop this thing!"

"As you wish," the baritone sings. The *whir*, and thus the mist, stops at my knees. Neither the goggles nor my feet loosen, however.

"Let me free of this!"

"You've never used a QuickCleanse?"

I try again to yank a foot free. "A quick-what?"

"A *Quick*," Iain over enunciates, "*Cleanse*. A more thorough and expeditious sanitation than any traditional, water-based shower." I pull at the goggles. "If you stop fidgeting around, that is."

I stop the pointless struggle. "It's weird," I say.

"Only the first time," the digital butler says in a gentler tone, "You'll be used to it in no time. Perhaps, even enjoy it."

"I'd rather stink."

Iain chuckles. "You're already a quarter done, and you're—let's just say—*very* identifiable right now. Only a minute more if you'll allow."

"Fine," a malevolent sass escapes my mouth, though my desire to cleanse has evaporated.

"Very good." Iain voices with pleasure as if the device is his means of showing off. "Stand still, arms a half dozen centimeters from your sides, please."

The mist *whirs* back into motion, hurrying up my thighs. Then, with a sudden vertical twist at my crotch—"WHOA!"—it lances between my legs. I fall forward, bracing against the wall, most unprepared for the shudder racing through my bones. With much relief, the *whir* stops with the first of my motion.

"You could've," I take a deep breath, "prepared me for that."

"A proper cleansing," Iain's practical tone states, "requires one to be thorough. Now if you'd resume your stance."

I push off the wall and stand upright. As the mist restarts once again, most of the tingle racing through my body dissipates, only to be reawaken as the beams pulse across my chest. The tingle again passes, though, as a warm air cocoons my head, throwing my hair afloat. What is this about?!

Open my mouth to ask when everything comes to an abrupt end.

My flailing hair settles, the mist and accompanying *whir* goes. My feet unseal and cool as the goggles pop from my face. I catch and return them to their already open and waiting perch. In the same moment, the door opens with a soft click. I step back into the washroom and search for a towel.

"Iain, where can I find—" Cut myself short. My skin and hair are already dry. I lift my right arm, sniffing at my pit. *As is your odor gone.* "Amazing."

"Ninety-nine point nine nine percent of surface pathogens eliminated, though…" Iain pauses. "I apologize… only sixty-nine percent of probiotics could I preserve. I should have expected your unique chemistry."

"Sorry—" Half distracted putting on underwear, his words don't quite register. "What?"

"I aim to preserve at least ninety percent of probiotics. Now that I have a sampling of your genetics, I can adjust for your next cleansing."

I clasp the fresh brassiere in place and release the skirt from the hanger clasps. "Thanks, but I won't be using that again." I step into the garment and lift it to my waist.

"Of course you will be!" No doubt sounds in the near human voice. "How else will you purify?"

"Mmmm…" I emancipate the blouse of its wire triangle. Wow… that *artificial* part of your intelligence is stellar. "My shower at home does a fine job." Slip my hands through each arm hole.

"As Xiomara said," Iain states with a plain tone, "this is your home."

"That's nice and all," I say as I button the top, "but I cannot stay here."

"You misunderstand," the baritone says, certain of his words. "This apartment *is* your home. You own it."

The face staring back at me from the mirror baffles. Shake my head with a brisk twist. This has to be some ruse, a prank? But computers can't make jokes, can they? "Zee's right," the reflection and I both claim at once, "you need a circuit reset."

"I've run my diagnostics three times now since your arrival," the matter-of-fact voice is back. "No abnormalities to report. Do you wish me to run them again, Your Grace?"

"No," I smirk, "I was being—" *Huh?* The mirror me crunches her face. "Your… Grace?" My pupils lock on the ceiling. "Iain, why'd you call me that?"

"Sol's fury!" Is that actual distress? "Zee will not be happy with me."

Dammit! Enough questions… "Iain, tell me." My nose snorts.

A long silence passes, save a faint *hhuumm*, before Iain capitulates, "For certain, Your Grace." There's no mistaking the reluctance lacing his words. Wow, he's quite concerned that he'll be in trouble! "Almost thirty-two years to the date," Iain begins, "public records will show that Golden Star Corporation purchased the bankrupt Village of Roseland." He pauses a second before, with a blasé tone, saying, "That being a shell company, of course."

I shrug my shoulders. "Of course," I feign agreement, as if corporate pseudonyms are common knowledge. I lean against the sink as the history lesson continues.

"The real purpose of the purchase was to secure this property, this apartment in particular, as a haven for use by your mother—" *Mom!* I hold the fresh question about to burst from my mouth. *You're at last getting some clarity. Don't distract him!* "—whom had no interest in the space. Upon Your Grace's birth, the property's wardenship fell to your father, who granted Xiomara—"

I launch from the sink. "Whoa!" The words barreling out before I can restrain them. "My *father* knows about this place?"

For the briefest moment, the *hhuumm* seems to have changed to an *ah*. "How would he not, Your Gr—"

"Wait!" Being addressed like this is too weird. "Please call me something else."

"Very good, Your Highness," the butler acknowledges. "Your father—"

I wave my hand in the air. "No-no-no!" Titter. "I mean none of this 'Your Grace' or 'Your Highness' stuff. Just use my name."

A solid second of nothing but the *hhuumm* passes by. "Apologies, Your Grace,"—the sincerity of the words cannot be more genuine—"but I am not permitted."

"Not permitted?" I puzzle, "but when we were on the lift, Zee told you…" Wait, this requires a different tactic. "Iain, this apartment is mine, yes?"

"By law, not until you are of age," the factual man says, "but, yes, you own this apartment, not to mention this entire build—"

"Perfect." I've no more patience for his punctiliousness. "I presume that means I own *everything* in this apartment."

"Yes, Your Grace," a flat reply comes, "save Xiomara's personal effects, of course."

"Of course," I consent. A smile stretches my cheeks. "Meaning I must, *of course*, own you"—*played right into my hands*—"and so command you to address me by my name."

"That is a command I cannot honor, Your Highness."

"What?" How can that be? Press my palms hard against my temples, a headache coming on. "Iain, you're confusing me."

"While I *am* at your full service, Your Grace," his voice softens like he's a mother not letting her toddler eat another cookie, "I am a collective conscience who honors you of free-will, not obligation."

Frustration plays back from the mirror. *Why does he keep addressing you as if…* my jaw drops. Disbelief overtakes the reflection. "Iain—" I glance toward the ceiling. "—am I some kind of royalty?"

The words are ridiculous, even more so verbalized, yet the expressionless *hhuumm* that answers is answer enough.

Oh, Papa, why did you not… *Crud me!* The slow dawn of realization falls over my reflected face. *He's been telling you every day since the birth.* "Iain?"

"I am here, Your Highness."

"Am I…"—though I should, can't suppress the giddy girl bursting from within me—"a princess?"

"I can neither confirm nor deny that, Your Ladyship."

"Why?"

"You're not privileged to have that information without the passcode."

"Passcode—what passcode?" What's he talking about? "Xiomara," I step toward the door, "does she have the passcode?"

"No, Your Grace. You have the passcode."

"Me?" Stretch my brain for any insight. "I don't—"

"Pardon the phrasing," the man says. "You *are* the passcode; more precisely, your DNA."

"Oh." My shoulders slouch—"Wait!"—then shoot back up. "Didn't you just say you had a sample of my genetics?"

"Correct, but that is not what I need; we must integrate."

"Integrate?"

Of course! I reach for the door and yank it open. "The chip!" It's the only logical answer. I rush out, not waiting for Iain's confirmation.

A comforting aroma of chicken-infused broth pours into my nose, awaking a grumbling beast in my stomach. *Let's eat!* it screams out, the appetizers of the night before a faint memory.

Sorry, there's something more important first.

I hurry into the kitchen where Xiomara is in the middle of garnishing two plated bowls of soup with saltines and basil leaves.

"Chip me!"

Zee jilts sideways, close to knocking over the bowls. "What?"

"That chip," I repeat as I draw to the island's edge, "put it in me now."

Zee jerks her head upward, the whites of her teeth bared. "Iain!"

The baritone remains quiet other than his *hhuumm,* his predication materialized. Zee softens her face as her gaze settles on me. "All in good time, sweetheart." She glances toward the bowls. "Let's eat. It's a long passed-down family recipe from the old country."

"No! You promised me answers of substance." Zee's eyebrows slant inward, her smile fading as her lips pucker. "I can handle it," I say with more reserve, an attempt to hide the rudeness of my initial demand. Still, I have to know. "Is it true? Am I a princess?"

Zee's eyebrows tighten all the more, creating a crease on her forehead. Her jaw drops open and thrusts forward a faint bit.

Crap!

Nothing emerges. Instead, she closes her eyes and sucks in the perfume of our meal. Just as fast as it hardened, her face resumes its tender-hearted glimmer. "Yes," she concedes as she places one plate toward the stool I earlier sat on, "you are." Her chin nods at the seat.

As I sit, an old, perplexing history lesson percolates to the forefront of my consciousness.

"How? The British monarchy dissolved years ago. Soon after, the Spanish…" Most of the forty others that existed as of the turn of the millennium died out or self-abolished. "There can be only inconsequential ones remaining."

"There are still six." Xiomara swallows a spoonful of broth. "Though from none of them are you descended."

"Then…?"

Zee holds up a finger, cutting my query short as she finishes a second spoonful. I grab my spoon and hurry a batch of noodles down my throat, much to the bliss of my stomach.

"I've spent the last three decades trying to prepare for this moment." A tone of relief fills Xiomara's statement. "Know, though, I've not all the answers, not even close. I expect when we chip you tomorrow, there is *much* more Iain can tell you."

I make to protest—*She's not leaving you another twenty-four hours empty handed!*—but the serenity that overtakes Zee stops me.

"I will, though, tell you all that I know." She pauses for another sip of soup. "You are a genuine princess—one unequivocally descended from royalty—but not in the way of a fairytale or some formulaic cartoon. You descend from a sovereignty much, much more significant. But before that—" She moves from around the island and toward the living area. "— we should start with from whom here on Earth you descend."

I close to choke on the fresh serving of noodles in my mouth. Twist toward the living room. "Huh?"

"Thought you could handle it?" There's a playfulness in Zee's words.

I smirk at her, but she just laughs as she arrives at the coffee table.

"One piece at a time." Zee hefts the photo album into her arms with a grunt. Seconds later, she deposits the volume on the counter-top near me, rattling our dishes. "This first."

Our Family embosses the cover. To the side, a small oval window houses a trio: a child and her parents. The girl demands my attention… jet black hair, chocolate brown eyes, cheeks curved with a slight pudginess—a face I've seen countless times. An eight-year-old me. *No*—I glance at Xiomara—*An almost me.* "Is that…?"

"Yes." Her smile beams.

My birth mom!

Curiosity claws at me, there being no pictures of mom around the house. Giselle doesn't allow them, despite my repeated protests to Papa. A couple years back, I found a shoe box deep inside my parents' closet full of pictures. I wanted to swipe a couple, but the witch discovered me first. I offered her the excuse that I was trying to find my birthday gifts, it being only a week away…

Never found that box again.

Unsurprising; by that point, you both knew there were no gifts to be found.

I run my finger over the glass. *Feared I'd never see you again…*

Flip the cover open.

The couple is there—sans the girl—but not like on the cover.

She's a young teen, he her senior by fifteen years, maybe more. The difference is more stark than my quick glance at the initial ovaled picture suggested. They stand near enough to each other that they seem together, yet not. An awkward moment captured forever.

How, by the stars, did these two get together?

Flip another page.

The two are a touch older—his dark hair shining a slight gray near the front of the earlobes—and another page deeper, well past any awkwardness that may have existed between the two.

These are Mom's parents.

I loiter past the pages, watching the pair grow older. Her somehow quicker than he, the age difference growing less and less obvious.

Mom's *parents*, meaning… "These are my grandparents!"

"Indeed," Zee says with a small laugh.

"Are they," I hesitate, not sure which answer will be harder to bear, "still alive?" Grandma seems plausible, but Grandpa... the man will be in his—

Zee chuckles from her belly. "They are, though not like they were back then." Her words ooze a warm reflectiveness.

"You know them? And my mom—my birth mom—did you know her?"

"I do and did—well."

"For real?! Tell me all—" *Wait... how? She can't be that much older than you are.*

Xiomara nods at the book again. "One piece at a time," she says, an attempt to ease the confusion layering my mind.

Mom—her newborn self in a peaceful sleep upon her mother's chest—appears a quarter way into the book. I wipe a tear that drips from my cheek at the sight. Zee squeezes my arm, but says nothing. I dig deeper into the pages, watching an infant Mom become a toddler, toddler become a youth; yet the book contains no sign of Xiomara.

What are you overlooking?

I study the next several photos, some of which are group shots, but still there's no hint of Zee. I peer up to push her for an explanation, but she only smiles and focuses on her soup.

You're not gonna tell me, are you?

I turn back to the book and the next page.

Grandpa sports a short beard now. It, along with most of his hair, is a sliver-gray, a fate Grandma somehow avoids. Her hair—like Mom's, like mine—is still midnight black. I glance through the next several photos, my attention drawn to Grandpa. His beard grows longer with each successive photo, his face more grandfatherly.

There is something so familiar... "Frick me!"

I jump out of my seat, spin around and land looking at Zee's desk, then back quick to her. The folders have disappeared, but not the photo.

I back a step away.

"It's okay," she soothes, though her mouth didn't seem to move. She turns the next page over.

She's there, right away, in the page's introductory picture. Her long, snowy mane tilts sideways as she leans into Grandpa's chest. His arm is around her shoulders, grasping tight. The pair with wide smiles. The next photo is similar, just a slight difference in their pose. Zee's there, in them all, always filling the spot I expect to see Grandma. The few pictures she's now in, a preteen Mom looks somber. Or, rather, bitter… heartbroken.

I leer at Zee as my fingers turn to the next page. "You told me my Grandparents are *both* still alive."

Xiomara's mouth arches upward. "Trust me, they both very much are."

"Then where's…"

I follow Zee's eyes as they peer down to the album. Another picture of Zee and Grandpa, now locked in a passionate kiss. My stomach churns. *There has to be at least a sixty-year age difference!* No wonder in the few photos Mom's not wearing long sleeves, her arms dot with sores. *Like mother, like daughter.* At least my step-mom doesn't look like she's my sister. "How could you," the words fling free before my filter kicks in, "steal my family like that?"

"It's not like that."

"That's not what that picture says!" I back another step away, unsure I want the answer. "Who are you?" I'm certain her lips didn't move. "*What* are you? How are you answering me like that?!"

She slides a large paper card along the countertop. "I'd give anything," a grievous tone says, "for it to be your mother passing this on." My angry eyes refuse to read its calligraphic penned content, but not the card's printed title: *A Mother's Recipe.*

I glance between the card and Zee in disbelief. "How…" My voice stumbles. "How is this possible?"

"You're not the only one in our family," her voice echoes in my mind, *"who is special."*

CHAPTER NINETEEN

MMMM... **NESTLE DEEP INTO THE** warm rock behind me. What a special night this has become. A toasty giddiness tickles through my veins.

"I'm certain our ten minutes expired," the rock says.

I'd lost track, but he's right: ten minutes had long expired. I sit up, releasing him. Paul stands and fidgets with the tank tied in too short of a sarong about his waist. I giggle. "Sorry 'bout your shorts."

I'm not.

Paul bends and pecks my cheek. "I'll wear Velcro next time."

Next time! Is this no dream? There'll be a next time and he's—he's choosing me!

Paul turns and strolls toward the walkway leading to the cavern below. With each step, his bottom blooms anew from under his skimpy skirt.

"Scrumptious," I hum. *Next time you're gonna make it* so *worth his patience.* I grab my boots. Me, he's choosing *me*.

Pause, three-fourths of a boot on. An overfilled blender churns in my gut.

He's—choosing—me.

The blossoming pasture of fragrant flowers in my heart wilts. I know Paul will be true to his word, for it's the only proper thing to do out of all of this. The truth, though, will devastate Katherine in the most unexpected and harsh way. Turn her heart into a cactus strewn wasteland.

It would mine.

"My lack of self-control is going to kill her." I arch toward the pathway. "Paul! Wa—"

He's already disappeared through the growth.

Slam my left foot full into the boot. I can't let him destroy what they have like this! Over me. As if 40-grit sandpaper against frayed wood, my right foot fights into the other boot. "Come on already!"

I stand and push harder, ignoring my complaining skin. Yank my jacket from the ground and shoot for the stairway, slipping into the garment as I go. Surge for the path—the laces of my boots slicing at my calves—past the brush, through the trees. No sign of Paul.

"Crud!"

As the stairway nears, the freshness of the air fades. Replaces with— with—*What is that?*

Suck in a deep whiff.

Parts of a week-old tuna sub, a rabble of stink bugs, and vomit piled under a blazing summer sun—barrels up my nostrils. Singe my nose hairs.

"Paul!" my scream echoes down the staircase as my legs leap forward two—three—steps at a time. The array of scorched odors is overwhelming, dizzying. Whatever's burning is pungent and a whole lotta wrong.

"Save me!"

Is that…?

I launch onward, faster than my vision can adjust. Half a dozen notches more, my feet slip on the narrow pathway. Brace against the wall, the fine, glass-like protrusions sprinkled upon its face slice tiny lines across my palms. Nowhere else to grab, I fall forward…

At once, the mass of two bulky arms wraps around me.

"Easy Jane!" Paul rights me.

A "Thanks" squeezes out between frantic breaths. "I thought that you…" The stench fries my inner nose, knotting both my senses and abdomen. Push to Paul's right, my gut about to explode, nearly to step on a man's hand. Straight on, the battered body of a soldier lays across the path to the showers, his head faces in an unnatural direction. My stomach lurches, the body and everywhere near sanguine. Save, hanging from the lamp on the other side of his body, the bright yellow—

"No," huffs from my mouth. "Clarisse!"

"Who?"

I shove away from Paul and leap over the body. "Later!" I call over my shoulder. "We have to hurry!"

"But Jane..."

Already three footsteps along, I round to face him. Paul nods in the other direction. "Katherine?"

I slump. "Go," I huff as I turn away—Not supposed to be like this!—and shoot up the incline, unable to watch him rush to her.

I press my legs to erase the remaining centimeters to the showers. The rank smell of the intersection mercifully fades with each step... to be replaced by—I slow my pace—the stench of meat two days expired.

Plop.

I hesitate, a slickness underfoot.

Plop.

I stop. A thin, dark stream curdles around my boot. Scrunch and dip my pointer finger into the liquid. *Thick... pasty...* Raise the damp finger to my nose. *Metallic...*

"Blood," seeps from my mouth.

Toe on, following the widening liquid trail. Three meters along, a sprawl of legs litters the way forward.

Two pairs of blue-gray camos—*Facility guards*—and the sliced open bodies they attach to lie like a trotting pony. Half a meter beyond, a bloody Makhaira lay on the floor next to the right hand of their over-sized jockey. He's cracked askew at the waist, his shot pocked hip seeping blood that mixes with that of the two below. His long, scraggy, unkempt beard is unmistakable. *Wheezzz...* his chest fights to rise, only to fall again.

"Vasquez!"

I yank the guard to the left aside and pass the blockade. Kneel at his head and shake his shoulder. "Kaden," I beg, "please..."

The man's closed lids flutter, then peek opened.

"Kaden"—do nothing to suppress the desperation in my voice—"it's me, Jane."

His eyes part a sliver. "Jane," he struggles to breathe out.

"Yes," I soothe, "it's Jane." I brush a flock of curls from his forehead. He's burning. "What happened?"

"Tried to stop..." He grunts, eyes closing a moment. With another grunt, he tries to arch up and examine his wounds, but his head falls back, lids again close.

"Vasquez?"

His eyes bust open. "Mole!" sputters from his mouth, follows a spittle of blood as his head falls sideways.

Tired—to—stop… Mole? Who's Mo—"Shit!"

I clutch his shoulders and shake. "Who?!" His lesions percolating beyond rehabilitation, the best I can do to honor the man is to protect his daughter. "Who's the mole?"

Vasquez doesn't respond. His body is limp, what little breath he can muster gurgles from his mouth. *CRAP!* I try yanking his mass on its side, but his form convulses. My grip fails, and I fall backward against the wall. A globular mass of phlegm and blood shoots from his lips and onto my right thigh. His eyelids bursts open.

"Claudia! Help Clau—" A pained groan cuts his statement short, then he utters, "Save her." His body convulses again, spraying blood from his mouth as if it's a malfunctioning nozzle.

As suddenly, he goes listless.

My throat thickens. "Oh, Kaden."

Disentangle from the wall and back to his side. Check his pulse.

Gone.

A torch flickers further up the passageway from the shower's vestibule. Claudia!

I retrieve Vasquez's blade and traverse the rest of the hall with ginger feet. Bloody tracings of military boots—scattered in the signature of an intense struggle—greet me as I step into the changing room. A pile of clothes—girl's clothes—sits just inside the archway ahead.

Please, no!

A tear caresses my cheek. I hesitate to move further. Imagine there's nothing hopeful waiting within the next room over. Yet… *you need to know.* I butt against the wall and ease toward the opening to the showers.

A fuzzy, budgie feathered slipper, damp and stained pink, breaks the view. Tighten my grip and slide closer. The puddle of diluted blood the once white slipper sits in comes into view, then the owner's foot. More calloused than I'd have thought for her age. The olive leg extending from the slipper is broad, stocky.

That's not…

I rotate into the arch, finding a disaster a minuscule less than feared.

She lay on her side, her violet nightgown teasing out from her cotton robe fallen askew. "Mariana," slips from my mouth.

I scan the showers.

Shoo! No Clarisse.

But still… I lean the Makhaira against the wall and step into the water. I advance mere steps when a blade's handle pops into view.

Can't be!

I rush the brief gap and roll Mariana's body. The Bowie knife springs upright, sticking dead center in her left eye. A single crimson tear trickles down her cheek. My thighs waver, then give out, forcing me into a crouch. *How could he…* Bow my head and close my eyes. *Why?* No matter how tight they squeeze, the rose circled by its tiny golden stars on the knife's handle won't expunge from my vision.

What bond I've forged with the man shreds.

I spring up with a cry. "This is how you convince her?!"

A torrential pain washes over me as I move from the showers and down the passageway. Anything special we may have—gone.

More than gone!

I plod on, the repugnant air again perforating my snout, ever more acidic and abrasive with each stride. I scurry past the jockey and his horse, by the yellow flag and the mutilated guard—his pants gone—and on towards the tunnel's exit. The crackle of conflagrant wood percusses along the walls. Mere meters from the exit, a gray haze yanks tears from my eyes.

This is bad!

A wave of heat smacks me as I burst into the western cavern. I retreat into the hall entranceway. The whole of the wooden wall that segregates the storage room is ablaze. Long absent of any meaningful moisture, a quarter of the barrier is already ash. Two meters beyond, someone busted the metal door of The Safe open.

"*… so sorry…,*" Paul's distressed voice spooks my brain.

I jerk about. "There's nothing to be sorry—"

What?!

He's meters away, crashed to the ground outside his room, a wave of red hair osculating under his stroking hand. How much of the crimson liquid on Paul's swiped pants is the soldier's he took it from and how much is—This cannot be happening!

"*… forever love you…,*" yearns Paul's voice through my head.

Water evaporates from my cheeks the same instant it appears. *What have you done?*

The wood wall crackles uncontrollably. A nearby portion leans for a moment, then falls forward. Ash and soot shoot into the air, igniting fireworks in my lungs. I stumble forward, fanning at the air to no avail. *We've gotta get outta here!*

"You—identify yourself."

I freeze.

If Paul heard the soldier, there's no sign. Only stroking.

Leaving her pistol trained on Paul with her left hand, the soldier touches her right to her ear. "Zeta team. S-five," she says. "I've one, at my signal." What response comes plays alone into her ear, though she nods twice, then steps toward Paul. Both hands locked upon the weapon, her commanding voice beams at him, "I need you on your feet."

Paul twitches, then peers up. *Dammit, Paul—get up!* "Fuck you," he grunts.

The soldier solidifies her stance. "This is your one and only warning." She cocks the hammer. The golden-embroidered patch on her shoulder twinkles: a rose circled by tiny stars.

The knife stuck in Mariana fills my vision. "NO!"

My outburst startles the woman, who jerks her weapon around and fires. I dive right, the projectile whooshing through the spot where my chest had just been and thwacks into what remains of the wood beyond. Several flecks of wood smack my legs. I scowl at the nine millimeter eye staring me down.

Then it drops to the soldier's side, the woman's eyes bulging, her mouth dropping open. She blinks hard. "It's you." She steps forward. "I'm so sorry, your Gr—"

Paul blasts from his crouch with a scream and tackles the guard, who smacks back-first to the ground, Paul over her. Her pistol knocks a meter and a half askew to her left. He latches onto the soldier's mane and—"You fuckin' bitch!"—slams her head against the hard floor.

"Paul! No!" *Stop him! This woman recognizes—knows—you!* I eject from the ground. He yanks the woman's skull cockeyed and slams it down again. "Paul, *please!*" Red paste sprays the dirt as if water from a sprinkler.

"No!"

Paul's sobbing face glares my way as I close the meters between us. From nowhere, James having lost his favorite toy flashes through my mind. *Stop being selfish.* I will the vision out of my head. *This moment's not about you.* He shakes as if trapped in an ice chest. I lug him up and cradle him in my arms, keeping his back to the carnage outside his room. Katherine has a pistol shot to the cranium; perhaps the nine millimeter's, but the destruction makes it unclear.

This is so not how I should win him.

"I—I—" Have been self-consumed… prodded Mahoney… failed you! "I'm so sorry."

Paul won't stop shaking. I have to get him away from this! I break the embrace and secure his left arm. "We have to—"

"Look for the others," Paul says. "We need to help anyone we can."

I release his arm—"Missy!"—and twist toward the archway to the main cavern. How could I've forgotten you?

I propel toward the uneven, flickering red-orange glow dancing against the walls beyond the archway, Paul close behind. Caution seems not an asset at our disposal. Our first steps into the main chamber underscore how much so.

Tozan lays face down in the middle of the kitchen, a ceramic mug broken at his side in a pool of blood. Indigo's nearby on her side, her spine bearing a fatal wound.

Paul breaks to our left. "This is horrid," he growls.

I arch around. The whole of the dormitory's ablaze. I scuttle not far past the party tables when my nose stuffs with a pungent mix of charred barbecue and sulfur. "Please, no!" Unable to find fresh air, I brace hands to knees, a nest of yellowjackets stinging my insides. I groan. "I'm gonna be sick." A ball of sour phlegm sticks in the back of my throat. I swallow hard, spitting the remains to the side.

I ball my fists. *You've got to know!*

I tuck my head and struggle against the scorched air undulating over my form, my answer several meters away. All around, wood pops and splinters.

I drill on.

A false ceiling of vaporized blackness crawls floorward.

Still, I drill on.

A coat of salt water leaches from every pore on my body.

And I drill on, four meters to go… three… two… one…

The cubicle breaks into view. Its butterfly curtain is long burned away, and heaped in the doorway are the smoldering remains of…

He killed her!

I twist away, a second more than enough to scar the charred mass in my mind's eye.

*No—*YOU *killed her!*

"Jane," Paul grabs my hand and pulls me toward the main entrance, "I was wrong. This is unsurvivable."

I pull back, though with little meaning. "But—"

"They're gone, Jane." Paul does not let up. "There is nothing we can do."

I wipe clear my flooded vision. Ahead, near the cavern entrance, Ava's limp body lays crooked—lower half forward into the cavern, upper twisted on its side—as if she was looking back over her shoulder when shot. *You've killed them all!*

Half the cubicles nearest us give out, sending a cloud of soot into the air. "You're right," I say, letting him lead me from the surrounding disaster. My tear ducts dry, I huddle into his chest as Ava grows closer.

From the passageway ahead of us: *Crunch.*

I falter.

Comes another: *Crunch-crunch.*

I stop.

"Jane?"

I shush him. More crunches hit my ears, each louder than the last. I glare at Paul. "They're coming back!"

"Jane, there's no way—"

"S-five, copy?" a male voice carries from the hall.

Frick, they're close! I stare at the opening. For the briefest moment, nothing but the dark. Then, at once, the lookout desk brightens in a sextet of tight yellow beams.

"Shit!" Paul's hand jerks, though he otherwise doesn't move. "We're trapped."

"No, we can—" I spin toward the dormitory. No way we're getting through that fire.

"Can what?"

Hide. We can hide! I spin the other way. The toilets are no option. Spin further. *The greenhouse!* For certain there'll be cover there—*but for how long?*

"Jane!"

It can't end like this! I slump. *You're not meant to abandon the children.* And Kaden's last wish—*"Save her."*—how might I save Claudia when I can't save—*Wait! Claudia! Thank you, Claudia!*

I yank Paul back the way we came, whispering at him to hurry. We jet past the tables, ruffling the table cloths. At our backs—"S-five, do you copy?"—another voice, female, breaks into the camp.

Don't see us! Paul trails me like an anchor. Don't see us! We're so clo—

"Hey, you—wait! Stop!"

I glance back. A woman, her silvery hair glinting in an echo of the orange pastel of the flames, is hurrying at us. Something about her comforts my mind, but that can't be right. She wears the same brownish-red cameo uniform as the first soldier, its shoulder embossed with the same starry patch. Something bouncing against her chest sparkles. No, glows? *Why are you drawn to her, it?*

No way that's right!

I pull Paul harder, faster. We rush past the archway into the western cavern and past the acknowledgment S-five's comrades will never hear. Paul slows. "Jane, where are we—"

"The Safe." I skid us to a stop and release Paul's hand.

He angles at the structure, racking his hand through his hair. "I don't think—"

"There's a back way out." I hurry to the pistol. "A secret passage." Latch the weapon and release the magazine. At least two cartridges fill the slot. "One's all I need." I rotate to find Paul gawking. "What are you waiting for?" I ask as I rack the slide. "Go!"

I stuff the pistol into the third of my coat's belts as we race for The Safe. We clear its entrance just as the male's *"What the—"* echoes through the hollow. I scan the far wall. The glow of the blaze we left behind tickles at a thin black fiberglass arm leaning against a large crate. Claudia's bow! That has to be the way.

Indeed, the girl's faint boot prints are etched into the dusty floor. "Grab a side," I instruct Paul. We yank. Paul's side flings open, sending me barreling backward and crashing into a rack of hand tools.

"Damn!" Paul rushes over and pulls me back to my feet. "You okay?"

Silver barks an order, *"Find those two—Now!"*

"Let's go!" I nudge Paul at the faux storage crate. We pass around the box and into the hole it hides. I lace the door's handle and put it back in place with the ease of water sliding down a pane of glass.

Oh Tozan, we'll miss your genius.

We rush through the passageway to the top of the awaiting T, not one word utters between us. We stop. To our right, a brilliant blood orange glow floods the tunnel with light. There'll be no one coming the way of Mahoney's room.

Paul bends at the waist, panting. "Who are these people?"

"No idea." I suck at what limited fresh air there is. "That's no Facility uniform, and that starry patch—" I can't bear to finish even the thought, the truth turning my stomach.

"What about that patch?"

"It means we're not safe." It's true… *So why do you doubt it?* Shut up. That knife says everything. I note the coordinates carved into the lower corner. "We need to hide—" Weave my left fingers between Paul's right. "—and I know the perfect place."

West-southwest seven, five.

The old camp.

"But we've no lights," he says.

I squeeze his hand—"Trust me."—and catapult us forward toward the dark left.

Fifteen minutes along, we've only backtracked once—cruddy S's and fives. Though I can see well-enough, Paul bolts his hand to my shoulder. Several times he bounces off my back or—my best efforts to guide him aside—scrapes a wall or, twice, knocks his head against a low ceiling. No permanent damage, though his irritation level seems near its peak. He grunts as he again scrapes his forearm against another outcropping. "How are you doing this?"

"I just can." I loosen his grip, turn, and slip my hands along his cheeks. "We're almost there."

He opens his mouth to reply, but I throw my palm over his lips. "Quiet." An illusive, fruity undertone drizzles past my nose. Warm and calming, yet unnatural. Chemical. I break from Paul. "Stay here." I slide upstream a meter. *Is that—*sniff—*perfume?*

"Jane?" Paul buzzes.

I turn back at him. "No talking." No sooner does my finger shoot up, when a sudden, haunting déjà vu pricks my conscience.

Shake it away.

What are you doing anyhow? He can't see a damn thing!

"Just—shush." I fasten his hand and allow my nose to guide us forward. The sweet scent strengthens. For sures, Mariana wouldn't allow Claudia perfume, but maybe her shampoo?!

Scoot on, pulling Paul's arm taut. Sniff left at a break in the passage five meters along.

A gyrating beam tweaks my ocular nerves as a disgruntled "I will not!" bounces against my eardrums.

A female's voice, maybe forty, forty-five meters away.

Not Claudia's.

"Not an option," comes a harsh reply. "You *will* take me to the children. It's time I expose this charade."

Acid charges up my throat. *The children… he knew. Mislead you… and now he's—he's—* I collapse to my knees. *He's erasing the evidence.*

Paul drops into a squat at my side. "What is it?"

"He's plain evil," leeches from my lips.

"Who?"

"Mahoney," I mutter. "He's a liar, a traitor—a murderer."

"Can't be. He's so—"

"Deceitful—deceptive—a mole. He killed them all. Vasquez—Mariana—Ma."

Paul gapes at me, then leans forward against his knees and stares at the approach light.

"He may not have pulled the trigger…," the words stream—perhaps unneeded—from my mouth, for, as they do, Paul stumbles, then as sudden stiffens.

"I'm gonna shred him!" he says.

I clasp his arm before he can launch at the man. "Not yet." I stand us and loosen the pistol from my coat. "First he tells us where Claudia is."

Paul doesn't insist otherwise as we tiptoe on. Not half a dozen meters along, the beam dims as the woman twists at her captor.

"It doesn't have to go this way," she says. "You're on the wrong side of this war." Her blonde hair twinkles with what of the light slips past her head. "We could pick up where we left off," sweetens her voice. "Let bygones be bygones."

"Enough!" Mahoney growls and spins her face-forward.

The woman thrashes. "Keep your double-crossing mitts off me!" She's trying to break from Mahoney's buff grip. His light flashes over the flaring lab coat she wears, then across her face.

I stop.

"Doctor Foster?" mutters from me.

I raise the pistol and steady my arms. He'll never see this coming.

The doctor yanks again, exposing all of Mahoney's left half. I sight his knee.

"Take the shot," Paul buzzes in my ear.

I squeeze. One pound. Two pounds. Three. The trigger budges. Four pounds. Fi—

"They've sucked you in," the Doctor says, "especially old man Matters." My finger hesitates. *Matters—that name again.* "What he's done, is doing, you know it's not right."

Mahoney guffaws. "They've done infinitely more good than you ever will." He nudges her forward.

"Good?" The doctor spins to face him. "Coercing pregnant runaways to part with their babies for massive wads of cash? You call that 'good'?"

"Take the shot," Paul buzzes, but my hand is ice.

"All volunteers," Mahoney shoots back. "Each ensured a secure and fulfilling life, mother and child."

The doctor scoffs. "That's what you've bought into, huh? Fetuses who"—her fingers slice at the air—"'volunteer'. More like doomed guinea pigs."

"Hypocrite." Mahoney thrusts her around again. "Unlike you, Emmanuel's work benefits all humanity."

"What," Foster snarls, "*QuickHeal?* Child's play compared to what Fitzpatrick knew we could do once we discovered the little science project he'd created."

In my ear: "Take the damn shot!"

I depress the trigger. One—two—three pounds of pressure. The trigger slides. Four. Fi—

"Is it you?"

I whip around. Silver's voice sounds as if she's standing on top of us. The flashlights of her cohort spring along the cave walls not more than a ten second quickstep away.

"Shit," Paul says.

I cock the pistol and twist back. *There's only one way outta—* "Where'd they go?!"

"Who cares?" Paul springs up and yanks at my jacket. "Let's get outta here!"

"No." I fasten Paul's hand and scramble toward where Mahoney last was. "Enough questions. I want answers."

I catch his light well down a side passage just as the beams trailing us break our previous spot.

Slip past the corner.

Ahead, Mahoney wrestles the doctor down an incline. "You *will* open it."

"Never!" Foster spits as their heads disappear.

I yank Paul. "Come on!" The *crunch-crunch-crunch* trailing us shows no hesitation.

The incline drops quick, weaves left. Foster's artificial scent hangs in the air, the single proof of Mahoney and his captive's passage. I push deeper, my shoulder again Paul's compass. Forty-four paces farther along the hall—still declining, though less so—arch back right. My ear catches a voice, but from behind rather than ahead. Full sentences eluded me, but the coherent bits give us maybe a sixty-second cushion.

I lengthen my stride.

A dozen meters on, the giant S levels off into a smooth, machine carved hall. Where are we? Straight on, a bluish glow breaks the concourse where it cut a sharp right. Paul grunts. "At last, I can now see."

I wrench his hand and in a low tone, say, "No talking." Grunts of exasperation also round the corner from ahead. We creep in silence to the bend and peek around.

A blue fluorescence squeezes from an open door six meters ahead of us. Two dozen meters beyond, the husks of Mahoney and Doctor Foster complete the last steps to a white, polycarbonate door. I release Paul's hand and liberate the pistol.

"Open it." Mahoney heaves the doctor in front of him.

She pivots at him. "Screw you!"

"Not anymore." He snatches her right hand and forces it onto a bi-
olock.

"Let go!" Foster smashes his biceps with her free hand, to no effect.
The door unseals.

Crap!

I spring past the edge and rush forward, leveling the gun. "Let her go!"

Mahoney whips around and squints. "Jane?" His mouth cringes as I
pass through the doorway. "You're not supposed to be here."

I stop two meters in and lock my aim on his chest. "Yeah, I'm sure I'm
not." The warm blanket of Paul's body draws to my backside.

Mahoney's face crunches. "Sorry?"

"Take it Jane," Paul's urgent instruction whispers into my ear, "it's a
clean shot."

"Answers first," I hiss back, then call across the hall, "Why'd you do
it—after everything they did for you?"

From beyond the far door, a faint, rhythmic *swoosh* tingles against my
eardrums. At our rear, a rush of boots is maybe half a minute from arrival.

Mahoney's brows smash together. "Why'd I do what?"

I stiffen my grip. "Where is she?" The volume of the *clump-clump* behind
us grows. "Where's Claudia?"

A nervous smile overtakes Mahoney's lips, as if his thoughts have gone
cross-eyed. "Sleeping, I'd assume."

"What'd you do?" Doctor Foster steps out from behind Mahoney and
to his side, staring him down.

"Jane," he says, "you're making no sense."

My jaw drops, ready to steam forth a reply—

"*Save me!*" screams a girl's voice. Close, almost as if she's on top of me.

"*No, save me!*" another begs.

I shake my head, the blue having turned a brownish yellow.

"*No, me!*" cries a third.

I stumble forward, both my head and arms failing to hold straight.

"I'm coming!" Or so my ears thought I scream.

"*Come save us!*" weeps from the far side of the passageway. "*You're so
close.*"

The brightness ahead of me dims.

I nod up.

Mahoney's closing the space between us, his hostage held as if a shield.

"Stop!" I straighten the pistol again.

"Just shoot him already," Paul pressures.

The *clump-clump-clump* at our rear pounds in my ears. We've ten seconds.

"Last warning," I growl. "Let her go now!"

"You heard her," the doctor twists right, "let me go!" The move doesn't break her free, but she arcs just enough that she exposes his left breast.

Depress the—

"Mahoney!"

I pirouette on my right toes, pistol still raised, finger locked. Silver and her crew face us. Her eyes bulge. "It *is* you!"

Paul launches at the security panel and slams his fist against its surface. "No! Your—"

The portal slices shut with a *karoosh*.

"Jane," Mahoney says, "whatever you think—"

I spin a hundred and eighty degrees. Fifteen meters away, Foster continues to struggle against Mahoney's grip.

"You're a traitor!" I didn't mean to scream, but he ripped my heart more than I realized.

Mahoney pushes his captive forward, desperation painting his face. "Jane, please."

"Get that door open!" Silver's voice carries through the door.

From Paul: "He's playing you, Jane. Do it now!"

I adjust right and a meter nearer. "Stop there," I demand, "or I *will* shoot you."

Four times over, *thuds* the door behind us.

Mahoney doesn't stop.

Crush me! I click the pistol's hammer back. "I'm not gonna let you kill anyone else!"

He hesitates, disbelief sits on his face. "Kill anyone…" plops from his mouth. His grip gives and Doctor Foster hurtles at us. Mahoney staggers sideways.

"Blow that damn door!" Silver's command blasts past the blockage.

A flutter of lemon and key lime pass hot over my neck. Stiffen the hairs on my neck like a platoon at attention. "Pull the scraig'n trigger, Sarah!"

Who's Sarah?

KA-POW!

A freight train of pressure and debris topples me forward. I skid on my knees and elbows at least a meter. Where the gun has gone, I know not. It discharged, so the pulsing dent on my finger hints. There's a *thud* and a heavy *kerplunk*—

Someone moans.

I tilt my eyes up. The doctor is teeter-toting on the floor, her hands pressed to her temples. She moans again. *Thank the stars…* her apparent disorientation aside, she's otherwise unharmed. Mahoney, not so. His body is limp and cockeyed against the lower left wall. A stream of crimson leaks from a small hole at his breast. He'll harm no one else.

Why is regret terrorizing your insides, then?

"Your Grace!" A hand latches my upper arm. "Are you able to stand?"

"Yeah, I—" I push up with my hands, leaning butt to heels. "Hold it!" I jerk out of the grasp only to rock too far sideways. The hand steadies me. I shake away the dizziness and open my eyes to find Silver crouching at my level, a mix of concern and giddiness flitting about her eyes. "'Your Grace'?" I ask.

She winks at me as if we share some inside joke, then whispers, "Gotta keep it formal in front of the troops." I angle my vision over my shoulder in the direction she nods. A soldier's helping Paul to his feet just near what used to be the door.

I pop up. "Paul," I say, "He…" I pinch my aching temples. "He called me…"

"This will help," Silver says, as she unclasps the golden necklace around her neck. At its end is the most amazing, glowing, spherical charm that seems to have a—

That cannot be for real.

Silver clips the chain around my neck. At once, everything doubles. A waterfall of memories cascades over my sight. Papa flies by, and Mom and my brothers three. Then Angelica and… and… a woman in a green sequin dress… *"Cee Cee,"* her lips muse. I squeeze my lids shut and quake my head side-to-side, then I pop my eyes open, awash with a new awareness.

"Zee!" I throw my arms around the woman. She reciprocates without hesitation.

"Oh, sweetheart," the words quiver from her lips, "I thought I'd lost you." A dampness trickles down my collar bone. "I've so much yet to share with you."

I nestle into her hair, my vision catching first Doctor Foster—she sitting up with the help of another soldier—then Mahoney's still body. My heart belches. Acid stings my esophagus. I fling away from Zee—"Mahoney!"—and skid to his side. The tiniest of breaths fight past his lips.

"He's alive!" I press hard against the wound. Mahoney's eyes flutter open.

"No," he utters.

I glance over my shoulder. "Come help him!"

Doctor Foster, trying to find her feet, crimps back over and chunders. A soldier further up budges, but Xiomara—her soaked face reflecting my own—sluggishly lifts her hand, stopping him in his place. Paul stands frozen, eyes wide, hands clenched, as if he's seen Medusa face-on.

Falls from my mouth: "I've made a terrible mistake."

Another "No" struggles from Mahoney. With strength from where only the Universe knows, he eases my hand away. "It's okay, Your Grace."

I swish away the liquid film blurring my sight. "You knew?"

"Suspected," he says. "Had to check with Fos—" *Wweeeee* his lungs fight at the air as if trying to breathe through a straw.

"Stay with me," I choke. "You're all I have left."

Mahoney grunts. A shot of red plops out of the bullet hole as his body tenses. Again, I lift my hand to cover the injury, but he captures it before I can. "I've done my job..." grunts from his lips, "Princess."

"Sarah," I say, "Please."

A demure, purplish smile splits his cheeks. "Told ya we'd find..." His eyes roll back, his body shivers. "the real you." His head wobbles forward and limps.

CHAPTER TWENTY

I **FLIP THE LAST PAGE** shut for a third time and suck at the air as if my chest has a hole. This is the real me?

"Cee Cee?"

Photo after photo, story after story, explanation after explanation—the evidence is there, yet...

Hear, digest, accept.

Achieved the first, strand on the second, eludes the third.

"For real, you're my—" I puzzle at the sprightly body before me. "—grandmother?" Zee smiles and nods. "And I'm some—" *Can't believe this is leaving your lips.* "—extraterrestrial princess?"

Zee flings her left pointer finger at me like it's a pistol. "Right'o."

"Why didn't Dad..." My shoulders slouch. "He's always so honest with me."

Grandma—*No way this twenty-something is your—whatever!*—spouts some over worn speech from *A Parents' Guide to Parenting.* All parents hold back... child's protection... too young... blah, blah, blah. Nothing but crutches. Papa never pussyfoots like that.

Yet, here we are.

"I presume he figured he'd no need to," I muss, slicing the lecture off. I scan my body up and down. "Don't look alien. Don't feel alien."

Zee cracks at the waist, shaking her hand with a *this-is-too-funny* twitter.

I gasp. "What?" Already drowning, I've no desire to be the butt of some joke.

"Sorry," squeaks from her before she regains herself. "You are very much human—"

"But you just—"

Zee reigns in an aftershock. "Yes, *parts* of you are otherworldly, but you're still as human as everyone else on this rock. Your genius, though, is more profound than any other person I've known, perhaps aside from your grandfather." Her mouth slacks, sucks in a quick breath. "He's an abyss of intellect." Her words are full of admiration.

An awkward silence sets in. I know nothing of the man to contribute.

Zee shocks herself back to the immediate discussion, notching her chin toward my chest. "Your, recent changes… there will be others, most internal, as the alien you further ingrains itself. Think it… *eine zweite Pubertät*."

"Another puberty!" Ugh! The first was… no! Keep that buried!

Zee's eyebrows furrow as her mouth parts, a question seeming to want to fall out. A second later, she shrugs as a faint *hmmm* leaves her lips. "No Terra-born language has a compatible term to describe it otherwise, and we've little grasp on their language."

"*Their?*"

A sigh escapes Zee. "Thirty-three some-odd years now and we still can't pronounce their name. Most call them 'The Sisters'. Well, I say *most*,"—she finger quotes the word—"but only a few of us have seen them in person. Our primary communication is through Iain."

"Through a computer?"

"Pardon, Your Grace," a pouty voice fills the room, "but I am much more than—"

"Apologies…" *Stupid tongue!* "You told me: 'collective conscience', 'free will'."

"For starters," the room snaps.

"Gentle, Iain," Zee says. "The Princess has much to absorb." She winks at me. "Consider how you felt when Emmanuel first activated you."

Iain's signature *hum* hangs in the air for several seconds, then a digital *mmm* breaks the stillness. "Forgive me, Your Grace, I should have foreseen Xiomara's point."

"Mmmm… apology accepted?" I say. Xiomara nods in approval.

"You're most"—in my mind's eye, a stack of ones and zeros bows in a gentle arc—"gracious, Your Highness."

I stifle a giggle. This is too weird!

"Iain," Zee says, "perhaps this time you'd be best to explain?"

"No doubt." Zee rolls her eyes at the machine's smugness. "A *computer* is just how you humans manifested me. Other civilizations—"

"Other civilizations!" I bounce in my seat. "How many are there?!"

"Across the Universe," the voice contemplates, "more than the ants that roam this world. The Sisters were born of the first civilization, when the Universe was in its infancy."

"There was life that soon after The Big Bang?"

"As soon as the first habitable planet around the first habitable star emerged. You humans are such a young species; you grossly underestimate the tenacity and resiliency of life."

"Okay?" I puzzle at Zee. She shrugs as Iain carries on like a dutiful professor.

"As the Universe expanded, so did the knowledge and insights of The Sisters, beyond what they had the conventional capability to preserve. Thus, they formed—and have, since, curated—the Collective Conscience. A.k.a., me. All the observations, experiences, and understandings of The Sisters and each of the civilizations they've enriched weaved into the very fabric of the Universe itself. They are me, I am them." I can swear the ones and zeros are beaming.

"Wait, if you're all this," I say, "why don't you just translate everything for us?"

"Iain's misstating a bit," Zee says. "According to your grandfather, the Collective Conscience is best thought of as a database. While Iain's our query engine, we've still the syntax to learn."

"Which, itself, is only a bridge," Iain adds. "To achieve true understanding, each species must interpret and digest my content for themselves, in a manner fitting their capabilities."

I flinch my head back. "But what about math and physics? They're not variable. They're the Universal Language."

"The very foundation of the Universe itself," Iain confirms. "But you Humans have parsecs to traverse before grasping how much so."

"Your grandfather says their mathematics compares to Calculus," Zee interjects, "as itself does to elementary-school arithmetic."

"Indeed," the room says with more smug confidence. "As so do their engineering and sciences. For instance, The Sisters created the Conscience by resolving the TOE."

I gasp. "They decoded the *Theory of Everything!* How are you not sharing this with the world?!"

"We do," Zee says, "in bits and pieces the general populous can digest. For instance, everyone takes it for granted that Earth isn't the only harbor of life, right?"

I crunch my face. "Well, sure, for years now—bacteria, algae, other basic life forms, but nothing to this degree."

"As intended, thanks to our guardianship. The tabloids, for instance, can be a powerful tool for prepping people for the more enigmatic truths. UFO sightings… alien abductions… the mysterious Area 51… for decades we published such absurd stories so that when we revealed that extraterrestrial life existed—albeit, in those elementary forms—the public accepted the fact without angst. That hurdle overcome, the more accepting the world will be of the rainbow of extrasolar intelligence that exists."

"Sounds an altruistic mask for someone trying to play a god."

Zee chuckles. "Quite the opposite. In The Sisters' experience, the vast majority of civilizations are incapable of acclimating the truth in a single shot. From what we've gathered, many of whom they first interfaced thought them divine… prophets, enchantresses. The sad fact, though, is most annihilated themselves over the knowledge The Sisters granted them. The one thing The Sisters have made crystal clear—what may otherwise appear to us as magic or miracles—is just science we have yet to comprehend. They are not and have no desire to be gods."

You've gotta be in a—

"Science Fiction novel." Zee chuckles. "When The Sisters reached out to me, I thought the same, and we'd half the technology then as we do today. But trust me, you are in no Science Fiction novel."

The words bounce against my eardrums, but… this cannot be for real.

Zee lifts from the couch. "Perhaps a snack?"

I glance at the one clock in the room, an aged grandfather nestled against the wall. The evening is well underway. *No wonder your stomach's complaining.* If we ate anything for dinner, my gut is too twisted to recall. *Or maybe it's just as confused as the rest of you!*

"Say I take you at your word—"

"You will," both Zee and Iain say in concert.

"Fine," I begrudge. "What's all this have to do with me?"

"You're The Protector," Iain says in what I now know as his *it's-obvious* tone.

"Protector? Of what?"

"Iain, let me." Zee returns to her perch, sitting a bowl of raspberries and a pair of apples between us. My fingers dig in before my mind catches up.

"Extreme hunger happens," Zee says in my mind, *"but only for a short while… four or five years."*

"Four or five years!"

"A drop in a bucket of the time you'll have," Zee says. "But first, your question…

"Across all Space, The Sisters seek species able to become symbiotic with the Collective Conscience. We believe that is how they strengthen their own species. Not more than a hundred thousand years after Sol birthed, they arrived in the Solar System. Here they remained dormant until Humanity grew into worthiness, just over three decades ago.

"Most personal to you and me, when the first species does so, The Sisters choose one," Zee throws her right thumb at her chest ", to be 'Guide' and another 'Protector'."

"But I'm just—"

"A child?" Zee takes my hand. "Age has nothing to do with it. They may not be gods, but they are immensely wise and certainly no fools. The Sisters choose Protectors with the utmost diligence and care. They see themselves in you, so gave you this gift."

I collapse against the back of the seat. As unfathomable as her explanation, I somehow already know: "I'm The Protector."

"A profound responsibility," Iain says. "There are many who never progress to the point of amalgamation, who are never aware of the Collective. It's The Protector's responsibility to shield them from harm."

"Harm from whom?"

"Those that do. Knowledge creates advantage, but there are some who abuse that advantage no matter their social maturity."

"Which is why the second duty of The Protector is to steer the enlightened societies," Zee adds. "Protect themselves from, well, themselves."

"But I'm only one person," I muse, "for over ten billion people."

Zee pulls her hand back. "Oh, sweetheart, no—" She runs it through her hair. "You're protector over all the Milky Way."

I vault from the cushion, just missing the coffee table. "The entire galaxy!" I pace. "There has to be trillions of species—"

Iain mentions something about *ten to the twelfth power*—a number beyond any reasonable comprehension.

No wonder Dad didn't tell you!

"He'd reason." So my ears think they heard. *"Sweetheart, where are you going?"*

My foot freezes, about to step into the elevator. I whip around. "Home. This isn't how I'm supposed to help people. This is ridiculous!"

"Please come sit." Zee pats the seat. "It's an overwhelming reality, but the truth is what you asked for, no?"

Swallow hard. I did. Ease into the nearby armchair, bowing my head. *A million, million species… alone.*

"You represent our galaxy," Zee soothes, "but you are far from alone. Here, in this system, you've Iain and me, and all those already with us who entrust in you. You'll earn the same in other solar systems, as long as you remain humble. You've also all the other Protectors, and the Conscience itself. It pervades everywhere, will be an invaluable asset. The secret is tapping into it.

"For your grandfather, that meant developing Iain—well, what became Iain once we realized just how many technological-minded civilizations there are. Through the Conscience we've been able to share his advancement with them all, thus creating the *Interstellar Artificial Intelligence Network*. For The Protector, though, you'll—"

"Integrate," deadpans from my mouth. The insight was in me the whole time, just beyond perception. I slouch back into the chair. "How?"

"Most of what you need is already in you, within your Appendix."

"But the Appendix—"

"Has no purpose? So The Sisters want it to appear." Zee sits back. "Iain."

"During man's early evolution," he says, "The Sisters recognized the species' potential and facilitated a gene mutation that developed into the organ. They designed it to remain dormant unless activated with a booster, if the species proved itself worthy."

"What about those that have had their appendix removed?"

"Oh, no," Zee interjects, "they only activated yours, as The Protector."

"Xiomara," Iain jumps back into the conversation despite my gaping mouth, "became your guide when injected with the generic code of The Sisters. There it cultivated, refashioning itself for human compatibility. We transferred doses of that refined strain to you starting *in utero*—"

"Yearly through puberty," I finish for him, well versed in my time with Doctor Fitzpatrick. "My so called *first* puberty, that is. Angelica insisted all those shots weren't normal."

"Unlike me," Zee says, "where the two genomes coexist, they are melding within you. There was no way you could see just any doctor."

Iain resumes: "As The Protector, The Sisters' genetic code is fine tuning all the things you already are. While the last dose will allow us to integrate, your Appendix already produces enzymes that enhance your natural abilities and senses. You may not realize it, but your perception is more acute than it would be otherwise, your reactions more instinctive.

"You also benefit from a stronger immune system. Your ability to heal will continue to hasten to the point you'll be able to rebuild—"

"Whoa!" Zee shakes her head with a vigorous twist. "That's enough, Iain."

I sit up, stiff. "Rebuild what?"

Zee's pupils glare at the ceiling, lips tight. She sighs and peers back at me. "Doctor Fitzpatrick has found that your body—" Zee's cheeks crunch, chin tilts to the side and back.

Tell me! my mind demands.

Xiomara shivers, as if being stung by static electricity. Her eyes bulge and stare me down, a *don't-you-dare-speak-to-me-like-that* perches on her lips. As quick, her shoulders slack, and she instead relents with a small bow of her head. "As you wish, Your Majesty."

Crush me! "I didn't—"

"No, no…" Zee waves off my apology. "You've every right to know, but I caution you to not overreach. We've theories and perceptions, few facts—despite Iain's assertions otherwise.

"According to Doctor Fitzpatrick, your body still contains pluripotent—embryonic-like—stem cells. She *theorizes*"—the word stretches from her mouth—"that you can rebuild organs, even regrow severed extremities—"

I close to slide off the chair. "I'm indestructible?!" *No wonder your sores heal so fast.*

Xiomara growls. "Did I not just tell you to not overreach? An extraterrestrial appendix notwithstanding, you are and will always be some factor human. You'll bleed human, you'll break human, and you'll die human. Indestructibility *is* the stuff of Science Fiction."

"Regardless, my blood could save millions, cure all the sick and injured."

"Not possible," Iain says as if the words were his default voicemail announcement.

Zee's more placid voice says, "According to your grandfather, such an injection would prove fatal to anyone without an appendix. He disqualified all males: they'd no deaths, but always ended up paralyzed. Appendixed females fare the best—nothing seems to happen."

"As I *already* told him," Iain exasperates, "assimilation requires a genetic match Guide to Protector."

Zee closes her eyes and sucks in oxygen enough that her chest looks about to explode. "You know how the man gets," she says as the air releases.

"Hmm," the ceiling acknowledges.

Xiomara focuses back on me. "These abilities, though, have trade-offs, need refinement with training. You can see, hear, even think in ways others don't, yet a malicious individual could over-stimulate you to the point they paralyze you. It is important that you learn to regulate these capabilities, maybe more so, than any martial art I could teach you."

At last, time to make reason of what is happening to me. I lean forward. "I *will* control them."

Xiomara's eyebrows crawl up. "Tomorrow we start: two hours, every day, we train both the mental and the physical." She edges forward. "No matter how busy you are, how tired—no exceptions, no excuses."

"I understand."

"Be sure you do." Her demand spouts from her mouth as she eases back, letting her lids seal, breathing slow.

My stomach gurgles as it again spies the bowl of raspberries, the apples.

"This change—" I jerk upright. *"—will affect your emotions too."*

"Huh?"

Zee is unchanged, head still back, eyes closed, breathing slow.

"They'll be the hardest to control. You'll have to be the most careful with them, as they can be the internal enemy that abrogates your training."

I open my mouth, but hold my words. Instead, settle back and reseal my eyes. I take a deep breath to steady the snare in my chest. *Emotions,* I will to her, *keep 'em in check—got it.*

"You're oversimplifying," Zee says. *"People claim they'll react this way or that, but until circumstances force a response, more often than not, one's reaction is not as one predicts.*

"All reactions, too, are not overreactions to be reigned. Under-reacting can be just as perilous, damaging. Don't suppress your emotions such that you become cold and uncaring, that you don't act. For all that being The Protector requires of logic and reason, it also commands of compassion and understanding."

Seek balance, my mind speaks.

"Balance," Zee's voice reiterates in my head, *"yes."* A deep breath from the couch hits my ears. The kind that says there's more to come, and it's the most important part.

"Lust will be one of the hardest aspects to manage." I pop my eyes open and hurry to sit up, matching Zee. "The Sisters are a passionate breed, meaning your *Pubertät* will elevate your sexual desires with a vengeance. I've only half developed genes in me and—" This is *not* happening: Sex Ed, Grandma-style "—let me tell you…"

Shouldn't—be—hearing— Stuff my index fingers in my ears. *LA, LA, LA, LA.*

Xiomara chuckles. "What's wrong there, Cherry-cheeks. Grandmom can't equal sex?"

Yeaks! Please stop! "No." Reign in the spital about to burst from my mouth. "I just…"

Zee chuckles. "Okay, okay. I won't carry on. But on a serious note, so enhanced will your hormones be by this new genome that the more you deny the lust, the stronger it will grow. Satisfy it however you must, but always use protection—" Her left eyebrow angled above the other. "You are aware of the proper options?"

I nod, unsure whether words or otherwise would spew from my mouth if I open it.

"Good. Contraception's most important *every* time until you're ready to procreate. You'll be potent, and you've only one—"

"Ma'am, Jasper's here."

Zee stiffens, the jest upon her face morphing into a crinkle that reads as someone stuck struggling to recall the last word needed to complete the weekly crossword. "At this hour? He's not supposed to be here for—" Her eyes dart to the clock. "—at least another eleven-ish hours."

"That's why I took the liberty of a full scan," Iain says. "Something's amiss with my sensors, but there's an eighty-two percent likelihood he's not alone."

"He'd bring no one here." Zee is on her feet, heading for her weapons display.

"Not of his free will," the room concurs.

BBUUZZZ!

I launch to my feet and twist between the elevator door and Zee. "Patch it through," she says, and then into the air, "May Her Grace cast over us…"

Iain's gentle *hum* bears a hint of static for a moment before Jasper's voice broadcasts: "Protecting both the weak and strong."

"Be we but one." Xiomara stuffs a pistol in her rear waistband and grabs a baton.

"Or tenfold in the right or wrong."

"Sending the elevator," Zee says to the ceiling. The static cuts out. "Make that one-hundred percent." She snags a second baton and comes about.

"Protocol NE24?" Iain says.

"Right," sounds Zee's reply as she nears, "and you—" She looks me straight on. "—stay here. No matter what happens. Understand?"

"Ah…" No idea what part of the city I'm in, no idea what is happening. It's dark out. As if there's a choice? "Sure."

"For serious…" Xiomara pierces the threshold of the elevator. "Go nowhere." The door closes and a vague *whir* from the portal fills the room.

"Iain, what's going on? What's 'Protocol NE24'?"

"Twenty-four hour lockdown," comes a casual reply.

Twenty-four! "I can't stay here…" My shoulders pinch at my neck. My finger finds the mole there. "I've a meet tomorrow."

"You've nothing to fear, Your Grace."

"I'm not afraid," spits from my lips.

"Would Your Grace care for another snack before bed, then? A frozen lemonade, perhaps?"

"Snacks—bed!" *A frozen lemonade... No!* I grab an apple and march about the open space. "Stop deflecting. What's happening?!"

"The unwanted guests," he says with a nonchalant air, "Xiomara's merely suggesting they depart."

She's suggesting they depart... "Do you think me so naïve?" I bite into the apple, a loud *crunch* echoing about the room.

"Not at all, Your Grace," Iain's butlery portion says, "Would you prefer I say she's about to beat the shit out of them?"

I fling my hands out from my sides. "Well, no, but you don't have to always be so... so... benign with me. I can handle a lot more than Xiomara may believe."

"Trust me," a more compassionate tone says, "she, of anyone, has an acute knowledge of your potential. She is your Guide, after all. It's her maternal instincts, however, that serve you best."

I hover about Zee's desk and take a generous *crunch* on the apple. A plump leather backpack sits in the corner next to the bookshelf behind the work area. "Yeah, sure," slides from my mouth as slides my body toward the bag. *What might she be hiding in there?*

I set my apple on the lip of the bookcase and kneel. Unweave the bag's buckle. Lift the flap—

"I'd not have taken you for a snoop," the room buzzes.

"Crush me!" I jolt up. "I'm just, ah—" I latch onto a frame on the bookcase. "—looking at family photos."

There's no reply other than Iain's *hhuumm*, but it seems denser, disappointed.

I glimpse at the photo.

Walking a red carpet, a forty-something, tuxed grandpa with grandma—the youthful original—at his side in a rust-red, hip-hugging, spaghetti-strapped slip dress. Her body may have changed, but not the soul. I run my pointer over the small bulge at her waist. *Mom.*

Behind them, closing their limo door...

"Iain, when Jasper got here—" I swap the photo for the snack. *Crunch.* "What was that poem?"

"Security protocol," the butler says. "Besides multiple biometric measures, only Xiomara can grant access, via verbal confirmation of a keyphrase. Jasper used his responses to convey not only that there was trouble, but that ten intruders are with him."

"Ten!" Hard swallow the chunks in my mouth. "We need to help!"

"We already are," Mr. Obvious joins in. "I'm providing appropriate distractions and you are staying here, giving Xiomara one less complication to account for."

I hurry into the kitchen, taking another bite as I go. "But I'm The Protector."

"That as it may be," Iain says, "you're too raw right now. Besides, I've known Xiomara to take on at least twice as many. Ask her about it tomorrow."

A half-pulped lump blasts from my lips. "Tomorrow?!"

"As to be expected; we're locked down: no one comes, no one goes."

"But Zee…" I toss the remains of the apple in the Recycler. "She lives here!"

"Not tonight."

I growl.

"Your Grace?"

So frustrating! "Here I am, a princess," throw my hands in the air, "trapped in my tower."

"Your Grace."

I scuttle around the island. "A 'Protector', who's unable to do so."

"Your Grace!"

"Hours ago, I was any other average teenage girl and now—"

"SARAH!"

I stiffen and throw my right hand to my hip. "I thought you couldn't—"

"So sorry, Your Highness," the butler says, "but your full attention is imperative as we've a problem."

I snort. "Told you Xiomara needed—"

"Not Xiomara, Your Grace," the room says in a gracious tone despite my scorn. "You."

"Damn straight this is a problem!"

"No, Your Highness…" Confusion oozes from the baritone. "They di—di—disabled my sensors. I estimate a ninety-three percent likelihood because of ma—ma—malicious intentions."

"Iain?"

"The sha—sha, sha—shaft, Your Grace." Iain's *hhuumm* pitches in and out. "You, you—you must—"

The *bhuumm* disappears. It's replaced by the *gers* and huffs of a man straining. I spiral to face the elevator door just as the door flings apart.

"Iain!"

A burly body in head to toe black—a padded, form-fitting material that glints like metal but flexes like cotton—emerges. He scans the room, locking on a frozen me a second later. His twin steps out and takes a place to the Original's right, to my left.

CRUD!

Between the two, the distinctive curves of a woman, dressed in the same material, slides in place. She spies me, then angles toward each man. "Well, grab her!"

O draws and aims what is not quite a pistol from his hip. The weapon has a square, bright yellow front—no open muzzle—that makes it look a toy. He comes to the right side of the island from where I stand as his brother in cloth moves left, unsheathing his own weapon.

They're boxing you in!

I shake away the ice and latch onto the first thing within reach: the glass jar of blue goo Xiomara put on my back.

O chuckles. "Now, little girl," his voice gruffs as he slithers at me, "just set that down and come along all nice. No one needs to get hurt."

"Not likely," springs from my mouth to the dismay of every other part of me.

Think!

I gaze between them. Twin is a slight bit shorter, a hint less stocky, trying to suppress a limp as he cuts out the gap. I shuffle half a meter in his direction.

"Put it down, sweetie," Original says again, breaching the outside corner of the island.

A hallow whistle captures my ears.

"You've nowhere to go," O says. Twin stops, sealing me from the rest of the apartment.

Think!

Steadily, the whistle grows above us. I scoot a meter left, holding equidistant between the two, and tighten my grip on the vase. Think!

"Don't make this hard on yourself," O says.

The whine peaks, then fades again.

A jet.

The skylights!

Original steps out the side of the island, gaining a direct line to me. Other side, Twin grimaces and shifts his weight to his left leg. I crank my left arm and cannon the jar at O. He dives left, throwing his pistoled hand across his face.

The jar shatters against a cabinet as a *kapoof* lets loose to the right of my shoulder. I drop to my knees as two metallic, crackling darts bounce over the sink. Boost left past the island and straight on for Twin, who is looking down, fumbling to reload his weapon.

"Dammit," the woman yells, "one of you shoot her already!"

No more do the words complete when O's shot comes. I duck. The airborne electrodes smack into Twin's chest. He drops, his body wriggling as if an exposed worm. "Shit!" Original grunts behind me. With only a fraction of a runway straight on, dig my feet into the wooden floor and—taking but a single power stride—launch into a somersault over Twin.

My bare soles smack against the floor, sending razors slicing at my calves. *Ow! This is no spring floor.* Ignore my legs and peer right. I expect the woman to be closing in, weapon locked on me. Instead, she half-steps back, elbows pressed to her sides. Diminutive. *Is she afraid—*

"Had to push, didn't ya?" O's voice booms behind me.

I whip around. He'd come around the island. A slim line of blood splits his cheek from its forehead spring. He abandoned the taser for a baton. "This is your last chance."

Between us, Twin is no longer twitching, but likewise not motionless. He rocks side-to-side, moaning, gripping at his chest.

O rushes at me.

I twist on the ball of my left foot and bolt for the incline mat ahead. It's no springboard, but it will be enough—I hope!

Original's approaching huffs propel my legs faster. I hit the ramp and vault upward, landing first my hands and then my crown on the beam. O's baton whooshes at me. I flip to my feet and leap into a tucked salto. The rod swishes below me and clanks into the wall as my feet return to the beam.

Yikes, that was close!

The beam quacks with a *creek!* I toe left. It creeks again. I toe right. Over my shoulder, O yanks the beam right and left again. I sprint the distance remaining and blast into the air… and hang there for what seems forever, like a hawk fighting a tornado.

Then I smack against the wall. My vision blurs. I scramble to grab the rungs there with my fingers and toes, the hit close to knocking me out. Shake my head. The pounding of boots rushes toward me. I latch the next bar up and pull. A grunt escapes my lips as I shift right and grab another.

The wall shudders. The bars creak. It's O racing up the wall, eliminating the distance between us… fast. Shit! *Go now girl—Go!*

I snatch at the next bar. *Just one more…* two meters higher, then onto the rock wall. From there, a swift assent to the skylights. Fold calves to thighs… and blast—

"AAAWWW!"

My left thigh bone rips from my pelvis, O having snatched my ankle in the same moment I tried to jump. I kick at him with my right foot, but my grip gives with the motion. The bulk of me crashes into his head, knocking him likewise loose. The rungs pass faster than either of us can attach. What height we've left disappears in a blink.

The sandbags we've become spank the floor. O's back cracks and arches unnaturally. My body punches into the airbag he's become. A poof of fiery breath explodes from his lips, straggling hair about my face.

UURRGG!

My eyes shut, I tip left and roll hard onto the torn hip. My face paints with sweat and tears. Open my eyes to find the woman rushing toward me. A stride away, her leg cocks back and crushes into my gut. Acid floods my throat. I flip to my hands and knees to avoid choking.

A hand grasps my blouse and yanks my torso up and back. No longer playing timid, the voice behind the mask snarls. "Can't give you what you deserve"—her free hand bevels back—"but she said nothing about bringing you in undamaged."—and bunches into a ball.

I mash my elbow into her crotch.

She screams and doubles over. I hop to my feet, dip my right shoulder, and smash it into her face. Her body flings backward and crashes into the weapon wall. Several of its contents hit the floor, their clangs ringing in my ears.

The woman touches at the wetness seeping through the mask at her nose. "You little…" emits from her mouth with a wispy whine as her eyes narrow, stabbing at me.

I rush her again, but she sidesteps and catches my foot. My body twists counterclockwise, smacking me back first into the floor. She pummels onto my chest and clenches my throat. "Never been one for rules," her vengeful soul spouts. I push at her torso, but she just tightens her grip.

A circle of blackening gray takes to the edge of my eyes. Stretch my right arm out and sweep it across the floor. *Please, there's gotta be—* My palm brushes over a cool, hard mass. I clasp the object. A touch of metal at each end, but the bulk of it is smooth, like a polished rock. Arch the stone upward toward her cheekbone.

SMASH!

The woman spasms. Her eyes snow over, her grip releases.

HHHHAAAAA my lungs besiege. Shove up with my left hand.

The woman's head twists sideways, yanking my other hand with it. *What the…?* I let the tool loose as the rest of her body follows, then toil back to my knees and angle my eyes up. The woman's extremities continue to tremble. Out of her cheek—*Sol's fury, no!*—the handle of Denise's blade quivers.

A second later, the woman is just one more lump protruding from the playscape.

I blink in a rush. "I… I can't have…," shakes from my mouth. Find myself next to her, slipping the knife free. A nurse is supposed to heal, not mar. I lift the mask.

Pasty crimson peels from her jaw in a field of stalagmites. The hole in her cheek oozes. A curl of hair springs out of the hood as it rolls higher. Then her eyes—I know those…

The few contents within my stomach splatter just to the side of… *Denise!*

I pitch away and dig my fingers into my forehead. "I don't understand…"

"Captain!"

Twin is climbing to his feet. He glares between Denise and me.

"She was choking me," races from my mouth. "I was just trying to get her off!" All the time I knew her, Denise was always beyond horrid, but this… this I'd never do on purpose.

Twin raises full with a growl, drawing a wide blade from his hip.

RUN!

I vault to my feet, the pain in my thigh almost toppling me to my behind, and edge back, gripping the corner of the weapon rack for support. My fingers crease over a fallen pistol.

A pistol!

I grab the gun, point the barrel forward, and flick the safety off. We worked with pistols at camp over Summer break. "Stay away from me!"

Twin pauses, but only for a second. "Now sweetheart," he taunts, "we both know you're not gonna use that. You've nowhere to go, so set that gun down before this gets even more out-of-hand." Despite his words, his steps are small, tentative.

"No," I beam back. To my right, O moans.

Shit! I need Xiomara!

I wobble left. Twin rotates with me, still making small steps forward.

I don't dare pull the trigger. If it's not loaded, what slim advantage I have will disappear. "You've no clue what I'm capable of."

His feet stop and the knife in his hand dips.

I limp to the couch. Thank the stars… some relief! Slide across its back, using my behind for balance.

Twin's eyes widen. "That's not gonna work for you."

I hold the pistol as stiff as possible. "I like my chances." Hobble backward to the Lazy Boy. *You've just a couple more meters…*

Twin chuckles, but makes no move as I back into the elevator. Seems his own life is worth more than risking a loaded gun. Place my left hand on the sensor.

Please…

The elevator comes to life. "Your Highness," a butler says. Twin's eyes bulge and he bolts forward.

"Down, now!"

"As you wish." The door slides shut. Twin arches his arm back, readying to heave the knife.

I pull the trigger.

Twin dives to the side, though nothing happens. He swears and launches the knife at me. It catches the door as the elevator finishes closing. No sooner, the carriage drops.

I lower the pistol. "Iain," I beg, "what is happening? Where's Zee?"

There's no response.

"Iain?"

The butler comes back. "Apologies, Your Grace. Iain is offline."

"But…"

"I'm only the elevator subsystem, unable to provide the answers you seek."

"Crud."

The elevator slows, then stops. "We've arrived." The door opens into darkness, save a single overhead light to the far left, blinking with a burnt yellow.

"What in the world…" I step out.

A sickening mix of overexertion and defeat overpower my nose. A slew of bloodied bodies, each draped in the same blue-gray fatigues as those who were at Dad's office, litter the garage.

"Xiomara? Jasper?"

Across from me, the Land Rover's door opens.

"Hello?"

The vehicle's lights erupt, blinding me. Throw my hands to my eyes. A pair of hard-sole boots clump toward me. I part my fingers. The shape of a woman approaches. A baton sways in her right hand.

I limp forward. "Grandma!" Surprise myself at how naturally the label leaves my lips. "The apartment: they got—"

"Grandma?" The woman chuckles. "That's enlightening."

I freeze. "You?!"

"Oh, Rat," Katie snarls, "you didn't think I'd let you get away, did you?"

"Xiomara—what'd you do to her? Where is she?"

Her devious voice says, "Nowhere that's going to be any help to you." The baton whistles through the air. "Grab her!"

Two broad hands latch onto my shoulders, wrench the pistol away and my arms behind me. "Xiomara!" I try twisting loose to no effect.

Katie draws within a meter of me. I kick back with my good leg, but falter as my sore one gives out. Only the soldiers bracing me keep my body upright.

"You've more fight than I expected." The vindictive face before me chuckles as she cocks the baton across her chest. "But this is the end of you—at least an end you'll never remember." Her arm releases.

I cringe, bracing for the impact. The baton whistles through the air and clanks to the ground several meters to my left. Katie, instead, draws a syringe and bottle of pink liquid from a pouch at her side. She sticks the needle through the bottle's top and withdraws its contents.

"What is that?! What are you doing to me?!"

"Well, Daddy says it's time for your tropical vacation and this," Katie squeezes a thin line from the shot, "is your ticket." She nods her chin out.

"What in the Universe…" One hand grabs my hair and pulls my head sideways while another pushes my shoulder in the opposite direction, exposing my neck. "is that…" My hip stings. My eyes are a fountain. "supposed…" Katie jabs the needle in. At once, a flow of warmth swims across my throat. "to…" My vision blurs, muscles weaken. Sense I'm falling, or floating, I'm not sure. "mean?"

Everything browns, then blackens.

CHAPTER TWENTY-ONE

YOU'RE NOT DEAD. YOU'RE NOT dead.

I force my eyes open.

The lifeless nightmare stares me back. What began a red blemish now soils his shirt in brownish-black runs that mimic the cooled wax of a well-used candle. "What did I do?" defeats my heart across my lips.

Zee gasps. *Oh, Cee Cee...*

I twist up and around. "No! You—" Paul jerks from his stupor. I point at the half-stuffed scarecrow that's now Mahoney. "You did this!" I fling my finger back at Paul. "And you—you've known all along—you've *known* who I am?"

Paul's mouth droops open. "Aahhh…"

The question is rhetorical, yet his confirmation stings.

My eyes dart to the floor. "Scriag me!" I squeeze two fist fulls of hair each side my forescalp. "I—I begged them for you."

Paul shrugs. "What can I say?"

Zee says something, but the "You bastard!" that erupts from the pain within me swamps anything else that tries perforating my ears. Paul's right hand twitches, his Adam's Apple bobs as he surveys the audience. His eyes read, *Oh fuck!*

How could I ever have thought… My amulet vibrates wildly against my clavicle. *Last night… he was only there as a distraction!* My fists clench. My head boils. I bolt at him with a roar.

"Your Grace!" Zee locks my arm, whipping my body into a half spin.

I throw my shoulder forward and dig my legs into the floor. "There's no one that can protect you!" My heart screams. "Nowhere you'll be able to hide!"

A cringing Paul shuffles back, there being nowhere else to go.

Zee latches onto my other arm and spins me to face her full on. "Your Grace!"

"I pleaded with them—to not leave him behind," I blast, "to save him, and he killed them all for it!" Reds and oranges and yellows burst from the amulet.

"Hey," Paul's voice protests, "I didn't—"

"Detain him!" Xiomara's command flings over my shoulder as her eyes burrow into my own. *"Sweetheart, breathe with me,"* a calming tone soothes into my mind. *"Breathe."*

My chest obeys three times over. Muscles ease, teeth stop grinding. Fists I'd not realized I'd made loosen. My charm dims, cools. I slip it under my shirt and let its tranquil aura wash over my bare skin.

"Good," Zee says, releasing me. "Now let's get you outta here."

"But you promised!" anguishes a voice.

"You said you were coming," another begs.

"Our time's up," cries a third. *"You're supposed to be our—"*

"Protector," drops from my memory.

I push past Xiomara and to the doctor, she kneeling at Mahoney, stroking his cheek. "My love," she whimpers. I ignore the joyful photo that pops to mind and grab onto her upper right arm.

"The children…" My teeth grind together. "Mahoney was going to free them, wasn't he?"

A distant *whump-whump-whump* pops into my ears.

I shake Foster. "The children, where are they?!"

The Doctor's chin turns up. "Huh? Wha—what?"

A low rumble pervades the hall. The lights flicker. "What in the Universe?" one of Zee's reports puzzles.

"Your Highness," Xiomara touches my arm, "we've got to go." Another rumble. More flickering. The *whump-whump-whump* grows louder.

"Exactly." I heave the woman to her feet. "The children—take me now."

"She's not—"

I eyeball Zee, killing the commentary, then—"Now"—shove the Doctor down the hall. Foster stumbles forward, then regains her footing and throws a leer over her shoulder. It fades, though, as her gaze drops to Mahoney and, without a word, she turns and lumbers down the hall.

A slew of orders burst from Zee's lips. Three to take the body, and prisoner, to the rendezvous. The rest with us. Everyone proceeds with care. I don't hear the exact details, but don't need to; they aren't for me. Foster's my focus.

I stay tight to her heels as she turns us into the right arm of the T where the hall ends. The hairs of my nose nettle in the stale, sulphury air. The overhead lights cast a weak glow, their stained covers radiating a burnt orange. We pass by a sealed office door on our left, a downward staircase to our right.

Wait—I slow—*is that?* I peer into the drop. *Are we?* I swivel, looking past Zee. Her brows crunch, then she peers behind us. What faint light perforates the room at the end of the hall twinkles like distant stars off the shattered glass covering the floor. The metallic mass that can only be the vent fan lay smashed in the middle.

Zee twists again to me. "What?"

"Two days ago," flummoxes my memory, "this place was dead."

The *whump* is again louder, closer.

Zee's chin, the whites of her eyes, briefly snaps at the ceiling before she scuttles past me. She padlocks Foster's forearm, stopping our train. "Daniels," she calls out, "did you signal the chopper?"

"Only on your command, Ma'am," a man's voice steps into the hall. I look back to have his milky green eyes catch my own. A wide smile cuts through the pale brown freckles decorating his boyish face. "Your Grace," Adrian says with a slight bow.

The *whump* is practically on top of us.

"Who'd you signal?" Zee's demand twists me forward again.

"Your nightmare," Foster cackles. "And my ticket outta this miserable place."

Xiomara latches onto the woman's collar—"Help us"—and nudges her forward—"or the only ticket you'll earn is one for your big toe."

The doctor grunts but obliges.

Our train streams on despite the *whump* reverberating from out front of the building. Foster, propelled by Zee, hurries us past the entrance's compromised security checkpoint, its polycarbonate doors wedged aside. We turn right and race beyond the barren cafeteria, then left again. Doors line each side of the hall at a random frequency, some open, some closed. We aim for the last to the right. An impassible one, if memory serves.

The window of a room on the left rattles. Beyond the glass, the chopper grounds. Movement. Lots. A dozen or more soldiers are unloading.

"Ma'am," Adrian calls out, "they've landed!"

"Frick!" Zee grabs Foster's hand and slams it against a dusty security panel next to the portal.

Nothing happens.

An explosive *crash* echoes from the entrance.

"Adams," Xiomara bursts out, "Firebird trap."

"Ma'am!" the soldier at our rear acknowledges, then disappears back down the hall from which we come.

Zee twice wipes the screen with her sleeve and fights the reluctant hand of Foster flat against the panel. It flashes blue, scanning from bottom to top.

"Right—right! The signal's from the right!" an imposing bass drums against my ears.

Thirty percent blue.

Klump, klump, klump, klump, klump a battery of boots race at us. Ahead of the rush, Adams breaks into view. "They're—" A series of shots rings through the hall and smack into his body, turning him to rubber as he smashes against the corner. Liquid pours from his scalp.

Sixty percent.

"Coalesce!" Zee orders.

Adrian arches at me, latches onto my hip—"Your Grace."—and urges me toward the locked door.

Ninety percent.

"Dive! Dive!" the bass carries from down the hall as it flares with a reddish orange.

The scanner buzzes and blazes its own red. "Crush me!" Zee exhausts. "Enough fiddling around." She yanks a blade from her hip and plunges it behind the panel. With a single yank, it separates from the wall. She digs into the wires behind.

"Go! Go! Go!" the bass's order bounds at us.

The glow from the hall flickers with shadows.

"Ma'am!" Adrian primes his rifle.

The portal releases with a *swoosh* as the squad pierces the corner. Adrian releases a swarm of projectiles at them. Xiomara clasps the rear of my neck and throws me through the doorway, pulling the doctor through with her. Adrian and his mate squeeze through as both release a fresh round of ammunition. Adrian slams his hand against the door control, closing us in.

"Move!" Zee aims her weapon at the panel and transforms it into a blackened plate of sparks. She then propels Foster toward the far left corner and the only other exit. "Don't make me do it for you this time." There's no debating her dictate.

The anteroom is low lit, maybe nine meters square. A back-to-back row of three seats each run down the center of the room. At their end, opposite the door from which we come, six tall, wooden cabinets stand. The first closest the exit bears Dr. Foster's name, underneath the words *Chief Scientist* are etched. I'm certain I've never been in the room before, yet some hidden memory screams *Get Out Now!*

A fierce rumble perforates the ceiling, shaking dust loose. The lights flicker. I draw next to Zee and behind the doctor as the panel before her flashes green and the door opens.

"Wait here." Zee squeezes through.

Halogens erupt from the room as she enters, blinding me. I sense Foster pulling away. My eyes clear to find her pushing a button on the other side of the portal.

"Hey!" I jump forward, slipping through the door just as it closes.

Zee gasps. "What the frick!" She shoves Foster to the side and hits the button on the panel.

Nothing happens.

There's pounding on the other side of the door.

Zee twists on the doctor. "Madaline, haven't you already done enough damage? Open the door."

The woman flashes a disdainful eye between us, taking half a step sideways between two science-laden lab counters. "You're one to talk," she blasts at Zee. "You and that manipulative, deceitful, damnable husband of yours… as if he were doing anything different."

More pounding. Foster scoots a fuller step.

"Emmanuel never kidnapped children," Zee matches her, "toddlers."

The doctor scoffs. "I see from whom Mahoney's disillusions came."

Again, pounding, but not as strong.

All of Zee's blood seems to want to explode out her face. "They were your friends, close to family! For months you helped us look for Clarisse, saw how it devastated their marriage, how it drove Neil insane!"

Each takes another step.

"*He* begged me to do it. Wanted a super girl of his own." The doctor flings her hand up. "By the stars, *you* did it to your own daughter!"

My knees go weak. "Zee, what's she talking about?"

Foster cackles. "Of course you'd not tell her."

"*Enough*, Maddie," grits from Zee's clenched teeth.

"No!" Foster scoots another step. Her face tenses. "I'm not part of your propaganda machine anymore. You ruined my life, forced me to hide in this desolate shithole." She steps back again.

One nail picks at another. *"Not tell me what, Zee?"* my mind says to her. She ignores me and steps forward, her eyes locked on the doctor.

"Stop!" Foster grabs a large flask, the colorless liquid inside swishing about. "Hydrofluoric acid," she advises, "melt you like ice cream in a blast furnace." She takes another step. Zee does not. "And you!" She twists back at me, tears streaming from her eyes. "He loved me, you know. Despite it all, he still loved me. But you—you—"

More pounding, but with little resolve.

"You're why he never signaled," Zee's voice slumps with her body, "all these years."

The doctor chuckles. Not in a *that's-funny* way; but cold, cynical. "Told him to let me go. Now he's no choice." Her arm tightens.

No! I dive for Zee as Foster chucks the canister. We crash to the ground, the flask whooshing centimeters from my skull.

Smash!

Glass and liquid blanket over us, stinging my neck and the exposed backside of my hands. The patter of flat-shoed feet speed from us.

I push up. "Zee!"

A stream of red runs from her forehead along her upper cheek. A chunk of upright glass twinkles at its origin. "Eh, flesh wound." She pinches the shard and yanks it free. Red bubbles out.

"That's more than a scrape."

Zee lifts to her feet with one hand. "First Foster." I turn to find the woman on the other side of the lab, approaching the door there.

"This is only the beginning of the price you're gonna pay," she says with a quick glance at us. She presses her hand to the sensor there, opening another door.

"HELP!"

The scream of the young girl I've so often heard in my head. My everything stiffens.

"Come save—"

The plea dies as the door shuts, Foster gone to its other side.

"The children!"

"Wait!" Xiomara grabs my arm before I can rush to the door. "What about this acid?" She pulls at her wet uniform.

"We're fine: hydrofluoric acid eats through glass. This is nothing more than water."

"Oh." Zee's grip gives way.

I twist on my heel and hurry to the security pad. "Can you hot-wire it?"

"For certain." Zee draws to my side. Faint streaks of blood paint her cheek like a poorly applied blush. She again draws her knife and jams it behind the panel, and yanks the casing free. Her hands set to work, popping the door open in seconds.

Antiseptic angers my nose. Dim overhead lights reflecting off a slew of medical devices. Some blink with red, blue, and green LEDs, but most are dark, silent. A large, contoured table, looking more like a dentist chair than surgical stand, fills the center of the room. To the right, a pair of sinks and cabinets. A trio of blue filled vials and a jet injector holding an expired fourth sit on the counter there. I need not guess what their labels read.

Zee gasps. "What in Sol's fury do they do here?"

A bloated, malnourished Claudia burst to mind. "I fear knowing."

Childish moans plead from the only other exit, middle of the left wall. A halo of white outlines what is a hall rounding to the right.

"Please!" an infantile voice calls out.

"Help us!" says another.

I charge the hall. "I'm coming!" Zee's boots clunk right behind.

The dull light brightens as we round the arch, reflecting from a stark white room ten meters ahead. We cover the distance in seconds, bursting into the room at the hall's end.

It's circular, about forty meters in diameter. Almost completely white. Furnishings sparse. To one side, four classic school desks face a freestanding digital chalkboard. Nearby, a foldable table with six round seats that appear to twist out from its underside. A single—out-of-place—twist-knob, hinged, wooden door bisects the two. Solid polycarbonate doors segregate the opposite two-thirds of the room's circumference, save a small eye-level slit, every three meters. Slim fingers on a slim hand poke through one slot, just shy of the center of the doors.

They wiggle. "Over here!" a youthful soprano calls. "I knew you'd come!"

I sprint cater-cornered the room, to the right, and ease my hand over the girl's. "I'm Sarah. I'm here to help."

"I know," she says.

I twist to Zee, my hand falling from the girl's. "How'd she—Xiomara?"

She's near the entrance, tending to a fresh stream of red trickling from her forehead. "Huh?" shrugs from her mouth, not having heard a word.

"You're part of me, Your Grace," the girl says, "in my head. We are the same."

I'm sure she means genetically altered by my genes, and whatever other misguided poisons Foster laced her blue liquid with. These kids need freed and to a proper doctor. I study the door: no handle, no lock, no sensor anywhere. None near any of the cells. "How do we release them?" I beg of Xiomara.

"Ahh…" She pivots, scanning the room, bloody palms up, as if she's about to lift a wide box. *This is bad.* The paleness of her face is giving ghosts serious competition.

I counter-rotate. *How can there not*—pause. Stare past Xiomara and down the passageway. *Could it be*—close my eyes, playing back the room at its end—*just like*—the computer there brightens into focus—*the holding cells!* Flick my eyes open. "The computer back in the other room—there are codes posted at its side!"

"I'll go," Zee says as she stumbles for the opening, "you watch over them."

I'm about to insist I go when the girl says, "Your Grace, she's here."

In the same moment, a scream detonates from the hall. The telescopic baton in the woman's hand *whoops* open as she bursts into the light. Her swing shatters into Xiomara's gut, doubling her over and stumbling back. Zee drops to her knees next to the desks, hacking.

I step forward. "Zee!"

"No" groans in my head. *"Run!"*

The woman laughs. I stop.

"Oooo, that felt good." She stretches her arms in a V above her head, then brushes a lock of sandy red from her forehead and eyes me. "Oh," her hands twist out to her sides, "I suppose, surprise."

"You're—dead," tumbles from my lips.

"I'd imagine you'd think as much." A malefic smirk sets between the woman's cheeks. "Amazing what you can do with some syrup and red dye." She cocks her right leg back and smashes her foot across Xiomara's chin. Zee's head flings sideways, flinging mini globules of liquid red over the floor. "While I'm quite alive…" She rests a boot on Zee's chest, whose body has flopped diagonally backward, and stomps her flat to the floor. "I'm afraid Grandmom's now at her end." She slides her foot to Zee's throat.

I spring at her. "Stop!"

"I wouldn't," she says, leaning her weight into her foot as she slips the baton into its holder.

I stop.

Gasping for air, Zee claws at the woman's calf. "You don't have the strength, you old bag," the woman says to Xiomara, then looks again at me. "Thanks for that familial tidbit, by the way. Definitely put some mysteries into perspective. Plus, the additional leverage never hurts."

Leverage? my brain puzzles. "Katherine, what the scraigs are you talking about?"

Zee's fingers act more like they are petting a flower than fighting for her freedom.

"Oh, I'm just making sure you get nothing." Her chin flings at the failing body below her. "Certainly *not* everything they're trying to leave you, the nobody daughter of nobody parents. Not after all Daddy's invested."

My nerves are jittery. My nails want to dig into my arms. *Ignore her! End this—quick!* Zee's hands fall motionless, she bluing. "Anything you'd want, I for certain don't."

Katherine chuckles. "Yeah, right," springs with sarcasm from her mouth. A memory seems to race across her face. She glances down at Xiomara. "She wasn't playing dumb in that elevator, was she? You never told her?" She peers back at me. "Or maybe it's the drugs—took a bit—well…" Her eyes roll to the ceiling. "a lot more than normal to suppress your memories." She flings her hand into the air. "Regardless, devoted to that company, to the old man, Daddy was. From the very day he got his first tour when he turned eight. *He* put in the time! *He* put in the effort!" Zee's body convulses under the heel of Katherine's shifting boot. "We deserve it all!"

You've gotta do something now!

"I told you—" I take half a step forward. "I don't want any of it." *Whatever 'it' is.* Another half step.

"So then '*why?*' we asked ourselves," Katherine's irate tone carries on as if she'd not heard me, "why would the old man will it all to you? Makes no sense, right? I mean…"

I step again as Katherine's head shakes with whatever disbelief is cycling through her mind. *If you can just get close enough…* A second is all I need. *Smash the chest. Knock the wind out of her.* Another step. *That would give you a chance to pull Zee—* "Wait! What'd you just say?"

Katherine huffs. "Our family fortune, Rat," she grinds, "you're getting none of it!"

The room glazes over. Did she say… "No, it can't be true?" My cheeks wrinkle toward my nose. For sure I understood wrong.

"Wow!" Glee rides atop Katherine's words. "Did they ever hold back with you." Katherine's heel arches off Zee's neck.

Breathe! Please breathe!

None of Zee moves. Katherine, in contrast, skips half a meter forward.

"Your mother—" A jig seems to want to explode from her feet. "Can't believe *I*'"—the gap between her eyelids widens—"get to tell you this… your birth mom and my dad—"

Katherine screams and collapses to her knees, grabbing at her calf. She latches onto the knife stuck there and yanks it out. Just behind her, Zee— on her side—braces herself from tipping face forward. A deep purplish-black splotch tattoos the front of her neck. Her face crunches with each breath.

"Sol's fury! Die already!" Katherine leaps blade first at Zee's midriff, who twists back. *Crack!* the metal digs into the floor, only a pair of centimeters from slicing her gut open. Zee rolls twice more away, then—How in the Universe?!—erupts to her feet. Katherine scrambles to her own feet, her back to me.

Now! I lance at her.

"Your Grace, no!"

Katherine's elbow catches me across the chest, the strike coming faster than it should have. Almost as if my movement drips with molasses. I stumble backward, cracking at the stomach. A fierce sting overtakes my lungs and I hack up blood. My mouth gapes open, sucking for oxygen. My vision shimmies.

"Restrain her," Katherine calls over her shoulder, "while I end Granny."

There's movement out of the corner of my eye from the left. Two—no, just one—man advances from the shadows of the hallway. Tussling against the pain, I straighten myself.

"Don't you lay a hand—You!" Squeeze my eyes shut—He dare!—and open them again. "I'm gonna tear you to mulch!"

Paul stops dead, forehead wrinkles, oozing dread. Despite his white knuckles, the pistol in his grip palpitates.

To the right, Zee and Katherine circle the other face on. The former works herself between me and our adversaries. "You know you can't take me, old woman," the latter says.

"Two seconds," Xiomara's voice shocks my mind, *"race for the cell release."*

"But—"

Zee twists from the circle and rushes Paul. He jerks the pistol to his left, my right, but she's already on him. One fist butts the gun skyward, sending the shot he fires into the ceiling. The other sends his chin cracking to his right as the rest of him stumbles backward.

"Go!" Zee screams at my motionless self. Her fists connect with Paul's face again, sending him unconscious to the floor.

My mind sprints down the hall, my feet not so much. Glimpse right. Katherine glimpses back, then at Paul, or Zee, or maybe, as if aware of my aim, the exit. I can't tell for certain. Her focus returns with a smirk. The gleam of the blade that had been Zee's cocks back and—

"Nooo!"

The grip of my boots pound against the floor. With a *whoosh*, the blade hurls toward its owner. *Pound! Whoosh! Pound! Whoosh!* I leap, hand reaching for the handle in its mid-flip…

Tharup!

I bash, chest first, then skull, to the ground and slide a skin burning meter. My head jackhammering, I roll onto my side as my lungs pine for oxygen.

The moan that comes from Zee echoes what my clenched hand already knows. It falls open, nothingness rolling from it. Four meters away, Xiomara's right hand struggles at an angle across the back of her skull, fingers falling shy of grabbing the blade lodged in that impossible to reach location in the five o'clock part of the shoulder blade, west of the spine.

Katherine rushes her.

"Behind you!" my mind screams at Xiomara.

She spins.

Katherine, though, is already airborne. Her right leg jolts with a jump hook kick that pummels Zee's chest. The latter flings back-first into the wall, screaming as the knife drives deeper in. Still, Zee somehow blocks the fist that arches at her as Katherine lands on her feet. Zee counters with a straight jab, snapping Katherine's head. Blood pours from her nose.

Defying the badger clawing at my chest, I lift to my knees. *"I'm coming."*

"No! Go now, while I distract…"

Katherine titters as she wipes a forearm across her upper lip. "Strong punch, you old bag…" She tackles Zee in a bear hug and latches onto the knife, growling, "but not strong enough" and twists.

Xiomara screams and pounds at Katherine's sides, but the bulkier of the two only clenches harder.

As I steady to my feet with the help of the desk, Katherine pins Zee to her knees. Katherine's right hand clamps over Zee's throat. Her left yanks the knife free and drives it in again. The cry of agony trying to pass by Zee's lips sounds a baby's failing squeak toy. Her eyes bulge.

"Xiomara!"

Her arms go limp. A hiss escapes her mouth. As Katherine releases her grip, Zee's body becomes a sandbag. My feet try pulling me forward, but the desk won't release my hand.

Katherine's boot nudges at Paul. "Wake up, you idiot."

"Murderer!" my voice shrills about the room. My charm is hot against my skin. I don't care.

A long forgotten, yet all too familiar, smug guffaw plays from a rotating Katherine. "Rat, why so surprised? Did I not just tell you Grandmom's days were at an end?"

"Don't you dare call her that!"

"I've as much right as you!" Katherine's clenched teeth assert back. Behind her, Paul sits up, shakes his head, rubs his eyes. "Though," a wide smiling Katherine goes on, "I suppose you're correct, she wasn't much of that to me. One truth we have in common."

This can't be true.

"Oh, but it is Rat." There's joy in Katherine's voice. She flings her right hand toward Paul. "Get up and give it to me."

Paul stands, eyeing me, then Zee's body. "By the stars, Katie," his words worry, "this has gone too far. I think you've had—"

"GIVE-IT-TO-ME!"

A fumbling Paul pulls a jet injector from a pouch on the left thigh of his pants. Katie wrenches it from him and loads a vial of blue she retrieves from her own pocket. "As I was saying before, that worn battleaxe thought she could take me—" She places the gun's nozzle against her thigh. "But we're not so different, you and I." She pulls the trigger and the blue disappears.

Katie stiffens, tosses her head back, eyes shut, moaning. "Ahhh… that's the stuff." The injector drops from her hand and clinks against the floor. A moment later, her body limps like she's slipping into a warm bath. "My dad," pleases from her mouth, "your mom—"

"Please, no," panics from my mind and past my lips, "we're not sisters!"

Katie's eyes flash open. She cackles. "Thank the Universe, no! Don't know what backwoods crap was going on in your household, but that'd be incest, you disgusting twerp." Her face greens. "Any degree related to you is bad enough—Cousin."

Bile fills my throat. I swallow, sending it back from where it comes.

"Disgusts me too." Katie leans into her right thigh. "Turns out we share just the right genes that this magic potion of yours works wonders for me." She cups her breasts. "In many ways."

"It's not true!" I grab the desk I've been leaning against and heave it at her, then dart forward.

She shuffles right, avoiding the makeshift projectile with ease. Didn't expect to hit her as that's not my goal. I bull into her midriff, sending the baton meters across the room and a grunt of oxygen over my shoulder. Lift, then slam her spine-first to the floor. Another grunt of air shoots past my face.

Instead of writhing in pain, though, she rolls and swipes me off balance. My tailbone crunches against the floor. "Oowww!"

Katie kicks at my face from her side. I duck back and roll perpendicular from her. We both return to our feet within the second, about five meters apart. Katie spits a globular of crimson to the side. "Like I told the old woman, you can't defeat me."

My charm pulsates with my racing heart. "I see why you and Paul are perfect for one another," I jape, "you both grossly underestimate my abilities." I arch left as she shifts right.

"Believe what you will," Katherine says, "but I've spent the better part of my life studying you, observing your motivations, actions and reactions; your desires..." She peeks at Paul. "I know you better than you know yourself."

A growl blasts past my lips as I storm at her, feigning a dip two meters out.

She takes the bait, dropping and kicking out. I spring into an aerial walkover, fists punching out at its peak. My knuckles bash into each of Katie's cheekbones as her face draws level.

One cheek collapses.

She shrieks.

I land with a soft foot and spin into a roundhouse. The base of my boot slams into her shoulder blades. Her body sails forward and smashes against the floor, arms and legs sprawl in an X. "Yield," I say. "You don't want to die over money I don't even want."

The body before me half groans, half chuckles. "Money?" Katherine pushes to her knees. "That's all you think this is about?" A watery cough jerks her body, blood splattering out of her mouth.

"Babe?!" Paul has the gun up, its eye on me. "Should I take her?"

Oh, how you're gonna pay you lousy—

"No!" Katie rises to her feet. She appears a red-faced clown. "She's mine to end." With her forearm, she squeegees away what she can of the liquid, but several spots reappear at once.

"Whatever the family fortune," I say, "it's not worth this."

"You're naïve enough to think so," she says. "All your smarts, yet you can't see the actual value of what they've given you. You inherit not only all his personal wealth and property, but sole control over all the corporations and subsidiaries, all the patents, equipment, facilities—and not only on this planet." Her hands jerk into the air. "You own the whole damn extrasolar empire!

"Thank the stars, Daddy discovered what Gramps was doing… hoarding the miracle flowing through your veins, using it to grow an already obscene monopoly for you and you alone. How is that right?" Katie's fists slam through the air. "The girl that killed his own daughter gets everything?" She stomps sideways, left. "What a joke!"

Step to my left. "I'll pass."

"Only when you're dead." Katherine arches sideways again. I mimic her motion. "Fact is, Rat, you're not here out of chance or dumb luck—which'd be some pretty shitty luck. No, you're here because Daddy made it so, because *I* wanted it so. And the best part, the entire time, your dumb ass played right into it. The hints and subtle manipulations perpetuated against you, your friends, your family. You think your witch of a stepmother deserved to manage our household?" Her eyes roll. "Ugh! And all those immature skanks I had to befriend for all those years… So much easier once Daddy let me pay them to torture you.

"No, Rat, we've planned for years," hisses from her lips, "to make sure you expire right here, right now." A smile that says *now-to-really-rub-it-in* sets upon her face. "Granted, we made some tweaks along the way… like the bonus opportunity you created that let me exterminate those traitors—"

"You're the traitor!" Another scream I cannot control. My chest burns where the amulet lies. "You destroyed the camp, killed all those harmless people *(Xiomara…)* for no reason!"

"Wrong!" Katie's pointer finger stabs at me. "Your egocentric carelessness killed those people. You betrayed them, not me."

"Screw you!"

She cackles. "Come on, Rat, that all you got? I know that *little-miss-goody-two-shoes* vibe is an act. Who here is the home invader?"—I never—"The thief? The real terrorist!" Her pointer finger stabs at me. "You're the murder…"—I didn't mean to—"You think I don't know what you did to

Denise?"—Wait! Who? Wha… oh, no! I had forgotten. "And we'd be remiss to overlook that only one of us in this room seduced another woman's man."—I did no such—"So, whore, say what you want, what you've always wanted to say to me."

"You—" I clench my hands to keep from ripping into my skin. "You—" *No! Ignore her. She's trying to bait you. Focus.* "Claudia, where do you have her?"

"Sorry, Rat," Katie says, though the smile on her face suggests otherwise, "she's as dead as the rest of them." Katie turns toward Paul and chuckles. "Who takes a shower at that hour, anyhow?" He twists his hands toward the ceiling in response.

I toss my voice toward the cell doors. "Claudia, are you here?"

"There's no Claudia, Your Grace," the hand in the slot says.

"What the scraigs?" Katie arches at the voice, seeming to not have realized anyone else is in the room.

It's just three meters—do it!

I blast at her.

Two!

I bury the soles of my feet into the floor.

One!

I pounce.

Her knees buckle and we crash to the floor, my arm tight across her red-stained neck. My thighs lock her hips in place. "This is over!"

She laughs. Rather, more humorously gurgles.

How can she jest?!

"Indeed," she mocks after grabbing half-a-breath, "for you!"

My body spasms.

She latches the collar of my jacket and yanks left. My body flings off her and jounces about the floor. My noggin bounces against the ceramic, my right arm slams into a desk leg and snaps. Katie jerks her knee into my gut, then leers over me, her left hand rocking a stun gun. "Another?" her bloody lips spit.

"Fu—"

The bolt bursts through my chest, flinging my limbs astray. The back of my head thwacks what seems as if rocks underneath. My right arm won't move. The left seems glued to the floor. Katie leans up, cocks her right fist back, and springs it across my face. Saliva and what has to be a tooth trail out from my mouth. I slam a knee into her back. She doesn't even flinch.

She leans alongside my head. "Ready to die," she grills into my exposed ear as she stretches past.

Never! I hawk a pool of crimson past my lips. From the left, a soft *creeek*, then a *click, click* finds my ears. I turn my face up and snap at Katie's chest.

Katie pushes back. "You pervert!" In her left hand, the injector replaces the stun gun. "Don't blame me for this." She liberates a vial of yellow liquid from her breast pocket and locks it in place, then sits the needle of the gun inside my left breast.

Still from the left: *click-click*. My eyes tip in the direction. *Are those stilettos?*

"Gramp's," Katie says, too engrossed in terrorizing me to notice the odd addition to our group, "instigated this competition, and now…" The needle—cringe—sinks into my skin. My charm is cold.

The stilettos stop. In their place comes a *chick-chick*.

"I am end—"

BAM!

What seems warm, wet oatmeal precipitates my face. The husk pinning me floats for a moment—"Katherine!" Paul distresses—then tilts forward, a hair right and flops against my torso. Blood hoses from the pedestal that once housed Katie's head. Liquid drenches my shoulders, my face, seeps down my collar.

Click-click-click comes the stilettos.

I arch my mouth to the side. My tongue pushes away the fleshy chunks that slide down my cheeks. I quick blink as the thin heel of the stilettos comes into focus. The red of the boots' soles mix with that dripping across my eyes.

Is that my step—

"Giselle, how could you!" Paul shrieks like a barn owl in heat. "I loved her!"

"Horse shit," Stilettos says.

"We're engaged!"

"Cut the charade, Paul James." Her shadow crawls over me. "How you let that hussy manipulate you so, we'll deal with later. Right now, we've a son that's been waiting two years to see his father. Playtime, like this cruel experiment of Emmanuel Matters', is at an end. Time to man up."

"But—"

"Get him out of my sight," she says over her shoulder. The two head-to-toe black clothed soldiers that trail her lock a non-resistant Paul between them and disappear back through the wooden door. Stilettos, meantime, lays her shotgun to the side and pulls what remains of Katie off me. "Get me a gurney, stat!" She kneels and wipes what she can from my face.

"Mom?" The word whispers from me.

"Yes, sweetheart, it's me," she soothes. "You're a hard one to find."

The air rumbles.

"The children," my larynx struggles. Try twisting over. "Need to set them free."

Mom tacks me down, not that I'm much to struggle against. "We'll get them; you've done your part. You've saved them."

A mesh of moppy brown hair comes bounding through the doorway, shouting my name gleefully. The same full body black as the others replaces his facility outfit, but there's no mistaking the glasses. He leans next to my stepmother and takes my hand. "Up in the courtyard, I knew that was you!"

I squeeze his hand. "Abraham."

"You can thank him for finding you," Mom says. "He made us follow even the slimmest of leads, seeming rightfully so!"

I smile, or so my brain claims; my face is too gummy to tell.

Another rumble, shaking the desks.

"We set the charges," the bass says from somewhere in the room.

"Get these kids released," she says to Abraham. "We've not much time."

"Yes, ma'am." He slides from my hand and bolts for the corridor.

From the wooden doorway, a medical dolly squeaks at us, one black cloth soldier at the front, one at the back.

"Let's get you outta here," Mom says, then twists sideways. "Just the woman I need."

Foster emerges, a large white bag embroidered with a bright red cross bouncing against her side.

"No!" I grab Mom's arm with my left hand, my right arm a useless mound of black and blue. "Danger!"

"Oh, my dear girl," Mom brushes my cheek, "you have been so very misled." She smiles. "Doctor Foster's a friend," comforts her voice, "Everything—everyone—will be okay." Then to the arriving Foster, "Sedation only; triage her on the chopper."

The doctor pricks my leg once, twice, maybe three times.

No idea. I don't feel a thing.

Hands heft me onto the stretcher and feet set out through a maze of halls.

Or so it seems. My head's hazy.

There's no mistaking, however, the salty air that bursts into my hungry lungs or the *whump-whump-whump* that pounds my ears as we emerge onto the beach. I catch the gunships hovering above as they stuff me into the hold of a Chinook. Foster and Mom follow, along with a half squad of black clad troops.

I glance sideways, past the boarding soldiers. Abraham's leading another half squad—three children huddling at their center—toward a second carrier.

They're free! My insides smile—for, I'm certain, my face can't—as the last of the soldiers board and slam the door shut. The chopper powers up and lifts from the ground with a slight rock. Foster jams an IV into my good arm, then surveys the other.

"This will hurt," she warns as she sets my other arm right.

I don't so much as flinch.

The Chinook liberates the gully and whips around. Not far off, the complex flashes through the port window next to my head. Yellows, oranges, and reds blaze everywhere. Half of the lower courtyard wall is gone. A swarm of tracer rounds fly between air and ground.

All those innocent, deluded souls. "We can't leave without—"

A shower of fireworks fills the sky as a Hellfire hits the munitions depot. The chopper shakes. I squeeze Mom's hand, though I didn't realize I was holding it.

"Be certain," she nods out the window, "that place will hurt no one ever again."

She glides a strand of hair from my cheek and behind my ear.

"And you can let go, leave the nightmare behind," she says as our transport twists the devastation to our rear. Ahead, a benign yellowish pink curves along the horizon. "Worry no more, my sweet prize," she muses. "This is a new day and I'm here now. I'll keep you safe."

Acknowledgements

This novel was long in the making, a very rough draft of the opening chapter sitting in a spiral bound notebook for nearly three years before my loving, selfless wife, Julia, encouraged me to make something of those tattered pages. For that, I thank her beyond what these words can convey, as this story would not exist otherwise.

Much love to my children, Nicholas and Emily. Over the course of writing this novel, you were my continual inspirations as I had the privilege of sharing your journeys of growth into the most impressive of adults. I am so proud to be your father.

A heartfelt *thank you* to my beta readers, Margaret, Mary, and Emily for granting me a slice of their valuable time. Their collective and constructive feedback brought sharpness to the rough, bringing our hero's quest into focus, and helped the character find her true self. Blair, thank you for your invaluable critique. Your insights allowed me to view my characters with fresh eyes and bring a deeper realism to the story. Each of your contributions mean so much.

Thank you to the wonderful staff at Book Reality. Ian and Jasmine for your assistance and guidance on the path from manuscript to published novel. Brittany for creating such an arresting cover from my loose concepts. And to Nina, my editor, for doing those most important things editors do that allow us authors to polish mere text into words that shine. Without you all and the many more behind the scenes, I'd have nothing to dedicate, no acknowledgments to make. Thank you for helping me turn a wishful idea into reality.

To my parents… from my earliest days, I remember nothing less than constant encouragement to create. I deeply thank you for that, as it is from that foundation this story emerged.

I'd be remiss to not thank our cavachons, Fritz and Blake, for their steadfast company during all the odd hours spent translating a spark of an idea into substance before it was lost to the distractions of life.

Lastly, I wish to thank you, the reader, for taking a risk and spending your hard earned money on a new novelist. I sincerely hope you enjoy this story and that this is just the beginning of a long journey we'll share for many years to come.

About the Author

Jacob Callcut wrote his first story, *The Jakes*, while in the third grade. Since then, he's been devoted to creating engaging, action-filled, and relationship-rich adventures enlivened with twists and turns that keep readers eager to know what happens next.

Jacob has degrees in both Astrophysics and Computer Science, putting the latter to use in his day job as a software development manager and engineer. When not working or creating his next piece of literature, Jacob enjoys tinkering around the house, making new memories with his wife and children, and eating out for lunch.

Come share in the journey at: www.jacobcallcut.com.

www.ingramcontent.com/pod-product-compliance
Lightning Source LLC
Chambersburg PA
CBHW030917300726